New York Times bestselling author Jill Shalvis lives in a small town in the Sierras full of quirky characters. Any resemblance to the quirky characters in her books is, um, mostly coincidental. Look for Jill's bestselling and award-winning books wherever romances are sold.

Visit her website at www.jillshalvis.com for a complete book list and daily blog detailing her city-girl-living-in-the-mountains adventures. For other news, find her on Facebook /JillShalvis, or follow her on Twitter @JillShalvis and Instagram @jillshalvis.

Jill Shalvis. Delightfully addictive:

'Sisterhood takes center stage in this utterly absorbing novel. Jill Shalvis balances her trademark sunny optimism and humor with unforgettable real-life drama. A book to savor – and share' Susan Wiggs, *New York Times* bestselling author, on *The Lemon Sisters*

'Jill Shalvis's books are funny, warm, charming, and unforgettable' RaeAnne Thayne, *New York Times* bestselling author

'With a fast pace and a lovely mix of romance and self-discovery, Shalvis's novel is chock-full of magnetic characters and seamless storytelling, rich with emotions, and impossible to put down' *Publishers Weekly* (starred review) on *Rainy Day Friends*

'Shalvis has crafted a wonderful summer read that will fit right in with beach blankets, flip-flops, and maybe a little moonshine' *Library Journal* (starred review) on *Lost and Found Sisters*

'I love everything about this book, the family dynamics, the humor, and the amazing romance. Just amazing!' Lori Foster, *New York Times* bestselling author, on *Lost and Found Sisters*

Almost Just Friends

Jill Shalvis

HEADLINE
ETERNAL

Published by arrangement with William Morrow,
an imprint of HarperCollins Publishers

First published in Great Britain in 2020
by HEADLINE ETERNAL
An imprint of HEADLINE PUBLISHING GROUP

1

Cataloguing in Publication Data is available from the British Library

ISBN 978 1 4722 6958 4

Offset in 10.93/15.20 pt Minion Pro Regular by Jouve (UK), Milton Keynes

Printed and bound in Great Britain by Clays Ltd, Elcograf S.p.A.

HEADLINE PUBLISHING GROUP
An Hachette UK Company
Carmelite House
50 Victoria Embankment
London EC4Y 0DZ

www.headlineeternal.com
www.headline.co.uk
www.hachette.co.uk

Almost Just Friends

CHAPTER 1

"Chin up, Princess, or the crown slips."

Piper Manning closed her eyes and plugged her ears against the horror. She'd known this would happen even as she'd begged against it, but sometimes there was no stopping fate. She shook her head. *You've survived worse. Just push through it. Pretend you're on a warm beach, and there's a hot surfer coming out of the water. Wait, scratch that. A hot Australian surfer coming out of the water, heading for you with a sexy smile and that accent—*

Someone tugged her fingers from her ears. Her best friend and EMT partner, Jenna. "The torture's over," she said. "You can look now."

Piper opened her eyes. No warm beach, no sexy surfer. Nope, she was still at the Whiskey River Bar and Grill, surrounded by her coworkers and so-called friends and way too many birthday streamers and balloons, all mocking her because someone had thought it'd be funny to do up her thirtieth in gloom-and-doom funeral black.

"You do realize that turning thirty isn't exactly the end of the world," Jenna said.

Maybe not, but there was a reason Piper hadn't wanted to celebrate. She'd just hit a milestone birthday without being at any sort of milestone. Or anywhere even *close* to a milestone. Certainly nowhere near where she'd thought she'd be at this age.

"Hey, let's sing it again now that she's listening," someone called out. Ryland, no doubt. The hotshot firefighter was always the group's instigator.

And so everyone began singing again, laughing when Piper glared at them and tried hard not to crawl under the table. She'd rather have a root canal without meds than be the center of attention, and these asshats knew it. "It's like you all want to die," she muttered, but someone put a drink in her hand, and since she was off duty now for two days, she took a long gulp.

"I was *very* clear," she said when the alcohol burn cleared her throat, eyeing the whole group, most of whom were also first responders and worked with her at the station or hospital in one form or another. "We weren't going to mention my birthday, much less sing to me about it. Twice."

Not a single one of them looked guilty. "To Piper," Ryland said, and everyone raised a glass. "For gathering and keeping all us misfits together and sane."

"To Piper," everyone cheered, then, thankfully, conversations started up all around her so that she was finally no longer the center of attention. Everyone was well versed in her ways, which meant they got that while she was touched that they cared, she didn't want any more attention. Easily accepting that, they were happy to enjoy the night and leave her alone.

"So, did that hurt?" Jenna asked, amused.

"What?"

"Being loved?"

In tune to the sounds of the bar around them—someone singing off-key to "Sweet Home Alabama," rambunctious laughter from a nearby table, the *clink* of pool balls—Piper rolled her eyes.

"You know one day those eyeballs are going to fall right out of your head, right?"

Ignoring this, Piper went back to what she'd been doing before being so rudely interrupted by all the love. Making a list. She was big on bullet journaling. She'd had to be. Making notes and lists had saved her life more than once. And yes, she knew she could do it all on a notes app on her phone instead, but her brain wasn't wired that way. Nope, she had to do everything the hard way and write that shit down by hand like in the Dark Ages. She flipped through some of her pages: Calendars, Grocery Lists, Future Baby Names (even though she didn't plan on having babies), Passwords (okay, *password*, singular, since she always used the same one—CookiesAreLife123!).

And then there were some random entries:

Life Rules
- Occasionally maybe make an effort to look nice.
- Don't cut your own bangs no matter how sad you are.
- Never ever, EVER, under any circumstances fall in love.

She also had a bucket list of wishes. Oh, and a secret *secret* bucket list of wishes . . .

Yeah, she clearly needed help. Or a little pill.

"New journal?" Jenna asked.

"Maybe." Piper's vices were simple. Basically, she was an office supply ho—a never-ending source of amusement to Jenna, because Piper was also a bit of a hot mess when it came to organization and neatness. Her purse, her car, her office, and also her kitchen always looked like a disaster had just hit. But her journals . . . those were pristine.

"How many journals have you started and either lost or misplaced since I've known you—a million?"

Piper didn't answer this on the grounds that she might incriminate herself.

Jenna pulled out the pack of stickers that were tucked into the journal. They were cute little thought bubbles with reminders like DOC APPOINTMENT, EMPTY DISHWASHER, and CAFFEINATE.

"I feel like stickers are cheating," Jenna said.

"Bite your tongue, woman. Stickers are everything." So were pens. And cute paper clips. And sticky notes . . .

"Come on. There're far more important things than stickers."

"Like?" Piper asked.

"Like food."

"Okay, you've got me there."

"And sex," Jenna said. "And that should go above food, actually."

"I'm going to take your word on that since it's been a while."

"Well, whose fault is that?" Jenna leaned in, trying to get a peek. "What's today's entry?"

"A list for figuring out what's next on fixing up the property." Piper and her siblings had inherited from their grandparents a house and some cottages on Rainbow Lake. "It still needs a lot of work. I'm in way over my head."

"I know." Jenna's smile faded. "I hate that you're going to sell and move away from Wildstone."

Wildstone, California, was Piper's hometown. Sort of. She'd moved here at age thirteen with her two younger siblings, Gavin and Winnie, to be raised by their grandparents. But in the end, Piper had done all the raising. It'd taken forever, but now, finally, her brother and sister were off living their own lives.

And hers could finally start.

All she had to do was finish fixing up the property; then she could sell and divide the money into thirds with her siblings. With her portion, she'd finally have the money and freedom to go to school and become a physician assistant like she'd always wanted.

So close. She was so close that she could almost taste it. "I plan to come back to Wildstone after school."

Because where else would she go? Her only other home had been following her parents all over the world, providing healthcare wherever they'd been needed the most. But her mom and dad were gone now. Her family was Gavin and Winnie, and everyone in this room.

"But why the University of Colorado?" Jenna asked. "Why

go so far? You could go thirty minutes up the road to San Luis Obispo to Cal Poly."

Piper shook her head. She'd been stuck here for seventeen years. She needed to go away for a while and figure some things out—like who she was if she wasn't raising her siblings. But that felt hard to explain, so she gave even her BFF the ready-made excuse. "U of C is one of the really strong schools for my program. And I think I'll like Colorado."

Jenna looked unconvinced, but she was a good enough friend to let it go.

"Don't worry," Piper said. "I'll be back."

"You'd better." Jenna took another look at Piper's list. "I can't even make a shopping list."

"That's because you don't go food shopping. You order in."

Jenna smiled. "Oh, right."

Outside the bar, they could hear a storm brewing. The news had been talking about it all week. Wild winds pushed against the building, making the lights flicker and the walls creak, but nobody even blinked. Wildstone people were a hearty bunch.

"Paint samples!" Piper remembered suddenly, and wrote that down.

"You know you're a bit of a control freak, right?"

When you ran your world, everyone in that world tended to depend on you to do it right. That's how it'd always been for her. She'd been in charge whether she liked it or not. Piper chewed on the end of her pen. "I'm forgetting something, I know it."

"Yeah," Jenna said. "To get a life."

"What do you think I'm trying to do here?"

Now it was Jenna's turn to roll her eyes. "Everyone else is talking about the new hot guy in town, and you're over here in the corner writing in your journal."

"Hot guys come and go."

Jenna laughed. "Yeah? How long has it been since you've had a hot guy in your life, or any guy at all?"

Piper looked across the bar to where Ryland was currently chatting it up with not one but *two* women. Her ex was apparently making up for lost time.

"And whose fault is that?" Jenna asked, reading her mind. "You dumped him last year for no reason, remember?"

Actually, she'd had a really good reason, but it wasn't one she wanted to share, so she shrugged.

"What you need is a distraction. Of the sexy kind," Jenna said. "You carry that journal around like it's the love of your life."

"At the moment, it is."

"You could do a whole lot better." Swiveling her barstool, Jenna eyed the crowd.

"Don't even think about it," Piper said.

"About what?"

"You know what. Fixing me up."

"And would that be so bad?" Jenna set a hand on Piper's writing arm. "You're the one always fixing everyone's life, everyone's but your own, of course. But even the Fixer needs help sometimes."

It was true that she'd gone a whole bunch of years now being the one to keep it all together. For everyone. Asking for help wasn't a part of her DNA. But Jenna did have a point. Today was her birthday, a milestone birthday at that, so she should do at least one frivolous thing, right? She turned the page of her journal and glanced at her secret bucket list.

- Take a cruise to Alaska.
- Get some "me" time every day.
- Learn to knit.
- Buy shoes that *aren't* nursing shoes.

"Okay, *no*," Jenna said. "You're not sitting at your birthday party eyeing a list about buying nursing shoes."

"About *not* buying nursing shoes," Piper corrected. "And this isn't my party."

"It's your party. And if you'd told Gavin and Winnie about it, they'd be here helping you celebrate too."

Just what she needed, to give her twenty-seven-going-on-seventeen-year-old brother and her not-quite-legal-to-drink sister a reason to party. "I told them not to come. Gavin's busy at his job in Phoenix, and Winnie's working hard on her grades at UCSB."

"They're lucky to have you, I hope they know that," Jenna said genuinely. "Look, you work so hard keeping all of you going. But today, at the very least, you should have some fun."

"I hear you. But keep that in mind." She pointed to the sign hanging above the bar:

WARNING:

**ALCOHOL MAY MAKE THE PEOPLE IN THIS PLACE
APPEAR BETTER-LOOKING THAN THEY REALLY ARE.**

Jenna laughed but wasn't deterred from taking in the closest table to the bar, where three guys sat drinking and talking.

"Don't you dare."

"Who here is single?" Jenna asked the table.

Two of the guys pointed to the third.

"You?" Jenna asked him, clearly wanting confirmation.

He took a beat to check Jenna out. She was channeling Beach Barbie tonight, with her wild blond hair rioting around her pretty face, her athletic build emphasized by tightly fitted fancy yoga gear.

"Yeah," the guy said. "I'm most definitely single."

"Good. Because it's my friend's birthday." She turned to gesture at Piper, who froze in the act of trying to sneak off.

"Why is she hiding in the corner writing in a book?" Single Guy wanted to know.

Jenna looked at Piper. "Well, we're not all perfect. But she's got a lot going for her. She's friendly . . . ish. And she's got all her shots, and is potty-trained to boot. I mean, yeah, okay, sometimes she hides out in bars writing in her diary. But hey, who doesn't, am I right?"

Looking alarmed, Single Guy turned back to his friends.

"Gee," Piper said dryly. "And you made me sound like such a catch too."

Jenna shrugged. "Maybe he's not a diary fan."

"Yeah. That's definitely it. And it's a *journal*."

"Don't you worry," Jenna said. "I'm not done."

"*Please* be done."

But Jenna was now eyeballing the man who'd just taken a barstool a few seats down. *Ohmygod,* she mouthed. *That's him. That's New Hot Guy!*

He was in military green cargoes and a black Henley that hugged his long, leanly muscled body. He had dark hair, dark eyes, and dark scruff, all of which went with his quietly dark expression that said *not feeling social.*

Jenna started to stand up for round two of Let's Embarrass Piper.

"Don't you dare!"

"Hey," Jenna said to the man, who nodded in return. "So . . . you're a guy."

"Last time I checked," he said.

Jenna jerked a thumb toward Piper. "It's my best friend's birthday."

Hot Guy's gaze locked on Piper, who was wishing for an invisibility cloak.

"She's made herself a list," Jenna said, and helpfully turned the journal his way.

Honest to God, Piper had no idea why she loved this woman.

Hot Guy read the list, rubbed the sexy scruff on his jaw, and then spoke to Piper. "Is this for you or your grandma?"

Jenna snorted. "That's actually her nickname. *Grandma.*"

"Some wingman you are." Piper snatched up the journal and closed it.

"What does the 'me time' entail?" Hot Guy asked.

"Pretty sure it involves batteries," Jenna said.

"Okay." Piper pointed at her. "You know what? You're cut off."

"Notice that she didn't answer the question," Jenna muttered.

"It doesn't involve batteries!" *Jeez*. No way was she going to admit what it involved was a nap.

Jenna took the journal, flipped to the right page, and added something to her list:

- Get laid.

Then she drew an arrow pointing at Hot Guy.

The guy nodded in approval. "*Now* you've got a list."

"Keep dreaming, buddy." Piper shook her head at Jenna. "And you. Are you kidding me? You wrote that in *ink*." Which meant it couldn't be erased. And Piper couldn't rip it out either. You couldn't just rip out a page from a bullet journal; it went against how she'd been coded. She supposed she should just be grateful Jenna hadn't turned to the next page and revealed her secret *secret* bucket list.

Jenna turned to Hot Guy. "Listen, don't let her bad attitude scare you. She's all bark and no bite."

He shrugged. "I like bite." And his and Piper's eyes locked. His were an intense, assessing hazel, a swirling, mesmerizing mix of green, brown, and gold. He was good-looking, but so were a lot of men. He was clearly in good shape—also not all that uncommon. But there was something else, something intangible that created an odd fluttering in her belly, and it took her a moment to recognize it for what it was—interest. Which made no sense. She wasn't looking for anything, and he . . .

Well, in spite of his easy engagement in their conversation, his eyes seemed . . . hollow, and he hadn't cracked a single smile.

Maybe they were kindred perpetually-pissed-off-at-the-world spirits, she didn't know. But one thing was for sure, he didn't seem uncomfortable in the least as she studied him. In fact, he didn't seem the sort to be uncomfortable in any situation.

Around them, the bar was in full nighttime fun mode. Music, talking, laughter . . . Everywhere came the sounds of people having a good time, not a one worried about the storm building. When someone called out for Jenna to join a darts game, she slid off her stool. "Okay, so, I'm going to abandon her now," she told Hot Guy. "Feel free to play the gallant gentleman swooping in to save the birthday girl. 'Night, Piper."

"That's *Grandma* to you."

Jenna just laughed and kept walking, and Piper pulled out her phone to thumb in a text.

"Bet you're telling your wingman that you're going to kill her."

Okay, gallant gentleman her ass. More like dark and dangerous . . . She hit send and looked up. "I might've mentioned she shouldn't close her eyes when she goes to sleep tonight. But you know what? Yours is better. Hold please." She typed a new text: *Don't forget, thanks to my dad, I know a ton of ways to kill someone with my pen.*

He read over her shoulder. "Nice."

"You find violent tendencies nice?"

He shrugged. "Being able to defend yourself is smart."

"You know I was just kidding about the pen thing, right?"

He cocked his head and studied her. "Were you?"

About the killing Jenna thing, yeah. But not about knowing how to do it with a pen. And yet no one had ever, not once, called her out on that threat as being real.

"Your dad military?" he asked.

"Was. He's gone now."

He gave a single nod, his eyes saying he got it at a core level. "I'm sorry."

She supposed it was his genuine and clearly understanding reaction that had her doing something she rarely did—saying more, unprompted. "We lived overseas in some seriously sketchy places. He made sure I knew how to defend myself and my siblings."

He gave another nod, this one in approval, and it had her taking a second look at him, at the calm, steady gaze that withheld any personal thoughts, at the way he sat at rest, but with a sense of tightly harnessed power. And then there was his build, which suggested he could handle whatever situation arose. "You were military too."

He studied her right back for a long beat, assessing. "Still am."

When he didn't say anything else, she arched a brow, waiting for more, but it didn't come. "Let me guess," she said. "It's a secret. If you told me, you'd have to kill me."

The very corners of his eyes crinkled. She was either annoying him or amusing him. "I'm actually a DEA agent," he said. "But also Coast Guard."

"How do you do both?"

"I was active duty for twelve years. Been in the Reserve for two. My DEA job schedule allows for the times I'm in training, activated, or deployed."

Man. She thought her parents had lived dangerous lives. This guy had them beat. And considering what had happened to her mom and dad, she decided then and there that she had less than zero interest in him, no matter how curious she might be. Because seriously, where was a hot easygoing surfer when you needed one? "How often does any of that happen? The training, activation, or deployment?"

"My unit trains three days a month in Virginia. We get activated at will. Deployed less often, but it happens." He shrugged, like it was no big deal that he put his life on hold at what she assumed was short notice to go off to save the world.

"The DEA doesn't mind you leaving at the drop of a hat?"

"They knew that when they signed me on. I had the skill sets they needed."

"And what skill sets are those?"

He gave her another of those looks, and she smiled. "Right. *Now* we're at the 'you'd tell me, but then you'd have to kill me' part."

With a maybe-amused, maybe-bemused shake of his head, he lifted his drink in her direction. "Happy birthday, Piper."

She blew out a sigh. "Yeah. Thanks."

He gave a very small snort. "You're really not a fan of birthdays."

"No. Or parties."

"I'm getting that." He was looking at her list again, and she put a hand on the journal to prevent him from flipping to the next page, which was even *more* revealing, and braced herself for the inevitable comment about the getting-laid thing.

But he surprised her. "It's way too cold in Alaska," he said. "If that were my list, I'd be aiming for a South Pacific island."

"Preferably deserted?"

He met her gaze. "Maybe not *completely* deserted."

Her stomach did a weird flutter, and that scared her. She didn't want to feel stomach flutters, not for this guy. "If you're flirting with me," she said slowly, "you should know I'm not interested."

"Good thing, then, that I'm not flirting with you."

How crazy was it that she felt just the teeniest bit disappointed? Plus, she didn't know how to respond. Reading social cues was not her strong suit. Feeling awkward, which was nothing new for her, she slid off her barstool and tucked her journal into her rain jacket pocket, surprised to realize they were still surrounded by people, *her* people, along with music and talking and laughter, and yet . . . for the past few minutes it'd felt like they'd been all alone.

"You out?" he asked.

"I think it's best if I call it a night."

He rubbed his jaw again, and the sound his stubble made did something to her insides that she refused to name. "Let me at least buy you a drink for your birthday first."

"Thanks, but there's the storm blowing in." As she said this, the power flickered but held. "I should keep my wits about me."

"Doesn't have to be alcohol." He glanced around them at the full, rowdy bar. "Are you a first responder like all your friends?"

"Yes. I'm an EMT."

"Well, I'm the new guy," he said. "Zero friends. You going to desert me like Jenna deserted you?"

She actually hesitated at that, until she caught that flash of humor in his eyes. "You're messing with me."

"I am."

She wasn't sure how to respond to this. It'd been a long time since she'd felt . . . well, anything. Just beyond him, she could see a group of her friends playing pool. CJ, a local cop, was winning. After Jenna, CJ was one of her favorite people. He glanced over at her, caught her eye, and gave her a chin nudge.

Guy speak for *Are you all right?*

She nodded and he went back to pool. Ryland was still flirting with two women, and she had to wonder: What was the worst thing that could happen if she let her hair down and enjoyed herself for a few minutes? After all, it *was* her birthday. "Maybe just one drink."

Hot Guy nodded to the bartender, who promptly ambled over. "A Shirley Temple for Grandma here on her birthday."

Piper laughed. She shocked herself with her reaction, making her realize how long it'd been.

Hot Guy took in her smile and *almost* gave her a small one of his own. "Or . . . whatever you want."

She bit her lip. What did she want? That was a very big question she'd tried very hard not to ask herself over the past decade plus, because what she wanted had never applied. In her life, there were *need to do's* and *have to do's* . . . and nowhere in there had there ever been time for *what Piper wanted's*.

Which was probably why she made lists like it was her job.

The bartender's name was Boomer, and she'd known him for a long time. He was waiting with a smile for her to admit the truth—that she loved Shirley Temples. But she didn't admit any such thing. She just rolled her eyes—honestly, she was going to have to learn to stop doing that—and nodded.

When Boomer slid a Shirley Temple in front of her, she took a big sip and was unable to hold in her sigh of pleasure, making Hot Guy finally *really* smile.

And, oh, boy, it was a doozy.

Just a little harmless flirting, she told herself. There was no harm in allowing herself this one little thing, right?

The lights flickered again, and this time they went out and stayed out.

She wasn't surprised, and by the collective groan around her, she could tell no one else was either. Boomer hopped up onto the bar. "Storm—one, the bar—zero!" he yelled out to the crowd. "Everyone go home and stay safe!"

In the ensuing mass exodus, Hot Guy grabbed Piper's hand and tugged her along with him, not toward the front door with everyone else, but through the bar and out the back.

Where, indeed, the storm had moved in with a vengeance, slapping them back against the wall.

"How did you know about the back door if you're new here?" she asked.

"I always know the way out."

That she believed. She took in the night around them, which was the sort of pitch black that came from no power anywhere and a dark, turbulent sky whipped to a frenzy by high winds.

"The rain's gonna hit any second," he told her, not sounding thrilled about that.

This tugged a breathless laugh from her. "Chin up, Princess, or the crown slips."

The look on his face said that he'd never once in his life been called a princess before. "Sorry," she said. "That was an automatic response. My dad used to say that to me whenever I complained about the rain. Do you know how often it rains in Odisha, India?"

"I'm betting less than Mobile, Alabama, where I once spent six months with my unit training the Maritime Safety and Security Team, and we never saw anything but pouring rain. Emphasis on pouring."

"Six months straight, huh?" she asked sympathetically. "Okay, you win."

His lips quirked. "Ready?"

"As I'll ever be."

And with that, he took her hand and was her anchor as they ran through the wind to her beat-up old Jeep. She was actually grateful since the gusts nearly blew her away twice, saved only by his solid, easy footing. The man moved like he was at the top of the food chain, with quiet, economical, stealthy movements that if you knew what he did for a living made perfect sense.

She and Jenna waved to each other from across the lot, and when Jenna gave her a thumbs-up, Piper shook her head.

"Thanks for the drink," she said, having to raise her voice to be heard over the wind.

"I'll follow you to make sure you get home okay."

"Not necessary, I'm fine." Because no way was she falling for that line. There was flirting, and then there was being stupid. "And anyway, as a local, I should be checking on you to see if you get home okay."

He laughed. And as it turned out, he had a great one, though she had no idea if he was so amused because he was touched by her worry for him, or because it was ridiculous, since clearly he could handle himself.

"I'm good," he finally said. "Drive safe." And then he stepped back, vanishing into the darkness.

CHAPTER 2

"Stressed is desserts spelled backward."

Piper headed out of the bar parking lot, her Jeep swaying in the harsh winds. She hit the highway to get to the lake, and the slightly dilapidated, old—heavy emphasis on old—Victorian house and four small cottages on the east shore. It was there that she, Gavin, and Winnie had lived when their parents had sent them home to the States after . . .

Well, after their entire world had fallen apart, destroying each of them in their own way. Although, in hindsight, that event had been nothing compared to what had happened next—all nightmarish memories she didn't want to face right now.

Or ever.

She'd been fixing up the cottages in between her shifts at the station. Once she got the property on the market and sold, they'd have some money to breathe, which would be a good thing because when she went off to school, she wouldn't be able to help her siblings financially anymore.

There was little traffic tonight. Or ever in Wildstone, which had an infamous wild, wild west past, played up for the tourists in all the glossy California tourist guides. The buildings on the downtown strip—two streets, one stoplight that almost always worked—were all historical monuments, and added to the infamy, including a haunted inn.

By the time she turned off onto the narrow two-lane road out of Wildstone, away from the ocean and into the lush, green, oak-dotted rolling hills, the storm had settled in. The wind continued to push at the Jeep, along with the rain slashing down now as well, making visibility tricky. The already-drenched land couldn't absorb the deluge, which had the roads slick.

Rainbow Lake was eighteen miles of bays and hidden fingers and outlets, a treasure cove of fishing, boating, hiking, and camping. Only the south and west shores were largely populated, and there was a nicer road to those areas, one that didn't go all the way around the lake to where she lived. Five miles in, she turned off where the road went from paved to gravel. There weren't many houses out here. It was relatively remote. Her closest neighbor on her left was ten acres away and she couldn't see the house from her own. On the right was another large ten-acre parcel that held a small marina and a residence for the man who ran it, leaving her sandwiched in between with her single acre.

She didn't care. She loved it here, always would. It symbolized safety and security, even if she was not-so-secretly terrified of the actual lake itself.

The power was out here too; she could see that right away. The two massive oak trees in the yard were nothing but dark swaying giants, sheltering her as she ran toward her front door. Letting herself in, she tripped over the boots she'd left on the floor—cleaning up the messy foyer was on one of her lists somewhere—and made her way blindly to the kitchen, where she pulled out her storm lanterns.

Dead batteries.

Well, shit. That was also on a list. She was searching through her junk drawer for spare batteries when she heard an odd *thunk*. Had that been against the side of the house? Freezing in place, cursing herself for marathoning all those horror movies the other night, she listened. Nothing. Drawing a deep breath, she decided the hell with it, if it was a mass murderer, well, at least she'd made it to the ripe old age of thirty. She'd had a good run, and hey, she'd gotten to have a Shirley Temple earlier. What more could she possibly want out of life?

Another *thunk*, and this time she nearly jumped right out of her skin. "Sweet Cheeks?" she whispered, hoping like hell it was the cranky stray cat Winnie had saddled her with when she'd gone off to college two hours south in Santa Barbara. "That's you, right?"

Nothing.

When the third *thunk* hit, Piper forced herself through the house, using her phone as a flashlight. Which is how she found the den window cracked about six inches, the slanted shutters banging in the wind against the wall, screen long gone.

Mystery solved.

She'd opened the window the other day when the sun had

been out and unseasonably warm for late January. Somehow, she'd forgotten to close it, and, she had no doubt, Sweet Cheeks had escaped, since it was her mission in life to mess with Piper's.

Okay, then, so no mass murderer. She'd live another day. But the adventure had made her tired. Or maybe that was just her life. Even so, she still had one more thing to do before she could relax. Well, two if she counted looking for Sweet Cheeks. With a sigh, she once again pulled on her rain jacket and went back outside and across the wide expanse of wild grass between her and the marina.

She'd grabbed her medic bag for the guy who owned and ran the marina. Emmitt Hayes was in his mid-fifties, ate like a twelve-year-old boy, drank like a fish, and had just been diagnosed as diabetic. He'd also recently suffered the loss of his son and wasn't taking care of himself.

So, since they'd been friends since he first bought the marina around five years ago, she was doing the caretaking.

Between the two houses was a runoff from two small tributaries, combining into one rivulet that fed into the lake. Ninety-nine percent of the time, she could step over the little creek when she needed to. Tonight the flow was heavier than she'd ever seen it, half water, half mud—another problem from the poor fire-scarred land due to last summer's terrible California wildfires.

It was one thing for her to step over a narrow stream, but another entirely to get past the rushing river it'd become, and she stopped, frozen to the spot. *Take a deep breath. Be logical. It's not as deep as it looks, it's just wide.*

And moving hella fast . . .

Sucking in a breath, she backed up a few feet and then took a running leap. The bad news—she landed a few feet short, leaving her wet and muddy up to her knees. The good news—she didn't drown.

But she wished she'd had another drink with Hot Guy.

A few minutes later she stood on the dark porch of Emmitt's house, drenched to the core. She knocked as loud as she could to be heard over the wild wind. "Emmitt," she called out. "It's Piper. You okay?"

The door opened, and at first all she could see was a tall, lanky shadow of a man who was wielding a flashlight, which messed with her ability to see clearly. "Emmitt?"

"Not quite."

Wait. She knew that voice, and she blinked in surprise because it was . . . Hot Guy? Had she manifested him here? Was she in an episode of *The Twilight Zone*? "What are *you* doing here?"

He was already pulling her in from the rain. "I was just about to ask you that same question."

"I live next door." She gestured vaguely behind her as he closed the door, shutting out the noisy storm. "I'm here to see Emmitt," she said. "He's my patient."

"Patient? I thought you were an EMT, not a doctor."

"I am, but he—" She shook her head, irritated, mostly at herself for being thrown off guard, because she prided herself on never being thrown off guard, by anyone. "Why am I explaining myself to you?"

"Don't worry," came Emmitt's voice from the depths of the dark living room. "He has that effect on everyone."

"What, charming people?" Hot Guy asked mildly.

Emmitt laughed. "More like irritating the shit out of them." He turned on a small lantern, smiling at Piper from the couch. "The apple never falls far from the tree, you know."

Piper stared at Hot Guy before turning back to Emmitt. "He's your son?"

"In the flesh."

She could see it now. Same dark hair and hazel eyes, and a somewhat imposing height and strength to match. But more than that, the sharp awareness they both had, the way they held themselves so easily, so casually, and yet seemingly utterly aware of everything around them.

She knew Emmitt had two sons, but she'd only known one of them. Rowan, who'd died three months ago in a tragic car accident. All she knew about his other son was that he lived on the East Coast. In fact, now that she thought about it, she didn't even know his name. "I'm sorry, I didn't realize."

"My fault," Emmitt said. "The divorce was eons ago. It was . . . tough, and there were problems. I raised Rowan. Camden stayed with his mom, to . . . help her."

She glanced at Hot Guy, who apparently was named Camden, but he'd lowered the flashlight at his side so she could no longer see his face. Beyond being startled, she was also realizing that Rowan had been Camden's brother. And much as she liked to fantasize about murdering her own brother in his sleep half the time, it was just that. A fantasy. She'd . . . well, she'd die if anything happened to him.

And suddenly Camden's grim mood made sense.

"Do you two know each other?" Emmitt asked.

"No," Piper said, at the same time Camden said, "Yes."

She stared at him.

He stared right back.

"Well, that clears that up," Emmitt said. "Cam?"

"We were both at the bar tonight."

"Yep," Piper added. "End of story. Now, tell me how you're feeling, Emmitt."

He flashed his son a grin, as if he found it hugely funny and satisfying that Piper wasn't interested in him.

As for how Cam felt about this, or anything, he wasn't revealing. "Why does she want to know how you're feeling?" he asked. "Have you been sick?"

"Nope. I've been healthy as a horse."

Piper shook her head. "Maybe a horse with—" She broke off, horrified that she'd very nearly outed Emmitt's medical condition, which was never okay, even when one was totally off-kilter.

Cam stared at her and then turned to his dad, who grimaced.

Piper sighed. *I'm sorry,* she mouthed to Emmitt.

"Don't worry about it." Emmitt looked at Cam. "I've got diabetes."

Cam's expression was disbelief. "Since when?"

"The doc tested me about five months ago. I was going to tell you."

Cam gave him a long look.

"Okay," Emmitt said. "So I wasn't going to tell you."

"Seriously?"

Emmitt huffed out a sigh. "Look, I'd have gotten to it eventually. But you've got to understand, my ability to remember to tell you things is far outweighed by my ability to remember every song lyric from the eighties."

"I'm so sorry," Piper said into the tense room. "I never should've—"

"It's okay, darlin'," Emmitt said. "You didn't do anything wrong."

"No," Cam said tightly, sending an incriminating look in his dad's direction. "You absolutely didn't."

"I know, I hear you loud and clear, but, son, you've had enough stress and grief, I wasn't about to add to it."

Cam closed his eyes and took what appeared to be a deep breath. Extremely revealing for the guy who had yet to show much emotion. "Dad—"

"And what does it matter anyway? I'm doing good," Emmitt said to both of them. "I'm feeling much better."

"Good," Piper said. "But your foot, where you cut it open last week. I'd like to check it."

"Cam dressed it for me just now. But I did drop a glass and he got cut dealing with the mess. Maybe you could take a look—"

"Of course," Piper said.

Emmitt nodded his thanks. "I'll be in the kitchen. My Jack isn't going to drink itself."

"Hey," Piper said to his back. "You're not supposed to be drinking alcohol anymore, remember? It's on your dietary restrictions list."

"I thought that list was more of a . . . suggestion sort of thing. You know, like a guideline." He turned and flashed a charming smile.

But Piper was charming-smile resistant. "Do you remember what I told you?"

"Shee-it," Emmitt said on a heavy sigh. "Yeah. Excuse me a minute."

When they were alone, Cam looked at her. "What did you tell him?"

"That if I caught him with alcohol or sweets, or anything not on his new diet, I was going to eat and drink it myself."

He snorted.

"So how bad are you hurt?" she asked quietly. "And where?"

"I'm fine."

He appeared okay but had his hands hidden in his pockets, so she suspected one of them was where he was cut. "I could just check—"

"Not necessary. I'm not your patient."

"Would that be so bad?"

"Yes," he said, his voice laced with good humor now, along with what her hormones tried to convince her was heat.

"Why?" she asked.

"Maybe I'd rather be something else."

Huh. Most definitely heat. She worked very hard at not responding to that but failed. "And what would that something else be?"

He just looked at her.

Oh, boy. She could deny it all she wanted, but she was one hundred percent attracted to him. She just wasn't sure she wanted to be. "You said you weren't flirting with me."

"And you said you weren't interested."

"I'm not." Shaking her head at the both of them, she moved to the kitchen in time to catch Emmitt hiding a box of cookies, two bags of chips, and a summer sausage. He was stuffing them into his pantry when she cleared her throat.

With a sigh, he turned to face her, looking only slightly ashamed of himself. "Hey," he said. "Stressed is desserts spelled backward."

Piper heard Cam's sigh behind her, and she crossed her arms. "I made you lists, Emmitt. One with a bunch of great food options. Another with easy recipes. And a third with the rules and restrictions." She pulled her journal from where it was still in her inside jacket pocket. "I kept the originals."

Emmitt took the journal and read out loud. "Things I can do to help control my blood sugar. 'Exercise three to four times a week, which can include walking, getting on a treadmill, or yoga.'" He swiveled a long look in Piper's direction. "Yoga's for uppity hipsters from California who eat avocados."

"*You're* from California. And I see you eat guacamole all the time. But fine. Skip yoga. Stretch instead. And eating right is everything."

"Here's another problem," he said, jabbing a finger at her journal. "This here says no white foods."

"Right," she said. "Like sugar and starch—"

"I know what white foods are. I love them."

Piper shook her head. "Emmitt—"

"I know, I know. You're just trying to help." Emmitt turned a few pages in her journal, and before she could reach to take it back, his brows shot up so far they vanished beneath his hairline. "'Top Secret *Secret* Bucket List.' Nice." He flipped another page. "And a list of personal rules." He started to skim them, smiling.

Piper snatched the journal and shoved it back into her pocket. "You did not just see that."

"What's it worth to you? How about a day of skipping testing my blood sugar?"

"You'd bribe your medic?"

"I'd bribe God if I could." He took in her expression and sighed. "Fine, I get it. And thank you. I'll work on things, I promise."

"You really need to, Emmitt. Your blood sugar has got to be more stable."

"It's not all my fault."

"No? Do tell," she said.

"I've been eating like shit for fifty-five years, and it's a known fact that you can't teach an old dog new tricks."

"Can I teach the old dog to want to live for his family?" she asked.

Emmitt's eyes cut to Cam. The two men exchanged a long look that had so many tangled emotions behind it, Piper couldn't even begin to interpret it.

"I'll work harder on it," Emmitt finally said.

"Good." She patted a kitchen chair and he sank into it. She checked his blood pressure, pulse, and blood sugar, all while avoiding looking at the elephant in the room.

The sexy, mysterious, and easy-on-the-eyes, dangerous elephant.

"He okay?" that elephant asked.

"He will be." She locked gazes with Emmitt. "If he behaves himself."

"Well, now, where's the fun in that?" Emmitt asked, flashing another of his charming grins, and in that moment Piper knew exactly where Camden Hayes had gotten his irresistible charisma.

CHAPTER 3

"Fear isn't a productive emotion."

It wasn't all that often that Cam Hayes mentally thanked the Coast Guard for his training, and given that he'd been with them since he was eighteen, being pushed to be the best he could be, there'd been a helluva lot of training. It wasn't just weapons and physical fitness either, though that was a big part of it. Reading a situation quickly and efficiently was as important, and as ingrained, as breathing.

Piper was clearly off-balance. He attributed this to the storm, but also to him. This wasn't ego talking; it was fact. Because he was just as off-balance.

Her name suited her. She was different. She was a quick thinker, fiercely protective of those she cared about, and—his personal favorite—also a smart-ass. "Tell me about the diabetes."

"You really didn't know?" Her censure was clear. She didn't approve of him being distant enough to not know.

He didn't approve either.

"My doing," Emmitt said. "He lives and works on the other side of the country. I didn't want to worry him."

"Dad. This is something we *should* be worried about."

Emmitt shook his head. "You had enough on your plate, son. With Rowan, and then getting called out to God knows where this past month. I didn't want you out there distracted."

Yeah, there'd been a lot going on, but this was something he should have known, no matter what, and he had to work at banking his frustration. "We can talk about it later."

"Only if it involves alcohol."

"No alcohol," Piper said.

Cam nearly laughed at his dad's expression. "You know," the guy said, "you two are a pair of fun-suckers."

Piper packed up her things and bent to give his dad a kiss on the cheek. "See you tomorrow."

Emmitt grumbled, but he hugged her. "Thanks, cutie."

Cam followed her to the door, intending to walk her out to make sure she got home safely, but she stopped him with a hand to his chest. "I'm good."

"It's a mess out there."

"Nothing I haven't dealt with before. Go deal with your family stuff."

Yeah, she was definitely annoyed that he hadn't known about his dad's medical condition. "We're on the same side in this," he said, wanting that to be clear.

"Then take care of him. And don't let him walk all over you."

Cam had to laugh. "No one walks all over me."

"Hate to break it to you, but your dad just did."

Shit. True story, born from not knowing each other that well, something they were working on fixing. Another truth—he liked how Piper wasn't intimidated by him in the least, and he mentally added *bossy* and *sassy* to her list of positive attributes. "His name should be Emmitt Stubborn-Do-Everything-on-My-Own Hayes."

She snorted in agreement, and he liked that too, but he wanted to make sure she understood something about him. "Listen," he said. "I try to call or text him daily. I specifically ask him what's happening and how he's doing. He's damn good at evading when he wants to be. But he should've told me."

"Hell, yeah," she agreed. "He should have." She cocked her head. "You're hurt because he didn't tell you."

Hurt? He'd long ago closed himself off to that particular emotion. To all of them.

"I shouldn't have broken it to you like that," she said with genuine regret. "It hadn't occurred to me that you wouldn't know."

"Apparently, I don't know a whole hell of a lot."

"You two aren't close."

"Not geographically, no. I thought we were working on emotionally." He shook his head. "Is he going to be okay?"

"He should be. Assuming he follows the plan regarding exercise and diet."

"Shit," he muttered, knowing exactly how stubborn his dad could be, which was a big part of how his family had ended up broken in the first place. His parents' divorce had been . . . tough, on everyone. But since Cam's mom hadn't been good at staying on her meds, he'd told the judge that he wanted to stay with her. Which was how he'd ended up on the East Coast with his bipolar mom, and his brother, Rowan, had ended up on the West Coast with their dad. There hadn't been much interaction between the exes, at least not until Cam had been old enough to travel back and forth on his own.

And at the thought of Rowan, a sharp pain went straight through his chest and gripped his heart, making breathing all but impossible. A visceral reminder that he hadn't managed to shut off his emotions at all.

"Hey," Piper said softly, putting a hand on his arm. "You okay?"

Hell, no. His guard was lowered. Actually, it was completely down. And he couldn't remember the last time that had happened outside of his unit. He met her gaze and decided he was just tired enough not to fight it. "If I say no, are we going to play doctor?"

She blinked. Paused. "You're . . . messing with me again."

"Am I?"

Still staring at him, she called back to the kitchen, "Emmitt? I'm leaving. Remember, I've got two generators and I'm right next door. Call or text me if you need anything."

"How about me?" Cam asked, having no idea what he thought he was doing, other than being incredibly stupid. Didn't stop him though. "What if I need anything?"

She bit her lower lip, like she was torn between panic and excitement at the thought of him needing something from her.

"You're a big boy," she finally said. "You seem like you can handle yourself."

"Yes, but don't forget, I'm on your list of things to do now."

That wrenched a laugh from her, and the air crackled with the storm—or maybe it was the tension between the two of them. Tension he hadn't seen coming and now wanted to chase.

"I'm getting rid of that list," she finally said.

He smiled. "That's a big fib."

"You don't know me."

"I know you break eye contact when you're saying something that even you don't buy. But if you don't want to talk about your to-do list, then let's talk about your secret *secret* bucket list. And that list of rules." He leaned in a little. "It's a naughty list, right? Tell me it's naughty. Tell me slowly and in great detail."

She gave him a shove, but not before he saw her shiver, as if she liked the idea. Then, shaking her head, no doubt at the both of them, she reached for the door before pausing to glance back. "Take care of him?"

He was surprised by her genuine tone, though he shouldn't have been. She clearly truly cared about his dad, and that above anything else she could have said or done told him all he needed to know about her. "Copy that."

She held his gaze for a beat and then she was gone, vanishing into the storm, which seemed to have doubled upon itself in the past few minutes. Crazy winds slammed sheets of rain against the roof and walls, making the house shudder.

Cam turned to the empty doorway leading to the kitchen. "You can stop eavesdropping and come out now."

Emmitt poked his head out, looking only mildly sheepish. "Just making sure you two didn't conspire against me."

"You deserve no less. Stay inside. I'm going after her."

"Is that because you're special forces Coast Guard, Deployable Operations Group, aka DOG—"

"Dad, I told you to stop googling that shit. I'm a Reservist now, but even if I wasn't, it's not something any of us would say. Plus, it's Deployable Special Forces these days, so DSF, not DOG."

"Semantics, son. Once special forces, always special forces—"

"We'd never call ourselves that."

"What would you call it? The elite? The best of the best? The—"

"*Dad.*"

"Oh, I know! Coasties, right? I saw that on a TV show once and—"

Cam drew in a deep breath. "I'm going to make sure Piper gets home in one piece. Just stay out of trouble until I get back."

With his free hand, his dad held up what appeared to be the Vulcan sign. "Scout's honor."

"I'm serious."

"No shit. You always are." Emmitt's smile faded. "But I'm sorry I didn't tell you about the diabetes. I didn't want to worry you."

Cam pinched the bridge of his nose. For years he'd been in command of a team of Coast Guardsmen who followed his every order without question. There'd been very little personal life, and when there had been any time at all, he'd done his best to spend it with his brother and dad. But it'd been mostly just Rowan because his dad had been busy trying to stay afloat financially. This meant they weren't as close as he'd like. Cam didn't feel animosity or anger toward either of his parents. He thought they'd each done the best they could. But he and his dad were still unfamiliar with each other, and a little awkward.

Cam was here because he had a few weeks off, his first leave since Rowan's funeral three months ago, and he had a mission, a personal one. He hadn't been able to get to it yet, but now he had to add to that mission—take care of his dad. "Just tell me you'll stay inside and safe until I get back."

"No problem, as I'm going to bed. See you in the morning." Emmitt turned back. "Oh, and one more thing. She's good people."

"Who?

"Piper. She's had a really rough go of things, all of it unfair, and it's been a burden that no young woman should have to bear."

"What do you mean?"

Emmitt slowly shook his head. "It's her story to tell. Or not tell."

"Then why are you mentioning it?"

"Because you tend to run roughshod over people to get them to bend to your will. You knew how to handle your mother, and I'm grateful, but I'm still learning how to handle you."

"I don't need handling," Cam said.

His dad smiled affectionately. "Maybe not, but by the looks of things, you've done nothing but irritate Piper. Thought you might want to change your tactic."

"All I'm trying to do is make sure she gets home okay. End of story."

With a smart-ass salute, his dad was gone.

Cam grabbed a light windbreaker from one of the hooks by the front door and the big flashlight from the bench. When he stepped outside, the storm immediately swallowed him up. He shielded his eyes from the driving rain and found Piper just on the other side of the rivulet.

Which had turned into a river.

She'd clearly jumped and fallen to her hands and knees, and didn't appear to be moving. Cam took a running start and leapt across, landing at her side.

She startled and gasped as she fell away from him.

"Just me," he said, crouching beside her, pulling off his hood so she could see his face. "You okay?"

"Oh, I'm just great," she said, wet and muddy and pissed off.

He rose and helped her to her feet, slipping an arm around her to keep her steady. "Come on, let's get you home."

"I can walk." She pulled free. "It's just a storm. Go take care of your dad. Speaking of that, why have you never visited him since he moved here five years ago?"

"I have. Twice. Both visits were very brief. I'm always gone, it's hard for me to get enough time to come all the way out west."

"Well, you're here now. So go back over there."

"Soon as I see you inside," he said. "It's not safe out here."

Planting her feet against the wind, she stared at him as if he'd lost his mind. In the glow of his flashlight, he could see the bright green eyes that had so charmed him in the bar were now flashing irritation. Only it was hard to take her seriously since she had mud on her cheek and nose.

"Maybe you don't know what the definition of first responder is," she said.

He felt his mouth twitch. "Actually, I'm quite familiar with the concept."

"So you do realize that I'm usually the one out in this kind of stuff rescuing people, not the other way around."

In his world, he was at the top of the food chain, his every command obeyed, his authority never questioned. So it took him a single surprised beat to realize she'd whirled on her heels and was moving away from him, calling out for someone.

"Who's missing?" he asked.

"Sweet Cheeks."

"Ah, thanks. Seems a little sudden, but I'm flattered."

"Oh my God, not *your* ass, I'm talking about my stupid sister's stupid cat. She loves a good storm, but I can hear her crying from somewhere."

Cam stilled and listened. Past the wind, past the driving rain, he heard it too, a cat's plaintive meow. Turning, he headed along the water's edge and stopped at the base of a huge oak tree doing its best to stand strong against the heavy gusts.

Thanks to the beam from his flashlight, he could see the cat in the tree, about twenty feet up, huddled miserably against a branch, looking more like a soaked rat than a feline.

"Oh, for—" Piper had come up to his side and was now swearing rather impressively as she dropped her medical bag to the ground and reached for the trunk of the tree.

"Stop," he said. "You can't climb it, not in this lightning storm, not without risking your neck."

"If Winnie finds out I killed her cat, I'm as good as dead anyway."

"Stay," he said, and with an inner sigh, started climbing the tree himself. It'd been a while since he'd done a rescue on land, even longer since the victim hadn't been human.

"Just FYI," Piper called up to him, "I'm only staying down here because there isn't room for two of us up there, and not because you told me to stay like a dog!"

He kept climbing.

"And also, Sweet Cheeks isn't exactly on the people train, so proceed with caution!" she yelled. "Or at least like you have a healthy fear of cats."

"Fear isn't a productive emotion."

He was pretty sure she snorted at that, but he was serious. He climbed for what felt like forever, and when he got to damn near the top of the world, cat and man stared at each other grimly. "Let's go," he told her.

The cat just glared at him, tail swishing back and forth.

"Yeah, well, I'm not thrilled either, but see that woman down there scowling up at me like I'm a pain in her ass? That's because I'm a pain in her ass. If I rescue you, maybe she'll soften a little bit. So what do you say?"

The cat declined to answer, so he snatched her off the branch. To say she wasn't pleased with this development was an understatement. She hissed and bit and scratched the shit out of him, nearly causing him to fall out of the tree twice. If his unit could see him now, they'd be rolling on the ground. It wasn't often he got his ass kicked, especially by a ten-pound, soaking wet feline, but by the time he had them both out of the tree, she'd most definitely won the battle.

When his boots hit the ground, Piper reached out for the she-devil masquerading as a cat. The she-devil who ... stopped hissing and clawing him and melted into her.

Piper lifted her gaze with a "thank you" on her lips, but broke it off with a gasp as her gaze locked on his hand, which he'd used to rub his chest through his soaked rain jacket. His fingers were streaked with his own blood.

"Oh my God, you're hurt."

"I'm fine." How was it that a cat scratch hurt more than a bullet? "Get inside. Unless there's another wild animal you need to rescue."

She didn't say anything to this, just tucked the now complacent cat under one arm and grabbed his hand, tugging him with her to run across the property toward her house, skidding to a halt twice in shock as lightning hit far too close.

Cam had been to war zones that were less hazardous than this hundred-yard dash.

Finally, Piper shoved open her front door and they stumbled inside. Kicking the door shut behind them, she set down the cat, who meandered off without so much as a thank-you glance.

"Ingrate," he muttered as Piper moved off as well.

She was back in less than a minute with a lantern that wasn't dead. Pushing a bunch of mail and an empty pizza box to one end of a coffee table, she set it down. "Should've cleaned up," she muttered. "It's on my list."

The lantern illuminated the room. Curious, he took a good

look around. The Victorian had been built what had to be close to a hundred years ago. The ceiling was high, the moldings original to the time period, the wood floor scarred but gorgeous. The furnishings were comfy and clearly well lived in, and plants thrived throughout the room. The bookshelves were filled, and there was just enough clutter and mess to give off the sense that this house had earned the right to be called a *home*. He didn't know why, but he loved that she was . . . well, messy. "Nice place. You live alone?"

"I grew up here with my brother and sister, but at the moment, Gavin's working in Phoenix, and Winnie's in school at UCSB."

"They didn't come for your party?"

She shrugged. "It's expensive for them to get home, and anyway, Winnie needs to spend the time studying."

"You need to start a fire. It's freezing in here. You'll never be able to sleep." He moved to the huge wood stove to do it for her, but she stopped him, her expression dialed to grim as she took in the blood seeping through his clothes. "I've got this." Hunkering low in front of the stove, she lit a match. In less than sixty seconds she had a fire going from what clearly had been a pre-prepped fire stack.

"Impressive," he said, insanely curious about this tough woman who, according to both his dad and the guarded look she wore like a cloak, had been through hell in her life.

He wanted to know more.

"Not my first time," she said. Rising, she came back to him, looking him over carefully. "She got you good."

He shrugged. "I've had worse."

She lifted a hand and touched his jaw, which was also burning now that he thought of it.

"Take off the jacket," she said.

"What, no dinner first?"

"Off," she said, not charmed, and then lent her hands to the cause, tugging at it until he took over and let it hit the wood floor with a wet *thwap*. They both looked down at his torso. Yep. Blood was seeping through his shirt in several places, on his neck, arms, chest. And not that he was about to tell her, but his right thigh too.

"Dammit," she muttered and grabbed her medical bag, which she dropped at his feet. *"Strip."*

CHAPTER 4

"I've been called worse."

The last time a woman had ordered Cam to strip had been a very different scene altogether, and it'd been a while. Generally speaking, he liked to be behind the wheel in most situations, but he'd never had any complaints about a woman driving in his bed. "Interesting bedside manner."

"Okay," she said. "How about strip, *please*."

He laughed, and he realized that until tonight, it'd been a damn long time for that too. "Well, since you asked so nicely . . ." But still he hesitated.

"Trust me, I've seen it all before."

He pulled off his shirt, wincing when the cotton stuck to the deepest slice across his chest.

Piper blinked, and for the first time all night, appeared short of words.

It was pretty damn cute, especially with the mud on her nose. "Thought you've seen it all before." She bit her lower lip, eyes suddenly hooded, and he couldn't resist teasing her. "So, how do I stack up?"

That got her, and she rolled her eyes. "Like you don't know. Sit."

The couch seemed too . . . personal, so he sat on her coffee table. She dropped to her knees at his side and doctored up first the cut on his left palm from where he'd nicked himself in his dad's kitchen, and then the two slices on his left biceps, and then the biggest one across his chest, during which time he did his best to ignore the feel of her soft breath on his skin and failed.

When she'd finished, she looked down at his cargoes and saw the blood seeping through from his thigh. Rising to her feet, she stepped back, gesturing for him to lose the pants too.

"Seriously," he said. "Doesn't even have to be dinner. An appetizer would work."

"If you're real good, I'll give you a sticker."

"How about letting me look at your secret *secret* bucket list instead?"

Her eyes narrowed. "How about we stop talking now?"

"Wait." He cocked his head. "Does this mean you also have a secret bucket list? And possibly a not-so-secret bucket list?"

She had hands on hips; a fresh, clean gauze in one hand, antibiotic ointment in the other, her expression dialed to Not Feeling Playful.

With a rough laugh, he stood and took the gauze and ointment from her. "I got this one, Doc." And then he gestured for her to turn around.

She did with a smirk, and then spoke over her shoulder. "Didn't peg you for the shy type."

"Oh, I'm not shy." He shoved his icy, muddy, wet cargoes to his thighs, and yeah, the cat had come within two inches of de-manning him. "Just didn't want to have to fight you off."

"Don't worry," she said. "I always get verbal consent first. And I bet you didn't want me to see your tighty-whities."

He gritted his teeth as he cleaned out the cut. Son of a bitch, that cat had gone deep. "They're not tight and they're not white."

"Batman undies?"

"Commando," he said, and that shut her up. When he'd fin-ished and pulled his pants back up, he lifted his head and found her facing him. His brows went up. "See anything you like?"

Instead of answering, she blushed. And he grinned because, yeah. She'd definitely seen something she liked.

Snatching the gauze and tube of ointment from his hands, she vanished into the kitchen.

A minute later, a burst of lightning lit up the living room like daylight, immediately followed by a thundering boom that shook the house and rattled the windows and actually changed the rhythm of his heartbeat.

From the kitchen came a cry and a crash, and he went run-ning.

Piper was at the sink staring out the window, both hands on her mouth, a broken glass at her feet, eyes wide and unseeing on the storm outside. There was a tree branch brushing against the window and he moved toward her, intending to pull her away in case it broke. But the moment he set his hands on her shoulders, she jerked and whipped around, catching him with a surprise roundhouse kick to the gut.

"Oh my God," he heard her gasp as he straightened gingerly. "I'm so sorry!"

"No problem," he said on a rough exhale, rubbing his abs as he eyed her. "And here I was worried about not sparring with my team while I was here. Maybe we should hit the mats together sometime."

She didn't smile. Her eyes were still huge and haunted, hollow in a way he understood better than he wanted to.

"Hey," he said. "It's okay. You didn't hurt me."

Closing her eyes, she nodded and turned away again, only to jump at the next flash of lightning and the immediate, earsplitting boom of thunder.

She was terrified of the storm. "Piper."

"I'm fine."

"I know," he murmured, gently turning her to face him. Slowly she opened those slay-me eyes of hers and leveled him with all the emotion swimming in them. "Bad memory?"

She hesitated and then gave a barely there shoulder lift. "The thunder gets me. Reminds me of the bombs."

Bombs? She was shaking almost violently now, and he ran his hands up and down her arms, realizing she wasn't all the way back with him, but somewhere else, somewhere far away. "You're cold and wet. Let's—"

"If you say get naked so we don't die of hypothermia, I might kick you again."

Feisty, even when she was down. He liked that, very much. "Actually, it'd be only fair since you've already seen me naked."

"Keep dreaming."

She said this utterly without heat, and he got even more worried. "Piper. What can I do to help?"

"I'm—"

"Fine. Yeah, yeah, I know. But maybe I'm not."

She stared at him, and then slowly stepped into him so that their bodies brushed together. Offering him comfort, he realized, going still at the shock of human contact. He'd been burying emotions for so long, he'd almost forgotten how to access them. Or how much he loved the feel of a woman. Almost. He closed his arms around her, remembering he hadn't put his shirt back on only when her chilled hands clutched his bare back. Allowing himself this, the contact he'd mostly shut himself off from, he let himself get lost in it.

When her phone buzzed between them, she pulled away and tugged the thing from her pocket, breaking eye contact to read her text. "Your dad says that according to the police radio, there's been a mudslide that wiped out access to our street, and that the creek is now a raging river of mud. He doesn't think you should try to get back until daylight."

That had better be true and not some misguided sense of matchmaking.

Clearly on the same page, Piper looked at him. "If he's playing Cupid, I'll kick his diabetic ass."

"I'll help."

"Good. So we're in agreement."

Cam knew he could get back to his dad's with no problem.

He could get just about anywhere under any conditions. It was what he did. But, even though Piper was clearly capable of handling herself, he hesitated to leave her alone.

She led them back to the living room and pulled up the top of the coffee table, revealing a compartment that held blankets and pillows. She threw one of each at him and gestured to the couch.

He'd slept on far worse.

"*Meow.*"

They both turned to look at Sweet Cheeks.

"The couch is his tonight," Piper told the cat. "You're with me."

Ten minutes later, Cam was lying on the couch, his feet hanging off one end, staring up at the ceiling wondering how one simple hug had felt like so much more. In the matter of a single evening, Piper had turned him around and upside down, taking him completely off mission. At the thought of that mission and what had precipitated it, he braced for the now-familiar pain. It hit on cue, slicing through his chest, making the cat's scratches feel like a caress.

He'd gotten *way* off mission tonight. He'd come to make sure his dad was okay after Rowan's death. Because God knew, Cam wasn't. Not even close. But the other part of his mission related to a promise he'd made to Rowan. Cam intended to fulfill that promise no matter what, at any cost. Just thinking about it, remembering he was never going to see Rowan again, his chest got so tight that he couldn't breathe for a long, torturous moment. When his lungs finally released, he sucked in air for a few beats. He was still concentrating on that when another crack of lightning and an ensuing boom of thunder hit, rocking the house on its foundation.

He heard running footsteps, down a hall, down the stairs. Bare feet . . . and then incoming, which was a woman landing right on him.

Burrowing in tight, Piper pressed her face to his throat.

Drawing her in as close as he could, he pulled her under the blanket with him, wrapping her icy form up tight, reminding himself that this was about comfort and absolutely not about her sweet, warm, curvy bod plastered to his. She was clutching something in her hand—her journal. "You sleep with that thing?" he asked.

"I was making a shopping list." Her voice was muffled against his skin, and he smiled.

"In the dark?"

"My phone's got a flashlight."

"Your phone also has a notes app," he said.

"I like to write by hand. It soothes me."

He'd laugh, but every time either of them shifted even a little bit, he could feel every inch of her against him. "How's that working for you tonight?"

"Clearly not so well. I'm . . . not a fan of these violent storms."

He was getting that. "Did something happen to you in a storm like this?"

Silence.

A tactic he'd used often enough, so he got it. "Storms used to freak me out too."

She lifted her face to look at him.

He was guessing she hadn't looked in the mirror because she still had mud on her nose and cheek.

"What did you do? To get . . . not freaked out?" she asked.

"My mom and I used to hide in the cellar. In hindsight, my fear probably came from her anxiety, but at the time I didn't know that. I just knew I was five years old and terrified because my mom was."

"Was your mom young?"

"Yes, very. And bipolar."

Her eyes went soft and sympathetic. "That must have made things really difficult for you."

He shrugged and ran a hand down her back. To soothe, he told himself, but she was still cold, so he wrapped both arms around her, and for the longest moment, they just stared at each other, sharing air. Until, once again, lightning lit up the room for a single heartbeat, with the inevitable crack of thunder right on its heels.

Piper remained rigid, silent and tense enough to shatter, until he slowly pulled her in closer, sliding a hand up her back to palm the nape of her neck, where he rubbed at the muscles that were tight with tension.

"I lost my parents in a storm like this," she whispered.

A shock of surprise went through him. "Ah, Piper. No."

"It was in the DRC—the Democratic Republic of the Congo. It was a crazy storm, and my siblings and I got sent home to Wildstone just as it started up because one of my brother's friends had just been killed by rebel forces."

Okay, and now he understood her earlier mysterious bomb comment, far more than he wanted to.

"My parents decided it was no longer safe for us kids," she went on. "Gavin was . . ." She shook her head. "In shock. Devastated. We all were." She drew in a deep breath. "So plans were made for the three of us to come here and live with our grandparents. We got out okay, and our parents were going to follow within the week, but . . ." She closed her eyes. "There was crazy flooding. The clinic was over capacity when the water rose unexpectedly and everyone inside died. It was a whole bunch of years ago, but violent storms like this one seem to bring it all back. The guilt and everything."

Yeah. He knew exactly. "If you'd stayed, you'd have died too, and Gavin and Winnie."

She nodded. "I know. But it's small comfort sometimes."

"I get that." *So much more than she could possibly know.* "Anyone who's been through what you have would be triggered by tonight's insane storm." His hand was still on the nape of her neck. Her skin was soft and he stroked his thumb back and forth, trying to comfort her, which wasn't something he'd thought himself capable of.

"I usually try to sleep through storms like this." As she said it, her hands slid up his chest. He wasn't even sure she was aware of what she was doing. "But my mind won't shut up," she whispered.

"No?"

She gave a slow shake of her head, watching her hands move on him.

Okay, so she *was* aware of what she was doing.

"Cam?"

"Yeah?" he asked, voice unintentionally low and husky.

"I need a distraction."

Several choice options came to him, all of them requiring a lot of nudity. Before he could get ahold of himself, her fingers dug into his biceps and she kissed him.

At the same exact instant, there came another bright flash of lightning and then thunder, but several seconds later this time. The storm was moving off. Still, he felt an instant rush, though he wasn't sure which to attribute it to, the storm or Piper's hot, sweet mouth.

When she let out a soft little whimper, he pulled her even closer, his hands making slow passes over her back, honestly meaning only to calm her. But she made another sound, a moan of desire that went straight through him, and suddenly it wasn't about comfort at all.

But so much more.

And then she shifted and one of his thighs slipped between hers, and things went straight to DEFCON 5. His fingers tangled in her hair as he deepened the kiss, which swallowed them up in an instant, combustible explosion of hunger and desire. There in the dark, they went at each other, their hands grappling for purchase, her heart pounding against his, assuring him she was in this every bit as much as he—until they broke apart for air to stare at each other.

She swallowed hard. "Scary."

"Yeah." Terrifying, actually.

She let out a huff of laughter. "Didn't expect you to admit it."

"What, that you're scary as hell?"

She laughed again and tilted her head back against his arm as she touched his mouth. "Maybe it's *you* that's scary."

"And maybe it's *this*."

She didn't try to pretend not to know what *this* was. Instead, she tucked her face into the crook of his neck. The safe zone, he presumed. As if anything about their chemistry was safe.

"You're quite the distraction," she whispered.

"I've been called worse."

He felt her smile against his skin. "So you're not insulted?"

"Seems like a win-win to me," he said.

"Mmmm." But instead of taking things further, she exhaled slowly and sagged into him as if she felt boneless, claimed by apparent exhaustion. With her breath puffing softly against his throat, he let his own exhaustion claim him as well. His last conscious thought was that it'd been a long time since he'd held anyone. Not since Rowan, as he lay dying in Cam's arms.

CHAPTER 5

"Next time put a sock on the door—leave me a sign!"

Mornings were always weird for Piper. One moment, she was deeply asleep, dreaming about a warm beach and her sexy, shirtless surfer— Hold up. Not a sexy surfer, but a guy in cargoes.

She opened her eyes and stared up close and personal at an Adam's apple and a scruffy jaw. A scruffy jaw with a deep cat scratch.

Then she realized she was wrapped around the body that came with that jaw, like he was her own personal body pillow.

Oh, shit.

Everything came back to her from the night before: going over to check on Emmitt, finding out his son was none other than the new Hot Guy, who then rescued Winnie's silly cat, and . . . the kissing. Good Lord, the kissing.

He'd then apparently kept her warm all night.

She wasn't sure what to do with that. He hadn't said much, but he'd held her in a way that had made her feel shockingly safe. He might be stoic and guarded and a little mysterious, but he was also capable and sure of himself in a way she strived to be and usually failed.

Plotting her exit strategy, she shifted, inadvertently rubbing up against him and . . . oops . . . not *all* of him was stoic and guarded and mysterious . . .

Her body parts liked this. A whole lot. But her brain was sure of only one thing—if he opened his eyes right now, she'd most definitely kiss him.

Again.

She didn't know what it was about him, but he kissed like someone who knew the act of mouth on mouth was meant to be erotic and sensual, and the means by which to take someone down in the very best possible way.

She was still off-center because of it.

Okay, so the bad news was that she wanted him. But there was good news too. And that was that he was temporary here, and temporary was her specialty. She didn't have the brain power to allocate to anything more. She was still staring at his throat, running the What-If game through her head, trying to decide if she was going to bolt or make the first move, when she heard someone clear their throat. She looked up to find Winnie standing by the couch, dripping rainwater all over the floor.

"*What are you doing here?*" Piper whispered.

Winnie shook her head. "Oh, most definitely you first," she whispered back, looking annoyingly amused. "Although I think

I can guess. It's the same reason why you didn't want me to come home for your birthday. You had your own celebration planned. Did you know you've got mud on your nose?"

Piper put her fingers to her nose and indeed felt dried mud. She tried to imagine what she must look like and decided it was probably best not to. She could also tell by Cam's alert body beneath hers that he was most definitely awake. She slid a look to his face, and yep, his eyes were open.

And on her.

"Oh my God," Winnie said, and slapped her hands over her eyes. *"Gross!"*

Piper looked down and saw that around their mid-body area, the blanket was moving rather suggestively. She lifted the blanket and Sweet Cheeks crawled out. "It's the cat."

"Sure it is," Winnie said, her hands still over her eyes. "You know, I wanted you to get a life, but next time put a sock on the door—leave me a sign!"

"It's not what you think!" Impervious to the drama, Sweet Cheeks was head-bumping Piper, demanding food, which got her booted to the floor, where, with narrowed feline eyes, she meowed her annoyance and stalked off, tail twitching.

"Hey," Winnie called after her. "Where's the love?"

Piper stood up and the blanket fell away, revealing she was fully dressed.

Cam sat up, also dressed. Well, mostly. He was still shirtless, and his cargoes seemed dangerously low on those sexy hips. And then there was the shaggy bedhead, which looked good on him.

As he moved, Piper's journal hit the floor, and Winnie burst out laughing. "Okay, now I *know* nothing happened. Seriously,

Piper, for your sex life's sake, join the twenty-first century and switch to the note app on your damn phone. Or better yet, figure out how to use the iPad that Gavin and I gave you for your last birthday."

Piper slid a look at Cam, who appeared to be holding back a smile.

Winnie wasn't holding back anything; it wasn't in her DNA. She was almost a mirror image of Piper, with the same shoulder-length light-brown hair—although Winnie's tips had been dyed blue—the same green eyes, and the same curvy build that never seemed to respond to exercise or diet.

But only Winnie had black circles under her eyes.

"Hey," Piper said. "You okay?"

"Peachy. Just wanted to wish you happy birthday, but you never answer your phone."

"There was no electricity last night. And we'd agreed you weren't coming home."

"No," Winnie said. "*You* agreed. But then I heard about the storm and you'd gone dark, so I got worried." She smiled at Cam. "Hi. And obviously, I'm the nice, considerate Manning sister."

With a sigh, Piper gestured to Winnie by way of introduction. "Cam, this is—"

"Winnie," he said.

Winnie smiled. "Hey, Camden."

Piper paused. Blinked. "You two know each other?"

"I met him at Rowan's funeral," Winnie said quietly.

Surprised, Piper glanced at Cam, who was giving nothing away, so she turned back to her sister. "You went to Rowan's funeral?"

Winnie's eyes filled, but didn't spill as she nodded. "He was my best friend."

"I know." Ignoring the ache in her own chest, she moved to Winnie and hugged her. "If you'd told me, I'd have tried to find a way to go with you."

"We talked about it at the time, remember? We couldn't afford for all of us to go, and I didn't want you to feel bad. Plus, I wanted to do it alone."

Then she and Cam exchanged a look that Piper couldn't translate. There was tension there. Not sexual, or at least she didn't think so, but that might've been wishful thinking on her part. Telling herself it didn't matter, she strode to the wood stove and stoked the fire back to life, adding wood, taking a moment to hold her hands out to the flames. Not that she was cold. Nope, Cam had been her own personal heater. She was just sorry she'd actually slept and slept hard, and hadn't taken a moment to enjoy being in someone's arms again.

"You shouldn't have come home just because of me," Piper said. "The flights are too expensive."

"I didn't fly."

Piper craned her neck to stare at her. "What do you mean you didn't fly?"

"I drove."

This took Piper aback. "You drove the POS we bought you in Santa Barbara, the one that was only for getting you around town?"

"And it got me around." Winnie smiled. "It got me all the way here. Well, to the gas station anyway. From there I had to walk in. Too many downed trees on the road."

"Are you kidding me? Do you know how dangerous that was, especially in the storm?"

"The storm's over. And think of it this way, if someone's stupid enough to steal the car, they deserve it."

Piper had a lot more to say about this, but she could feel Cam watching them curiously. "We'll finish talking about this later."

"Oh, goodie," Winnie said. "Because talking always works out so well for us."

She didn't know how her sister did it, how she managed to step on Piper's one sore nerve every single time. Step on it, stomp on it, kick it . . . "I didn't want you missing any classes."

"It's teacher conference week, or something like that," Winnie said with a shrug. "I'm not missing anything."

"You should be studying—"

"Piper, I'm twenty, not twelve. I think I know how to handle my life."

"Gee, I must be home," came a new voice. "Because there's fighting. Also, I didn't fly either. I took a bus. Because when you're alive, Piper, you answer your damn phone."

Gavin . . . ? Piper whirled toward the door. Yep, her brother stood there with that always-present easygoing smile he gave the world.

Winnie made a happy sound and flew at him for a hug.

Gavin sighed dramatically, but hugged her back. "Win, you look like shit. You okay?"

"Wow." Winnie pulled back. "If you ever want to be humbled, ask your brother how you look."

"Happy to help." Gavin looked just like Piper and Winnie,

except to Piper's ever-loving annoyance, he was lean to the point of looking underfed.

She'd never looked underfed a day in her life. "My phone died," she said, and hugged him too.

"There's a bunch of mud and downed trees blocking the street. Took me forever to walk in." Gavin looked at Cam. "Who are you?"

"This is Cam Hayes," Winnie told him. "Emmitt's son."

Gavin immediately lost his smile. "Hey, man. I'm sorry about Rowan."

Cam gave a short nod and rose to his feet. "How bad's the road?"

"Mud slid down the creek and into the lake. Missed your dad's house and the entire marina, and this place too, thankfully. But yards are decimated and the street isn't going to be operational until the county gets out here with a crew."

Cam nodded. "I'm going to go check on my dad."

"Let me know how he's doing. And . . ." She grimaced. "Sorry about both the cat and me trying to kill you."

He met her gaze, and she felt herself blush. He smiled, then headed to the front door.

"I'm going to go get some stuff from my car," Winnie said, and followed Cam out.

"Didn't she just say she'd left her car at the gas station?" Gavin asked.

Piper rubbed her forehead. "Yes, which means she's lying to us about something, but hey, what's new."

Gavin nodded with a low laugh. "Like I said, home sweet home."

Piper shook her head. "You hate it here. You couldn't wait to leave."

"I was a child."

She laughed. "And now you're not?"

He looked at her, not amused, his eyes far more grown-up than she'd ever seen them. "I'm twenty-seven. I might've taken the long, slow route to Adultville, but even I had to grow up sometime."

True, but the last time Piper had seen him had been eight months ago when she'd had to bail him out of a DUI.

Clearly reading her mind, he grimaced. "The *really* long, slow route."

She sighed. "None of us knows what we're doing. We're all just stumbling through."

"Huh." He gave her a half smile. "That's actually almost comforting."

"Good. So are you going to tell me why you're really here?"

He let out a breath and met her gaze straight on, which was terrifying, because he only did that when there was bad news. "Maybe I just needed you."

She laughed. "You barely even like me."

"We're family," he said simply.

This was true. Gavin and Winnie were all she had in the entire world. And past her gruff exterior, past all those years of being the bad guy while attempting to mold them into decent people, she loved them both madly. "Tell me, Gav."

"I took some time off. I . . . needed to be home."

"But you're okay?" she pressed, worried, always worried.

"I'm okay. But you should probably know, whatever the opposite of having your shit together is? I'm also that."

Her heart started pounding. There'd been many, many years where she'd truly doubted she could get him to adulthood alive. If there was trouble to be found, he found it, and shockingly easily too. But she'd thought after he'd gone to IT trade school and gotten a solid job, that he was in the home stretch. "Are you in trouble?"

"Not at the moment."

Okay, that was something, then. She let out a relieved breath. Maybe he and Winnie really were back for just a visit. "How long are you staying?"

"Couple of weeks."

Couple of weeks was no big deal. And it wasn't as if they were coming back to stay. She could do anything for two weeks. She was pretty sure anyway.

CAM SHUT THE front door of Piper's house and stood on the covered porch a moment, surveying the crazy destruction of the storm. It was still raining, though very lightly now, while at the same time a good part of the sky had cleared. Branches, leaves, and debris littered the wild grass acreage between the house and the lake, as well as the distance to the marina and his father's place.

He'd been to a lot of places in a whole bunch of countries, but even with the mess, this view was one of the most breathtaking he'd ever seen. From where he stood at the top of the slope looking down at the water, he could see miles and miles of green rolling hills dotted with sprawling oaks, and a very weak sun trying to rise above them all, leaving the land cast in a golden glow tipped with orange flames. The sky was awash in mingled shades from the entire family of blues, light to dark, and tumultuous gray.

After the night before, it all seemed . . . quiet. Just the sounds of the light rain hitting the already oversaturated ground and a couple of squirrels having a tiff in the trees.

Not all that unlike the one in the house behind him.

He'd watched the reunion between siblings with great curiosity. He'd been surprised at the dynamic between Piper and Winnie. They hadn't greeted each other like siblings. More like irritated parent and wayward child. There was clearly a lot of resentment built up there, both in the way they spoke to each other and in body language.

Same with Piper and Gavin.

Having not grown up in the same house as his brother, it felt oddly familiar. Cam was thirty-two now, and Rowan had been twenty when he died. That twelve-year age gap had seemed huge for most of their lives, putting an almost-parental spin on their relationship.

So, though Piper didn't know it, he felt connected to her on a core level.

In between the two houses, the so-called creek was still flowing like a wild river. He turned to head up to the street, taking his chances by going around to the back of the houses—and came face-to-face with Winnie.

"Hey," she said, looking over her shoulder as if to make sure no one was watching.

"Hey," he said back. "Want to tell me why no one seems to know you're pregnant with my brother's baby?"

"Oh my God, *shhh*!" She looked over her shoulder again,

then grabbed his hand and yanked him down the steps and into the light drizzle. She pulled him around the corner to the side yard, where they stood beneath the overhang protecting the air-conditioning unit.

She wasn't showing at all, which made sense. She'd gotten pregnant three months ago, just before Rowan's death. "You left the funeral without saying good-bye. I'm taking it that was on purpose," Cam said.

Winnie closed her eyes and then opened them again, revealing a grief that Cam understood all too well. "I appreciate you telling your dad to let me know about the funeral. I also appreciate you sending me the money for the flight and hotel costs to get there."

"What money?"

She gave him a *get real* look, gentled by a small smile. "I know it was you, Cam."

He lifted a shoulder. "Rowan would've wanted you there."

Her eyes went a little shiny as she nodded and looked away.

He gave her a moment, mostly because seeing her grief triggered his ever-present pain as well. "He wanted me to take care of you," he finally said, putting his mission out in the open. He'd promised Rowan, and Cam never broke a promise. At least not anymore. In the past, he'd let down his mom. He'd let down his brother. And now they were both gone, and he could never make it up to them.

And hell, he'd also let his dad down, by not even knowing the guy was sick. That was especially hard to take, because he didn't think he'd survive failing someone else he cared about.

But Winnie was shaking her head. "Thank you, but I don't

want to be anyone's burden. This"—she pressed her hands to her still-flat belly—"the Bean . . . it's on me."

"You're not a burden." He waited until she looked at him, this woman who was still mostly a girl, but had been encumbered with a responsibility that he was pretty sure she didn't yet fully understand. "And I want to do this. You're carrying my future niece or nephew."

She stared up at him. "So . . . you don't think I'm a screw-up? Just a girl who was stupid enough to get herself pregnant?"

"Is that why you're not telling Piper? You think she'll call you a screw-up?"

"Yes, because I am."

"Winnie . . ." He searched for words to put meaning behind the emotion clogging his throat. "I lost time with my brother," he finally said. "I don't want to make the same mistake here. As far as I'm concerned, you and your baby are family."

She seemed surprised but also relieved. "What will happen when you go back to work?"

"We'll stay in contact," he said. "I'll still be there for you and the baby, however I'm needed."

She looked torn between wanting to believe him and being utterly unable to do so. That was okay; Cam was used to proving himself.

Finally, Winnie sighed and squeezed his hand. "What you did for me, helping me get to the funeral, means more than you'll ever know. Thanks for letting me say good-bye to him with you. But I absolve you of any further obligation. Really. It's not your fault Rowan's gone."

Her honest grief hurt. Not that his grief wasn't honest. It was, and that shit went soul deep, so much so that he wasn't sure he could ever climb out. But his grief was tainted by guilt. So much fucking guilt. Because it *was* his fault Rowan was gone, and his alone. He hadn't realized how much that would hurt, or how it would twist everything inside him, leaving him feeling lost and alone. He'd gladly give up everything to see Rowan again, to tell him how fucking proud of him he was for following his heart, for not letting circumstances dictate his direction in life. But he couldn't. So he'd do this, watch over what Rowan couldn't. "You shouldn't keep this a secret from your siblings."

"Gavin knows," Winnie said.

"But not Piper."

"Not yet, no."

"Listen," he said. "Take it from me, secrets like this tear families apart."

"It's . . . complicated."

"Secrets always are."

Winnie sighed. "She also doesn't know I dropped out of college."

"Why did you drop out?"

She shrugged. "I was never into it."

He absorbed this for a beat, worried that the real reason was money. Rowan wouldn't have wanted her to quit because of that. "Is it too late?" he asked. "Because I can help you with the costs."

"It's not about the money. I only went in the first place to make Piper happy. I hated it. I wanted to be back here. Having morning sickness meant a lot of lying on the bathroom floor thinking too much, but the truth is that staying in college isn't practical. I couldn't graduate before the baby came, so what's the point? Plus, I really want do something with my hands. I want to be useful. And I'm going to do that from here. Somehow."

"Are you sure? Because seriously, whatever you need—"

"All I need," she said very gently, "is for you to promise *not* to tell my sister any of this. Not until I'm ready."

Fuck. "Don't ask that of me, Winnie."

"Please," she said softly, meeting his gaze. "It's just all too much right now, okay? First, losing my best friend—"

"Seems like Rowan was a little more than that."

Winnie swallowed hard and looked down. "Maybe. We didn't know, we didn't realize until after we sort of accidentally slept together one night. Things might've changed then, but right after, he went back East to visit with you for a few weeks, and he . . ."

"Never came home," he finished quietly.

She nodded and bit her lower lip. "And then I was in school, realizing that nothing felt right anymore, not class, not being out on my own, nothing . . ."

"So you came home."

She nodded again, looking very young and very unsure.

"Have you been continuing to see your doctor, the one you mentioned at the funeral?"

"Yes. I had my patience tested. I'm negative."

He snorted. "Copy that."

"Doc said mama and baby are fine."

"Good. And I mean it, Winnie, when you need anything, just let me know. We can work out a way for me to cover your bills without any invasion of privacy. But . . ."

She looked into his eyes, her own incredibly vulnerable and young. "But . . . ?"

"You need to tell Piper."

"I know. I will," she promised. "When *I'm* ready."

He drew in a long breath. "I'd do a lot for you, Winnie, but I'm not comfortable with lying to her."

"Well, I don't feel comfortable throwing up every morning, but sometimes we have to deal with our lot in life. Promise me, Cam. Or I'll leave, no forwarding address."

Shit.

"I'm sorry," she said, sounding like she meant it. "But I can't be pushed around on this. I'll do it—when it's right. Okay?"

What choice did he have? He gave a reluctant nod.

Winnie let out a shaky exhale. "Thank you. Now I'd better get back inside. I'm sure Piper has more she needs to gripe at me about."

"She cares about you."

Winnie cocked her head and studied him. "Huh."

"What?"

"You like her."

"I've known her for all of twelve hours." They both knew that was a non-answer, but the truth was, it didn't matter if he liked her or not. He was here to help his family. Other than Winnie and his dad, "the Bean," as she'd called it, was all the family he had left.

CHAPTER 6

"My alone time is for your safety."

Gavin walked through the big, old house. It was midnight, and very dark and quiet. Too dark and quiet for him, but he had nowhere else to be. The roads were somewhat cleared, but he didn't want to go out looking for trouble. Hell, half the time he never even had to look—trouble always just found him.

Piper and Winnie were sleeping, and he'd planned to do the same. But he'd long ago learned that he had to be exhausted first, or the dreams hit. There'd been far too many nights he'd bolted awake after an ugly nightmare to find himself curled up on the floor in the fetal position, rocking himself.

It was his second night home, and he'd slept like the dead last night, which had been a miracle. And yet he was afraid to hope that would be the norm here. Mostly, he was afraid to hope for anything at all.

He'd spent the past two days moving mud away from the foundation of the house and the cottages with Piper and Winnie. Both he and Piper had been stunned when Winnie had put in time, actually getting her hands dirty.

Winnie was a lot of things, most of them pretty great, like crazy fun, crazy wild, and . . . well, just plain crazy. But she'd never been big on putting forth a lot of effort. Into anything.

So when Piper and Gavin had stared in shock at Winnie showing up to help, it'd of course started a fight. Winnie had been insulted, reminding them both that she'd always preferred dirt and bugs to dolls and playing dress-up.

In turn, Gavin had reminded her that she'd spent the years between age three and eighteen both causing *and* raising holy hell on the world.

That was when she had "accidentally" thrown mud at him.

Naturally, a mud fight had ensued, and Piper, covered in mud and with steam coming out of her ears, had yelled at them to help or, better yet, get the hell out.

That was when Gavin had first realized that he wasn't the only one standing on the very edge of a cliff looking down . . .

Restless now, he moved around the house. He didn't need lights to make his way through the only home he remembered.

Except that wasn't quite true.

He'd been ten when he, Piper, and Winnie had been sent home from the Democratic Republic of the Congo in the middle of that storm from hell, back to Wildstone to live with their grandparents. Whenever he'd been asked, he'd told people he couldn't remember much before that.

But he could. He could, and did, and even now, alone in the

dark with the nightmare of that time ringing in his head, playing like a movie he couldn't pause, he could feel the shudder of horror and grief go through him.

"Survivor's guilt," a therapist had told him and Piper a long time ago.

No shit . . .

Hearing a sound in the den, he headed that way, not all that surprised to find Winnie curled up in the window seat in the living room, head bent, reading something on her phone.

"Hey," he said.

Winnie jerked and her phone went flying. "Hey yourself, creeper. You nearly scared the Bean right out of me."

He moved close and sat with her, looking out into the night and seeing nothing, because there were no city lights out here, no billboards or traffic. Nothing. "The Bean's okay." He slid her a crooked grin. "Its mama, though . . ."

Winnie rolled her eyes.

Gavin bent and scooped up her phone for her, which had a YouTube video playing on how to become a handyman. He glanced at her in surprise. "What are you doing?"

"What does it look like?" She snatched the phone from his fingers.

"It looks like you're trying to learn how to be useful."

"And?"

"And . . . that seems unlike you."

"Shows how much you know. I want to help. Piper's working so hard, and she's trying to fix this place up all on her own. That's not fair."

"Never bothered you before."

"Yeah, well, I was a child." She sighed. "And now I'm having a child. Need to get my shit together. I'm glad you decided to come home to do the same, but you were late. You were supposed to beat me here and soften her up for me."

He shrugged. "I nearly decided against coming home at all."

"Glad you didn't." She paused. "And just out of curiosity, what *does* seem like me?"

Even he recognized a trick question, but this was Winnie. They didn't pull their punches with each other. "You're covert. Sneaky. Like"—he raised a brow—"pretending to be in college this whole past semester when you're really hostessing at Chili's."

She grimaced.

"Or getting pregnant and then hiding it."

"I never should have told you. It was a weak moment, I'd just peed on a stick and freaked."

"Understandable. But it's a long time to be keeping these secrets from Piper. It's your superpower."

She flipped him off.

"Oh, don't worry," he said. "I've got the same superpower."

"Yeah, you do." Winnie lost her animosity and reached for his hand. "Only your secret shouldn't be a secret, Gav. It's not good for your recovery."

"Yeah." Feeling claustrophobic, he rose, hating the feeling that he was trying to climb out of his own skin. "But I'm not who you should be worried about."

"Then who?"

"Your sister, when she finds out how little you trust her not to freak out."

"You mean we," Winnie said. "How little *we* trust her not to freak out."

But it wasn't about trust for Gavin. Not with Piper. It was about how much of her life she'd already given up for him and Winnie. All she'd ever wanted was for them to turn out okay. Instead, she had a baby sister having a baby and a brother with an addiction problem.

And she didn't know about either.

"So you're going to tell her?" he asked. "Yeah?"

"Yeah."

"Anytime soon? Cuz he's been gone a little over three months now."

Winnie didn't respond to this.

On the one hand, he got why she wouldn't readily open up to their older sister. Piper had liked Rowan okay. She'd thought him sweet and affable, and good for his dad. But she'd also thought he'd been lazy and trouble, and not a great influence on Winnie, and as usual, she was right on the money there. Rowan *had* been all those things as well. But Gavin liked to think that in the end, he'd have changed for Winnie.

But now they'd never know.

He ended up in the middle of the kitchen, hands fisted at his sides, eyes tightly closed as he breathed through a desperate need.

For a pill.

Six months. He'd been out of rehab for six months, and after being secretly hooked on pills for three years, he'd told himself he was doing great. But it turned out great was relative. Yes, compared to the Category 5 hurricane he'd turned his life into last year, he was great. But compared to where he wanted to be— a whole person, which he had no idea how to make happen—he suspected he had a long way to go to get to great.

For shits and giggles, and to torture himself, he went through the cabinets. The place was a disorganized mess as always. Piper could find anything she wanted in here, but he had absolutely no idea how. She was a great sister, but a complete slob.

He looked around, shook his head, and began to clean up. He couldn't help himself. He apparently had been the only Manning born with the neat gene. Above the toaster that wasn't working, the one he'd promised to fix but hadn't, nestled between the sugar and the flour, sat aspirin, Tums, and . . . *bingo*, an old prescription of OxyContin from when Piper had sprained her ankle on the job a few years back. Because his sister was anal and a control freak, it appeared not a single pill had been taken.

He ran a finger over the bottle with a shocking, bone-deep yearning. It'd be so easy. So damn easy. For a painfully long moment, he stood there, during which time he'd have paid any amount of money to have his mom or dad appear to tell him that he had this. To tell him they believed in him. To hug him, just one more time.

But because wishes, like lightsabers, butter beer, and Prince Charming, weren't real, he remained alone. Swallowing hard, he shut the cabinet. But he was shaking when he took out his phone and sent a text to his sponsor.

He got an immediate response: *You need me?*

Did he? All he wanted was to be of value, but everything he touched turned to shit. And God, he hated a self-pity party. So he forced in a deep breath and shook his head. He was stronger than this. He was. So he texted back: *No, I'm okay now, thanks.*

He received another text that read: *Anytime, you know that . . .*

And he did. He was shoving his phone into a pocket when he heard something, a crinkling sound, like maybe there was a rodent riffling around in the pantry. After that last storm, he wouldn't be surprised if an entire colony had moved in. Moving silently to the pantry door, he accessed the flashlight on his phone and . . . yanked it open.

Not a rodent.

Piper. She was sitting on a five-gallon container of cat food, inhaling a family-sized bag of cheese puffs and—shock—writing in her journal. Not as jumpy as Winnie, not even close, his bad-ass sister merely lifted her gaze, casual as you please, and her brows went up.

"My alone time is for your safety," she said around a mouthful of cheese puffs.

How well he knew. Growing up, she'd hidden in this very closet whenever she'd needed a moment from him and Winnie, which with hindsight he totally understood. They'd been a couple of wild, feral kids, and she'd been saddled with them. As they'd all gotten older, she'd continued to hide whenever she'd had a problem, especially if she'd gotten broken up with, something that tended to happen once a guy got to know her.

"You get dumped?" he asked.

In a move that proved she wasn't that different from Winnie at all, she flipped him off and went back to munching and writing.

"So that's a yes." He leaned against the doorway.

"I don't know if you know this," she said in a frosty tone that he knew meant imminent death—his, "but alone time is when you're, you know, alone."

"I thought maybe it was more of a I-don't-want-to-talk thing," he said.

"That too. Definitely that."

He nodded, but didn't go away. "So who was it? You had some major sparks bouncing between you and what's-his-name."

"What's-his-name who?"

"Rowan's brother."

She gave herself away by jerking her gaze back up to his.

"You with him or something?" he asked.

"Of course not. No. Nope. I just met him."

"That's a lot of denial. And you know what they say about double negatives, they cancel each other out."

Piper pinched the bridge of her nose. Shorthand for Gavin was driving her nuts again. It was a short drive, and there'd been a time in their lives when he'd taken great pride in sending her on the trip. But he was too miserable at the moment to even be proud of himself. "Sometimes the amount of time you've known him doesn't matter. Shit happens."

"It matters to me." Piper drew in a deep breath. "I don't have time for a relationship."

"Who's talking about a relationship?"

She snorted. "One-night stands are more *your* thing."

Touché. "*Were* my thing." He tried to take a few cheese puffs, but Piper hugged the bag to her chest the way his grandma used to clutch her pearls. He considered wrestling them from her, but she could probably take him.

"Last time we had any sort of real conversation, you were seeing like five different guys," Piper said.

"Like I said, things change. And don't turn this on me. If you didn't get dumped, what are you doing hiding in the closet, stuffing your face and writing"—he looked at her journal—"a list of why emotions suck." She'd written three items so far:

1. They're annoying.
2. They're a waste of time.
3. They're stupid.

"All true," he acknowledged. "But that doesn't tell me why you're here. In the pantry. At midnight."

"Go back to bed before you turn into a pumpkin." She accompanied this with a go-away shooing gesture.

"And what about you? You won't turn into a pumpkin?"

"I'd have to believe in fairy tales for that," she said.

"Pretty cynical for thirty-one."

She slid him a death glare. "*Thirty*. And I *will* kill you where you stand."

He laughed, and it sounded rusty even to his own ears, but it felt good. "I missed you," he heard himself say, startling the both of them.

She stared at him for a beat and then into the bag, like it held the secrets of life. "Funny way of showing it, staying away for so long."

Two months of rehab. Six months of trying to make it stick. He'd hit a bit of a pothole in the making-amends portion of his recovery. Like the rest of his life, this part wasn't going to be easy. "Yeah. Sorry about that."

Worry was a groove between her brows. "You ever going to tell me what's wrong?"

"Nothing, now that I'm home." He paused. "Do you miss them, Piper?"

She didn't pretend to misunderstand. "Mom and Dad? Of course. Always."

"You don't talk about them. You never talk about them." And he needed to. Wanted to.

But she'd closed up on herself. "Of course I do."

"Yeah? When was the last time?"

"On Mom's birthday last month. I texted you that I'd put flowers on their graves and sent you a pic."

Which wasn't the same thing as talking about them, remembering them, keeping them alive in their minds, but Gavin knew better than to push Piper when she had that stubborn expression on her face.

"Are you homesick?" she asked. "Is that why you're here?"

"Yes," he said bluntly, wishing he could reach her, knowing he couldn't.

"I missed you too, Gav. I did. But realistically, how long do you think the three of us can live together without bloodshed?"

He shrugged, knowing she was right and hating that. "It'll be a crapshoot. Come on," he said, suddenly exhausted. "At least go find somewhere more comfortable to be alone."

She shrugged, and it gave him a chest pain, because he realized she honestly didn't think she deserved to have even a few real moments to herself. She had to hide to get them. Until now, he hadn't been exactly sure what had brought him home, but he thought maybe, just maybe, it hadn't been a solely selfish undertaking to save himself. Maybe, he hoped, he could do some saving of his own.

CHAPTER 7

"Our history is water under the bridge. It's
gone, and I'm not into regrets."

Piper's next shift was a doozy. She and Jenna transported a violent drunk who'd walked through a glass door. He'd been opposed to the ride, in spite of the fact he'd been cut up pretty good, and Piper had gotten punched in the jaw for her efforts. Now her head hurt and she wanted food and a bed, but first she did as she usually did: she went to the marina to check on Emmitt.

And maybe also hoping for a glimpse of the last man she'd slept with. Even though all they'd done was kiss, it—and him—had been starring in her daydreams ever since. She was almost afraid to see him, afraid she'd turn back into the woman who'd thrown herself at him because of a lightning bolt. She had no idea who that woman had been. Not her. At least not the grown-up version of her.

She found both Emmitt and Cam outside the marina office, buried headfirst in the engine compartment of a boat.

They came up for air when they heard her footsteps, and her gaze landed on Cam. He looked at her right back, and she wondered if he even realized that she'd revealed a far-too-vulnerable side of herself to him that for the most part she'd managed to hide from the rest of the world.

Emmitt cleared his throat, sounding amused.

Piper shook her head to clear it and pointed at him. "You're not supposed to be doing this sort of thing."

"Because of the diabetes?" Cam asked with a frown.

Emmitt sighed. "No. Because of my leg. I'm not supposed to be on it for any length of time due to the neuropathy."

"Jesus, Dad," Cam said. "What if you fell into the lake? You could've drowned."

Emmitt rolled his eyes and wiped his dirty hands on the bottom of his T-shirt, which, for the record, read: I MIGHT BE OLD, BUT I GOT TO SEE ALL THE COOL BANDS. "I was practically born in the water," he said. "I could swim if I was dead."

"Which could happen if you don't start taking better care of yourself," Cam said. He took what looked like a screw gun out of Emmitt's hand. "I've got this, okay?"

"Come on, Emmitt, let me check you over," Piper said.

Emmitt made a universally male sound that said she was a pain in his ass. "You know I love you, but damn, woman, you're bossy as hell. Anyone ever tell you that?"

She couldn't help but take a quick glance at Cam—who'd also made note of her bossiness. He was rubbing his jaw, fighting either a smile or a grimace of agreement.

"This boat's gotta be fixed now," Emmitt said. "The marina's closed midweek until spring, but I need to get the equipment ready for this weekend. It's going to be warm. People are gonna come out in droves."

"I've got it," Cam said.

Emmitt hesitated. "Uh . . ."

"What?"

"Remember that summer we were in North Carolina and you sank my canoe?"

"Of course I remember," Cam said, his patience seeming a little strained. "We were on our one and only vacation together, before you and Mom split. I was a thirteen-year-old pain in your ass. Which you mentioned about a hundred times in the space of an hour. It was the last summer I ever got to spend with you."

Emmitt's face fell with genuine regret. "Camden—"

"No." Cam held up his hand. "I got it. I was a handful, to say the least. But I grew up, Dad. And I can fix any boat. Hell, I could build one from scratch. Let me handle this for you."

Emmitt was looking like he had big regrets and something to say, so Piper started to turn and walk off to give them some privacy, but Cam said, "It's okay. Just check him over, I've got this."

Emmitt shook his head. "You weren't a handful, Camden. It was me. I was the handful. Your mom and I split, and she was adamant that I leave her alone to handle herself. I had Rowan, and I wasn't all that great at just being me, much less trying to raise a baby, but those are excuses, and I'm sorry. I'm so sorry."

Cam tipped his head back and stared at the sky for a long beat before meeting his dad's gaze. "Forget it, okay? It doesn't matter. What matters now is your health. Let's move on."

"This first." Emmitt took a step closer to him. "I wish I could go back in time."

"It's done. Why would you want to relive it?"

"So that I could try harder. I'd try to make it work with your mom so that we could've stayed a family. I'd do better by you, Cam. I would."

"Dad . . ." There was no anger in Cam's voice. No censure. "Our history is water under the bridge. It's gone, and I'm not into regrets. I'm here now, and so are you."

Emmitt slowly nodded his head. "And I'm glad for that."

"Me too. So get your ass inside and let Piper do her thing."

Emmitt turned to her and smiled. "He's been here only a week and already found the best woman in town." He paused and looked at Cam. "She's a keeper, son. Remember that."

"Uh, no, I'm not." Piper shifted her weight uneasily. "A keeper."

Both men looked at her. "Dad, could you give us a minute?"

"Sure," Emmitt said. "Take your time." He gave Cam a meaningful look. "And I mean that. Women like when you take your time."

Cam's grimace said he'd maybe finally found the end of his patience.

Emmitt held up a hand. "I know, who wants to take advice from your dad, right? But, son, I've been on Tinder for two years now, and trust me. I know these things." He turned and headed up to the house, and Piper nearly laughed at Cam's expression. The perpetually-in-control man had zero idea how to react to this.

"You think this is funny?" he asked. "Me coming face-to-face with my dad's sex life?"

"I think it's hysterical."

He shook his head, but he smiled too. Reaching out, he took her heavy duffel bag from her shoulder and slung it over his. "So you really do come over once a day to check on him."

"I try," she said, prepared to feel a little defensive about that. "I missed yesterday because my shift went late."

He squeezed her hand. "It means a lot, so thank you." Gently, he cradled her jaw, his thumb skimming along the bruise she could feel forming.

"Don't ask," she said. "Rough transport earlier."

Leaning in, he pressed a kiss to her temple, and then her forehead. "You okay?"

What she was, apparently, was a lover of forehead kisses . . . "Yes."

He held her gaze with his.

"What?" she asked.

"I'm working on my inner caveman, who wants to come out and deal with whoever gave this to you. They'd never find his body."

His easy expression had turned intense and determined, looking every inch the trained warrior she knew he was. "He's been arrested."

"Good." He looked her over, eyes assessing her. "Any injuries I don't see?"

He asked this lightly. Calmly, even. But there was an edge to him, and a visible set to his jaw.

"No," she said. "I'm okay. Really."

She got a nod, and he made a clear effort to shake off the tension. "If you were hurt, would you admit it?"

"Would you?" she countered.

That got her a wry smile. "Touché. Okay, how about this. We play doctor again, only this time *I* get to be all bossy and in charge."

She laughed for the first time all day. Laughed and . . . felt a little frisson of arousal go through her at the thought of playing anything with this man. "Maybe some other time."

"I'm going to hold you to that."

They started walking up the hill toward the house.

"You doing okay with your brother and sister being back?" he asked.

She glanced at him, not expecting the personal interest in her life. Distractions weren't supposed to do that. "Well, we haven't killed each other yet, so . . ."

He smiled. "That's good, right?"

"Yes."

"You sound surprised."

"I am. I guess sometimes I expect the worst."

"Hard way to live," he said.

True, and she gave a slow nod. Maybe she should start a list of how to have a better attitude . . .

"Have you and your sister had a chance to talk? Catch up?"

"Win's not big on talking, at least not with me."

He started to speak, but then stopped to pull something from her hair. "Why are you wearing pieces of glass?"

"Probably from that last call. The guy who . . ." She gestured to her face. "He walked through a glass door first."

His smile faded. "You get cut?"

"No, and considering the last time you saw me I was wearing mud, this has to be somewhat of an improvement."

He gave a very small smile. "I liked the mud. You looked good in it."

She rolled her eyes, but stilled when he brushed something off her shoulder, then her collarbone. "Why are you grooming me like a monkey?"

"Monkeys do it to show interest."

She paused. "I'm . . . not a good bet, Cam."

He locked his gaze on hers. "That just makes us even."

Okay, so they were on the same page. She liked that. A lot.

"You're staring at my mouth again," he said. "Last time you did that, you kissed me."

She felt her pulse spike and bit her lower lip.

He studied her. "Or maybe you want me to kiss *you* this time."

She reached up and touched his mouth. His lips were somehow both soft and firm. And warm and—

His hand wrapped around her wrist, holding one of her fingers to his mouth so he could close his teeth over the tip. Sort of gently, sort of not. Sucking in a breath, she squirmed as heat bolted through her, and then went still when his tongue soothed the nip he'd just given her.

She actually shook with need. She wasn't one to do this, to . . .

yearn and *ache*, like maybe she'd pass out if he didn't touch her. Mostly she rushed through her day for the simple pleasure of going to bed, which she did alone. Yes, she'd had relationships, even serious ones. But she had a problem with true intimacy that she could hide for only so long before she self-destructed and ruined the things that made her happy.

Ryland being her last example. The firefighter had told her he wanted more, he wanted her everything, and if she couldn't give it to him, others would.

Apparently, that had been very true.

But this, a small voice inside her said, *this isn't like that*. This, with Cam, wasn't going anywhere. It *couldn't*, so there was no pressure to think about the future, no pressure to make a promise to love someone when she wasn't even sure she could. There were no what-ifs. There was no chance of hurting anyone, or worse, getting hurt. Buoyed by that realization, she stepped into Cam and ran her free hand up his chest.

"That doesn't feel like a no," he murmured.

"It isn't."

He stared at her for a single breath, and then pulled her into him and kissed her, a succulent, sensuous, delicious kiss with a lot of tongue that had her instantly forgetting about the stress of her job, her siblings, her life. Everything.

When they'd run out of air, they pulled back and stared at each other. "Still scary," she whispered.

"Yeah." He was breathing no steadier than she was, which was reassuring. If he'd been as confident about this as he appeared to be in every other aspect of his life, she might've had to hurt him.

By mutual silent agreement, they entered Emmitt's house through the back door and into the kitchen, where Piper checked his vitals.

"Looks good," she said, amazed to find her voice still husky, her body still humming. "And I brought a surprise."

"Tell me it's food," Emmitt said.

"It's food." She pulled out the stuff from her duffel bag that she'd gotten on the way home. "How does breakfast for dinner sound?"

"Perfect," Emmitt said.

Cam came up to her side. "What can I do?"

She smiled at him. "Just stand there and look pretty."

Emmitt took a look at Cam's face and laughed his ass off.

"I'm not pretty," Cam finally said, as if she'd insulted him.

"Have you looked in the mirror?" his dad asked.

"Have *you*?" Cam countered.

"Yeah, and I'm pretty as hell."

Piper laughed, but it wasn't just that they looked alike. Both held their bodies in a way that conveyed confidence and an easy athleticism. And those matching intense eyes that could seem cold when they were thinking, but warmed when amused.

And in Cam's case, she happened to know they also went scorching hot when he was aroused . . .

They also had the same square jaw, both scruffy at the moment, and matching facial expressions, currently dialed to Hungry Males. She imagined her siblings would be wearing matching hungry expressions about now too, but she'd texted them both asking if she should bring dinner and neither had responded.

"Don't tease me," Emmitt said seriously. "You know breakfast for dinner is my favorite thing on the planet. But you forbid me from having it."

"I didn't forbid you." She began whipping up the ingredients and heating up pans. "I said you were doing it wrong. Too much fat, too much sugar."

Cam pulled out some chocolate milk and poured a glass for everyone before setting the table.

Emmitt sniffed suspiciously at the turkey bacon and gluten-free, sugar-free pancakes now cooking. "It looks good."

There was a knock at the back door, and Gavin walked in. "I smelled bacon."

"I tried to reach you," Piper said. "Go away. People who don't respond to texts don't get free food."

"Come in," Emmitt said, overruling her.

Cam set another place.

Two minutes later, Winnie showed up too. "Oh my God, I knew it. You're all eating without me? You suck." She sat at the table.

"Seriously?" Piper asked her.

Without missing a beat, Cam set another place.

"Sorry for the Manning family invasion," Piper said to the room.

"Yeah," Gavin said. "As a whole, we have boundary issues. I read that in one of Piper's journals once."

Everyone laughed except Piper, who pointed her fork at him.

"I like this," Cam said. "A big family dinner. Rowan was always two thousand plus miles away. I felt like an only child."

"My fault," Emmitt said. "Your mom and I really thought it

was best to each go our own way, and she couldn't have handled a baby, and you were already almost grown, so . . ." He shook his head. "I don't know what we were thinking. Honestly, we were only thinking about ourselves. It's not right how we bungled things. I'll never quite forgive myself, Cam, but I promise I'm working on being better."

Cam eyed him for a long beat and then nodded. Easy acceptance, easy forgiveness.

Piper wasn't at all sure she could have done either of those things.

They all served themselves and then sat as a group to dive in. It took Piper a minute to realize all chatter had died, replaced by silence. "What's wrong?" she asked.

"Nothing," everyone said in unison, with no eye contact. Gee, not suspicious at all. She took a bite of her gluten-free, sugar-free pancakes and . . . choked.

"Oh my God. That's"—she fought against wanting to spit it out—"*disgusting.*"

"Thank God," Emmitt muttered.

"It's gross," Winnie whispered.

"What's in the pancakes, sand?" Gavin asked.

Mortified, Piper started to gather the plates. "Maybe if I tried coconut sugar—"

"Sis, nothing could've saved that breakfast." Gavin rose. "My turn." And he headed to the kitchen. "Holy shit," they heard him say, and he popped his head back out. "You left me a disaster in here."

Piper shrugged. "I clean up afterward."

"As you go," Gavin said. "*Always* as you go." He vanished again.

Winnie looked at Cam. "When do you leave?"

"I've still got several weeks off."

"I meant the Coast Guard thing. You could get deployed at any time, right?"

"More likely to get activated. Deployment happens less often."

Piper set down her glass. She knew he'd been activated probably more times than it was worth counting, but it was one thing to think it, another to live it. "Where would you have to go?"

"Could be anywhere."

"Where've you been?" Winnie asked.

"Lots of places. Puerto Rico, Afghanistan, Kuwait, Cuba . . . Sometimes we don't do land at all."

"You stay on the water," Winnie said. "Right? Like when you're fighting pirates?"

His brows went up.

"Come on, I know you fight pirates."

He just gave a small smile. "Okay, maybe I've had some missions where we boarded and took down foreign freighters for possessing drugs and weapons."

"Pirates," Winnie repeated, looking pleased.

Piper and her siblings had been to a whole bunch of places too. For Winnie, that had happened from birth until the age of three. That meant she didn't have real memories of any of that time, just stories she'd been told. Practically fairy tales.

Not to Piper. Those times were all too real in her mind,

which meant the danger of what Cam did out there was not lost on her.

"It's not always like that," he said, speaking to Winnie but looking at Piper, as if he knew where her thoughts had gone. "Sometimes we're simply the humanitarian aid or law enforcement, and sometimes we're guarding oil fields and setting up ECPs—entry control points."

"I read that the Coast Guard is the only military branch that can carry guns on American soil without martial law being in effect," Winnie said.

"Because we're part of the Department of Homeland Security, not the DOD."

"What's your specialty?"

"I'm an ME1," he said. "Maritime Law Enforcement Specialist, First Class."

"Is that like the Big Cheese?" Winnie asked.

"My rank's E-6. If I went up one more to E-7, I'd be a chief. A chief runs the field, but usually from an office."

"Not as exciting," Winnie said.

"I'm not an office kind of guy," he said on an easy shrug.

Gavin came to the table with egg-and-sausage burritos. He squeezed Piper's shoulder. "Not trying to steal your thunder, just want to take care of you once in a while."

Touched, she smiled at him, and the rest of them stopped talking to eat and give the occasional moan of pleasure.

The burritos were amazing. Restaurant quality. "Okay," Piper said. "You win."

"It wasn't a contest," Gavin said modestly, and paused. "But do make sure to note this down in your journal. I want it on record to offset the next time I screw something up."

"Hey, we're all adults now," Piper said. "So there's no screwing anything up. We're all on the same page. No secrets equals no fights."

No one made eye contact.

"What?" she asked.

Emmitt lifted his glass of chocolate milk. "To family."

Winnie and Gavin quickly grabbed their glasses and lifted them too. "To family."

And even though Piper knew she'd once again missed something, the moment was gone.

CHAPTER 8

"If you feed me now, no one dies."

A few mornings later, Piper staggered downstairs in search of caffeine, pausing just outside the kitchen at the sound of voices.

"How did we all get so ridiculously broken?" Winnie asked.

Gavin laughed roughly. "You really need me to answer that? At least we're home with our glue stick, Piper."

Winnie was quiet at that, her silence seeming to suggest that while Piper *might* be the glue, she was also a little *unglued* . . .

Fair. Piper felt distinctly unglued lately. She'd just started to enter when Gavin spoke again. "When are you going to tell her, Win?"

"Never."

Gavin made a sound of disappointment.

"Whatever, Gav. People in glass houses shouldn't throw stones."

Piper would've liked to hear more, but Sweet Cheeks chose that very moment to wind around her legs, letting out a very loud series of chirps that said, "If you feed me now, no one dies."

Piper winced as both siblings turned toward her, startled. "Hey," she said casually. "What's going on?"

Gavin and Winnie looked at each other. Then Gavin shrugged. "Might as well admit it, since she's about to find out."

Winnie shifted her weight. "Gav—"

"Winnie burned breakfast."

Piper could have called that out for the lie it clearly was, but . . . she could smell it. She eyed the kitchen, stopping short at the realization that the place looked like a cyclone had hit it.

"I tried Rowan's banana muffin recipe and nearly blew us all up," Winnie said. "He was so great in the kitchen." She bit her lower lip. "Sometimes I forget he's gone."

Piper felt her heart squeeze. "I'm sorry, Win."

"I know you didn't like him. You thought he was a bad influence on me."

He'd been a terrible influence, introducing Winnie to a partying lifestyle that Piper hadn't approved of, but that didn't mean she didn't like him. She had. He'd been fun-loving, charismatic, and sweet. "He was a good kid. I know you miss him."

Winnie nodded. "I do. And since baking no longer holds any appeal, and I suck at cooking in general, I'm going to stick to what I'm good at—fixing things."

"You're good at fixing things?"

"I'm learning. And Emmitt taught me a little bit about gardening. I thought I'd help with the vegetable patch."

"Grandma's vegetable patch?" Piper asked. "The one no one's maintained for years?"

Winnie shrugged. "Thought it'd be nice."

"But we don't know the first thing about gardening."

"Duh. That's what YouTube's for." Hopping up to sit on the counter, Winnie began flipping through a stack of bills. "And yikes, we're poor."

"Like that's anything new," Piper said, still taking in the devastation zone.

"It wasn't my fault," Winnie said. "The oven's messed up."

"I'll put a new oven on my list for Santa."

"It looks like a bomb went off in here." Gavin shook his head. "She got that from you."

"Well, excuse me," Winnie said. "We can't all be neat freaks."

"How about just neat? Can you all be just neat?"

This was an age-old argument between the three of them. Gavin hated a messy house, but especially a messy kitchen. Funny, because he didn't object to having a messy life.

"Why are you guys up so early?" Piper asked.

"Cam finished fixing Emmitt's boat yesterday. So Emmitt took us fishing," Winnie said.

Piper laughed at the idea of her siblings getting up early on purpose. "Come on."

"It's true," Winnie said. "The sunrise was gorg."

"Yeah. Probably because it was the first time you've ever seen one."

Gavin laughed and bumped fists with Piper.

"Hey," Winnie said, pouting. "I've seen a sunrise. Once. When I got the stomach flu and was up all night puking . . ."

"That was a hangover," Piper said.

"Oh. Right."

Piper looked at Gavin. He was still smiling, looking young and carefree, and it pinched her heart. "And you. You used to hate mornings."

He shrugged. "I caught us dinner. You'll love it."

"Emmitt's been wanting to get out on the water," Winnie said. "You gotta remember, he's only owned the marina for five years. Rowan handled most of the boat maintenance, but he got behind. I had no idea, but it turns out Cam's the one who taught Rowan everything he knew." Winnie's eyes went a little shiny. "He's a really good guy too."

Piper suspected that was very true. Which wasn't the comfort it should've been because she didn't want to fall for him. She just wanted to get naked with him.

Quite badly.

"You guys don't even live here anymore," she said. "How do you know more about my neighbors than I do?"

Winnie shrugged. "Because we don't break out into hives when we have to be social?"

Gavin winced and gave her a small head shake. "Harsh."

Winnie sighed. "I'm sorry. Piper knows what I mean." She hopped off the counter. "I'm going to shower. Don't anyone use hot water. For a few."

"You mean an hour?" Gavin asked her back. "Cuz that's how long your showers last."

"Shut it!" came down the stairs.

Piper looked at her brother, who was now on his laptop, fingers racing across the keyboard. "Weren't you going to look into the hot-water tank situation for me?"

"Actually, Winnie's on it. She's really becoming quite the handyman. Er—handywoman."

"Okay." Piper didn't actually believe this, mostly because Winnie wasn't big on manual labor. Or any kind of labor. But whatever. "How about the toaster? You get a chance to fix that?"

"No. But later, I promise."

She waited, but he didn't say anything more. Or even look up at her. "Gavin, what's going on?"

"Nothing."

"Something," she insisted.

He shrugged. "I'm just tired."

She got that, but this was more. "It's unlike you to be so . . ."

He looked up. "So what? Useless?"

"Not the word I was going to use."

"Good, because I'm not useless, at least not completely. For instance, I can be used as a really bad example." He was trying to lighten the mood. He'd been doing that all his life.

"What I'm trying to say is that you're not acting like yourself." Yes, he was still the same laid-back and easygoing "no worries" kid he'd always been, and sharp and funny as usual, but there were haunted shadows in his eyes, and that worried her. "What's wrong?"

"Nothing."

She perched a hip on the kitchen table. "Try again."

He sat up, shoved his hands through his hair, and then rose to his feet. He looked her right in the eyes and said, "Listen, I get that you mean well, but it's okay. You did it, you got me to adulthood. I'm now tired by eight P.M., mostly pay bills on time, and love ibuprofen. Happy? I can make you a certificate of acknowledgment if you like, noting that your mothering duties are hugely appreciated and have been credentialed, signaling the end of your obligation."

This cut her to the very core, but she pulled a page from Cam's book and remained calm, holding eye contact. "I'm well aware. Just as I'm also aware you're acting weirdly defensive. Did you get another DUI?"

"No. Christ." He started to stalk off, but stopped to look at her, into her, and she felt anxiety crawl up her throat and block her air passageway.

"What do you remember of Mom and Dad?" he asked.

This completely threw her. "What? We just talked about this."

"No, I talked, you evaded. Because in fact, we *never* talk about them."

"Gavin, where is this coming from?"

He sat back down, heavily, like his legs were lead. "I'm losing my memories of them and don't want to."

The air in her lungs escaped in one *whoosh*, and she sat down too. "Oh, Gavin." She drew in a deep breath. "Sometimes . . . sometimes forgetting's the only way to lose the pain."

"Wow." He shook his head. "That's some serious bullshit right there, Piper."

"It's called a coping mechanism."

"It's denial, and trust me, denial's bad for you." He stood and walked off.

Okay, so once again, she'd said the wrong thing. She was getting really good at that, but then again, she'd had a lot of practice.

AT WORK, PIPER rode shotgun to Jenna. The day had been full already and it was barely noon. They'd patched up a trucker who'd picked up a hitchhiker and then gotten robbed and beaten up for his efforts. Then there was the contractor who'd stepped on his own shovel and gotten whacked in the face. Now they'd just left the hospital after a drop-off—a teenage pregnancy gone wrong thanks to an overdose.

Choices. It was all about choices, and every one of them had a consequence. Frankly, it was exhausting.

On the way to grab lunch, a call came through that had them taking off fast, following a fire truck to a multicar accident. They weaved and bobbed through traffic, Jenna being very liberal with her horn while muttering about idiots who should have their licenses revoked.

Reports were coming in about injuries, but no specifics, which meant they had no idea what they'd be running into.

Sort of the theme of Piper's life.

She felt her phone buzz with a text and eyed the message. It was from a real estate agent friend of hers, whom she'd contacted several months back for advice on selling the property. Alaina had suggested Piper give the house and cottages a light makeover for curb appeal, and in the meantime, Alaina would hunt down some potential buyers. Seemed she'd found a possible buyer, who'd be in town in two weeks.

Piper slid her phone away. Two weeks . . . perfect timing.

She'd talk to her siblings about selling, something she hadn't found time to do yet, and they'd continue to get the place ready, together. Then Gavin and Winnie would go back to their lives, and she'd be on the way to hers.

"So?" Jenna asked.

"So . . . what?"

"You still haven't told me what's happening between you and Hot Guy. You've ignored all my questions."

"And you think now, heading to the scene of a major accident, is a good time?"

Jenna took a sharp left turn that had Piper practically kissing her window. "Hey!"

"Start talking."

"I texted you the other day that everything's fine, I've just been busy."

"Yeah, and that's not suspicious at all . . ." Jenna took another hard turn and Piper braced herself.

"You do know that you can't afford another driving warning, right?"

"My driving's perfect," Jenna said. "Back up to what happened on the night of the storm last week. You've been cagey about that ever since. Ryland said he saw you and Hot Guy talking at the back door for a bit. Did he follow you home?"

"He has a name. It's *Cam*. And what does my ex care who I was talking to?"

"Back up," Jenna said. "Repeat that."

"What does Ryland care who I—"

"Not that," Jenna said. "The other thing."

Piper blinked. "Are you hungover again?"

"I'm referring to the fact that you're on a first-name basis with . . . Cam." She waggled her eyebrows.

"He's Emmitt's son."

Jenna looked confused. "Emmitt . . ."

"My neighbor. The guy who runs the marina."

Jenna's smile faded. "Rowan's brother?"

"Yes. He's a Coast Guard Reservist and with the DEA, though he's on temporary leave from that at the moment."

"Okay, let me see if I've got this straight. You're boning a sexy DEA slash military hottie, who happens to be the marina owner's son . . ."

"Oh my God, you're a child."

"Just tell me you got some," Jenna said. "Wait, never mind. If you had, you'd be smiling."

Jenna was her best friend, but how Piper felt about Cam was complicated. But he'd definitely made her smile . . .

"What aren't you telling me? Wait a second, are you suddenly smiling into the window?"

"You can't possibly see that."

"Maybe not, but I can hear it."

"I'm not smiling." But she wanted to. "Look, there might've been a kiss." Or two . . . "But that's all I'm telling you."

"Shut up. No, don't shut up! Tell me everything! You buried the lede! Did he throw you down on the bed and jump your bones? Oh my God, I want someone to throw me down on the bed and jump my bones!"

"If a man threw me down on my bed," Piper said dryly, "it'd better be followed up with him telling me to stay put because he's going to clean the whole house for me."

This was a big fat lie. If she had Cam in her bed, they'd absolutely not be talking about cleaning.

"You're ruining the fantasy. Back up and start at the kiss."

"We're done talking about this."

"Are you *going* to sleep with him?"

Piper tossed up her hands. "What part of 'we're done talking about this' don't you get?"

"Come on. If he's only here for a couple of weeks, you need to hurry up and blow off some steam. Or just blow."

Piper laughed; she couldn't help it. "You did *not* just say that."

"Look, he's perfect for you. He'll be gone before even you can screw up any real relationship with him."

Is that what she did?

"Yes," Jenna said, reading her mind. "It is. See Ryland as an example. He wanted more, you bailed. Also, you put everyone's needs ahead of your own, making yourself the lowest priority. You need to stop, by the way. And you should also put *that* in your journal under your ridiculous list of rules for yourself."

"Shh," Piper said, and turned up the radio connecting them to the scene of the accident. "They're calling for another unit."

"That'll be Noah and Sonya."

They both groaned at the name Sonya. She'd gone to school with them and was Jenna's nemesis because she was dating Jenna's ex, whom Jenna wasn't over yet, though she wouldn't admit that upon threat of dismemberment.

At the intersection ahead, police were already working on handling the traffic and blocking off the scene. CJ was one of them. He and Piper had been friends for years now. Ever since he'd had his heart broken by Gavin years ago.

Noah and Sonya's rig came up beside theirs and they all hopped out. The four of them grabbed their gear and were directed by CJ to one of what looked like a three-car pileup.

"Toyota ran a red," he said. "T-boned a semi, which got rear-ended by the Ford. The Toyota spun off the semi, rolled a few times, and then slid into a pole. The truck driver made the call, says he's uninjured, but has blood pouring down his face from a head wound." He pointed to the guy sitting on the curb, being watched over by another cop. "The driver of the Ford took off. We're in pursuit now. Firefighters are attempting to extract the guy in the Toyota, who's alert and very chatty."

"Like DUI chatty?" Jenna asked.

CJ touched the tip of his nose.

"Divide and conquer," Piper said.

"Be careful," CJ said, and she smiled at him.

"Always."

Noah and Sonya headed to the trucker sitting on the curb. Piper and Jenna jogged over to the firefighters at the Toyota. It was Ryland and Xander. She'd gone to school with Xander, and Ryland . . . well, they were both professional enough to leave their past where it belonged. Both firefighters were working the jaws of life, trying to get the crumpled and clearly jammed driver's door open. Inside was a male, early twenties, hanging upside down by his seat belt. He was yelling and swearing and waving his fists at what appeared to be the semi and the Ford.

Chatty indeed.

Xander and Ryland gave Piper and Jenna a chins-up greeting and kept working to free the guy. Piper bent low and cocked her head to the side to try to assess their patient. One, the inside of his car, even with the windows busted out, reeked like a brewery. Two, no blood that she could see. Which wasn't to say he hadn't been injured. She'd seen people walk away from car accidents thinking they were fine, only to collapse and die hours later from internal trauma.

"Hey there," she called out. "What's your name?"

"Suck it," he yelled. "I've got my rights, you know."

"And what rights are those, sir?"

"To be treated professionally and not like a criminal."

"That's all we're trying to do here. Are you in any pain?"

"No, but *you* will be if you don't get me outta here."

Both Xander and Ryland reacted to this with barely perceptible body language suggesting they were ready to subdue the guy once they freed him if needed. But neither would interfere with Jenna and Piper getting their jobs done unless it was deemed vitally necessary. It was a respect thing, and though Ryland might not respect the decisions of her heart, he absolutely respected her on the job and she appreciated that.

"Get me the fuck outta here now!" the guy yelled.

Piper looked at Jenna, who gave a tight smile. They usually ro-sham-bo'd for the shit jobs, and this one qualified, but it was Piper's turn and they both knew it. She squatted low to get eye to eye with the driver. "Sir, we're going to need you to cooperate so we can get you out of here, or—"

"Or what, you *won't* save my life? I'll sue your ass, dead or alive!"

Nice. But before she could respond, Xander and Ryland finally broke into the car. It took all four of them to get the guy out and subdue him, because it turned out he was also high as a kite, and whatever he was on had given him some serious superhuman strength.

She felt completely done in by the time she got home after her third hellish twelve-hour shift that week.

It was habit to bypass her house and head across the property to check on Emmitt. She jumped over the creek that was thankfully small again and knocked on the back door. As she waited, she flashed back to the other day, when they'd all had dinner together like they were a unit.

But it wasn't the memory of dinner that had butterflies taking flight in her stomach, or why she was suddenly starting to sweat. Nope, she knew *exactly* what was up and his name was Cam.

No one answered, but she could hear talking, so she turned and followed the voices down to the marina and the lake, where she found Emmitt and Cam on one of the docked boats.

Along with Winnie.

Winnie was talking a mile a minute, and laughing too, and Piper stilled, feeling a little left out. Of everything. How long had it been since she'd seen her sister looking happy like that? She honestly couldn't remember, and she knew if she intruded now, she'd ruin it.

So she started to walk off, but Cam called her name. With a grimace, she turned back and found all eyes on her. "Hey," she said, as casually as she could.

Winnie waved with great cheer, which from experience Piper knew was mostly guilt. But what the heck could her little sister be feeling guilty about?

Winnie rose and brushed a kiss to Emmitt's cheek. "Thanks for the tips. I'm going to go get started right now."

"Started on what?" Piper asked.

"It's a surprise."

"What kind of a surprise?"

"A surprise! Jeez!"

"The last time you surprised me was when we ran into each other in the middle of the night. I was going to the bathroom, you were sneaking out to a party."

"I was fifteen!" Winnie tossed up her hands. "Give me some credit."

Piper watched her stalk off, feeling the heat of humiliation on her cheeks as Cam and Emmitt moved to join her. "I can't seem to engage with her without a fight."

"The only thing that ever worked on Rowan was *not* reacting," Cam said.

"Advice you didn't learn from your mom," Emmitt said dryly. "Her favorite thing was reacting. Usually *over*reacting."

"True," Cam admitted. "I learned in the Coast Guard. Sometimes the guys in my unit act like a bunch of middle-school boys."

"Don't you mean girls?" his dad asked.

"Nope. Middle-school girls are smarter than middle-school boys. And that doesn't change with age, by the way."

Which gave Piper her first laugh of the day.

CHAPTER 9

Choose your own adventure!

Cam stood by while Piper checked his dad's vitals, noting that his dad looked good.

Piper looked exhausted.

"She takes better care of everyone around her than she does of herself," Emmitt said.

Yeah, Cam was starting to get that. He waited until his dad had hugged Piper and walked off before turning to Piper.

Who'd also started to walk off, toward *her* house.

"Hey," he said, gently catching her hand, pulling her back around to face him. He bent his knees a little to look into her face. "You okay?"

"Of course."

Of course. He shook his head. "You're the only person I know who could work the long shifts you do day after day, and then come home to put in some time fixing up your place, and say of course you're okay."

"But I am."

He ran a finger along her temple, tucking an errant strand of hair behind her ear, not missing the little shiver his touch gave her. "You hungry?"

"No."

"You tired?"

"No."

"Okay then," he said, knowing she was lying on both counts. "Do you trust me?"

She slid him a look. "I mean . . . maybe situationally."

He laughed at that. "Blunt. I like it."

"Most people don't."

"I'm not most people."

She stared up at him. "You might be right."

"You think you can turn off your mistrust enough to come with me somewhere? You won't have to think or do anything other than enjoy."

"Is it a one-way trip to a deserted island? Because that's on my list."

He smiled. "I thought Alaska was on your list."

"I've decided to become more adaptable."

He studied her. "Would you actually get on a plane with me right now?"

"No."

"Would you get into my truck if I promised you less than a thirty-minute drive, and then an amazing time?"

She arched a brow. "You think you're an amazing time?"

He laughed. "It's possible I have my moments. You'll have to come with me and decide for yourself."

She snorted, but some of her exhaustion seemed to lift away as she nodded. Smiling, he sent a quick text, then took her hand and started for the truck he'd rented while in Wildstone. On the way to the destination he had in mind, he stopped and got Mexican takeout, which, in spite of claiming not to be hungry, Piper inhaled.

"Oh my God," she moaned around her grilled-chicken-and-cheese burrito. "Amazing."

"I like that you're easy to please. It bodes well for me."

She laughed, as he'd intended. "You can't make me buy that you're not cocky as hell," she said.

"With you? It's actually the opposite."

She bit her lower lip. "For the record, ditto. But you always seem so sure and confident."

He shrugged. "You know how it is out there on the job. You've got a decision to make, sometimes many decisions all at the same time, and often with less than a second in which to make them. You've got to think fast, and own your actions. Sometimes, I guess that ability wrongly comes off as cocky."

She took another bite, chewing while she studied him thoughtfully. "To be fair, you're the only one of the two of us putting your life on the line every single second of the day you're on the job."

"That's not true. As a first responder, you put your neck out there, just like I do." He glanced over at her, taking in the fading bruise along her jaw.

When their gazes met, hers was warmer now, no wariness to be found, and he felt like he'd won the damn lottery.

"Thanks," she said quietly. "So where's home base for you? Near your mom back East?"

"Yes, but she's gone now."

Her eyes flew to his, stricken.

"About ten years ago," he said. "Accidental overdose." At least that had been the official verdict, but he knew the "accidental" part was up for debate. She'd not been able to manage her mental illness, and she'd suffered so much that he wasn't sure she hadn't just given up.

Something else he blamed himself for. Because maybe if he hadn't left for the Coast Guard, he could have helped more. He missed her, but he felt bad the most for Rowan, who'd never really gotten to know her.

"I'm so sorry." Piper's voice was soft. "So your dad . . . he's your only living relative left?"

Except for the baby her sister was carrying. The baby she didn't yet know about, no matter how much he bugged Winnie to tell her. And while he'd promised not to give away the secret, he wouldn't, couldn't lie outright to Piper. She didn't deserve that. And as always when his mind went down that path, he deeply regretted giving Winnie his word. Holding back from Piper didn't feel good, but when he factored in how attracted to her he was, how much he wanted her, it felt even more wrong.

Piper apparently took his silence as the need for a subject change, so she turned to the window and her brows went up as they exited the highway at Pismo Beach.

"Why do I feel nervous?" she asked, when he pulled into a parking lot.

He got out of the truck and came around for her, taking her hand. "Maybe it's me. Maybe I give you butterflies."

"You don't," she said, so quickly that he grinned, because now he knew that he totally did. "Whatever," she muttered. "It's not like you don't know that you melt bones when you kiss."

And now he kept grinning, because he was incredibly flattered that he could melt her bones. But it was more than that. When he touched her, kissed her, he got flashes of the real Piper, the one she liked to hide from the world. The real Piper was softer, sweeter, and reached him in a way no one else ever had. "You're good for my ego."

"Like you needed help in that arena."

He laughed as they walked to the beach. Hills made of sand spanned in either direction, making this a beach people tended to come to for four-wheeling rather than sunbathing.

"What are we doing here?" she asked, eyeing the choppy deep-blue water and heavy surf. "Don't tell me we're going swimming."

"Why?"

"Because I'm"—she appeared to fight herself for a moment—"not super comfortable around the water, which I know is ridiculous, since I live on a lake."

"For the record, I'd never say that. But what are we talking about here, a general light fear of the water, or full-blown phobia?"

"Just a light fear," she said, her breathing a little fast from just talking about it.

Okay, then. Phobia it was. He thought back and realized he'd never seen her on the docks at the marina. Earlier, she'd remained on shore, not taking a single step onto the dock at all. "We're not going in the water," he promised, leading her down the stairs to the beach and then about a hundred feet to a small shack with a huge sign that read:

CHOOSE YOUR OWN ADVENTURE!

"Oh, boy," Piper whispered. "Um—"

"Are you . . . *uncomfortable* with sand?" he asked.

"No."

"Are you uncomfortable with wind in your hair?"

She bit her lower lip again, possibly to hide a smile now. But he wasn't sure; it could be to hide her urge to murder him. "No," she finally said.

"Are you uncomfortable having a good time?"

She turned to him, utterly serious. "I'm not sure I'd recognize a good time."

He smiled and cupped her face as he leaned in and gave her a soft kiss. "Then trust me to show you one. One hour, Piper. Yeah?"

She stared at his mouth for a beat, like maybe she wanted it back on hers—which made two of them—and then nodded. "Yeah."

CHAPTER 10

"That was possibly the most thrilling ride of my life."

Piper had no idea what she thought she was doing. She didn't treat herself to fun very often. Or ever. But it *was* on her list of things to do, so that made her feel better, because tonight she'd be able to check off a box. She loved checking off boxes.

"That looks good on you," Cam said.

"What?"

"The smile."

She nearly tripped over her own feet. She was starting to realize that he saw her as someone far more adventurous and fascinating than she really was. Maybe . . . for this little while at least, she could be the woman he saw.

The guy standing at the shack waiting for them looked like every cliché of a surfer dude Piper had ever seen, sun-bleached hair to his shoulders, sunglasses, no shirt, board shorts, and no shoes. He grinned at Cam and gave a smart-ass salute. "Got your text. Your adventure awaits."

"Piper, meet Brodie," Cam said. "We were in initial training together, eons ago."

Brodie smiled at Piper. "Did he tell you that I beat him in every training exercise?"

"No," Cam said. "Because that's a lie. And anyway, who tapped out after his four years?"

"Guilty," Brodie said easily. "Wasn't cut out for the life. Or for walking about battle rattle when just trying to grab grub."

"Battle rattle?" Piper asked.

"Yeah. When you, like, have fifteen minutes to get food, so you run into a takeout place with so many weapons and tools that you rattle. Get it? Battle rattle." He smiled at the look on her face. "Yeah, you're in the presence of two serious badasses."

She looked at Cam, who shook his head, like he was nothing but a sweet teddy bear.

Uh-huh.

"Your chariot awaits," Brodie said, gesturing to the two . . . vehicles . . . off to the side on the sand. They were three-wheeled buggies that looked like they went really fast. She swallowed hard. "Um."

"They're trikes," Cam said. "Don't worry, they stay on the sand."

"Well, unless you take a jump and get some air," Brodie said. "Which I highly recommend."

Thirty minutes later, after a lesson and brief training about things like jumping and tacking—which supposedly was the art of slowing down by steering into the wind—Piper was in her own trike and doing a great job of pretending not to be terrified. Then she was flying along the beach while seated only a few inches off the ground, the wind in her face, whipping her ponytail, and she felt like she was going faster than she'd ever gone in anything ever before. Up and over the sand hills she went, no longer bothering to hide her whoops of sheer adrenaline-rush joy every time she got a bit of air beneath her tires.

To her left, another trike came into her view. Cam. She glanced over and found him looking hot as hell in dark sunglasses and a wicked smile.

She smiled back.

He kept pace with her for a long moment, then pulled ahead to lead her into a series of hills. There was a gust of wind and she felt the trike hurtle forward. She heard a roar from the tires on the sand and the wind around her, and found herself grinning from ear to ear at the rush.

When it was time to return to the shack, she pulled in next to Cam, who helped her out.

"Well?" he asked.

She grinned. "That was possibly the most thrilling ride of my life."

He pulled off her helmet, the look in his eyes saying that he knew he could give her an even more thrilling ride.

She had no doubt. But she hadn't managed to raise her siblings and give them all relatively decent lives by following a whim, sexy as that whim might be. She'd been afraid of commitment with Ryland because . . . well, she still wasn't one hundred percent sure. But she thought it had something to do with the knowledge that committing to him would mean becoming something she wasn't—a person capable of further dividing her heart, handing yet another chunk of it off to someone and in turn giving them power to hurt her.

But looking into Cam's gaze, she couldn't see him ever trying to make her into something she wasn't. Life with him would only get better.

But they weren't going to go there. And if that caused a little teeny, tiny spark of sadness, she shoved it aside. This wasn't the time to dwell. She needed to live in the moment, which normally she could do only by writing a reminder in a journal. Easy enough to do, since her journal was ever present. Right now it was in her purse. "Do you have your keys to the truck?"

"Yeah. What do you need? I'll get it for you."

Okay, she had two options: admit her crazy or keep it to herself. But maybe to prove that this wouldn't—*couldn't*—last, she gave him the truth. "I need to write something in my journal."

"Sure," he said without blinking an eye, and turned toward the stairs to get to the parking lot.

She stared after him, dumbfounded. Just the fact that he'd go get it made it possible to stop him. "Actually, it's okay. It can wait." Then she stepped into him and pressed her face in the crook of his neck to just breathe him in for a moment, willing herself to remember.

Live in the moment.

After all, there was no sense in thinking about the future, because as she knew all too well, not everyone got one. So why ruin the here and now by running ahead of herself? Besides, she thought with a happy sigh as Cam's arms came around her, the here and now was pretty damn amazing. "Thank you," she whispered against his skin, and then, unable to resist, she kissed his throat.

He took a deep breath, and his arms tightened a little. She thought he'd kiss her, but he didn't, maybe because Brodie was suddenly there, taking their helmets, grinning, asking them how their ride was.

"Great," she said, stepping back from Cam. "Thank you."

"Don't thank me. It was your man here. He dragged me in on my day off. Said I owed him." His smile was lopsided and very genuine as he looked to Cam. "And I do. I owe him my life. Several times over." And with another quick salute, this one not sarcastic, he turned and vanished into his shack.

She looked at Cam, but he didn't say anything, just took her hand and walked with her back to the truck.

"Did you enjoy yourself?" he asked when they were on the highway.

"Yes, in case you couldn't tell by the grin on my face." She squeezed his hand. "Thank you, for reminding me to take time to fly."

He brought her hand up to his mouth and brushed a kiss against her palm, which hit her heart. And also decidedly south of her heart. "What did Brodie mean, he owes you his life?"

His eyes were on the road now, but she sensed a rare hesitation.

"You can't say," she guessed.

"There's a lot of my military past that I can't talk about."

There was something in his tone now. Wariness? "I understand," she said.

He glanced at her. "You do?"

"Of course. Your missions are probably mostly classified."

"This one wasn't. It's just hard to talk about. He was on a training mission that went horribly wrong. His parachute didn't open correctly. He got separated from his unit, landed in unfriendly waters, and then it became a rescue situation."

"And you were the one who rescued him," she guessed.

"My unit, yes."

"You're a close-knit bunch?"

"Very." He shot her a smile. "A unit spends more time together than most families ever do. We get into, and out of, a lot of shit together."

"So what does a day as a Coastie look like?"

"At the unit, or deployed?"

"Both," she said, giving in to her ridiculous curiosity about him since he seemed willing—somewhat—to answer her questions.

"If we're at the PSU—our Port Security Unit," he clarified, "we start at 0500. It's training, training, and then more training, most of it brutal. Muscle memory's everything. We conduct muster, shoot guns, meet with the division, shoot more guns, clean boats, drive boats, and shoot even more guns. Then we go to the range to shoot again until we can't hold our arms up." He glanced over at her. "Sensing a trend?"

"Definitely. When do you eat and sleep?"

"Oh, all that's just the first part of any given day. There's also division-specific training and inspections. We eat or sleep whenever there's a spare second. Then wake up and do a wash and repeat."

Hard life. "And when you're deployed?" she asked.

He rubbed a hand over his jaw. A rare tell, she'd discovered. He wasn't uncomfortable often, but he definitely wasn't a fan of talking about himself.

"Sometimes it's almost a relief, because there're no inspections. Rule number one: keep weapons clean at all times. A dirty weapon'll get you killed. There's mission planning, equipment checks, reports. And then rule number two: sleep when you can and eat anything other than an MRE when you can. We take eight- to twelve-hour shifts, either driving boats, working in a TOC—tactical operation center—or manning an overwatch with mounted machine guns protecting high-value assets."

"High-value assets."

"Such as a navy ship, or Guantánamo Bay, or even a liquefied natural gas ship if the US has intel that it might be used in a way that could be detrimental to a highly populated area."

She boggled and was in sheer awe at the core strength of this man and all the others like him. "Do you ever get downtime?"

"Sometimes. We Skype home, chase any kind of ball we can get ahold of, and drink. In general, if there's trouble or merriment to be had while we're gone and left to our own devices, we will find it."

This she could believe. "Do you know what I think?"

His expression went slightly wary, the equivalent of a normal man's full-out wince. "Do I want to know?"

"I think you're incredible." She saw his surprise, something she was pretty sure he didn't normally experience. She smiled. "What?"

He shook his head. "Let's just say I've been in a few relationships where me not being able to talk about specifics was a huge issue, like I didn't trust them enough."

"Were any of these serious relationships?"

"I thought so once or twice," he said. "But I was wrong. I know it's hard for people to understand that it's not about trust. Sometimes it's literally my job not to tell."

"I get it," she said softly.

"That easy?"

"For me, yes." Then it was her turn to pause. "But I'm sorry if the people in your past weren't able to understand it and you got hurt."

A very small smile touched his lips, but he kept his eyes on the road. "My mom used to say that the past was just building blocks to the future. That all regrets, mistakes, and miscalculations were the foundation, and as necessary as air."

She smiled. "I'd have liked your mom."

"She'd have liked you too."

CAM HAD JUST turned onto their street when Piper got a page calling her back in to work. He parked and walked her to her car, though he really wanted to feed her again and tuck her into bed because he knew she was tired. But he hated being babied, and he knew she'd hate it too. So he opened her door for her and said, "Be safe."

"I will. And thanks again." She went up on tiptoe to kiss him, sliding a hand to the back of his neck, a touch he still felt as she drove away.

"You're still limping," he said to his dad, as the man came up beside him.

"Show-off. And I'm much better, thanks to that woman who just drove away." He paused. "And you."

"Was that an actual, almost thank-you?" Cam asked, amused, because his dad rarely bothered with niceties such as *please* and *thank you*.

"Maybe." Emmitt's gaze was still on the road, even though Piper was long gone. "I told you she's had a rough go of it. But I never did tell you how or why."

"You said it was her story to tell."

"Yes," Emmitt said. "And I still believe that. But I also know that she's likely to shut you out instead of letting you in any closer. So I'm going to give you a leg up and tell you some of it. You're welcome."

"Dad—"

"She had to raise her siblings on her own. Well, she had her grandparents around at first, but by the time Piper was eighteen, she was on her own with them. And Gavin and Winnie did as kids do and put her through the wringer."

"Their parents were killed overseas."

"Yes. She told you that?" his dad asked in surprise. "She never talks about it. She works hard and sacrifices to take care of everyone else, even on the job. It's not great pay, and she deals with a lot of people's BS. It's hard work, mentally and physically, something I'm sure you can relate to, given your own vocation. But for Piper, it goes on both at home and at work, and wears her down because she's the sort to take everything on her shoulders, no matter the weight."

His dad was right; she hadn't talked about any of this much, but he could read between the lines. She was resilient. Smart. Loving, though he had a feeling she'd deny that. And . . . well, amazing.

"You were so self-sufficient and insistent that you were okay on the East Coast with your mom. I let myself believe it, because I felt like I was drowning raising Rowan," his dad said. "But in hindsight, it was easier than I thought, and in fact, I might've been too easy on him." His good humor faded. "I miss that kid like crazy." With a long exhale, he turned to Cam. "I read the police report and the news, but you and I haven't talked about it. The car accident."

Cam tried to swallow, but there was a sudden lump in his throat the size of a regulation football. So he shifted, turning so he could see down the hill, beyond the house, to the lake.

"Sometimes I close my eyes at night," his dad said, "and it's all I can think about. Was he in pain? Did he . . . suffer?"

Cam felt his heartbeat change, start a heavy thudding that he still woke up to in the middle of the night. Panic. Fear. Terror. He'd been trained by the military on how to deal with all of that, and he'd gotten good at shoving his feelings deep.

Real good.

But that one night . . . Hell, that one half hour with Rowan had ripped through his training like it was nothing, and he'd not been able to get back to that numb place since.

His dad was still facing him, but Cam didn't move or stop taking in the sight of the water, one of the only places he felt at peace.

The car had T-boned them at sixty miles per hour. Rowan

had taken the hit and he'd been bleeding . . . everywhere. Two major arteries severed. There hadn't been time to do anything but crawl to where he lay and pull him close.

"No, he wasn't in pain, he promised me he wasn't," Cam managed to say. He could still see himself sitting in the middle of the dark street, the car horn going off and utter destruction all around them while he held his brother as he bled out faster than anyone should be able to. They'd had less than two minutes. That was it. "He made me promise him to look after Winnie and the baby they'd just found out she was carrying."

His dad remained quiet for a long moment. "And so you're here, honoring that promise," he finally said raggedly, and when Cam looked over at him, he saw tears on his cheeks.

Twisting the knife.

"Dad—"

That was all he got out before his dad yanked him into a bear hug. "Thanks for not dying too," he whispered thickly.

Emmitt Hayes was thirty-three years older than Cam, but strong as hell. There was no escaping. So Cam wrapped his arms around his dad, and they both set their heads on each other's shoulder.

After another long minute, his dad finally released him and stepped back, swiping his eyes with his arm. "So . . . want to help me clean out the fish guts?"

CHAPTER 11

"When I say *whatever*, I really mean screw you."

After another sleepless night, Gavin found himself in the kitchen at the crack of dawn. In the old days, Piper had been the one to put together meals for their little *Bad News Bears* family of three. Simple stuff, like mac and cheese and hot dogs. Sometimes she'd chop up some broccoli and try to hide it in the cheese, but he and Winnie had always been good at sniffing out anything green, stomping all over Piper's hope that they'd eat healthy.

Truth was, he and Winnie had been blissfully ignorant, not understanding their precarious position, which was that Piper, a kid herself, was doing the best she could to keep them together. He hadn't appreciated it then.

Actually, he hadn't appreciated it until he'd gotten out of rehab with a relatively clear head, if not a still-confused heart.

Piper had single-handedly saved their lives and he hadn't ever given her enough credit for it.

He'd been such a dick back then, to everyone. He liked to think he'd changed, that he'd grown up, though it'd taken him a lot longer than it should have. But hey, better late than never.

This time around, he wanted to be of value. Toward that goal, he made breakfast, the one thing he was good at. He whipped up southern eggs Benedict, with maple bacon on sourdough toast, only he completely forgot about their shit toaster being broken.

The thing was the devil incarnate. The last time he'd been here, Piper had threatened to throw it out, but he had fond memories of the thing from the early, *early* days when his grandparents had still been alive. Grandma had made him cinnamon-sugar toast every night until she died when he was fifteen, and he'd refused to let Piper ditch it. Instead, he'd promised a million times to fix it.

Which, of course, he'd never done. And sure enough, the minute he turned his attention to the pan, the damn thing sparked, smoked, and then . . . burst into flames.

The fire alarm went off, screaming at him in a decibel so loud he couldn't hear himself think. He stared at it for a single beat, and Piper rushed past him with the fire extinguisher and . . . killed the toaster dead.

"Seriously? You knew it was broken!" she said, or more accurately yelled to be heard over the still-wailing smoke alarm.

In a big, faded T-shirt and boxers, she climbed up onto the counter and began waving a towel in front of the alarm.

Feeling stupid, he climbed onto the counter as well, taking

the towel. He was taller and had a better reach. "Get down, I've got this."

Jumping down, Piper opened the window and back door, then surveyed the disaster while he continued to wave air at the fire alarm until it stopped going off. This took a good ten minutes.

"Dammit, Gavin," she said in the blessed silence.

"I'm sorry. I really was going to fix it."

"Gee, I've never heard that before."

Okay, he deserved that. But he really hated how she could make him feel like a stupid kid again. "So you were just standing in the hallway waiting for me to fuck up?"

"Of course not! But when I smelled breakfast, I knew what would happen."

He let out a breath and nodded. "Because I always screw up."

Before she could react, there was a knock on the opened back door. Gavin turned and time stood still.

CJ.

He was in full cop gear, including utility belt with handcuffs and gun—the whole nine yards. "A fisherman called in," he said, speaking directly to Piper without even glancing at Gavin. "Said he thought one of the empty cabins' burglar alarms had gone off. I was in the area and followed the screaming alarm. Everything okay?"

Piper said something, but Gavin couldn't have repeated it because he didn't hear a word of it. He couldn't talk either. Or breathe.

CJ, the only person outside of his family whom he'd ever loved, and also the only other person besides Piper on his list of people to make amends to.

Which he wasn't exactly doing a bang-up job of.

He hadn't seen CJ since they'd been, what, twenty years old and on top of the world? For one thing, he'd not come home often, and for another, CJ had left Wildstone for a while too. They needed to talk, but knowing what a prick he'd been, he'd felt uneasy and awkward about doing so.

Vaguely, he realized Piper had made some excuse to leave them alone and was gone. CJ still stood in the doorway, looking neither uneasy nor awkward.

Made sense. Gavin had been the one to screw up. He'd made a lot of mistakes, and he was here to own them. But as it turns out, saying that to himself and actually doing it were two very different things. "Are you hungry?" he heard himself ask. "I've got breakfast. Well, minus the toast. There's more than enough. I could make you a plate—"

CJ was already shaking his head and turning away, without a single word to the guy he'd once claimed to love, and Gavin died a little inside.

"Ceej."

He stopped but didn't turn back. Tall, leanly muscled, tan on top of his Puerto Rican coloring, all of it stealing Gavin's breath.

"I'm . . . sorry," he said.

That got CJ to turn around, his dark gaze looking . . . haunted and sad, which didn't match his carefully distant tone. "For?"

Okay, so he was going to make Gavin say it. Fair. "For leaving. For staying gone. For not returning texts or calls. Pick one. Or don't. Whatever, it's your choice."

CJ took that in a moment. "When I say *whatever*, I really mean screw you."

"Sometimes me too," Gavin said, relieved because they were at least talking. "But right now it means I really am sorry, and I don't know how to make you believe that."

"That's because I don't give a flying fuck."

But see, that had to be a lie, because CJ *always* gave a flying fuck, about everything, and it was that, the sarcasm and lie combined, that gave Gavin his first little bubble of hope since the day he'd left rehab. "Okay," he said, nodding. "Understood. But you used to give a whole bunch of fucks, at least about my homemade breakfasts, and I have to tell you, I've only gotten better."

CJ's gaze slid past him to the stove, and Gavin bit back a smile. *Gotcha.* "I can hear your stomach growling from here," he said softly.

"That's because I'm just coming off a twelve-hour shift."

"So you're starving. Why make yourself suffer when it's me you're mad at? Here." Gavin stepped back, giving CJ plenty of room and space to enter on his own terms, like he'd have done for a hurting stray animal. Meanwhile, he piled up a plate with food and set it at the table, gambling on the fact that CJ wouldn't spite himself just to snub his long-ago ex.

After a long hesitation, CJ took the bait. He came in and sat heavily, like maybe he was exhausted. Probably for the same reason Piper always was. Budget cuts had caused hiring freezes, leaving the police, fire, and other emergency response agencies far too understaffed.

CJ began to inhale his food, and when he caught Gavin watching, staring really, because he couldn't seem to help himself, he quirked a brow. "What, you've never seen a guy eat before?"

"You look good, Ceej."

CJ looked away, but not before Gavin caught the slight color to his cheeks. "You forgot the crepes," CJ said. "We always had crepes for dessert."

Gavin's breath caught at the memories. "Crepes were *your* specialty." Crepes and tacos. There was just something about the way CJ put his heart and soul into anything he cooked, but especially those two things. "I haven't had them since . . ." Gavin trailed off, feeling a shocking desire and longing for that time in his life. Back then, everything had felt so complicated, but had really been the simplest—and best—years of his life.

Without another word, CJ rose, and Gavin thought that was it, the guy was out. But instead, CJ made himself at home at the stove and began to make crepes.

Watching him move in the kitchen like he'd been born to it brought back a whole bunch of memories. It'd been CJ who taught him how to cook in the first place. He could probably run any kitchen in the world and yet . . . "So. A cop, huh?"

CJ froze for a single beat and then kept whipping the eggs and flour. "You're just surprised because you have authority issues."

Yeah, he did. Serious ones. He watched CJ carefully pour the first crepe into the pan, wait until it bubbled and got to the perfect color, before using nothing but the pan handle and a flick of his wrist to flip the crepe.

Four minutes later, it was CJ's turn to hand Gavin a plate, with a rolled crepe stuffed with the raspberries and blueberries he'd found in the fridge, topped with powdered sugar.

Gavin took one bite and moaned.

CJ's gaze went straight to his mouth.

"And I'm surprised," Gavin said quietly, picking up their conversation where they'd left off. "Because I seem to remember the *both* of us running from the cops. More than once."

CJ's eyes hardened. "We were two feral kids who thought that nothing could stop us. We were dumbasses."

True. Gavin had been grieving for his loving parents and seeking ways to forget his pain. CJ had been kicked out of his house for being gay. No warning, no anything, just forced out with only the clothes on his back, leaving him to the streets.

Luckily, his older brother had taken him in, and Gavin had been grateful. Even then he'd known he was going down the rabbit hole, feeling lost and completely unable to help CJ, because he himself had been so troubled. And he'd found his trouble, often. The memories gave him the opening he needed. "I screwed up."

CJ nodded. "Yeah, you did." He turned to go.

Unable to let him leave, not like this, Gavin pressed him up against the door to stop him, but something else happened. A bolt of not-so-forgotten hunger and desire coursed through him.

And given the way CJ sucked in a breath, he felt it too. Slowly he turned to face Gavin.

"I was young and stupid," Gavin said, looking him right in the eyes.

"And now you're . . . not young and stupid?"

Taking heart that CJ hadn't shoved him away, he shook his head. "Well, I'm working on it."

They stared at each other, the air crackling between them. Yeah, the spark was still there. And by spark, Gavin meant out-of-control, raging wildfire.

But CJ shook his head. "Not going to fall for that again, Gavin. Or you."

Gavin tried not to react, because he knew that was hurt talking. And yeah, he had a lot to make up for. He'd known what CJ's family had done to him, how they'd turned their backs on a sixteen-year-old kid, leaving him to fend for himself in the world. And then, several years later, Gavin had done the same damn thing. He didn't deserve forgiveness, but he wanted it anyway. "You don't feel anything?"

"Didn't say that."

Gavin looked at him, really looked. CJ had changed, going from lanky kid to one hundred percent man, and Gavin was shallow enough to admit that the new muscles and rugged, tough look was hot as hell. But besides the superficial shit, there was more. CJ's eyes weren't as cold and unfeeling as they'd been at first. The cop had given way, making room for his old best friend and first lover.

And like Gavin, CJ was most definitely not having coplike thoughts, because his eyes darkened the way they always had when he'd been aroused, and relief and hope filled Gavin. "You know if thought bubbles appeared over your head, you'd be screwed, right?"

CJ snorted. "Yeah. But luckily I no longer act on my impulses. You should try that." And then he shoved Gavin away and walked out the door.

CHAPTER 12

"Is that what the kids are calling it these days?"

The next afternoon, Cam stood in the alcohol aisle at the grocery store, picking out his poison. He'd driven his dad here, because, for one thing, the man drove like a menace.

"You going to follow me through the whole store?" his dad asked.

Which brought Cam to the second reason he was here. If left to his own devices, Emmitt would stock the kitchen with junk food, which was apparently killing him. "Unless you think you can behave."

"I've told you, son, there's no fun in behaving."

Cam pinched the bridge of his nose. "Dad."

"Fine. For you, I'll try."

"Not for me. For—"

"My grandkid. I know." His dad nodded. "Don't worry, I plan

to be around long enough to drive him crazy in the way I wish I could've driven you crazy."

"Don't underestimate yourself," Cam said dryly. "And maybe the baby's a girl. You ever think of that?"

His dad looked horrified. "What will we do with a girl?"

Cam laughed and shook his head. "I haven't the foggiest. Just go get what you need from Piper's list."

"You ever going to tell me what's going on with you two?"

"How do you know something's going on?"

"I got eyes in my head, don't I?"

Cam gave him a look, and his dad laughed and ambled off with the cart. He knew his dad thought Cam was being a hard-ass, and he was. He didn't care. He was done letting down the people who mattered to him. First his mom, whom he hadn't been able to save. Then Rowan.

But not his dad too, dammit. Or Winnie and the baby. Or their future livelihood—which was the marina.

And that brought him to the third thing. He'd put in a request at the DEA for a West Coast transfer. They had an office in San Luis Obispo, only thirty minutes from here. He'd still have to travel back East once a month for a weekend of Coast Guard training, and then there'd be the occasional activation and deployment, but the idea of being based near his dad was shockingly appealing.

For many reasons.

But there was no guarantee he'd get the transfer anyway, so he had no plans to tell anyone about it unless it came through, but he was surprised by how much he wanted it to.

And if he was being honest, it wasn't just about the baby, or his dad, though both those things were huge factors. It was also about Piper.

He hadn't seen her coming. At all.

And then, as if he'd conjured her up by wishes alone, she came around the corner, head down, eyes on something in her hands. A list, no doubt.

He eyed her cart—a box of tampons, ice cream, and wine—and bit back a smile. "Rough day?"

She lifted her chin. "What makes you think that?"

He took in her flashing eyes that were lined with exhaustion, and decided not to point out that it was all over her face. And in her cart. "Just asking."

She sighed. "I'm making dinner tonight," she said, as if she were faced with walking to her own guillotine.

"Interesting menu," he said, nodding at the contents of her cart.

She stepped in front of it, blocking his view. "You making fun of me?"

"Wouldn't dream of it."

She sighed and sagged a little. "It's family dinner night. Used to be tradition for the three of us. But now . . ." She shook her head. "I don't know what to make. I'm completely out of the habit of cooking."

"What did you used to cook?"

She gave him a small smile. "Mac and cheese and hot dogs."

"Sounds good to me."

"You think?" she asked, looking so adorably hopeful, he nodded. "Okay, then," she said. "Thanks." She started to move off, but he put a hand on her cart.

"You probably don't know this," he said, "but it's customary when someone gives you a suggestion for what to cook for a dinner party that you invite them to attend."

She blinked. "You want to come to the Manning shit show? Like, on purpose?"

She was a confident, strong-willed, strong-minded woman in every part of her life. Except, apparently, in recognizing when a man wanted her. Really wanted her. "I like your family," he said. "You're all . . ."

"Cray-cray?"

"Real."

She looked at him for a long moment. "Dinner's at six."

He smiled. "See you then."

Twenty minutes later, he'd driven his dad home and ended up in the marina office, where he'd been trying to make sense of the mess.

Apparently Rowan had done everything here, which made Cam feel even worse, because he'd accused his brother of being irresponsible and immature. Of giving up on college without even giving it a try, to hang out on the lake and do nothing. Of not giving a shit about his future.

Turned out, Cam had been dead wrong, about a lot of things. He hadn't realized how hard his brother had been working, or how without him, the marina would have fallen into disrepair and disorganization.

His dad was lost without someone to run the place, and Cam intended to fill that gap until he had to go, hopefully hiring someone to help before he left.

But the real question was, how did one apologize to a dead man? Because Rowan hadn't been slacking. Chances were, he'd felt he *couldn't* go off to college. He'd *had* to stay here and help out their dad, holding the marina together so the guy would have an income.

And he'd never let on to Cam, not once, not even the smallest complaint. Cam didn't know what to do with that, with knowing exactly how badly he'd failed his brother.

Running a marina, even a small one like this, took an incredible amount of work. They had several dozen slips, a gasoline pump, repair services, rental equipment for people who didn't want to own but wanted to go boating, and all of it required constant upkeep.

It was about creating relationships and customer service, about being good enough, kind enough, helpful enough to encourage repeat business.

And no one understood that more than his dad and Rowan, because at their core, they were both social, charismatic creatures. Attributes that Cam hadn't gotten from the family gene pool.

For years now, boating and being out on the water had been about work, about keeping the world as safe as possible, about stopping atrocities that most people would thankfully never have to think about. It hadn't been about fun, not for a long time.

He wasn't sure he could get there, but he was sure as hell going to try. For his dad. For Rowan. For the legacy he'd left.

Over the past week and a half, he'd spent a lot of time going through the office. Rowan had surprised him there too. He'd had an org chart, broken down into service categories. Dockage, fuel, repairs, etc.

What his brother hadn't been able to do, probably due to lack of time, was calculate revenue and expenses. He hadn't been able to see where they were bleeding money or what was working. So Cam had dug in. He'd focused on the largest revenue source first: the slips and storage. First problem was they had too many empty slips.

Gavin appeared in the office doorway. "Hey."

"Hey yourself."

He came in and sprawled out in the chair facing the desk. "I could hear you swearing from the docks."

Frustrated, Cam pushed away the laptop. "Give me a boat to repair, or anything over paperwork any day of the week."

Gavin turned the laptop to face him. "Bookkeeping not your thing, huh?"

"I'd rather go back to boot camp and get tortured by the sadistic training officers all over again."

Gavin glanced over the numbers. Clicked on a few tabs. "You got an existing customer list?"

"Yeah. I need to hit it hard to get all the slips filled for the upcoming season."

Gavin nodded. "Yeah, you do. I'd start by reducing the rate—offer a special promo rate. Then rinse and repeat until seventy-five percent of the slips are filled. Keep the rest available as transient slips and charge more for them."

Cam took a second look at him. "Great advice. Okay. What else?"

"Once you get your slip inventory paid for, you'll be in better shape. The service and fuel should be easy profit, assuming you stay on top of it. Which means someone taking better care of these poor books."

Cam didn't think twice. "You available to handle that part?"

Gavin's brows went up. "You trust me with your bookkeeping?"

"Why, you going to skim off the top?"

"Hell, no. I'm not aiming for prison." Gavin rubbed his jaw. "But you should know, I'm . . . a drug addict. I'm in recovery. Out of rehab six months now."

Cam leaned back, surprised. "Piper know?" When Gavin gave a slow shake of his head, Cam swore. Piper was going to be pissed, and rightfully so. "What is it with you and Winnie?"

"I'm going to tell her."

Cam groaned. "You're both killing me."

Gavin snorted. "Not my first time hearing that." He paused. "Look, for what it's worth, Piper deserves better than what Winnie and I have given her. I'm working on that."

"Maybe you could work faster."

Gavin nodded.

Cam studied him for a minute. He hoped Gavin just needed a second chance, one his brother wouldn't ever get. "The job's yours if you want it."

Gavin blinked. "Serious?"

"*Dead* serious. I'm leaving here in less than two weeks, with no guarantee when my next extended leave might be."

Gavin looked him right in the eye. "You going to break my sister's heart?"

"Winnie will be fine. I'll make sure she's covered financially, and she'll have you and Piper for support too."

"I wasn't talking about Winnie."

Cam drew in a deep breath. "I respect your asking, but whatever's happening—or not happening—between Piper and me is not up for discussion."

"So that's a yes, then," Gavin said. He stood and turned to go.

Shit. "No," he said to the guy's back. "I'm not going to break your sister's heart." She might, however, break his . . .

Gavin turned around as if he couldn't quite believe what Cam was saying. Frankly, Cam couldn't believe it either.

"We did *not* have this conversation."

Gavin nodded, respect in his gaze, attitude gone. He nodded toward the laptop. "I could definitely take over the bookkeeping. Shouldn't be more than a few hours a week, and I could use the extra money." He paused. "And if we're divulging things that we haven't said out loud and that are scary as fuck, you should know that I'm hoping to talk Piper into turning the property into a B and B. By renting out the cottages and using the bottom floor of the big house to serve breakfasts to guests, we'd all have some relatively easy income."

"Have this conversation with her *soon*, Gavin."

"I will." He looked at the mess of paperwork on the desk. "Want me to start now?"

"God, yes. But tomorrow's fine."

They spent a few more minutes together, with Cam handing over everything Gavin would need, hoping he was doing the right thing by Piper. By all of them.

After, Cam walked up the hill to his dad's back deck and

found a couple of steaks on the barbeque, which he knew for damn sure weren't on his dad's list of acceptable foods. He headed into the kitchen via the back door and found his dad making out with some woman up against the refrigerator.

Cam slapped a hand over his eyes, which heightened his sense of hearing, and what he heard was clothing being quickly rearranged. *"Are you kidding me?"*

Emmitt cleared his throat. "Son, this is Margaret. She's a librarian. Runs the Books on Wheels van."

"Nice to meet you," said Margaret, a pretty, redheaded, fifty-ish woman who was flushed and breathless.

Her blouse wasn't properly buttoned but Cam would die before mentioning it. He did his best to hold eye contact as she offered him a hand to shake. "You too," he murmured, giving his dad a look when Margaret scurried to the oven to pull out cupcakes.

She smiled at Cam. "Honey, do you like cupcakes?"

"My dad's diabetic. He's on a low-sugar, low-fat diet."

Margaret looked horrified. "So . . . you don't like cupcakes?"

Cam looked at his dad, who had the good grace to grimace.

"Today's a cheat day," Emmitt said.

"Dad, we need to talk." Cam gestured toward the living room.

His dad grinned at Margaret. "I think I'm in trouble."

"I love trouble," Margaret said, and gave him a wink.

In the living room, Cam rubbed the bridge of his nose where a headache was forming.

"I just realized why kids are considered great birth control," his dad said mildly, following him in.

"Dad, you're not taking your health seriously."

"Of course I am. Sex is good for you."

Cam squeezed his eyes shut. "You're about to eat a whole bunch of red meat, and then have cupcakes filled with fat and sugar. And just to remind you, this baby that's coming has already lost her dad."

Emmitt's face went solemn. "Or he. *He* already lost his dad."

"Either way, they're going to need you."

"So what the hell am I supposed to eat?"

"You already know this," Cam said. "You've got a list. You can eat anything we just bought at the store. Salmon, chicken, vegetables—"

"Ugh. Fine." His dad started back into the kitchen. "Oh, and you might want to wear earplugs to bed tonight. Unless getting lucky is also against the rules."

Cam just stared at him.

"By getting lucky, I mean having sex. In case you needed that spelled out."

And to think, he'd left war zones to be here. Right about now, he'd prefer a good fire fight to this. "Dad, for future reference, I *never* need it spelled out." Cam followed him back into the kitchen, nodded politely at Margaret, and then grabbed the gallon of ice cream from the freezer.

"Hey," his dad said. "That's mine."

"You can't have ice cream anymore, remember? We bought you coconut sorbet as a replacement." Next Cam went into the fridge and took out the bottle of chocolate syrup.

"I know what people do with that," his dad said. "And, *nice*. You getting lucky too?"

Margaret winked at his dad, and Cam threw up in his mouth a little bit. "It's for *dessert*."

"Ah. Is that what the kids are calling it these days?"

Cam decided walking away was for everyone's safety. A few minutes later, he knocked at the house next door, but no one answered. Probably because the occupants were yelling at each other. Loudly. So he let himself in and followed the commotion to the kitchen.

"It was just a charger," Gavin was saying.

"It was my *last* phone charger," Piper said. "And you didn't even ask."

"Remember that time I cut myself with the pocketknife you gave me for Christmas?" Gavin asked. "And the doctor thought I needed a blood transfusion? You were willing to give me your blood that day, remember? And now you can't even give me a charger?"

"I'd give you my blood *and* my charger," Winnie interjected. "But I lost my charger. I also lost my phone, so . . ."

Gavin looked at her. "Again?"

"Do you want to die?"

Piper growled at them both and tossed up her hands.

Cam opened his mouth to announce his presence, but right then Gavin cleared his throat and spoke first, quickly and a little breathlessly, like he had to get it out fast or not at all. "Speaking of blood and chargers." He looked at Piper. "I, uh, lied when I told you I was on vacation from the IT job. I'm not on vacation. I'm on extended leave." He paused. "No, wait. That's a lie too. Sorry, bad habit." He shook his head. "After the DUI, I got fired. And then I went to rehab. I've been out for six months, but I haven't been able to get another job that makes enough to support myself." He spread his arms out a little. "So . . . here I am, and I realize I need to make amends to you. I'm sorry I lied. Or omitted. I'm sorrier than I can say. I never meant to hurt you."

Utter silence.

Cam took a step back to give them privacy. Flying under the radar was definitely the way to go, and he turned to leave, but that's when Piper saw him.

So did Gavin, who seemed hugely relieved. "Oh, good. Some-one not related to me, *and* you've got chocolate." He turned to Piper. "Before you kill me, you should know that I've been hired by Cam to handle the marina books. So if you kill me, you'll screw over Cam and Emmitt."

So much for flying under the radar.

CHAPTER 13

"Wanting to kill each other is sort of
the definition of being siblings."

Piper was reeling. She was aware of Cam standing there, and that a part of her recognized him as both someone to be careful with and an ally, but she didn't take her eyes off Gavin. Couldn't. "What did you just say?"

"That Cam hired me."

"Before that," she said tightly. "What did you say before that?"

Gavin lost the smile and let out a long breath. "Please don't ask me to say it again. It was hard enough the first time."

"But . . ." She shook her head. "Rehab? For what?"

"Remember when I broke my wrist a few years ago? They gave me a bunch of pain meds."

"Yes," she said slowly, her mind doing the opposite and going a hundred fifty miles per hour. "The same ones Winnie had been given the year before for her appendectomy. And me for my sprained ankle."

"I know. I stole Winnie's leftovers because I couldn't find any more and I needed them."

Sadness and worry joined her fear and panic. "Oh, Gavin," she whispered. "Two years ago? You've been taking pills that long?"

"Actually, three years, and yes."

Winnie, who hadn't said anything during this exchange, and who knew the whole story but only since he got out of re-hab, suddenly burst into tears. Huge, gulping, loud sobs.

Before Piper could do anything, Gavin pulled Winnie into his arms. "Like old times," he murmured, stroking her hair. "You always used to cry every time we'd fight."

Winnie buried her head in his chest and kept crying.

Piper felt the urge to do the same. But she was the oldest, the one in charge, a failure apparently, and to make it all worse, Cam was a witness to all of it, all of their crazy, messy life.

"It's going to be okay," Gavin told Winnie. "Don't make yourself sick."

"It's not going to be okay!" Winnie hiccupped through her tears and pushed away to point at him. "*You're* not okay, and I don't know how to make you okay! And I need you to be okay, Gavin!"

"Win," he said quietly, but with utter conviction, "I got ahold of the demons, I promise you."

Piper could hear her heart pounding in her ears, because she hadn't even known he had demons. What kind of sister didn't know this about her own baby brother, the same sweet boy who'd been through hell before they'd landed back in Wildstone? Such hell that she hadn't been sure she'd ever be able to reach him. Her biggest fear had always been that she'd fail, and she had. She reached for his hand. "Gavin—"

"I really am so sorry I didn't tell you the truth," he said quietly. "That I hurt you."

He looked anxious and . . . nervous, and she realized what he needed. "It's in the past," she said just as quietly. "You're forgiven."

"You don't have to let me off the hook that easily. I hurt you."

"You hurt yourself more." She squeezed his hand. "But now you're not alone."

Winnie swiped at her eyes, which made her mascara run. "This is all so scary," she whispered soggily. "Everything's so scary."

And that was another thing. Piper hadn't known they were scared. How had she not known?

"What's scary is your face right now," Gavin told Winnie. "You look like a raccoon."

On the stove was the pot of mac and cheese she'd made, along with a plate of sliced-up hot dogs, ready to be stirred into the mac and cheese. Winnie picked up a little round and flung it at Gavin.

It bounced off his chin, and he stared at her in shock before scooping a spoonful of mac and cheese and flinging it at her.

It hit her square in the forehead.

The next one hit the wall because Winnie ducked. "This is why we can't have nice things!" she screeched, and picked the piece of macaroni from her forehead and ate it. "Good stuff, though."

"Are you kidding me?" Piper said. "*Stop.*"

They didn't. And it was like trying to hold back the tide. They'd lost their minds.

"Seriously," she yelled, refusing to look over at Cam, because she could only imagine what he must think. "*Stop!*"

Winnie, who'd caught a spoonful of flying mac and cheese with her cheek, pointed at Gavin. "You're so dead."

In the next beat, the skirmish was full-on war. Piper opened her mouth to yell again and got hit in the face and chest with mac and cheese.

Sweet Cheeks was cleaning up the floor, chirping in happiness as utter chaos reigned. Until a piercing whistle stopped them in their tracks, and they all turned in unison toward the source.

Cam. He shook his head in shock. "I've been in battles that were less harrowing. What the actual hell?"

He sounded so uncharacteristically surprised and shocked that under any other circumstances, Piper would've laughed. As it was, it was all she could do not to cry. But she hadn't cried in years. If she lost it now, she'd never recover.

"Man, you don't have any sisters," Gavin said. "Be grateful. They're . . ." He circled a finger at the side of his head, the universal sign for *loco*. Then he reloaded his spoon with another scoop of mac and cheese and turned to Piper with a raised brow.

"Don't. You. Dare," she said. "You were an addict and you couldn't tell me?"

"Not past tense. Once an addict, always an addict." He gave her a knowing look. "Just like once a control freak, always a control freak."

Piper blinked. "Are you referring to me?"

He pointed to her ever-present journal lying on the counter. "Yes, Ms. Has-to-Make-a-List-for-Everything, I am."

She resisted the urge to hug the journal to her chest. Instead— and she had no idea what came over her; maybe it was the heavy weight of sorrow and rage and guilt—before she could think or stop herself, she grabbed a hot-dog bun and pitched it at him.

He ducked, and it hit Winnie in the nose.

"Hey!" Winnie shrieked. "*I'm* not the druggie. That's Gavin and Daddy!"

In the act of reaching for another bun, Piper froze. "*What?*" she whispered, sure she'd heard wrong.

Winnie turned to Gavin. "Tell her."

"Okay, but remember," he said to Piper, "I warned you not to let me off the hook that easily and you forgave me anyway." Gavin grimaced, and a piece of macaroni fell off his chin. "So, fun fact . . . I was going through Gram's office earlier while you were working."

Piper stared at him. "You had no right to do that."

"I've got as much right as you."

Piper blinked, but only one eye reopened, because the other was crusted shut with cheese.

"I found a file of medical stuff," Gavin said. "Doctor visits, prescriptions, stuff like that. Turns out, Dad was addicted to Oxy too." He gave a wan smile. "Apple and tree and all that, I guess. Who knew, huh?"

Piper, whose legs had lost all their bones, sank into a chair and swiped at the glued-shut eye. "Dad was addicted to drugs?"

"Prescription meds," he said, and when she stared at him,

he shrugged. "He was getting help for it, though. I actually thought you probably already knew. Winnie was too young, and I guess I was too."

"Oh my God," Piper whispered.

"Okay, so you definitely didn't know." With a sigh, he sat next to her. "Sucks, right? But I gotta admit, it's nice to see you showing your feelings instead of hiding them and pretending they're not there at all in some misguided attempt to be strong for us."

She shoved her hair away from her face—and *gross*, there was mac and cheese in it—and glared at him. "This is not about me and my feelings." Upset, she got back to her feet. "This is about you, Gavin, and your drug addiction. The one you hid from me. How is that healthy? Isn't that against recovery advice, having secrets?"

Gavin's face closed up, and to her shock, he stood as if he wanted to say something, but in the end he kept his mouth shut and just walked out of the room.

Winnie, after an accusatory, tear-filled glance, followed.

Piper huffed out a breath. "I'm sorry," she murmured to Cam, and then, needing a moment, stepped out the back door. Deciding maybe she needed several moments, she walked along the hill, going just far enough to stare at the turbulent, choppy lake.

Cam followed her. She heard his footsteps, and was grateful he hadn't spoken. She turned and looked at him and had to let out a rough laugh.

He was holding the bottle of wine she'd bought at the store earlier.

"Good call," she said, and took a long pull. She swiped her mouth on her arm and looked him over. "How the hell did you manage to not get a single drop of food on you?"

"I wasn't in the line of fire." He took her hand in his. Which meant that he now knew she had sweaty palms, and he could probably hear her pounding pulse as well. "Are you okay?"

"Yes." She shook her head. "No." She breathed for a minute. "I did warn you it was going to be a shit show. I mean, I know they're my siblings, but sometimes it's like we're strangers."

"Maybe if you guys talked some more, got everything out."

"Gavin lost his job and went to rehab. And Winnie is completely unconcerned about missing school . . ."

"*Talk* to them," he repeated softly.

"But I don't even know where to start, at least not without sounding like a judgmental idiot."

"Start with something easy," he suggested. "Like . . . Gavin, Winnie . . . you're my brother and sister, and your life choices are yours to make, and I'll support you no matter what."

She choked out a laugh and took another long sip of wine. The liquid courage had her whispering her fear out loud. "What if I can't say that?"

"Well, then . . ." Cam gave her a very small smile. "Piper, you're my neighbor, and your life choices are yours to make, and I'll support you no matter what."

She started to smile, but felt a sob coming on, so she turned away.

Cam slowly pulled her back around. And then into him.

"Careful," she said. "I'm covered in—"

He didn't stop until she was plastered up against him and he was hugging her. He held her like that until she stopped vibrating with pent-up emotion and devastation. Then and only then did he slide his fingers along her jaw and tilt her face up to his, lowering his head to give her a sweet kiss that she felt all the way to her toes. It seemed to infuse her with a strength she'd forgotten she had, and when he pulled away, she drew a deep breath.

"Thanks," she whispered, and eyed his shirt. She'd mashed some mac and cheese into him. "I'm so sorry."

"Don't worry about it."

"Let me guess. You've had worse?"

"Yes. And you're stalling."

She drew another deep breath and nodded. "I am. Talking's never really worked out for us as a family."

"Maybe it's not about talking. Maybe it's about listening."

She looked at him.

He looked at her right back.

"You . . . think I don't listen," she said.

"I think you're smart as hell. Which means you almost always have the right answers. But sometimes people need to find those answers on their own. They need to make their own mistakes. They need to know that when they admit those mistakes, they're going to be loved and accepted anyway. And before you think I'm smarter than I am, you should know I only learned all that when it was too late. Don't be too late."

His smile was kind and tinged with pain, and her heart ached for him. *And* he was right. She didn't listen very well. Or at all.

"I do accept them," she said softly. "I mean, Winnie's . . . amazing. Resilient. She'll always come out on top, I know it.

And as for Gavin, he's smart, resourceful, charismatic . . . He's got so much potential. Addiction's a disease, he didn't do it on purpose."

Cam gave her a small smile. "And here you thought you had nothing to say."

SHE WENT LOOKING for Gavin first. She found him in the very kitchen she'd just abandoned. He'd cleaned up the mess and was surrounded by what looked like all the ingredients she'd had in the pantry. "What are you doing?"

"Cleaning and organizing our pantry." He hadn't looked at her, but his voice dared her to contradict the *our* part.

"I'm sorry," she said quietly. "I didn't listen before, but I'm listening now. Please talk to me."

"I'm busy right now."

Racked with guilt, she got between him and the pantry and met his gaze, which was both hollow and haunted. "Gavin," she whispered, and wrapped her arms around him. "I'm so sorry. I should've known. I hate that I didn't. You needed me and I wasn't there for you."

"It's not your fault." He stood still for a moment, and then sighed and hugged her back. "We're not big on sharing our feelings. There's no way you could've known."

And the dagger just slid in deeper, because Cam was right. She didn't listen enough. "Gavin." He pulled back, seeming tense again. Braced for a fight, she realized. "You're my brother," she said quietly. "And your life choices are yours to make, and I'll support you no matter what."

He looked at her for a long beat. "I doubt that would still be true if I told you that I fell into my job because I just happened to be good at it, but it got stressful. And then more stressful. And to deal with that stress, my roommate—a pot dealer, by the way—helped me out now and then. But it got a little out of control, because I was already using illegal prescription meds to relax and cope. And then I got the DUI and everything snowballed."

"I hate how that all happened to you."

"It didn't happen to me. I did it to myself." He looked her right in the eyes, not shying away. "I used up all my money for lawyers and rehab. Ran credit cards up too. By the time I got out, my world had imploded, leaving me jobless and just about penniless. And if it helps, Winnie didn't know any of this either, not until I got out of rehab." He lifted his hands. "Anyway, so here I am."

She drew a deep breath and nodded. "Okay."

"Okay?"

"Yeah," she said. "You're my brother. You're home, and being home will help. You'll get through this, but you won't be alone."

Gavin looked at her, disbelieving.

"I mean it," she said.

"You're not mad?"

"Not at you."

"We need more flour." Then he wrapped his arms around her and buried his head against her shoulder. She felt his emotional shudder run through him.

She hugged him close. "We'll get more flour."

"We need more sugar too," he said, or at least that's what she thought he said, muffled against her shirt.

She swallowed hard. "Whatever you need."

"Then I really need a new KitchenAid food processor in candy apple."

She snorted through her thick throat.

"Piper?"

"Yeah?"

"What if what I really need is to be here with you and Win for a little bit?" He lifted his head and met her gaze.

She drew a deep breath as she realized her own hopes and dreams of going off to school were getting further and further away. "Then we'll all live together again for a little bit."

"And if we want to kill each other?"

"We already do," she said. "Wanting to kill each other is sort of the definition of being siblings."

He hugged her again. "Love you, Pea."

His old nickname for her, from the early days when he hadn't been able to say Piper. He hadn't used it in so long that just the sound of it was like coming home. *It's enough,* she told herself. *This life's enough.*

"Love you more," she whispered.

CHAPTER 14

"Sorry not sorry."

Gavin waited until late that night when the house was dark and silent to sneak out. Back in the days of his wild and crazy and very confused teen years, he'd snuck out a lot. That had involved escaping through his second-story bedroom window, climbing along the ledge to the corner of the house, and shimmying down a tree.

On those nights, he'd rarely had an agenda. All he'd known was that he'd grown up in a world so far from this one, a wanderlustful, amazing, crazy world in which he'd seen every continent and more cultures than most people knew existed. He'd not known anything different until he'd been sent here after hell had broken loose.

A hell of his own making that had started and ended in the DRC. There'd been strict rules for him and his sisters there, and a "yard" they'd had to stay within. Going past that into the jungle had been forbidden. In fact, that had been Winnie's first full sentence when she'd been three years old: "Don't leave yard."

So of course Gavin and his BFF, Arik, had gone into the jungle in the midst of a storm. And they'd walked right into a gang of local drug runners. In the ensuing fight to get away, they'd been separated. Gavin had heard the shots and run until his side hurt. He'd tumbled into the yard. Alone. It'd been hours later, when the storm had been gaining steam by the minute, that Arik's body had been found.

The very next day, he and his sisters had been sent home by their parents, who promised to follow shortly.

They'd died in the flooding from the storm before they could get out.

To say after all that, that Gavin had been a hard-to-handle kid, one who was angry and grieving and generally pissed off at the entire world, was an understatement. Suddenly his skin had felt several sizes too small, and he'd been crawling up the walls, his brain filled with so much inner turmoil he didn't see how he could possibly go on.

So he'd escaped every night, thriving on the illicit freedom. A freedom he'd known he didn't deserve, not when Arik would never know the same, or Gavin's parents either. Still, he'd done his best to make sure the world knew he was angry, hurting, and racked with guilt. God, the stupid things he'd done, but he'd been a walking, talking death wish. He'd gone swimming in the lake by moonlight, alone, even in a storm with a three-foot chop. He'd stolen his grandma's car and hit up the bars around the Cal Poly campus looking for easy, fast hookups.

His grandma had never caught on to him, and then she'd passed away right in the middle of his assholery.

Now as a dubious grown-up, he wasn't still mad at the world. Maybe at himself, but he was slowly getting over it. And he sure as hell wasn't going out the second-story window. He intended to go out the back door, but he found Winnie in the kitchen. She had the toaster's parts strewn across the kitchen table. Her phone was propped up against the napkin holder, playing a YouTube video on how to fix a toaster. Sweet Cheeks was asleep in her lap. "What are you doing?"

"What does it look like?" she asked.

"Okay, I'll rephrase. Do you *know* what you're doing?"

"If I did, would I have watched this YouTube video ten times?" She sighed. "Emmitt told me what to do, but I can't remember all he said." She met his gaze and frowned. "What's wrong?"

"Nothing." He headed to the door. "Don't get electrocuted."

"Don't find trouble."

He turned back. "What does that mean?"

"You're heading out, right? I thought people in NA aren't supposed to go out alone."

Yeah, and he was also supposed to be working on his steps, making amends. "I'm not looking to get wasted."

"Promise?"

"Yes."

"Pinky promise?" she asked.

He realized she wasn't kidding. She was utterly serious and also worried, which made his chest ache. "Hey," he said. "I really am okay. You know that, right?"

"You keep saying it, but you lost your job, your place, and near as I can tell, all your friends."

"That was last year," he quipped. "This year I'm trying something new."

She still didn't smile, and he let out a long breath and came back to sit next to her, wrapping an arm around her.

"Is this about the fight tonight?"

She set her head on his shoulder and pressed her hands to her belly. She was three and a half months along, and even with her hands holding her shirt tight to her, there was only a very slight curve to her stomach.

"I haven't told Piper yet," she said.

"Gee, I hadn't noticed."

"Cam wants me to."

"Uh-huh."

"And Emmitt wants me to."

He looked at her.

"And *you* want me to," she said.

"Yes. I do."

"No one's ratted me out."

"It's your secret to tell, Win."

"I know. I'm working my way up to it."

The irony didn't escape him. He was working his way up to certain things as well. "Sooner than later," he said, eyeing her belly. "Or you won't be telling. The Bean will announce her own arrival."

Winnie rubbed her stomach. "You think it's a girl? The doc said it's hard to tell before twenty weeks."

"I don't care what it is as long as you and it stay healthy," he said. "But yeah, I figure it's a girl. Karma for your teenage years," he teased.

She finally smiled, and he felt his own smile curve his mouth.

"We're going to be okay, Win. You know that, right?"

"Yeah. But what about Piper?" She jerked her chin toward the window, and when he looked out, he saw Piper had set up lights and was painting the outside of the last cabin.

"You don't think she's okay?" he asked.

"Uh, hello, it's midnight and she's out there painting the cottages."

Good point.

"I think we drove her insane, Gav. Actually, I think we still do. She needs someone in her life."

They watched Piper paint. She dipped her roller into the pan and lifted it high to reach the eaves. A few drops must have hit her because she swiped her arm over her face, which only smeared the paint.

"We should fix her up with someone," Winnie said. "As a bonus, it'd distract her from us."

"Think so?" Gavin asked doubtfully, eyeing Piper's crazy hair, the paint-streaked face, her ancient, holey jeans, and the too big, long-sleeved T-shirt that read SORRY NOT SORRY across the front.

A shadow crossed the yard and Gavin rose before realizing who it was.

Cam. He said something to Piper, who tipped her head back and laughed.

Laughed.

His hard-ass sister rarely did that anymore.

"Huh," Winnie said. "Maybe he can't see too well."

Cam ran a finger over Piper's paint-covered jaw and said something else. Piper didn't laugh this time. She bit her lower lip and stared at Cam's mouth. And then . . .

"Shit." Gavin shut his eyes. "They're going to make out."

"No, it's even better."

Gavin opened his eyes. Cam had taken his hands off Piper—thankfully—and now the man had the roller and was painting in long, smooth strokes. Piper had picked up a paintbrush and was working on the windowsill.

Winnie boggled. "Oh my God, do you think she somehow managed to find a guy all by herself?"

"They grow up so fast," Gavin said, which made Winnie laugh.

"You do realize she'll mess this up, which is why we have to help."

"No. You're not going to interfere."

"But—"

"She's okay," Gavin said firmly.

Winnie didn't look convinced. "She's gonna need help."

"Maybe, but that doesn't mean she'll thank you for it. You stay out of it."

"Gavin."

"Yeah?"

She looked worried again, but tossed him her keys. "Be careful?"

"Always."

He headed into town, driving aimlessly for a while. He

avoided the Whiskey River Bar and Grill. He was getting his life together, so why tempt fate?

It was one in the morning when he found himself in front of CJ's house. Yes, he'd stalked his ex, figuring out which house was his thanks to a combination of Instagram and Gavin's knowledge of every square inch of the county.

He wasn't sure why he'd come here. Or why he got out of the car and stood on the front porch. It was stupid. It was beyond stupid really, especially when he heard footsteps come up behind him. He whipped around and froze.

CJ stood there, gun out. "Good way to get yourself killed."

Just looking at the first and only love of his life was a gut punch. And a heart punch. And a soul punch . . .

God, he'd been so stupid. And wasted so much time. "Getting killed isn't the plan," he said mildly, even with his heart in his throat. "At least not tonight."

CJ just shook his head as he shoved his gun into the waistband of his jeans, at the small of his back. The jeans were the only thing he wore, and the difference between the too-skinny eighteen-year-old CJ and the now ripped twenty-eight-year-old CJ was . . . eye-opening.

"So what *was* your plan?" his past asked, still looking pissed off.

Plan? Gavin had no idea. So he went with his first instinct. He yanked CJ close and kissed him, the man's erotic growl of surprise spearing heat through Gavin's entire body. His hands came up to slide into CJ's hair, against his scalp, tugging him closer still, the kiss a haunting, almost forgotten combo of promise and connection.

"Stupid plan," CJ said when they came up for air.

"No shit."

"I should kick your ass."

Gavin smiled. "You could try."

CJ shook his head. "You're not even the slightest bit sorry you tried to sneak into a cop's house undetected."

"I'm a little sorry," he said with a shrug, adrenaline still pumping through him. "But probably not nearly as much as you think I should be . . ."

Swearing roughly, CJ gripped Gavin's biceps hard.

Shoving me away or pulling me in?

They stared at each other until a rough groan tore from CJ's throat and he yanked Gavin inside.

CHAPTER 15

"Careful, payback's a bitch."

A few days later, Piper was exhausted and just leaving the station after a long twelve hours at work when she got a text from Winnie.

Meet me at the lake at the tire swing. p.s. maybe change first. Nothing personal, but it wouldn't hurt you to up your game from your usual fashion sense, which screams "I'm cold and tired."

Piper looked down at her fleece-lined stretch pants and oversized flannel button-down. Okay, so maybe her sister had a point. When she got home, she upgraded to jeans, but stuck with the flannel shirt because *comfort*.

Besides, there were other things to worry about. Like her siblings. Her motto had always been, if she couldn't fix it, she put it on a list and set it aside for later. Some people might consider that denial, but she called it survival.

But she and Winnie had a lot to work on.

The swing was about a half mile around the north side of the lake where the landscape was open wildland. The three of them had spent many, many summer days there, chasing the ducks, swimming, and using the tire swing—which hung from a huge old oak tree—to jump into the lake. Well, Winnie and Gavin had. Piper never jumped into the lake.

As she walked, she told herself that Winnie's text seemed like a white flag, a way to meet in the middle, in a place where there were only good memories. She had no idea what to expect, but when she got there twenty minutes later, there was a cute picnic basket at the water's edge.

But no Winnie.

Piper sat down on the blanket, and while she waited, pulled out her journal. She thumbed to her Home Depot list and what she needed in order to finish upgrading the cottages, but quickly got bored with that and flipped the pages to her secret *secret* bucket list.

So many things to add . . .

But she realized that all of them, the things she'd written and the things she hadn't, represented one thing.

Loneliness.

It was a hard pill to swallow. She'd purposely protected her heart to save it from the pitfalls of life, and in doing so, had closed herself off.

The truth was, she wanted to be wanted. She wanted to feel something. She wanted passion and hunger and desire, but more than any of that, she wanted someone to feel those things for her.

It'd been a long time since something or someone had moved her. She stared out at the water. It was still warm. This entire winter had been warmer than any she could remember. The lake sparkled from the late-afternoon sun, the water a deep blue. But that wasn't what she saw. She was seeing, remembering, Cam coming out of the shadows late at night, as he had a few nights before, to help her paint the cottages. She was seeing the muscles in his arms and shoulders bunch and stretch the material of his shirt taut as he moved so effortlessly with the roller, making more headway in minutes than she had in hours.

She was seeing him grin at the paint on her face, looking so playful and relaxed that she "accidentally" painted her hand and then patted him on the back as he worked.

And then his butt. "Oops," she'd said. "I just got paint on your best body part."

He'd flashed her a full wolf grin. "That's not my best body part."

After they'd finished painting, he'd kissed her good night, and it'd been her to deepen the kiss. He'd given a low, rough, sexy male growl of approval and pressed her up against a dry wall to free up his hands. And goodness, those talented, knowing hands . . . She'd been desperately trying to get down to bare skin when her phone had gone off. One of the other EMTs had gone home sick and they'd needed Piper immediately.

Now, in the light of day, with her good spots still quivering at the midnight memories, she added a new item to her list:

- Discover Cam's best body part.

When she realized she was smiling wickedly, she shook her head. She'd finally cracked, no doubt from a deadly lack of orgasms. But hey, that was a fixable problem. And if she got it together before Cam left Wildstone, she could fix it with him. *Hmm*. Maybe she should start a list on how exactly to make that happen. Or *where* she wanted it to happen . . . With a grin, she wrote: *Have sex* not *on a bed* . . . Then a shadow fell over her.

She jumped and slammed the journal shut as Cam sat down next to her.

He studied her face, his own amused. "I'd give a lot of money to know what you were just writing."

She lifted a shoulder. "Making a shopping list."

He shook his head. "You're a terrible liar."

This was true, and she felt her cheeks burn. "It's got nothing to do with you."

"Wow. Lies on lies. Now I really want to know." Leaning in, his mouth brushed her earlobe. "Bet I could get it out of you."

If he kept doing that, the truth wasn't the *only* thing he'd get out of her. And where was Winnie? She looked around. No sister in sight. What the hell?

"You waiting for someone?" Cam asked.

"Winnie. And she's late. What are you doing here?"

He opened his mouth, but her stomach growling loudly beat him to it.

With a smile, Cam opened the basket and pulled out the cheese and crackers, and got busy with a knife.

She devoured the first cheesed-up cracker he handed her, and he quickly made her another.

This time she managed to slow down enough that he was able to make one for himself in between feeding her. When he stopped to suck some cheese off his thumb, the sound made her shiver.

Noting her squirm, he smiled, and his eyes seemed to darken with heat. "You okay?"

She decided not to answer on the grounds she might incriminate herself, but when he held out another loaded cracker, she bit his finger, making him laugh.

"Careful," he warned. "Payback's a bitch."

That gave her an anticipatory shiver. Seriously, his voice alone could give her an orgasm. And by the look on his face, he knew it too. She busied herself with eating, and he laughed again, softly, knowingly.

Next time she'd bite him harder.

"You've been putting in long hours." With this, he gave her yet another cracker. "Both at work and at home."

He was making sure she was eating, she realized, discombobulated by the barrage of sweet and sexy from him. He made her dizzy, in the best of ways. "I need to get everything fixed up sooner than later."

He nodded. "Are you going to rent the cottages out, then?"

"Sell. I need out from the huge overhead."

"Oh," he said, seeming surprised.

"Why?"

He shook his head. "Nothing."

"Feels like something."

"Have you talked to Gavin and Winnie about selling?"

"No. Up until this latest visit home, they've shown no interest in what happens to the place. So I figured they'd be excited about having their portion of the profit."

"Maybe you should talk to them about it."

She shrugged. "As you've seen firsthand, we don't do 'talk' so well. Oh, and I tried the listening thing. It's . . . a work in progress."

He looked like he one hundred percent understood that. And she knew he did, and that also, he missed Rowan. Scooting closer, she reached out her hand, which he took in his and squeezed in silent thanks. And now suddenly she didn't want to bite him so much as she wanted to hug him.

Digging into the basket, he came up with some grapes, which he shared with her. "What happens if you sell?"

"We'd divide the profit three ways, which should leave me with more than enough to follow my dream of going to college to become a physician assistant. The sale would hopefully cover the move and tuition at the University of Colorado."

"When do you start?"

"The program has six start times a year, so it just depends on when I get it all together. It's about the money at this point. I need to have enough to cover myself for the two-year program, and I need Gavin and Winnie to have enough that they won't need me to supplement them."

He ate a few grapes. "You're a good sister."

"One who's made a lot of mistakes."

"Such as?"

"Being too tough on them, and maybe not affectionate enough. I never had the time to really listen to them. I was just hyperfocused on not screwing up all our lives."

"You did your best." He shrugged. "Besides, we all have our faults."

"Yeah? What's yours?"

He looked at her for a long moment. Instead of answering, he went back into the basket and pulled out a bottle of wine. He held it up and she nodded, so he poured them both a glass.

"Are you trying to say you have *no* faults?" she asked.

He snorted. "I'm definitely not saying that."

"Well, then?"

He cocked his head and studied her. "Maybe I don't want to tell the woman I'm insanely attracted to exactly what those faults are."

That gave her body a shot of pure lust. How many times had she been told by a sexy man that he was insanely attracted to her? Exactly zero. To cover up her reaction, she gestured at him with her glass of wine. "But you do admit you have them."

"I'm human, aren't I?"

She'd been teasing, but her smile faded because he wasn't. He'd fooled her for a moment, distracting her, but yeah, he was still grieving. And who wouldn't be? She lightly nudged her shoulder to his. "I've got lots of faults. I'm impatient, single-minded to the point of distraction, hate to be vulnerable, which means I avoid real conversations, and . . ."

He raised a brow when she trailed off. "Don't stop now, it's just getting good."

Drawing a deep breath, she admitted her truth. "Despite what you seem to think, I'm not a great older sister."

He cocked his head, his gaze warm but curious, and utterly devoid of judgment. "Let me recap what I know. You came here with Winnie and Gavin when you were just a kid yourself. You had your grandma's help for a while, but you mostly raised them on your own. Yeah?"

She nodded, and he squeezed her hand.

"In my book, that makes you a *great* sibling, and possibly the best person I've ever met."

She took a deep gulp of the wine. The shockingly good wine. She looked at the bottle. "Wait a minute. Winnie hates wine. Why would she buy herself such a good one?"

"Probably because she didn't buy it."

She lifted her head and stared at him. "Because . . . *you* bought it? *You* set all this up?"

He held the eye contact. "No."

She stared at him some more, and then it hit her. "Ohmigod, you think *I* did this?"

"Didn't you?"

She closed her eyes. "She set us up. I'm going to have to kill her." Standing, she looked around, certain they were being spied on by her annoying, meddling, interfering sister.

Cam stood too. "Okay, so you didn't do this."

She moaned. "I don't know what's worse, that you think I did and then denied it, or that Winnie thought I needed so much help getting your attention that she had to put it all together for me."

That got her a smile. "Trust me, you do just fine attracting me all on your own."

"Yeah?"

"Oh, yeah." He nodded his chin toward the tire swing. "That thing safe?"

"I hope so. Gavin and Winnie spent a bunch of years on it. If you get some good momentum going, you can fling yourself pretty far into the water."

"As competitive as you are, I bet you went the farthest."

"I'm not *that* competitive."

He practically rolled his eyes out loud.

"Okay," she conceded with a laugh. "I am. But I never used the swing."

"Why not?"

Well, this was awkward. She started to turn back to pack everything up, but he stopped her by taking her hand in his.

"Hey," she said. "If you don't have to tell your secrets, I sure as hell don't have to tell mine."

He considered her for a beat. "How about this? A secret for a secret."

She narrowed her eyes in doubt, but he looked genuine, and she realized this might actually be too good a deal to pass up. "Okay," she said, but then grimaced, because this was embarrassing. "I misdirected you when we were at the beach. The water thing . . . it *is* a phobia. I'm . . . ridiculously and overwhelmingly terrified of deep water."

His brows went up in surprise.

"What, you think I'm not afraid of anything?"

"I don't think you often admit it," he said. "That's what surprised me. As for the phobia, that was perfectly clear."

She moaned and covered her face.

He pulled her hands free. "Tell me what happened."

"Why do you assume something happened?"

"Call it a hunch. Plus, you just crossed your arms and looked away."

Dammit. She dropped her arms. "One secret at a time. And it's your turn."

"Okay . . ." He paused. "I called in a favor and got some extra leave time. I've got another three weeks from the DEA, though I'll still have to fly out for Coast Guard training for a few days. But I'll be back."

She stared at him, absorbing that news.

"Look at that," he said. "I just left you speechless."

Yes, and he'd also just changed the rhythm of her heartbeat. "To help your dad?"

"Among other things."

"Such as?"

He just looked at her.

Oh. Oh, wow. She went a little warm and mushy in some spots, while other areas, such as her brain, started to panic, snagging the very air in her throat so that she couldn't breathe.

"Yeah. Now you're getting it," he murmured, apparently a mind reader now, and he touched his wineglass to hers with a soft *clink*.

They drank, and then he set his glass aside and took hers to do the same. He pulled her into him and was lowering his mouth to hers when she put a hand on his chest.

"Problem?" he murmured.

Um, she wasn't sure. Her heart was pounding, and then there was anxiety and worry chasing each other through her veins. To distract from that, she said, "If Winnie did this, she's watching."

Cam looked around and shook his head.

"Trust me." She hurriedly began to gather everything, shoving it all back into the basket.

He was sticking around for longer.

For her.

He liked her, maybe as much as she liked him. Which was a good thing, right? So why then did she feel the need to retreat and take a moment to think too hard? "Sorry," she said as they walked back.

"For?"

"For cutting things short."

He gave her a long look.

"What?"

"I thought maybe you were going to admit you just freaked out when I told you I'm going to be around for a bit longer."

She stared at him, mouth ready to deny it, but . . . she couldn't.

Because he was right.

CHAPTER 16

"Let's see what you're packing."

Gavin led an annoyed, grumpy CJ through the dark on the trail around the lake.

"When are you going to tell me what the hell we're doing?"

It was midnight, quickly becoming Gavin's favorite time in Wildstone. "You work too hard."

CJ laughed roughly. "What does that have to do with anything? You showed up at the end of my shift, insisted I come here to the lake with you, that you had something of vital importance to show me. So? What is it?"

The cop was in street clothes tonight. Sexy jeans. Long-sleeved button down opened over a T-shirt advertising CJ's brother's motorcycle shop. Bad 'tude all over his face, which came, no doubt, from a tough shift. And possibly a general pissiness from feeling things for Gavin that he didn't want to feel. Overall look: hot as hell.

CJ hated to be managed. Gavin knew this because he was the same. So if anyone in the world understood CJ's current mood, it was Gavin. He stopped and stripped out of his shirt, then kicked off his boots.

CJ just shook his head. "Are you crazy? It's February."

"Yes and yes. It's also still sixty degrees. We've done this in far colder weather."

"*This* being . . . ?"

"Skinny-dipping." Gavin smiled. "You telling me you don't remember?"

CJ didn't budge. He also kept his emotions close to the vest. Whatever he was thinking, he wasn't about to share. "The last time we did this," he finally said, "we were young and stupid. *And* high."

Gavin laughed. "Come on, old man. Strip. Let's see what you're packing."

"You already know. You've seen it all before, most recently the other night."

Gavin had no idea why, when the guy was acting all buttoned up, that it totally turned him on. Clearly, he was mental. Proving it, he just smirked. "Some things bear repeating." He unbuttoned his jeans.

CJ raised a brow.

A challenge. And Gavin Manning had done a lot of things, but he'd never backed down from a challenge, even when he should have. So he shoved his pants down and off, and then gestured for CJ to get on with it.

CJ took in the sight, which was more than slightly gratifying.

"Well?" Gavin asked. "Am I doing this alone?"

"You avoided my question."

No shit. "Which one?" he asked innocently.

CJ just shook his head at him.

"Right. The whole 'what are we doing' thing." Gavin decided not to press his luck. "Spending time together."

"We already tried that when we were kids. It went spectacularly wrong."

It had. And all of it had been Gavin's fault. "Maybe I want to see if it could go spectacularly right this time." He held his breath while trying to look cool and nonchalant—not easy when bare-assed naked, by the way.

Their gazes locked and held for a long beat. Gavin waited for another objection, but one didn't come. Finally, CJ swore and muttered to himself, but tugged off both his shirts and tossed them aside.

Gavin smiled.

CJ rolled his eyes and lost the rest of his clothes, and Gavin blessed the moonlight that gave him a front-row view of the only body that had ever driven him crazy.

Beneath the moon, they stood on the tire swing together and catapulted themselves into the water. They raced, swimming their asses off to the rocks about a hundred yards out. They body-surfed on the swells. They spent time, hours of it, just . . . being.

Later, much later, lying flat on their backs in the wild grass staring up at the stars, CJ reached for Gavin's hand. "Thanks."

Gavin turned on his side and propped his head up with a hand, smiling. "Anytime."

This tugged a rough laugh from CJ. "I meant for . . ." He shook his head. "Look, I don't make time for this stuff anymore. I don't make much time for myself at all."

"All work and no fun?"

"There's more to life than hookups and fun, Gavin. I'm still not sure you get that."

"I do." Gavin ran a finger along CJ's set jaw. "I'm done with that life, Ceej. There's nothing for me there anymore, nothing but emptiness and loneliness and trouble."

"How do you know you're done with it?"

"Because I've been lucky enough in my life to have it all, and then stupid enough to throw it away and have to live with that. I've seen both sides. I guess some of us have to sink as low as we can sink before understanding what life's really about."

"And what's life really about?" CJ asked.

"It's about being with the people you care about most, about living in the present with honesty and no regrets." Gavin managed a half smile. "Or at least as few regrets as possible."

CJ stared up at him for a long beat and then pulled Gavin on top of him. "Then here's to as few regrets as possible."

And that was the last time they communicated, at least with words, for the rest of the night.

THE NEXT MORNING, Piper groaned her way out of bed at the crack of dawn. The new locks for the front doors on the cottages had arrived the day before and she wanted to get started on installing them.

And not because she hadn't slept, thinking about Cam's accusation that she was running scared. True, by the way, and she hated that.

She staggered into the kitchen seeking caffeine. She stopped short at the sight of Gavin and Winnie. "Seriously," she said. "The two of you are starting to worry me."

"I've got work," Gavin said. "I'm working with Cam on the books. The job's small, only a few hours here and there, which is great, but not enough for me. So I've also got a few other job interviews today."

Piper blinked. "In Arizona?"

Gavin and Winnie exchanged a look. "No," Gavin said. "Here. One in Wildstone, another in San Luis Obispo. Both IT entry-level positions with sucky wages, but they're something. I want to be able to contribute to the household."

"And I'm working too," Winnie said.

"Oh? On another ambush?"

Winnie had the good grace to look a little contrite. "I was just trying to help."

"Well, don't."

"Fine." Winnie rose. "I've got to get to work too."

"Where?" Piper asked.

"Here. And the good news is that I'm cheap. Free, to be exact."

That's when Piper realized her sister was wearing a toolbelt. And it actually had tools in it. The leather creaked and the tools clanked when she crossed the room to the toaster.

"You're working here," Piper repeated, confused.

"Why not? You're working your ass off, right? And you can't

do it all on your own." She pointed at herself, looking prideful and a little wan, which Piper attributed to her being up at this previously unseen hour.

"Okay," Piper said. "Who are you two and what have you done with my real siblings?"

"I know, right?" Winnie put a piece of bread in the toaster. "Guess we grew up after all—"

"Wait!" Piper said before Winnie pushed the lever. "You'll start a fire."

"I fixed it."

Piper blinked. "You fixed it?"

"Yeah. I keep telling you, YouTube's amazing. Oh and the Wi-Fi—"

"—is crappy," Piper said. "I know. I keep meaning to call—"

"Fixed that too."

Piper stared at Winnie. "What?"

"Yeah, you had the wiring all screwed up, and also you weren't password protected, so everyone and their dog was using your connection. Rookie mistake."

Piper blinked. "Are you making fun of my tech skills?"

"Yes."

"Just remember, I taught you how to use a damn spoon."

Winnie grinned, and it looked so cute and carefree that Piper felt a burst of emotion. *Happiness,* she thought. She was so unused to it, she'd barely recognized it.

Winnie started to say something else, but went suddenly still, a hand on her stomach. Her color was way off. As in green.

"You okay?" Piper asked.

"Yep." Winnie paused, then shook her head. "Nope." And she went running out of the room.

Piper looked at Gavin. "The flu?"

Gavin shrugged. "Hey, do you think Mom and Dad would like the idea of all of us being back here together as adults?"

Her chest got a little tight in the way it always did whenever he tried to get her to talk about their parents. Just thinking about them hurt like hell, much less talking about them. But she managed a tight smile. "I do." Then she left the kitchen and moved to the downstairs bathroom door, which was shut and locked. She knocked softly. "Winnie? You okay?"

"Go away."

Ah. There she was. Piper went and got a can of ginger ale and a sleeve of crackers, and left them outside the bathroom door. Then she got one of the cottage front door locks replaced before she had to take off for work, where she spent twelve straight hours seeing the worst of humanity. But on the upside, she and Jenna got a whole fifteen minutes for a midday break, and they hit up 7-Eleven for hot dogs and chips.

Score.

After work, she drove home and climbed out of her car, taking a moment to just look at the lake and unwind. Other than that one bad storm, winter hadn't been much of a threat. She hoped it stayed that way. Right now it was windy but a downright balmy sixty-two degrees. The sun was setting, casting the choppy lake and the surrounding rolling hills in a kaleidoscope of colors.

Grabbing her bag, she headed toward Emmitt's house for her daily check-in. Halfway there, she caught sight of someone on the docks. A tall, built someone sitting with his feet hanging over the side, staring at the water the way she'd been.

Cam. He was in a wet suit that he'd peeled off his torso and shoved down to his waist. His hair was wet.

It was ridiculous how he could affect her mood. *And* her pulse. She'd told herself this was a bad idea, *he* was a bad idea, but there seemed to be some sort of disconnect between her brain and heart. Not to mention decidedly south of her heart.

Her life was chaos, always had been. But somehow Cam had become the calm in the storm. He was easy to be with. He was slow to anger, steady, determined, focused. And best yet, she didn't have to take care of him. She could just enjoy him.

The knowledge felt . . . freeing and fun, a lot like the freedom she'd been yearning for and dreaming about. She'd like to keep things just as they were. Well, okay, maybe with a whole lot more nudity and orgasms. But other than that, just like this, no complications.

Complications continued to ruin her life.

It was then that she realized Cam's shoulders were set with tension, and even from this distance, she could tell that something was wrong.

Emmitt was going to have to wait.

She got down to the marina and came to a halt just before the docks. Because of course Cam was on the longest one, which jutted straight out at least a hundred feet over the lake.

If she wanted to get to him, she'd have to walk it.

Oh, boy. She took a few more steps, but stopped right before stepping up onto the actual dock itself.

She was already sweating. "Hey."

He didn't hear her.

Damn wind. She drew in a deep breath and stepped up onto the dock. She swiped her clammy hands over her thighs and took another step. Suddenly she felt ill. Maybe she'd caught Winnie's flu. Maybe she should turn around and go straight home.

Except Winnie had texted her earlier not to worry, she didn't have the flu. Maybe food poisoning, but whatever it was, she was fine now.

Great. So Piper couldn't even use "close to death" as an excuse. "*Cam.*"

He still didn't turn around. *Well, shit.* She managed another few steps, getting past the sandy shore now. Which meant she was directly over the water, specifically the waves lapping at the beach. Perfect, and now she was starting to hyperventilate right on cue.

Which was of course when Cam turned and caught her standing there, very carefully dead center of the dock, hands to her pounding heart.

"Hey," she managed with a pretty good false cheer, if she did say so herself. "Whatcha doing?"

"Swimming."

This had her fear momentarily forgotten. "In the lake?"

"No, in the air." He shook his head, a small smile playing around his mouth, but not making it to his eyes. "Yes, the lake. I swim it every day."

"The whole thing?" she squeaked. "On purpose?"

He lifted a shoulder. "I've always used swimming to blow off steam."

Well, hell. Something most definitely wasn't okay. "What's wrong?"

He didn't answer, which meant—dear God—she was going to have to move closer.

CHAPTER 17

"I remember all my promises."

Cam heard Piper's question; he just had no idea how to answer. What was wrong? *Every-fucking-thing*, but that seemed overly dramatic, and he didn't do dramatic. Or emotions. Not since he'd bottled everything up, including Rowan's death, and shoved it down deep.

For him, it was the only way to deal. *Keeping* it deep, however, was proving all but impossible. Three-plus months. Three-plus months Rowan had been gone, and whoever had said time heals all wounds was full of shit.

"Cam?"

She'd taken another step toward him but was still only halfway to him. She was standing oddly, as if every muscle in her body was strung too tight and on high alert. He realized the wide-eyed look she was wearing meant she was too petrified to walk out on the dock to get closer to him, and yet she was doing it anyway, inch by inch.

For him.

He shook his head. "Go home, Piper. You've had a long day, you're exhausted."

She swallowed, but didn't retreat. "Something's wrong." Her eyes were now once again locked on his, like he was the only thing keeping her sane, telling him without words what trying to support him was costing her. "I'm coming to get you."

With a sigh, he rose and met her. Wrapping an arm around her shoulders, he started to lead her back to the shore.

She gulped hard and stopped him. "No. The other way. You weren't done sitting out there."

"You sure?"

She nodded, and not about to argue with her, he walked her to the end of the dock. He once again sat and hung his legs over the side, waiting for her to do the same.

Slowly, arms out, legs bent at the knees like she was a cat on ice skates on linoleum, she lowered herself onto all fours. She paused in that position for a long beat, then finally sat, hugging her knees to her chest.

To her credit, she didn't push him to talk; she just reached out and took his hand in her clammy one and held tight, whether from sheer terror or wanting to comfort him, he wasn't sure.

"You seriously swim the lake?" she asked.

"Usually twice."

She gasped in horror, and in spite of what he was feeling, he smiled. "You think I'm nuts."

She managed a small smile. "You're my friend, and no matter what life choices you've made, I support you. Even if I think you're nuts."

He actually laughed when he hadn't thought he could, and his frozen heart thawed a little bit. "Thanks for supporting my choices. FYI, I've just made another one." Cupping her face, he kissed her, a soft kiss with a hint of a promise that he hoped she took him up on sometime. But it was her move to make, not his.

She put her hands over his and kept her eyes closed as she slowly pulled back. "You're good at that. And I'm betting you're good at all the stuff that goes with it."

"There's only one way to find out."

She smiled. "I'd like that. But . . ." She opened her eyes. "Something's wrong."

He shrugged. Yeah, there was something wrong with him, probably a whole bunch of things, actually. But he didn't have words for it right now. So he leaned back and stared at the water.

Piper leaned back too, carefully *not* looking at the water. "Winnie's working on the house. And Gavin's taking on some small jobs."

"And you're telling me this because . . . ?"

"Because we're friends."

"We are, but I know you now," he said. "You're telling me this because you want me to open up as well."

"Yes." She smiled, but her eyes remained serious. "Because otherwise I'm risking heart failure for nothing out here."

She wasn't joking. He could see her pulse leaping at the hollow of her throat. "I'm fine, Piper." A lie, of course. He wasn't fine. He'd been going through Rowan's things. A macabre task, but his dad had asked him for help packing it all. Memories were one thing. Walking past Rowan's bedroom every single day, which was practically a shrine to him, was another.

So Cam had taken that task on for his dad, which was how he'd found the engagement ring Rowan had bought to give to Winnie. His chest hurt at the thought. "I packed up Rowan's things today."

"Oh, Cam." Her expression said she was still flipping out on the inside, but she was determined to help him. She scooted closer so that they were thigh to thigh, whispering "Oh my God, oh my God" to herself the whole time, before very slowly lowering her feet over the side of the dock to match his position.

He brought himself out of his own head enough to be impressed. "Are you doing what I think you're doing?"

"Trying not to die? Then yes, I'm doing exactly what you think I'm doing." She took a deep gulp of air. "We have this deal, a secret for a secret, right? So . . . I'm going to tell you another secret."

"Now? While you're shaking in your boots and trying not to throw up?"

She slid him a look.

He didn't laugh, because she was serious.

"I'm afraid of the water," she said.

"Hate to break it to you, but that's still the same old secret you've pawned off on me three times now. I'm beginning to think you're cheating."

"Yes, but you asked what happened." She paused. "I had a near miss here on the lake. Almost drowned."

Ah, hell. Reaching out, he took her hand in his. "That would do it. When?"

"The year after my parents died. It was my fourteenth birthday party. My grandma had invited all my friends, and we spent the day outside by the lake. We were in canoes. I was with two other girls in one that was meant for only a single occupant."

"Never good," he said. "You rolled."

"Oh, yeah. And panicked. One of the girls who I didn't know very well held me down. She thought it was funny, but I was a terrible swimmer to begin with . . ." She shook her head. "I got turned upside down and couldn't figure out which way was up, and I lost it. Spots were dancing around in my eyes, and just before everything went dark, I was scooped up and shoved to the surface."

"The girl?"

"No. My grandpa." She smiled a little. "He was sick and had been sitting on the porch of the house. He never paid any attention to us kids, but he had an eagle eye." She shuddered with the memories. "It was the most terrifying moment of my life." She paused. "He passed away shortly after that," she said softly. "And I know it sounds melodramatic, but that was the last time I ever felt really safe."

He thought about all she'd said, and all she *hadn't* said. By age fourteen, she'd lost both of her parents and her grandpa. She'd been helping to raise her two younger siblings.

She'd never had a real childhood.

Chances were, that birthday party was the last time she'd ever been a kid or done something frivolous for herself. He squeezed her hard. "I'm feeling very grateful for your grandpa."

That got him a small smile. "Me too."

"And no wonder you hate birthday celebrations."

She snorted. "No, I hate birthday celebrations because it reminds me that another year's passed without any headway."

"Toward what?"

She bit her lower lip.

"Is this about your secret and secret *secret* lists?" he asked.

"Some," she admitted. "But now it's your turn."

Right. He nodded. Then he said the words that never failed to beat the shit out of him. "The car accident that killed Rowan? I was driving."

She sucked in a breath. Still clutching his hand in hers, she brought it up to her heart. "Were you badly hurt?"

That her first words were worry for him told him everything he needed to know—she was far too good for him. "Not even a little bit," he said, hearing the bitterness in his voice.

"Oh, Cam." And with that, she crawled into his lap and hugged him so tight he couldn't breathe. Or resist hugging her back. Then she set her head on his shoulder and did one of his favorite things. She let him be with his own thoughts. It was a rare beat of desperately needed quiet, and in that moment she was able to do for him what swimming the lake twice over hadn't done.

Give him some badly needed peace.

PIPER FELT WHEN some of the terrible tension inside Cam drained a little. Not enough to suit her, though. He couldn't walk around this way, she thought. It'd kill him.

That she often did the same thing didn't matter.

He was hurting, and she was someone who at her core

wanted, needed, to heal people. She was still on his lap. His arms were loosely around her, her head on his shoulder, his jaw pressed against her hair. She drew a deep breath. "Growing up, there were so many times I wanted to strangle Gavin and/or Winnie. But the truth is, if something had actually happened to one of them . . ." She broke off when her voice cracked and had to clear her throat. "In hindsight, I think those were the moments where love showed the most, because they were the only people who could get beneath my skin and into my heart."

Cam slid a big, warm hand up her back and into her hair, wrapping it around his fist to tug lightly so he could see her face. "Has anyone else ever gotten beneath your skin?"

Their gazes were locked. No place to hide. "Not since my parents died."

He nodded, as if she'd simply verified what he'd already suspected, that she'd turned off her heart from further hurt, and she'd been very successful at it.

"It's a shame," he said.

"Why?"

"Because I see how fiercely you love." When she tried to pull free, he tugged a little bit harder, holding her to him. "You've got so much love to give, Piper. It's hard to see you closed off."

They stared at each other, during which she felt a shift, a cataclysmic one, at least for her. She'd thought of him as the fun-time guy. After all, he was going to leave soon, and hell, for that matter, so was she. They'd probably rarely, if ever, see each other again. Which was why he'd seemed like the perfect distraction.

But in that moment, she felt the lock on her heart loosen,

even open, which meant this wasn't anywhere near as casual as she'd planned.

Cam whispered her name softly, with a longing that stirred her own to an almost unbearable level inside her. And then— she wasn't sure who moved first—they were kissing, long, lingering kisses with lots of heat and tongue. Her hands tightened on his biceps, then ran up to cup his face before going south and landing on his bare chest.

He froze, then pulled free.

"Oh, crap, sorry." Mortified by his response to her touch, she tried to scoot away, but his hands were immediately back on her, his voice sounding strained as he held her to him.

"*Piper*—"

"No." She covered her face. "Forget it, okay? It's been a while, and I'm really bad at this part, at reading what a guy's thinking, and—"

He pulled her hands from her face, so she played a three-year-old and closed her eyes.

"Look at me," he said, in a voice she imagined he used on his men, because she obediently opened her eyes.

"Are you listening?" he asked very intensely.

Listening. *Dying* . . . "Yes."

"Good. I want you, Piper." He waited for her to realize she was literally up against the proof of that wanting. "Badly. But . . ."

"I'm not a big fan of buts," she whispered.

He smiled. "Piper, we're outside."

"And?"

"And by the time I get you inside, I suspect you'll have changed your mind."

"Try me." She had no idea where those two words came from. No, scratch that. She knew exactly. And she meant them too.

He looked at her, and she did her best to seem like something he couldn't go without right this very second.

He took a deep breath and started to speak, but with the feel of him so hard against her, she was done with the speaking portion of this event. Especially because he looked so turned on and stern at the same time. So she leaned in and kissed him again, very seriously.

With a rough groan that spoke to all her good parts, he wrapped her up tight and kissed her back. At some point, he rose to his feet with her still in his arms. His big hands went to her ass to hold her against him as he walked, and she gave an involuntary squeak of terror as she remembered they were on the docks, surrounded by water.

"Close your eyes," he said.

"You just told me to open them."

"And now I'm telling you to close them again."

He walked only a few yards, it seemed, before taking a big step onto something. Something that rocked.

A boat.

Oh good God. Her heart thumped heavily in her chest, and not with lust this time. "Cam—"

"Keep 'em closed, Piper."

She heard a door open and then shut, and what she thought might be the click of a lock before she was finally settled on something soft. Before she could decide what, Cam's big, warm body came down over her. Entangling his fingers with hers, he slowly drew her hands up to either side of her head.

"Okay," he said.

Her eyes flew open to find his dark and heated on hers. "We're on a boat," she whispered.

"Yes. Away from anyone's view. Unless you're changing your mind."

Not in this lifetime. "No."

He nodded, but still looked so . . . solemn. "I don't have a condom."

She couldn't remember ever feeling so disappointed about anything ever. "Why?"

He almost smiled at that, she could tell. "Because I'm a very stupid, stupid man."

"*So* stupid."

That did get her a smile. "I realize you've got zero reason to trust me, but I'm disease free. Are you on the pill?"

She gave him a bobblehead nod. "And I've been checked too."

She felt his thumb glide over her lower lip. "Tell me to stop," he murmured huskily. "And I'll stop."

"Just like that?"

His fingers sank into her hair, his eyes softening. "*Always* just like that. I mean, there might be some grown-man crying, but this is your show, you're in the driver's seat here."

Since her body was already damp and trembling for him, stopping was the *last* thing she intended to do.

"Piper?"

"The only thing I want you to stop doing is talking so you can do stuff to me and make me forget that we're on the water."

"Bossy. I like it."

"Then you're going to love this. Lose the wet suit, Cam. Quickly."

He lifted up and did just that, leaving her speechless for a moment, because just like that first night in her house during the storm, he was commando.

He, however, was *not* speechless. "Just so you know," he said, his mouth making its merry way along her jaw to her ear, "you can be bossy in my bed anytime."

She nodded and started to answer, but he dipped his head and licked the hollow of her throat at the same time that he stroked his hands down her body and then back up again, this time beneath her shirt.

And then the shirt was gone.

Everywhere he touched, her skin came alive with fiery trails, and she shivered as he lingered as if wanting to remember every second of this.

She most definitely would. She heard a soft, breathy moan and realized it was her, as her fingers curled into the muscles of his back. He shifted, angling their hips closer so she could rock up into him, and the friction . . . the delicious eroticism of it had her halfway to orgasm. His mouth claimed hers again, the kiss ratcheting up her body temperature, and when he pulled back, she nearly cried. "Don't you dare ask me if I want to stop," she gasped.

He let out a rough laugh and nipped her earlobe as his hands worked to liberate her from her pants. They got caught on her steel-toed work boots, making him swear. She sat up to help, laughing at the sight of him sliding off the bed—and they were on a bed, on a boat, *good God stop thinking about it*—and onto his knees. Naked, he bent over her boots to work the hopelessly tangled laces. Swearing again, he finally just muscled the boots off, tossing them impatiently over his shoulder, where they hit the wall with twin *thunks*.

She was grinning when he freed her pants from around her ankles and crawled back up her body.

Seeing the man in clothes had been heart-stopping. The sight of him without was perfection.

"I'm tired already," he murmured, smiling into her laughing face. "You wore me out."

"Poor baby. Does that mean I get the top?"

"Next time," he said, and bent his head to her body, where he proceeded to rob her of the ability to speak more than words like "oh God" and "don't stop" and "please, more" for a very long time.

When she was boneless and still gasping for air, he entered her and revved her up all over again, their wild kisses moving in rhythm with their bodies.

It was shatteringly intense, and this time they lost themselves together. When she could finally uncurl her toes, she blinked the real world back into focus. There, for a moment, she'd forgotten her own name, though she was pretty sure all the wildlife on the lake now knew his. "Wow."

At her side, Cam laughed roughly, sounding lighter than she'd ever heard him. "Yeah." He pulled her into him and buried his face in her hair. "You just destroyed me. You know that, right? You own me now, Piper."

He was just teasing; she knew that. "We're going to do that again, right?"

"Oh, yeah." He came up on an elbow and stroked a finger along her jaw and down her body, the calloused pad catching on a nipple, watching as it tightened for him.

"Now?" she asked hopefully.

"Now." He rolled onto his back, pulling her on top to straddle him.

She grinned down at him. "You remembered."

"I remember all my promises."

IT WAS FOUR in the morning when Piper snuck into the house. She blamed Cam for exhausting her so thoroughly that they'd fallen asleep. Luckily, the morning wasn't particularly cold, so when she shivered, she knew it wasn't a chill. It was the memories of one Camden Hayes, all hard muscle under firm skin, the feel of his mouth on hers, the taste of him, the sound of his deep, rough groan in her ear when she'd touched him.

It was still dark, but she didn't need to turn on any lights as she tiptoed up the stairs and down the hall, stopping short at the sound of someone throwing up.

She pushed the bathroom door open and found Winnie on her knees, hugging the porcelain god and puking her guts up. Sweet Cheeks was winding her way around Winnie's legs with worried little cat chirps.

Piper nudged Sweet Cheeks aside. Then she pulled out her own hair tie and used it on Winnie's hair to hold it back for her. Turning, she grabbed a towel, wet it in the sink, and set it against the damp, heated nape of Winnie's neck.

Winnie moaned, flushed, and lay her cheek on the side of the toilet seat, eyes closed, skin green and clammy.

"Okay," Piper said, dropping to her knees at her sister's side. "This isn't food poisoning. It's time to get you to a doctor."

"You're a doctor."

"I'm an EMT."

"But you're going to be a physician assistant once you finish school."

"Which I haven't even started yet," Piper pointed out. "And why are we talking about that instead of you? Something's clearly wrong, Win."

"Yeah." Her sister closed her eyes. "But it's not what you think."

Piper stared at her, and when her own stomach dropped to her toes, she leaned back on her heels. "Oh my God. You're pregnant."

"Yeah. But trust me, God had nothing to do with it."

CHAPTER 18

"When I told you I caught the spider
in your bathroom . . . I lied."

At Winnie's shocking statement, Piper's legs collapsed. Luckily, the wall kept her propped upright. Numb, she stared at her sister. "You're really pregnant?"

"According to the ten pregnancy tests I took in the Target bathroom." Clearly feeling the opposite of numb, Winnie got to her feet and turned to the sink to rinse out her mouth.

"When?" Piper asked from the floor. "How?"

Winnie met her gaze in the mirror. "Well, when two people like each other, they—"

"Oh my God. You think this is funny."

"No," Winnie said. "I really don't. But while I'm spilling my guts literally and figuratively, you should also know something else. I quit college." She paused. "Last semester. Oh, and the other day when I told you I caught the spider in your bathroom . . . I lied. Whew." She let out a long breath. "I hope you feel as good as I do now."

Piper wasn't firing on all cylinders, so it took a moment to process. "You'd better not be serious about the spider."

"I am."

"This really isn't funny."

"No shit."

Piper could do nothing but stare at her sister, her pregnant and college-quitting sister. They were still staring at each other when they heard the front door open and close.

And then Gavin was coming up the stairs. He started down the hallway, but stopped short at the sight of them in the opened bathroom. His shirt was on inside out and his shoes dangled from his fingers. He was wearing a smile that Piper hadn't seen in ages.

"Now, see," Winnie said, pointing at her brother. "*That* I find funny."

Gavin eyed them both. "You told her," he said to Winnie, and Piper gaped at him.

"You knew?" she breathed.

"Well, yeah. She's been eating like she's growing an entire litter, and she's actually been mostly cheerful. Hasn't tried to kill me either."

"So you . . . just guessed?" Piper asked.

"No, she told me."

"When?"

Gavin looked at Winnie.

Winnie grimaced. "From the beginning."

Piper stared at her in hurt disbelief.

Winnie tossed up her hands. "I'm sorry! But I didn't tell you sooner because I knew you'd freak out. And hey, Gavin's sleeping with his ex! Why aren't we all talking about *that*?"

"You suck," Gavin said.

Piper held up a hand. She honest to God felt like she was thirteen and in over her head all over again. Or still. "You could've told me."

"Sure," Winnie said. "But we all know how that conversation would've gone. And I get it, I'm the baby of the family. I'm the extra, the one who doesn't have to grow up as fast, or try very hard." Her smile was sad and regretful. "And that's all me. Because what did I do when I found out I was pregnant? I came home with my tail between my legs."

"Oh, Winnie," Piper said softly. "I—"

Winnie shook her head and held up a hand. "I know that I barely remember Mom and Dad, that we had a whole life on the other side of the planet that I also can't remember. But I know how much I owe you, Piper. How much trouble and angst I've caused over the years. So, yeah, I should've told you. You certainly deserved to know. But I guess I just wasn't ready to hear the spiel. That I'm smart, but don't apply myself enough. That I've got a whole bunch of potential, but never live up to it. That I need to focus on what's important. But see, Piper, I do. I am. I'm *very* focused on what's important to me. You just don't always agree with me."

That this might be true shamed Piper. "I'm sorry," she said. "I never meant to make you feel bad about your choices. I just didn't want anything to hold you back, ever."

Winnie gave a crooked smile. "Have you met me?"

Piper gave a soft laugh and so did Winnie.

"So . . ." Piper paused. "What are your plans?"

Winnie took a shaky breath. "I'm still absorbing all of this myself, and I know we need to talk about it, but I hope you can try to understand that I'm not quite ready to." Never comfortable with deeply emotional moments, Winnie proved it by pointing at her big brother. "So CJ took you back, huh?"

"Nice diversion," Gavin said, but smiled. "And yeah. He took me back. For now anyway."

"I didn't realize you two had even remained in touch," Piper said carefully. Gavin had been the one to leave CJ, but that didn't mean he'd gotten off pain-free. Because he hadn't. And in fact, he still grieved over losing CJ, and she wasn't sure he was strong enough to survive it again. "I'm not sure this is a good idea—"

"Stop," Gavin said gently. "You've spent enough of your life worrying about me. You don't need to do that anymore. CJ and I both know what this is, and what it isn't."

She hoped that was true, because she didn't want to see either of them hurt. But then again, she and Cam also knew what they had and what they didn't, and that wasn't going to stop her from being hurt when it was over.

"Seriously," he said quietly, giving her a one-armed hug. "You've got other things to worry about." He jerked his chin in Winnie's direction.

"Hey," Winnie said. "I'm fine."

"Right. We're all just fine." Piper sighed. "Who's the baby daddy?"

Winnie's smile faded. "That's one of the things I don't want to talk about right now." Or ever, her expression said.

Piper paused, surprised. "Why not?"

"Because it doesn't matter."

Piper was confused. "Of course it matters."

"It doesn't," Winnie insisted. "I've got this, Piper. I do. I mean, how hard can it be?"

"To be a mom?" she asked in disbelief.

"Yeah."

Piper didn't want to scare her, but neither did she want her to look at this with rose-colored glasses, with absolutely zero idea how hard parenting could be.

Winnie was watching her and shook her head. "Don't discount me, not on this."

"I'm not trying to, Win. I'm trying to be supportive." *While not freaking out completely.* Because she'd already raised two chicklets. She was in the home stretch of being free. Or at least, she had been. "What about college? You'll need a degree if you're going to raise a kid. You could get another semester under your belt before you give birth."

Winnie shrugged. "Maybe I'll do it online, but I like fixing things. I want to do that instead."

"You're getting good at it too," Gavin said.

Winnie beamed at him.

"We're selling this place," Piper burst out.

Her sister gasped. "What?"

"*Why?*" Gavin asked.

"Think about it," Piper said. "We'd each get a third of the money. Winnie, you'd be able to pay off some of the college debt and have a nice nest egg for your baby. And, Gavin, you'd have financial security." She paused, expecting excitement.

"But I want to raise my baby here," Winnie said. "Be a family. Like *we* were."

Gavin looked like he agreed with that.

Okay, so no excitement. What was happening?

Gavin drew a deep breath. "God knows, you deserve to get something out of all the work you put into this place. But if you're doing this for me, don't. The last thing an addict needs is financial security and discretionary money burning a hole in his pocket."

"Okay." *Don't panic.* "So what *do* you need?"

"Honestly? To be right here in this house with both you crazy people."

Wow. This was not how Piper had seen this going. At all. "So we're, what, going to live together, until we're old and gray?"

Gavin and Winnie looked at each other and then at Piper. "Yes," they said in unison.

Winnie put her hands on her still-flat belly. "I need this, Piper," she whispered.

Gavin nodded, and at the touch of fear in his gaze, Piper softened. Ached. "But—"

"We're a unit," he said. "The three of us. We're all we have left because our parents are gone. And I get it, that very fact forced you to become the Fixer, and don't get me wrong, you've *always* done the right thing by us. You put your life on hold to make sure we grew up okay, but you've never liked it. Even now I can see you panicking on the inside, scrambling to figure out how to get us gone again." He hesitated, and when he spoke, his voice was unusually solemn. "Do you have any idea what it feels like to be a burden to someone you love?"

God. He was right. As awful as it was, there'd been times when she'd felt overwhelmed and out of control, and had looked at them as a burden, and that was all on her. She wanted to reach out, hug him, say something to ease the pain in his eyes, anything, but they'd never been a huggy sort of family. And now she knew that it was her fault they weren't.

"You were my mom, my dad, my friend, and oftentimes also my enforcer," Gavin said. "But you've never been my sister. You've never let me be your brother. You've never let me be there for you, Piper, not once. You need to stop protecting me. I'm grown, I'm good, and that's all thanks to you. But I *want* to be siblings. I want to be equals. I want to be the one to help you for a change."

"I don't need help."

He nodded. "Yeah. You're an island and an army of one, believe me, I get it. But do you realize we've never even grieved together for all we've lost?"

Her biggest fear. If she let out the grief, it'd consume her. So she shook her head, her mind dark with memories. "I can't."

"I know," Gavin said. "Because you never could. Not even when I needed you to."

She opened her mouth, to say what, she had no idea, but Winnie started shoving them out the bathroom door, face green. "Oh God, hurry. Get out. Get out, get out! Save yourselves!" she yelled, and slammed the door on their noses to throw up again.

CHAPTER 19

"You mean other than your sweet, sunny nature?"

Midmorning, Cam sat in the tiny marina business office, staring at the ancient metal filing cabinet. Up until today, it'd been filled to the brim with paperwork shoved into each drawer so tightly, he'd had to pry them open one at a time.

His dad's filing system.

Rowan had been going through it all and leaving notes, but paperwork hadn't been his strong suit. Hiring Gavin had been one of Cam's smartest ideas ever. Piper's brother had gone painstakingly through each bill and receipt, slowly making progress and some sense of the bookkeeping.

Or lack of it.

It gave Cam relief knowing that when he got called to head back to work, he could go with the confidence that Gavin would be able to keep things up to date. What didn't give Cam a sense of relief? Everything he'd be leaving behind.

Or whom.

Scrubbing a hand over his face, he leaned back in the chair, closing his eyes for a second as he remembered the feel of Piper's body against him, how she'd responded to his touch like he was the very breath in her lungs.

Being with her had been magic. And addictive. And yet he would still have to leave, no matter what he wanted. It was inevitable.

But his return would be as well. He was no longer surprised by that realization. What he had been surprised by was all he'd found here in Wildstone. Last night, something in particular had driven him to swim the lake, needing both mental and physical exhaustion.

Turned out that being with Piper was all he'd needed.

But in the light of day, what he'd found yesterday in Rowan's things was still shocking him. It'd been hidden in the old metal filing cabinet.

The chair Cam sat in was also metal and far too small, which meant his knees were jammed up too close to his chest. He felt like a giant playing in a dollhouse. Not the best place for an epiphany.

When a knock sounded on the door, it was a welcome diversion. It opened before he could even get up, and there stood Winnie, hair in two ponytails, the ends dipped in blue, wearing jean shorts and an oversized T-shirt, looking fourteen years old, tops.

"I told her," she said, leaning dramatically against the doorjamb. "Piper." She came into the office, filling it with the level of angst only a twenty-year-old woman-child could. She plopped into the metal chair across the desk from him.

He stood. "Is she okay?"

"Well, *I'm* fine, thanks for asking."

Cam shook his head at her. "You know what I mean."

"She's . . . shocked." Winnie rubbed her stomach. "She can join my damn club."

Suddenly suspicious, Cam sat. "When you say you told her, you mean you told her all of it, right?"

"You make it sound like there's so much to tell."

He leveled a look at her. "For nearly two decades, she raised you and Gavin with hopes and dreams for you both. I'm pretty sure those hopes and dreams didn't include you quitting college, returning to Wildstone, or getting pregnant so young."

Winnie sighed. "I know. And yeah, I told her everything. Well, except the Rowan being the daddy part. I mean, why drag a dead guy into it, right?"

"Why wouldn't you tell her?" he asked, boggled by the mysterious workings of the female mind.

Winnie tipped her head back and stared up at the ceiling. "You knew your brother. He was . . . awesome, but he marched to his own beat, you know? He wasn't exactly the most responsible guy around. I know this because I'm not either. And Piper knew it too. But what she doesn't know is that I'm changing, for the Bean." She cupped her belly. "But I have to show her, Cam. Show, not tell. I'm going to prove myself to her, for me *and* Rowan. I just need time to do it."

Cam opened his mouth, but telling her she was making a stupid choice was what he'd have done to Rowan. And look where that'd gotten them. So he bit his tongue. Hard. Because Piper wasn't wrong about Rowan. The kid had been slow to grow up, really slow. And living here on the lake with his dad, who wasn't exactly Mr. Responsible himself, hadn't helped. But in the end, Rowan had at least been trying. Hell, Cam had the proof of that sitting in his pocket.

Winnie was growing up too, getting a crash course in adulting while she was at it. By all counts, she was doing her best. It'd be of no use to tell her how stupid it was not to tell Piper, that it'd only blow up on her in the end. Chances were that she already knew. Or, more likely, she just didn't care, because in Winnie's world, it was still all about Winnie.

That would change too, soon enough, but she'd have to figure that out on her own. He was here for her, no matter what. He'd made a promise, and he took those incredibly seriously. But first and foremost, his responsibility was to the baby she was carrying. "Rowan had *definitely* started to grow up," he said. "For you both."

Winnie gave him a look that held a mix of doubt and hope. "Really?"

"He was in it with you, Winnie. All the way in."

"What do you mean?" She straightened up and leaned toward him now. "How do you know?"

"Because I found this." He pulled the little black box from his pocket, the one he'd found shortly before Piper had come to him on the dock last night.

Winnie took the box and stared at it for a long moment.

When she finally opened it and found a very modest but pretty diamond ring, she covered her mouth with shaking fingers. "He wanted to marry me?"

"Yes."

She clutched the box to her chest like she was hugging it, but didn't make a move to put it on.

"You're not going to wear it?"

She pressed her lips together. "Did he tell you how we got together? I mean together, together?"

"No."

"We were BFFs. Ride or dies, you know? And though we toyed with an attraction, we'd always ignored it." She shook her head. "I think we were both scared. Even stupid kids like us recognized when two souls were meant for each other, and that was . . . well, terrifying. So we kept it platonic."

Cam glanced down wryly at the hand she held over her stomach.

"Yeah, well, I'm getting there," she said. "He came down to Santa Barbara to visit me just before he went to see you. I wasn't expecting him. He showed up at my place just as I was getting home from a date with a guy who had turned out to be an asshole." She sighed. "The truth is, Rowan sort of saved me that night. I was upset, and . . ." She closed her eyes for a long moment, lost in her thoughts. "And, well . . . one thing led to another." When she opened her eyes, they were wet. "That was the last time I saw him."

They'd been on the verge of something, something that might've been really great for both of them, and it'd been taken away from them. Cam hated that.

Winnie ran her finger over the ring, then met his gaze, her own surprisingly adult. "We weren't in love. At least not yet. But I loved him in my own way, and I know he loved me too. And I like to think we could've made it work."

Cam stood up, pulled her to her feet, and hugged her as she started to cry. "I think so too," he said softly, his own throat tight from listening to her pain.

Finally, she sniffed and pulled back to swipe a hand across her face. "I know we already had a funeral, but it was with a bunch of people I didn't know. I want to do a really small thing here, with Piper and Gavin, who couldn't afford to go to the first one." She looked at him. "Would you be okay with that?"

"Of course, but are you sure you want to put yourself through it again?"

"No. But I want to do it anyway. For closure."

Cam nodded. "Then that's what we'll do."

"Next weekend," she said. "With your dad and my siblings?"

It was the last thing he wanted to do, open up the wound and grieve again, but he nodded. "Sure."

There was a knock on the doorjamb. Gavin. He took a look at his sister's tear-streaked face. "What's wrong? You okay?"

"Rowan got me a ring," she said. "He loved me."

"Well, of course he did," he said, and gave her a one-armed hug. "We all do."

"Stop being nice." Winnie sniffled some more. "Or I'll never be able to turn off the waterworks."

"Were you looking for me?" Cam asked Gavin. "Or did you come to put in a few hours?"

"Both."

"He's upset because Piper wants to sell the property," Winnie said. "He just got back together with his ex and doesn't want to leave town."

"That's not why I don't want to leave town," Gavin said. Paused. Shrugged. "At least that's not the whole reason anyway."

"So Piper's definitely selling?" Cam asked.

"She wants to," Gavin said. "And I get it. She needs out. She deserves that."

"I tried to get us a loan," Winnie said.

Both men looked at her, shocked.

"Yeah," she said. "Look at me adulting, right? But Piper's not trying to run from *us*. She's just trying to get herself a life now that we have one." She looked at Gavin. "I thought if I got a loan and paid her for her third of the property, she could go away to school in Colorado like she wants. And then maybe we could stay and rent the cottages out, like you thought about doing, and . . . I don't know . . . do a B and B thing."

Gavin looked stunned. "You'd do that with me?"

"In a heartbeat. With you as the people person and me as the fixer-upper person, we couldn't go wrong."

"You sure, Win? I mean, you get that I'm all sorts of fucked up, right?"

"Hello," she said with a soggy smile. "Have you met me? Because same. But in the end, it doesn't matter, because I was declined by the bank. I don't have any credit history, and apparently I'm also a huge risk. I know, shock, right?"

Gavin laughed a little bitterly. "Well, I've got plenty of credit history, it's just all bad credit history. In fact, it's so bad they'll probably run the other way. But I'll try anyway. We'll figure it out somehow, okay?"

Winnie smiled and nodded. "I believe that."

Cam did too. The Mannings were a force to be reckoned with, and he wouldn't bet against them. But . . . "You guys need to talk to Piper. Tell her, all of it. She'd find a way to help you guys make this happen."

"You think so?" Winnie asked.

"I know so. I realize neither of you are here for advice, but I'm going to give it to you anyway. You want to prove to her that you can handle things? Then *show* her." He turned to the door.

"Where are you going?" Winnie asked.

"To find your sister."

"Wait!" She ran to the door and stepped in front of him. "You're not going to tell her about Rowan, right? Because remember, it's *my* story to tell. You promised."

He wondered if Piper felt this same pinch in the chest as he did whenever dealing with her siblings, like a thousand elephants had just run over him. He'd felt it with Rowan too. "And *you* promised you'd come clean. With everything."

"I am. I will!"

"You do realize the position you're putting me in, right?"

"But I'm the mama of your niece," she said, going right for the emotional gut punch without remorse. "And you promised Rowan you'd take care of me."

"Niece?" Cam asked, now feeling a different pinch in his chest entirely. This one came with an unexpected rush of emotion. "You're having a girl?"

"I don't know," she admitted, dipping her head, rubbing her stomach. "But I'm kind of hoping. I want her to have Rowan's eyes." She looked up again. "But also I want her to have my hair, because . . ." She waved a hand at it. "Well, look at it."

Cam blew out a breath. "You've got to promise me you'll tell Piper everything before I have to go back to the DEA."

Winnie nodded.

"I want the words, Winnie."

"I will. I just need a little more time to show her who I am, who I want to be. Then I'll tell her everything. I promise I will."

Cam looked at Gavin. "Look after her." He left, crossing the properties to knock on Piper's door. No answer. He walked past the cottages but didn't see her working on any of them. But her car was in the driveway, so she was here somewhere.

He was quite certain that after finding out about the pregnancy, wherever she was, she wanted to be alone. She'd just had a big shock, and she was very used to dealing with those on her own. From a very young age she'd been responsible for just about everything. She'd buttoned herself up and kept her head down to make it all happen. She'd learned to be organized and type A just so Gavin and Winnie would make it to school fed and clothed, and the bills got paid. Frankly, he was in awe of her and all she'd done, and also proud of her.

But he wanted to be there for her, however he could. If she'd let him.

And that was a big if . . .

When he realized she was probably walking around the lake and that it'd be easier and faster to find her with the boat, he went back for it. He putted toward the north shore and caught sight of her from several hundred yards out. She was sitting on the tire swing, writing in her journal.

He understood. He hadn't grown up here, but the sparkling water, the rolling hills, the trees, the scent of all of it gave him such a sense of peace.

Piper glanced up at the sound of the engine, and even from this distance he could read her. She was not pleased with his arrival.

He turned off the motor and drifted in close, beaching the bow, tying off, and then leaping to shore. "For a woman who's deathly afraid of the water, you sure like to be near it."

She didn't budge. His favorite female badass just slanted him a long look. "Just because I don't want to be in it doesn't mean I can't love it," she said. "The scent and sounds of it make me happy."

"You're a conundrum."

That got him a small smile. "So I've been told, and not as nicely."

"I talked to your siblings."

"Yeah? Did they raise your blood pressure with just their presence?"

He smiled, but it faded quickly.

She stared at him. "She told you?"

When he didn't answer right away, she repeated the question, but without the question part. "She told you, just like that." She shook her head. "Am I hard to talk to? Is that it?"

"No."

She sighed. "You're just saying that because I slept with you."

"Technically, there wasn't much sleeping involved."

She tipped her head back to look up at the sky. "I'm not doing a good job at life-ing right now."

"I disagree. You amaze me, Piper, every day."

"So why do both my siblings go to you with their problems instead of me?" She looked confused and hurt.

"Sometimes it's easier to talk to someone with a little distance, who can look at things more rationally, with a different perspective."

"Why are you doing this, Cam?"

"Doing what?"

"Getting close to them."

"I like them," he said.

"And me. Why are you getting close to me?"

"You mean other than your sweet, sunny nature?"

She didn't smile. In fact, she stared at him like she was seeing him for the very first time. "I keep people at arm's length for a reason," she said, getting to her feet. "Because I don't need or want anyone in my business or my life."

"Maybe I care about you."

"You shouldn't. I don't want you to. And I don't know why you would." She chewed on her bottom lip for a beat and then shook her head. "I'm sorry. Clearly, I need a time-out."

And with that, she turned and walked off. Not toward home, but the other way, farther north. He let her get a good head start before following on foot, just wanting to make sure she was okay. A minute later, she stopped and turned to face him, swiping at tears that broke his heart.

He closed the distance between them, never breaking eye contact. "Why do I care?" he asked, echoing her words as he stroked her cheek with his thumb. "I care because I want you to have a happy, fulfilling life. I care because I know you're hurting. I care because I'm emotionally attached to you. Hell, Piper, I just want to help you, but I can't because you won't let me in. Let me in."

She closed her eyes, and he thought she was denying him, but then she whispered, "No one's ever said anything like that to me before."

His chest was tight when he put his hands on her hips and pulled her in. "Then I'll keep saying it."

She swallowed hard and went up on tiptoes to press her forehead to his. "It means more than you'll ever know." She paused. "I . . . overreacted. I'm sorry. I'm just having a hard time shutting down my emotions. They keep spilling out of me. It's like an avalanche. A tsunami. I can't seem to control them."

"Then don't shut them down. Let them come out. Then let them go."

"I can't. Not here. Winnie and Gavin will come looking for me eventually. I need to talk to them, but . . . Winnie's having a baby. God." She appeared to try to beat back the panic. "I need to process first, and I need to be alone for that."

"I've got just the place."

CHAPTER 20

"It turns out that I *am* going to hit on you again. You should brace yourself because I'm going to be very convincing."

Piper walked with Cam back the way they'd come, not realizing that his destination was the boat. Stopping, she shook her head. "I might've given you the wrong idea. I'm not exactly in the mood—"

"I know. We're not going there."

Wait . . . they weren't? If she had any brain power left, she'd allocate some to figuring out why he didn't want to sleep with her again.

"You wanted to be alone," he said. "I'm trying to give you that."

"Great, but can't that be anywhere other than the boat?"

"Name one place in this town we can go where your siblings aren't going to be able to find you."

Good point. Dammit. She eyed the boat, and then Cam again. The water was calmer than it'd been in days. But still . . .

His eyes softened. "I've got you, Piper."

She sucked in a breath at the words that felt so . . . comforting. Why? What was it about him that gave her strength? She had no idea.

But getting on the water . . . Yes, she'd been onboard with him before, but that had been . . . different. For one thing, they hadn't actually been moving; they'd been tied up to the dock. It had taken several mind tricks to allow herself to be okay, although once Cam's hands and mouth and body had gotten on her, she'd forgotten they'd been on a boat at all.

But at the moment, she was in the middle of a pity party for one, thank you very much, and she wasn't ready to be over it.

Ahead of her, Cam untied the boat with quick, practiced ease, and she took a moment to appreciate the way he moved because she wasn't dead. But then, holding the rope in one hand, he held out his other for her.

She shook her head.

He was smart enough not to rush her. And she knew he'd never make her do anything she didn't want to. Nope, his tactic was even worse.

He waited for her to come to him.

Welp, he was about to wait until hell froze over. She clutched her journal close and shook her head again.

"What if your future niece or nephew fears the water like you do. Wouldn't you want to help them get past it?" he asked.

"Wow. You fight dirty."

"I do a lot of things dirty."

She felt a hot flash rush through her. "You're trying to distract me."

"Yes. Is it working?"

"No."

"Piper, I've got you," he repeated.

Said the spider to the fly.

With a huff of air, she walked toward him, stopping several feet from where he waited with what looked to be all the patience in the world. "Do you just command the bad guys to hand themselves over to you too?"

His lips twitched. "Yes, but it doesn't usually take this long for them to do it." He wriggled his fingers.

She stared at his hand. It was strong. Calloused. And, she knew from experience, all warm and extremely talented.

"Trust me." He flashed a smile. "You know you want to."

Hoping she wasn't going to regret this, she put her hand in his.

He didn't pull or in any way suggest that he wanted to direct her movements. He was being sweet and gentle. She met his gaze, half touched at his tolerance, half irritated as shit that she was feeling the urge to please him. "I really don't want to board."

"Because the last time you were on a boat was so . . . unenjoyable?"

She felt her face heat, but she lifted her chin and hoped he never got a peek at her latest journal entry where she'd listed the ways he'd melted her bones. In great detail. "It was . . . okay."

He laughed, and the sight was so unusual and so amazing, she stared at him. Damn, he had a really great laugh.

"Just okay, huh?" he finally asked.

She forced a casual shrug. "It was . . . *fine*."

He laughed again. And dammit, he was one hot son of a bitch. "I'm going to make you take that back," he said, voice like sex on a stick.

So much for sweet and gentle.

He squeezed her hand reassuringly. "I've got you," he repeated softly.

Yeah, he kept saying that. And she wanted to believe him, but she was short on trust at the best of times, which this most definitely was not. "Are we going to leave the cove?"

"Only if you want to, but I suggest yes."

She bit her lower lip.

"Piper." His voice was terrifyingly kind. "I'm not going to let anything happen to you. I've got life vests. I've pulled one out for you. See?" He lifted one for her perusal. "You can wear it the whole time."

She gave a jerky nod. "Thanks. But that feels . . . lame."

"It's not lame. Not even a little bit."

"I seriously don't think I even remember how to swim."

"You're not going into the water," he said.

"You don't know that. A catastrophe could happen."

"Such as?"

"A big storm could hit and capsize us," she said, eyeing the cloudless sky.

"Been there, done that, wrote the training manual on how to keep everyone alive," he said very seriously.

She stared at him. "I'm not sure if you're kidding or not."

"Kidding about the manual, not kidding about keeping people alive."

"You've saved someone from drowning before?"

"Seen a guy do it once or twice."

She realized how dumb her question had been. "You probably have a lot of stories to tell."

Instead of answering, he jumped onboard—without letting go of her hand, she noted. Apparently he recognized a flight risk when he saw one. Turning back, he waited for her to join him.

"Can you tell me any of your stories?" she asked.

He looked surprised by her interest. "I can't give specifics, but there was one time when my unit saved a hundred-plus people who were stranded in cold, frigid waters, and no one had a door to cling to."

She blinked. "Did you just make a *Titanic* reference?"

"Yes."

"There was room for two people on that door, Cam."

He smiled. "We got everyone back on shore safe and accounted for. Didn't leave a soul out there, door or not. Does that help?"

"How many times have you done something like that?"

He shrugged.

"So, like, more than . . . ten?"

"Yes."

"How many more?"

"Too many to count," he said, still with the laid-back voice, no sense of growing impatience. And she realized he wasn't putting on an act. This was him: calm, stoic, steady as a rock. Period. He wouldn't fail her, he wouldn't abandon her, and he wouldn't turn his back on her.

"Any more concerns I can help you with?" he asked. "Or can we . . . ?" He gestured to the boat.

"What if you have to make a sharp turn and I fall out? I wasn't kidding. I'm not a good swimmer."

To his credit, he didn't even smile. He just held eye contact and very seriously said, "Luckily for you, I am. I'm good enough for the both of us."

Right. Okay, then. With no other reason to stall, she tightened her grip on his hand and jumped onboard, gasping as the boat rocked beneath her feet. Cam immediately wrapped her up in a flotation vest and bent his head to give the buckles his full attention.

"In case I'm somehow incapacitated," he said with a smile.

"Are you laughing at me?"

"I'm taking care of you."

Something *else* no one had ever said to her.

Then he pulled her up against him and kissed her. He kissed her until she didn't remember she was terrified, or that her siblings were driving her crazy. Hell, she didn't remember her own name and she didn't care.

He pulled back. "You okay?"

Huh. She actually was. "I think so."

"You look surprised."

"It was the kiss. Too bad you can't bottle them up."

He laughed and turned to the controls. She stood at his side, and when he hit the throttle, she gasped and clutched at what she had to assume was an Oh, Shit bar.

"Aren't we going over the speed limit?" she called out. "Maybe you should slow down."

"We're going five miles per hour."

"Oh." She didn't realize she was gripping the bar so tightly that her knuckles were white until he reached out and covered her hand with his.

"Loosen up, Piper, or you'll have sore muscles from clenching so tight."

He hadn't meant it as a command, she knew this, but it still made her laugh. "Aye, aye, Captain, my Captain. Whatever you say."

His gaze swiveled briefly to hers. "Feel free to repeat that for the rest of the day."

She couldn't help herself—she laughed. How could a man be so kind and gentle, and yet utterly commanding and impossibly confident at the same time? "Sure," she said. "But then tomorrow's my turn."

Never one to back down from a challenge, he flashed her a sexy grin. "You're on."

Oh, boy . . .

They had the lake to themselves. Water sprayed up and hit the windshield in front of them. The wind went over the windshield and brushed her face, blew back her hair, and she braced to hate it, but . . . hold up. She didn't hate it. In fact, it was kind of a thrill. So much so that she found herself grinning from ear to ear.

Cam caught sight of it, and she expected him to grin right back at her. Instead he went quite serious, reaching out to touch her jaw, his thumb rasping over her bottom lip. "Making you smile like that is the highlight of my day. Hell, my year."

Her stomach clenched. Or maybe that was her heart. "Same," she said, so softly she was certain he couldn't have heard it over the roar of the engine or the wind.

But he smiled as if he'd read her lips, and it made her forget herself for a moment. The wind was in his hair too, and he wore mirrored sunglasses that were sexy as hell. So was his stubble, as was the way the gusts had his clothes plastered to him, showing off that leanly muscled physique to mouthwatering perfection.

When he caught her staring, his smile turned a little hot and a whole lot wicked.

A few minutes later, he turned into a deserted cove on the unpopulated north shore and slowed way down.

"I love it here," she said. "I don't often walk this far out to see it, though." She looked at him. "Thanks for doing this, for taking me out of my own head. I had no idea what I needed. How do you always just know?"

He laughed. "I don't. When it comes to you, I'm always off balance and guessing, hedging my bets." Coming close, he ducked his head to see right into her eyes. "But I like doing things for you. You always get this sort of surprised expression, like you never expect anyone to go out of their way for you, or make you feel special."

She'd never let her thoughts go down that path, but that he had was incredibly . . . well, incredible.

By the time he shut the engine down and moored them, she was ready to jump him. When he took her hand, she stepped eagerly into him. Had she said she wasn't in the mood? She'd been wrong. "Yes."

He smiled. He knew. "Hold that thought." He led her to the front of the boat, but instead of jumping down to the beach, he settled them on the top deck, lying back to stare up at a serene blue sky that stretched as far as the eye could see.

"What do you think that cloud looks like?" he asked, with a jut of his chin toward the sky, hands cradling his head, his long legs stretched out, boots crossed. "I think it looks like a pizza."

When she didn't answer, he turned his head and looked at her. "You okay? Do you need to get off the boat?"

"No, I'm okay." A surprise all on its own. "I'm just"—she had to let out a low laugh—"still processing the fact that I was going to make a move on you and you shut me down."

He came up on his side and curled an arm around her, tugging her into him. "I didn't shut you down. For the record, I'd never shut you down."

"Because you're a guy?"

He smiled. "Because I'm never going to *not* want you."

At that declaration, she felt herself still.

"Okay, don't read too much into that," he said, his smile fading at whatever he saw on her face. "I just mean that you've got to know I'm extremely attracted to you. Emotionally attached as well. So you don't need to ever wonder if I want you. I do." He braced himself over her and kissed her. Soft. Sweet. And then not so sweet, before pulling back. "I just didn't want you to think I was a sex fiend."

"But you are, right?" she asked hopefully.

He let out a low laugh. "Well, yeah. But I thought we'd . . . talk."

"*Talk.*"

"Yes. It's a thing, you know," he said, looking adorably uncertain for the first time ever. "Women like to talk, right?"

She laughed. "Yes, unfortunately. Are you telling me you're the one man on the planet who actually likes to listen?"

"Well, I like to listen to *you*," he said.

That flowed through her, making her feel wanted, cherished, and special. Not quite sure what to do with those emotions, she stared up at the sky. "Definitely looks like pizza," she said. "A pepperoni pizza with peppers on it, because peppers are a veggie and that makes the pizza healthy."

He laughed, and God, she loved making him laugh.

"I haven't done it very much lately," he said, making her realize she'd spoken out loud. "Not until I came here and met you." He shook his head. "There's not been a lot to laugh about."

Her heart rolled over and exposed its tender underbelly. "You miss Rowan."

"Yeah."

She set her head on his shoulder. "I'm sorry."

He pressed his jaw to her hair. "We were still pretty new to the sibling thing, since he was always so much younger than me." He turned his head to hers. "You didn't like him."

She stilled. "Winnie tell you that?"

"No. Just a feeling."

"Actually," she said, "I liked him a lot. He was kind and sweet, and was good for your dad, kept him on the straight and narrow. He was Winnie's BFF. After she left for college, he'd go down to see her sometimes. They didn't tell me much because they knew I didn't like how hard they partied. But he was a good guy."

"But . . . ?"

She met his gaze and knew honesty was the only way to go here. "But . . . I felt he had a lot of growing up to do."

"He wasn't a good influence on Winnie."

She gave a slow shake of her head. "No. But for what it's worth, I think he was changing. I think he was growing up, and I hate that he'll never have the chance to become whoever he was meant to be." She swallowed hard at the look of grief on Cam's face.

He turned to stare up at the sky.

She squeezed his hand, and he squeezed back, but other than that, he didn't move, didn't talk for a long moment. When he finally spoke, he did so without opening his eyes, voice low and gruff, filled with emotion.

"You know we didn't spend a lot of time together, that he was too young for me to really connect with given that there was thousands of miles between us. But in the last few years, we got better at it. We called, texted, and there were a few visits here and there." He paused. "I left my mom's when I was sixteen, did I ever tell you that? I did the whole 'angry at the world' thing for a while."

"Where did you go?" she asked, because she knew it hadn't been here, to his dad's.

"I stayed with friends," he said. "I could've come here, my dad wanted me to, but I was still pissed off at him for abandoning my mom. It wasn't until later that I realized it wasn't like that, that he'd legitimately tried, but she was way worse when he came around. I think it was guilt over not being able to raise Rowan. She . . . she wasn't well. She got a late-in-life diagnosis of being bipolar, and she preferred to self-medicate with alcohol rather than take her meds. She tried rehab a bunch of times, but it never took. Eventually, she went to live in a half-way house, and stayed there until she died."

"You were already in the military."

"Yes."

Piper had spent a lot of years thinking no one really understood what she'd been up against when her parents had died. But now she knew Cam understood, that he got it in a way she wished he didn't have to. "I can't imagine how hard it was for you, growing up like that."

He shrugged. "She did the best she could. Same with Rowan. And I was still way too hard on him." He shook his head, eyes tortured. "And now he's gone, and the last thing I said to him was in anger."

Her throat tightened at the emotion in his voice. "I'm so sorry, Cam. What happened?"

He let out a long breath. "We fought about his future. It's hard to forgive myself for that, that his last memory was of me being mad at him."

"He wouldn't want you to be holding on to that. You know he never held on to anything negative. That wasn't his way."

When he didn't look at her, she gently turned his face to hers.

"I hear you," he said. "But it's hard."

"I know."

He met her gaze. "You too?"

"Oh, yeah." She gave him a grim smile. "When my parents sent us home, I was furious. Even though they'd promised to follow us and arrive as soon as they could, I didn't understand." She drew a deep breath because it was always hard to think about, the memories of how awful she'd been. "I just saw it as they were dumping us because we were too much trouble. I told them they were terrible parents who were tired of lugging their children around, so they were sending us away to be selfish." She let out a long, shaky breath. "They died before I got to talk to them again, to tell them I loved them. That I was sorry."

"They knew," he said firmly.

She gave him a small smile. "Because you want it to be true for me?"

"Because you're an amazing person and they knew that, or they'd never have trusted you with Winnie and Gavin."

She'd never looked at it that way, but it did soothe something deep inside her. They *had* trusted her. And now . . . now Gavin was in recovery and Winnie was pregnant at twenty. Yeah, she'd done a bang-up job.

"None of that's on you," he murmured, and squeezed her hand again.

Maybe not. But it was going to change her world, in a big way. Because the Mannings were a unit, like it or not.

They remained silent for a long few minutes, no sound except the water lapping at the boat, the squawk of birds, and the occasional buzzing of an insect.

"You're going to be okay leaving this place that you love?" he asked. "For Colorado?"

She looked around at the gorgeous, lush green rolling hills edging the lake, dotted with ancient oaks and the occasional lost cow from neighboring ranches. "Living here isn't exactly a hardship. And I love my job. I love helping people. But it's . . . immediate, so there's no closure. I want to do more."

"You'll make a great physician assistant."

She wasn't sure she'd get the chance now, but she played along. "How do you know? You've never seen me in action."

"Actually, I have."

She laughed. "In your bed doesn't count."

"Hell yeah, it does." He smiled, but then got serious. "But I've seen you in action on the job too. The other day, you arrived on scene for a guy who'd had a heart attack at the little diner in town. Caro's. I was across the street getting gas when you and Jenna arrived. You dropped to your knees and began working on him, and you were amazing. From a hundred feet away, I could see your determination, could tell you wouldn't give up on him, on anyone."

She didn't know what to say to that, so she turned back to the sky, then pointed to a cloud. "That one looks like an elephant. I love elephants."

"You really will make a great PA, Piper. You can do anything you want to. I know it."

She sighed. "Maybe I should hit on you again."

"So we'll stop talking?" he asked, sounding amused.

She glanced over at him. "You make me sound like a better person than I am. Because what I didn't say was that I wasn't all that sorry to be getting away from Wildstone for a bit."

"Past tense?"

"Well, obviously I can't go now. Winnie's going to need me."

"Don't sell yourself short. You'll find a way."

She let his words wash over her. She'd told him her deepest, darkest shame, that she wanted to run away, from the house, her siblings, everything. And he hadn't judged her, not even a little bit. "Cam?"

"Yeah?"

She came up on her elbow and met his gaze. "It turns out

that I *am* going to hit on you again. You should brace yourself because I'm going to be very convincing."

"I brought you out here so you could get away."

"Captain, my Captain," she whispered. "Whatever you say."

He sucked in a breath. "You're fighting dirty again."

"I get it, you don't want to take advantage of me, blah blah. But . . . how do you feel about *me* taking advantage of *you*?"

His eyes went heavy lidded, his expression smoldering as he lay back, interlacing his fingers behind his head. "You know what? You're my neighbor, and your life choices are yours to make, and I'll support you no matter what . . ."

She was laughing as she climbed him like a jungle gym.

CHAPTER 21

"Sucks to be the one left behind."

Later, much later, now in the small interior of the boat, Piper and Cam dozed, lulled by the heat they'd generated. The windows were steamed and night had fallen, blocking the outside world, creating an intimacy that she wasn't sure she was ready for.

Cam was terrifyingly amazing, and it wasn't just because he knew his way around a woman's body. Even out of bed, he was a distraction, and she enjoyed spending time with him.

Which wasn't good.

But it didn't stop her from sighing in pleasure as he murmured something inaudible in his sleep and tightened his arms around her, as if to keep her from sneaking off.

Which had been her plan.

But there was nowhere to go unless she wanted to swim

back. But even if she could do that without drowning, she'd misplaced all the bones in her body thanks to the orgasms. Content for now, she pressed her face into the crook of Cam's neck. Just for a few minutes, she told herself, and let herself float away.

She awoke sometime later, violently aroused, with Cam's mouth working its way down her writhing body. Her fingers were digging into his shoulders and she was making the same "yummy" sounds she made when she ate ranch-flavored popcorn with extra butter.

She already knew he was as incredibly instinctive in bed as he seemed to be everywhere else. He knew exactly when and how to effortlessly take her to the very edge and hold her there just long enough to make her slide her fingers into his hair and tug.

The bastard just huffed a soft laugh against her and then . . . sent her flying. She came back to herself to feel him right there, kneeling between her thighs.

"Open your eyes, Piper."

It took her a moment to find the right muscles, but she finally managed to meet his dark, wild gaze.

"I didn't expect you," he said. "You open me up."

She might have argued that *she* was the one opened up at the moment, but she couldn't joke, couldn't tease, couldn't do anything but soak in the sincerity of those words, which filled her both emotionally and physically as he pushed inside her. She gasped his name in a shockingly needy voice, exposing a vulnerability she never liked to reveal. But he was right there with her, laid bare, letting her see everything he felt.

It didn't take him long to shove her over the edge again, but this time she took him along with her. As she closed her eyes and let herself float away, she smiled, because it seemed she'd found the one thing to make Cam Hayes lose his famed control.

Her.

A fact that was both thrilling and utterly terrifying.

CAM WOKE UP to a low but fervently uttered *"Shit!"* and opened his eyes. His arms were empty of one warm, soft, sated woman. And yeah, he didn't have any doubts on the sated thing, because he'd heard every single sexy sound she'd made when he'd been deep inside her.

They hadn't slept much. It'd been midnight when he'd taken them back to the marina, gliding into a slip without the motor so as not to wake anyone at either house. Docked, they'd started to dress, then gotten distracted by naked bodies under moonlight, and afterward had fallen asleep again.

Now, given the light slanting through the window—or the *lack* of light slanting through the window—it wasn't even dawn. When another low feminine oath sounded, he rose from the bed, grabbing his jeans as he did. Pulling them on, he found the source of the cursing.

Piper, trying to get off the boat.

She'd apparently been going for stealth, which, considering she'd gotten out of bed without waking him, was impressive. The fact that she'd put on the life jacket to go from boat to dock made him smile.

It'd snagged on a hook, leaving her trapped and fighting to free herself. Damn. He was going to fall for this woman hard if he let himself. Trying not to laugh, he came up behind her. "Sneaking out without a good-bye?"

"Hey, I said good-bye." She was tugging on the vest for all she was worth. "You just didn't hear me."

Taking mercy, he untangled her and turned her to face him, holding on to the straps of the life vest. "Nice touch."

"Yeah, well, I figured it'd be just my luck to fall in and get eaten by a lake monster," she muttered into his chest. "That adventure is most definitely not in my journal. Which, by the way, is in my pocket. There are whole days I fantasize about tossing it into the lake, but it's going to be on my terms, and *not* because I was stupid and fell in."

He laughed and shook his head. "Tell me why you're sneaking off." He bent his knees a little so he could see her face better. "Let me guess. Things got so good you got scared. Am I hot or cold?"

Her pretty eyes narrowed.

Yeah, he was hot.

She lifted her chin. "Maybe it was so bad that I couldn't do it again, you ever think of that?"

"I've got ten fingernail indentations in my ass that say otherwise."

She blushed. Cute. "Okay, fine, whatever." She tossed up her hands. "It wasn't . . . bad."

He laughed, and she huffed out a sigh and a reluctant smile. "You're an ass."

"Noted," he said. "Now tell me why you're running away."

She turned her head and eyed the lake, gorgeous and smooth

as glass at this time of morning. "I like you," she said to the water, quietly, as if admitting a state secret.

"Piper." He waited until she looked at him. "I like you back."

She bit her lower lip, and he tilted his head. "Help me out here. I'm not sure I get the problem."

"I said stuff."

"You mean like 'oh yeah, Cam, just like that' and 'harder, please, harder' . . . ?"

She pointed at him, her cheeks blazing. "You know what I mean."

"Actually, I don't." His smile faded because suddenly she seemed way too close to tears. "What's wrong? If you tell me, maybe I can fix it."

She closed her eyes. "I said that I need you."

"Yeah? And what's wrong with that? I'm right there with you."

She crossed her arms over her chest. "You do realize I was sneaking out so I didn't have to have this conversation, right?"

"Humor me," he said. "What's wrong with needing someone once in a while?"

"I've never said it to anyone before," she admitted. "In fact, I do everything I can to *never* need or depend on anyone. So if I say it, it means . . . things."

"Like the fact that you trust me?"

She nodded miserably.

"I trust you too, Piper. Or you wouldn't be in my bed."

She sighed, a sound that managed to hold all the memories from their time in his bed, as well as exasperation, probably at the both of them. "I can't do this now," she said. "I'm too hungry.

I need pancakes and I've got a batter mix at home. They're not going to be homemade, but if you—"

"Yes," he said. Then he leaned in and put his mouth to her ear. "I *need* pancakes too."

With a laugh, she shoved him away.

Grinning, he followed her up the hill. He thought about pointing out that she was still wearing the life vest, but decided it was best not to.

He followed her into her kitchen, having no doubt that she expected her siblings to still be sleeping. So the surprise couldn't have been a good one when she realized everyone was there. Gavin was at the stove making pancakes—not from a mix—and laughing with CJ. Winnie was there too, with . . . his dad? The two of them were at the table, heads together watching a YouTube video on how to fix a leaky pipe. They were both dirty, suggesting they'd actually been working.

Everyone stopped in their tracks and stared at Piper, and then at Cam.

Eventually, the shock wore off. Gavin gestured with a spatula at his older sister. "I want you to note that I'm a feminist, and also I think sex is good for the soul, so I'm not going to point out your walk of shame, even though you pointed out mine. But good God, woman, the least you could do is wipe that smile off your face so your brother doesn't have to throw up a little in his mouth."

"I'm not smiling!"

"Whatever, sis." Gavin expertly flipped a very large pancake with a flick of his wrist. "Also, did you wear that life vest while getting that smile? Because that must've taken real dedication."

Piper tore off the life vest and glared at Cam, like it was all his doing. It took a lot not to smile.

"I hope you used birth control," Winnie said. "Did you know condoms are only ninety-eight percent effective?" She pointed to her stomach. "Meet the other two percent. I mean, who knew, right?"

"It's on the box," Piper said.

Winnie frowned. "Are you sure?"

"Yeah."

Winnie shrugged. "Like I said, who knew."

"Glad we don't have to worry about percentages," Gavin said to CJ, who smirked.

Piper closed her eyes. "Okay, first, it's not the walk of shame when it's your own house. And being of age, it's *never* a walk of shame. Period."

Winnie grinned. "You might want to turn your shirt right side out and try saying that again."

Piper aimed another glare at Cam.

He lifted his hands in a sign of surrender. "You were the one sneaking out on me. I was asleep when you put that thing on."

Gavin was looking pained. "I just realized you're doing my boss. There's a high 'ew' factor here."

Piper looked down at herself. Yep, shirt was inside out. She put the life vest back on. "And second," she said, while everyone was still laughing, forcing her to point at all of them, including Cam. "I'm allowed a life."

"Amen, sister," Winnie said. "And it's good to see you going for it."

Cam watched Piper turn to Winnie, the irritation draining

from her eyes, replaced by an affection he knew was years and years in the making. "Thanks," Piper said.

Winnie smiled back. "So . . . we're okay?"

"We're okay."

Looking relieved, Winnie nudged her chin toward Cam. "So are you two a thing now or what?"

"Or what," Piper said noncommittally, and gestured to the opened laptop. "What are you up to?"

"Oh! We've got a plan!" Winnie looked at her brother, who gave her a nod of encouragement.

"Should I be scared?" Piper asked. "Cuz I am."

"You were right before," Winnie said.

Piper blinked. "I'm sorry, did you just say I was right about something?"

Winnie rolled her eyes. "I know, I know, you've never heard that from me before." She rubbed her tummy. "But guess what? I'm going to be a mom. A really great one too, and moms are mature. I'm trying to work on that. I want to be taken seriously, and before you speak, I realize I've never tried hard at . . . well, anything. But that's going to change. I'm getting really good at fixing stuff. So . . . meet your new handywoman." She gestured to herself. "Which is me, in case I wasn't clear."

"And I'm taking over cooking duties," Gavin said. "And not just because you suck at it, but because I miss cooking."

"You're just saying that because I messed up the chocolate chip cookies the other night," Piper said.

Gavin nodded. "*Never* let a recipe tell you how many chocolate chips to use. You measure that shit with your heart, Piper."

"Noted. But you don't have to do it all. I can always get Girl Scout cookies."

"You mean buy ten boxes at a time and eat them alone in the pantry?"

"Hey," she said. "It's called supporting young female entrepreneurs."

"Also," he went on, "Winnie and I want to rent out the cottages and turn this thing into a B and B, like Grandma's parents did a million years ago. I mean, they're even furnished. Besides, my blueberry pancakes should be shared with the world."

"One hundred percent correct on that," CJ said around a bite of pancake.

"And something else that should be shared with the world," Winnie said. "My newly found handywoman skills."

Piper gaped at them. "Do you have any idea how much work goes into running a B and B? We're not Great-Grandma. We'd need a website, and an accounting program, and a whole bunch of other stuff I can't even imagine."

"I know," Gavin said. "And I've been building a website. It'll be ready by next week. And I've got a good bookkeeping program. I can set us up, just like I'm doing for Cam at the marina. It wouldn't require any work from you. For once, I can step up and do something for you for a change." He gave a lopsided smile. "Look, we all know our childhood was . . . well, royally fucked up. But look at us making something of ourselves regardless."

CJ was looking as impressed by Gavin as Cam felt. But Piper looked . . . dizzy. She turned to Winnie. "What about your still-unnamed baby daddy? How's he going to feel about you sticking around here instead of going back to Santa Barbara? Is he going to relocate to help you? Is he even interested in being part of the baby's life?"

Tell her, Cam willed. Because the longer Winnie waited, the bigger the feeling of betrayal would be, and Winnie would be taking Cam right down with her.

"All that matters is that *I'm* staying here," Winnie said, disappointing Cam along with Piper, if her expression was anything to go by. "I'll figure out everything else later."

"Me too," Gavin said.

Emmitt looked at Cam. "Any interest in making like these two, and sticking around for your old man? I'd love that."

Cam grabbed two plates and held them out to Gavin to fill. "Thinking about it," he said, unwilling to hide a damn thing from Piper—that he could control, anyway.

His dad beamed.

Piper whipped her head around so fast to stare at him that Cam was surprised it didn't just fall off.

"I put in a transfer to be DEA West Coast," he said. "San Luis Obispo office. It's a long shot. I've got no idea if I'll get it. But yeah." He shrugged. "It'd be nice."

"When did you do that?" Piper asked.

"Last week." He didn't want to be two thousand miles away, worrying about his dad, about Winnie. Piper . . . He'd known what he needed, *wanted* to do, almost from the moment he'd set foot in Wildstone.

Piper came closer, and with her back to the room, asked softly, "Why didn't you tell me?"

"Haven't had much time alone."

She shifted even closer and whispered, "We had plenty last night."

"After you freaked out about me extending my leave, I thought I'd wait and break it to you gently if it happened. Besides, we were . . . busy last night."

"No really," Gavin said. *"Ew."*

Piper didn't take her eyes off Cam.

"Do we have a problem?" he asked.

The look on her face told him they did indeed have a problem, a big one. And he knew why. She'd been comfortable with this thing between them when it'd been temporary. But if he stayed, it suddenly made their no-strings fling complicated.

And she hated complicated.

Emmitt went to the fridge to pour some more OJ. He turned to Piper. "Need anything?"

"Actually, yes. I need my sister to be realistic about what she's facing. And I need my brother to understand that putting too much pressure on himself right now is a bad idea. And I need them both to be honest with me when shit happens, because how can we be a family if we're not honest with each other?"

"I feel like he was just offering you a refill, not counseling," Gavin stage-whispered.

"Food's getting cold," Emmitt said, and everyone started eating.

Cam was impressed. He had no idea his dad could command a room without trying.

Halfway through eating, Gavin cleared his throat and looked at Piper. "I know you think I'm in trouble and shouldn't overextend myself, but I do better when I'm productive. I've decided I'm going to hire myself out to build websites on the side."

"You'll have to schmooze and wine and dine people," Winnie said. "Not exactly a smart idea for a recovering druggie."

"Says the teenager who's pregnant," Gavin retorted. "And when exactly did *that* seem like a stellar idea to you, huh? I mean, it's right up there with that time you tried to trap a pile of ants with peanut butter, and then thought you could still eat the peanut butter."

"Hey, I was *four*," Winnie said. "Don't even get me started on the stupid things *you've* done."

"She's got you there," CJ said into his mug of coffee.

Gavin rolled his eyes. "Thanks."

"Anytime."

"And also," Winnie said to the room, "I'm not a teenager anymore. I'm twenty."

"Pass the syrup," Piper said.

CJ tossed her the squeeze bottle. "Nice refereeing."

"Not my first time."

They ate. They laughed over Gavin's recounting of his adventure to the grocery store via Uber, with a driver who wanted fashion advice since everyone knew gay men were "fashionistas."

"Did you tell him that your gay fashion sense was broken?" CJ asked with a straight face, as they all eyed Gavin's Hawaiian board shorts and surf-shop T-shirt that had seen better days a decade ago.

Winnie then told everyone she'd fixed the downstairs bathroom's plumbing with Gorilla Tape, and had submitted a video of it to the people who made the tape because she was convinced she belonged in a commercial.

Emmitt just seemed happy to be included. Cam looked around the table, watching the heckling, the laughter—even the bickering all felt . . . good. He knew there were huge problems lurking just beneath the surface, but for now it felt like a happy family moment, and he made eye contact with Piper. And while he knew his expression probably said he was enjoying this, hers was *Oh, shit, I'm enjoying this.*

CJ's phone went off. He read a text and rose, giving Gavin an apologetic look. "Sorry. I've gotta go."

Piper's phone went off as well. "Me too. There's been a shooting at the convenience store. Everyone stay home until I know more."

Cam had spent his entire adult life being the one to be called in, being the guy in charge of emergencies, always the one to tell people to stay back and let him handle things. Being the one in danger, being in the center of the action and in charge was the only way to control the outcome and make sure everyone stayed safe.

So watching Piper walk out the door toward danger while he stayed back was one of the hardest things he'd ever done.

"Yeah," Gavin said quietly, putting a hand on his shoulder. "Sucks to be the one left behind, doesn't it?"

CHAPTER 22

"As it turned out, there really were several layers of stupid."

Gavin sat at the kitchen table, Sweet Cheeks asleep on his lap as he worked on his computer on the B&B website. He was tentatively calling it the Rainbow Lodge and was having fun with that at midnight when Piper finally got home.

She practically crawled through the door, exhaustion etched across her face. And something more too. Grief, probably, for whatever she'd seen on the job. Though upon second glance, it seemed deeper, like it'd brought up remembered horrors from her past.

Their past.

His own memories were extremely conflicted, and he liked to pretend he didn't remember a lot of it. But that was a big, fat lie. He remembered everything.

The thing was, that even right up until the very end, he'd

loved every minute of his family's vagabond, wanderlustful life. He'd seen parts of the world that few ever would, and he'd soaked up the different cultures like he'd been born to it. And hell, he had.

But he'd lost Arik. And in the ensuing chaos and insanity, he'd also lost his childhood.

Once he and his sisters had landed in Wildstone, Piper had done everything in her power to bring it back to him, and in a lot of ways, she'd succeeded. But a part of him would always be that terrified ten-year-old who'd lost everything.

He stood and took Piper's heavy bag off her shoulder, hanging it up on a hook by the front door. Then he pulled her into the kitchen and pointed to a chair.

She sat in it so mindlessly, he knew she probably hadn't sat or eaten in twelve hours. So he did the only thing he could do for her. He fed her. He was flipping her favorite—a grilled triple cheese and turkey sandwich—when she took a deep breath.

"I've got something to tell you," she said. "I'm not supposed to. I promised a friend and a work associate that I wouldn't." She held his gaze across the stove. "So I need you to promise me that you're not going to run out of here. You can't. You're not supposed to know. It's not my place to tell you, but . . . I know you. I know what haunts you, and I know why. So I can't . . ." She closed her eyes. "I can't not tell you, Gavin."

Heart suddenly pounding, he turned off the stove, slid the sandwich onto a plate, and brought it to her. Then he squatted at her side and waited until she looked at him. "You're scaring me, Piper."

"I know, but if I say nothing and you find out . . ." She gave a slow shake of her head, her eyes shiny. "I'm afraid of what it might do to you. To your recovery."

He sat back on his heels. "Not making me feel any better."

"The shooting in the convenience store. It was an attempted robbery. When we all arrived, the shooter was still active. The cops created a diversion so several of them could enter the store. One charged the suspect. And he took the guy down too. But not before he was shot."

Gavin had stopped breathing. "*CJ.*"

"Yes, but, Gavin, this isn't the DRC, okay? It's not Arik. CJ isn't going to die—"

Gavin surged to his feet and headed to the door, but Piper caught him with surprising strength, holding on to him, refusing to let go. He could have fought her, but his knees were wobbly, and he realized she was talking to him.

"He's going to be okay. Gavin, are you listening to me?" She added a shake. "The GSW was a through and through. He's probably already been released from the hospital by now. He bitched all the way there in the ambulance, saying he didn't need to go. And I imagine he bitched all the way through getting patched up too. The only reason we got him to go at all was because it was his shoulder and he'd lost a lot of blood."

Gavin closed his eyes and reminded himself that he did in fact know how to breathe.

"Gavin? You okay?"

Sure. His biggest nightmare was coming true, but other than that . . . "Yes. Let go of me."

She slowly backed up and gave him some space. He met her

gaze and was reminded that she was dead on her feet. "Go to bed, Piper."

"But—"

"I promise not to do anything stupid."

She stared at him for a long moment, and then gave him a hard hug. "If you need me—"

"I know. I'll come get you if I do." He waited until she went upstairs. Then he waited some more to make sure she was asleep.

He called CJ first and was sent to voice mail. He texted. No response.

If CJ had been in danger of dying, Piper would've told him. He knew that. The sun would come up tomorrow. The sun would also go down tomorrow. And Piper would never lie to him. These things he knew for sure. His sister did the right thing, always. Never the easy thing.

So . . . why wouldn't CJ answer?

Maybe Gavin had gotten too close too fast for comfort, and he'd spooked the guy. *That* he could deal with. What he *couldn't* deal with was losing him.

Shit. He had to make sure he was going to be okay. He had to see it for himself. He simply couldn't breathe until he knew. Which meant, as it turned out, there really were several layers of stupid. Sending a silent apology to Piper, he grabbed Winnie's keys and headed out. He was banking on the knowledge that CJ hated hospitals and would never stay one minute longer than he had to. And honestly, unless he'd been shot in the mouth, he'd have demanded to be let go, AMA or not.

He found himself in CJ's driveway without remembering the trip. Because everything he feared—the helplessness, the not knowing, the gut-wrenching certainty that life was too fucking short, knowing he could lose someone he loved in the blink of an eye—it was all back with a vengeance.

There were lights on inside, but CJ didn't answer the door. Gavin didn't grapple with his admittedly loose morals. He broke in. The living room was empty, but there were discarded boots on the floor near the entry, and just beyond that, a shirt with blood on it.

Gavin's own blood froze. He could hear swearing from farther inside. Reassured by that, he moved toward it.

He located CJ in the bathroom, stripped down to a pair of jeans resting dangerously low on his hips. He was leaning heavily on the counter while trying to twist to see his back in the mirror. He had gauze bandages in front and back, both blood-stained, and he appeared to be trying to cover the whole thing with Saran Wrap, presumably so he could get into the shower.

Gavin stepped into the room, shoved CJ's hands clear, and took over the task. "How bad?"

"It's not," CJ said through teeth gritted in pain.

Tough guy. Normally, Gavin loved that, but now he just shook his head. "You sent me to voice mail and ignored my texts."

"Wasn't ignoring you."

"What then?"

"Didn't want to freak you out."

"Too late." Gavin pressed his forehead to CJ's. "Are you okay?"

"Are you?" CJ asked.

"If you are."

CJ let out a rough breath. "I will be."

"Are you even allowed to shower?"

"Who's going to stop me?"

"Me, if it's against medical advice." Which he suspected it was. CJ was trembling, so he pressed up against him, bracing him against the counter. "You're bleeding through," he said quietly.

"I'll change the bandages after the shower."

Gavin didn't bother arguing with the guy, because next to himself, there was no one more stubborn on the entire planet than CJ. So he finished covering the gunshot wound—just thinking those two words made him woozy—and turned on the shower. Then he unbuttoned and unzipped CJ's jeans and pushed them off.

"Usually I get dinner first," CJ muttered, but he was ashen and propped up against the counter, all talk and no go. Gavin shook his head at him and then quietly and quickly stripped himself as well.

CJ did a slow body scan, showing more life than he had a moment ago.

"Hold that thought," Gavin said, and got them both into the shower, where he washed CJ down with warm water and soap until the water stopped running pink. After, he gently toweled CJ dry and pointed to the bed.

Pale now and trembling like a leaf from the exertion, CJ climbed in and closed his eyes. "Don't get used to calling the shots."

Gavin huffed out a laugh at the sly reference to their sex life, in which CJ was almost always the aggressor. "I don't know, man, I'm kinda liking this new meekness from you."

Without moving anything but his hand, not even opening his eyes, CJ flipped him off.

Gavin went back to the living room to find what he was looking for. Near where CJ had tossed his keys was a pharmacy bag with meds. And a leather bracelet that Gavin recognized. He'd given it to CJ a whole bunch of years ago. Picking it up, he rolled it between his fingers, memories slamming into him.

They'd been at the carnival the summer after ninth grade. He'd won the bracelet at some stupid darts game and CJ had put it on. Said he'd never take it off.

Gavin took it and the pills, along with a bottle of water, back to the bedroom. Sitting on the bed, he waited.

CJ opened his eyes, looked at the leather band, then closed his eyes again.

"You kept it," Gavin said quietly.

"It meant something to me." CJ swallowed and Gavin watched his Adam's apple bounce. "I had put it back on after the other night."

At that, it was Gavin's turn to swallow hard. CJ was no longer the same boy he'd loved, but a grown man and a hell of a lot more honest about his feelings than Gavin could ever hope to be.

"They made me take it off again at the hospital," CJ said. "I can't put it back on until the abrasions on my wrists heal."

Gavin eyed CJ's wrists, which were bruised and cut up, probably from where he'd fallen after getting shot. So he put the bracelet on himself. CJ watched, his mouth slightly curved like he was amused at both of their stupidly sentimental asses.

"Until you can wear it again, I'll wear it for you," Gavin said.

CJ's smile faded. Looking unbearably touched, he nodded.

Gavin blew out a breath and read the med bottles. "You're supposed to start these antibiotics right away." He handed one over with the water and then turned to the pain meds.

"I don't need any of those," CJ said.

"Really? Cuz you're shaking with pain, and you're also paler than your sheets. Quite the feat for a Puerto Rican. Look, just take a damn pain pill. I'll stay and watch over you—"

"No."

"Why not?" Gavin asked, exasperated. *Worried.*

"Because *you* can't have any pain meds, not ever again."

And because he couldn't, CJ wouldn't allow himself to have any either. In solidarity. The surprising support had Gavin's throat too tight to talk again. He slipped the bottle back into the pharmacy bag. "You weren't supposed to even be on duty."

"Yeah? And?"

"And you stepped in front of a bullet. You stepped in front of a goddamn bullet."

"There were kids in there, Gav. A ten-year-old boy standing frozen in terror, not five feet from me. If I hadn't charged that asshole with the gun . . ."

Then a kid might've gotten shot.

Gavin bolted up, staggered into the bathroom, and threw up. Now *he* was the one shaking and sweating, and also—oh, goodie—in full flashback mode, when he felt CJ drop heavily to his knees beside him and pull him in close.

Gavin didn't even have the strength to fight him.

"You would've done the same thing," CJ said quietly. "The bullet went right through me. I'm going to be fine." He ran a hand down Gavin's back. "Tell me what this is really about."

Gavin dropped his head to CJ's good shoulder and squeezed his eyes shut. "Did I ever tell you why me and my sisters got sent home to Wildstone?"

CJ shifted so they were both leaning back against the wall, their legs out in front of them, their arms holding each other upright. "You know you haven't," he said quietly. "You've always said you don't really remember, that you were too young."

Back in the old days, Gavin had suffered horrible flashbacks. As his best friend, CJ had seen what Gavin was going through, but hadn't understood why. He'd tried to get Gavin to open up, but he simply couldn't. His grandma hadn't believed in therapy, but when she'd passed, Piper had made him go.

It'd helped. A lot. But by that time, he'd already detonated his and CJ's relationship.

And here they were, all these years later, and he still hated to talk about it. "You know my parents were killed overseas."

CJ's arms tightened around him. "Yes. And you and your siblings came here to Wildstone."

Missing a lot of details, but that had allowed Gavin not to talk about what had preceded his parents' deaths. "We lived in a village. The yard wasn't fenced, it was basically just a clearing. Our boundaries were determined by the jungle. We weren't allowed past the foliage. But, shit, you know I was an asshole."

"Still are," CJ said mildly, making Gavin laugh a little, which he supposed was what CJ had been going for.

"My best friend, Arik, and I didn't like being confined," he said. "So we made a plan. Or rather, I made the plan, knowing Arik would do whatever I wanted. We were going to wait until dark and sneak into the jungle and see what the big deal was." He closed his eyes. "We ran into rebel forces. They shot at us for fun." He realized he wasn't breathing, so he sucked in some air. "Arik got hit." His voice caught. "He died and it was my fault."

CJ was quiet for a moment. Just sat there and slowly rubbed the tension from the back of Gavin's neck before finally speaking. "So today played right into your demons."

"Let's just say that I'd give everything I own for a pill right about now. Luckily, I don't own shit."

"Arik wouldn't want you to blame yourself. He went with you into the jungle of his own free will, and if he's anything like your current best friend, you couldn't have stopped him even if you'd tried."

Gavin lifted his head, unable to worry about the tears he felt on his cheeks. "You think you're my current best friend?"

"I know it."

Gavin let out a long, shaky breath and nodded. "It's more than I deserve."

"You know what I think?"

"No, but I bet you're about to tell me."

CJ held his gaze. "So far, you've survived one hundred percent of your days. Which means you're doing great."

Gavin had to let out a low laugh. "Yeah, well, *great* is relative."

CJ gave a small smile. Because the guy knew what he meant, maybe even more than Gavin. CJ had suffered through life plenty. His goddamn parents had forsaken him, just up and kicked him to the curb not five minutes after he'd been forced out of the closet by some cruel kids at school.

At least Gavin had known his parents had loved him.

CJ had no such comfort. And in spite of everything, he had the biggest heart of just about anyone he knew. And he was staring right at Gavin, daring him to take notice of him.

For the record, Gavin was taking notice.

"I fell for you on day one," CJ said. "You took my breath away with your wildness, your sense of adventure, and that wary who-the-fuck-are-you look in your eyes. Nothing much has changed." He paused. "You going to break my heart again?"

Gavin stilled. "I didn't know I could."

"You think you have a lock on screwing up?" CJ started to laugh, and then sucked in a harsh breath and stilled for a beat. "Jesus."

"Don't laugh."

"No shit."

"You need pain meds," Gavin said.

"*No.*" He paused. "You know you were my first. That I loved you."

CJ had been Gavin's first too. His everything. But even so, back then he'd been unable to fathom a real relationship. It had been beyond his comprehension. He hadn't cheated. What he'd done had been almost worse. He'd up and left town with no forwarding address. And then he'd gone on to shove all emotions deep.

A Manning specialty.

"You destroyed me," CJ said softly, and Gavin started to get up.

CJ stopped him. "No, listen. I'm not trying to make you feel bad. You weren't okay. Your best friend was killed. You lost your parents. You played it cool, but you were wild and so very angry. I was drawn to that because . . . well, because I knew the feeling. When my parents found out I was gay, they stopped being my parents, just like that. From one moment to the next, I was suddenly abandoned just for being me. I became wild and angry too, and we . . . well, we fit in that moment. But I always knew I'd have to let you go when you were ready, and I did. And then, somehow, I slowly changed. I came to the questionable wisdom that I was missing out on life. I went to LA for a while. And"—he shook his head—"I slept with anything that moved."

Gavin felt the vicious bite of jealousy, but he nodded because he got it. "I'm sorry. I did love you, but I was scared. I wasn't ready for a commitment. Hell, I couldn't have committed to a dentist appointment back then. I was a hot mess and unable to let myself care, about anything."

"Where did you go?"

"Arizona. The job was high pressure, the competition was fierce, and I struggled to keep up. I cared way too much about everything and . . . I couldn't function."

"That's why you started abusing the pain meds," CJ said. "You were trying to not care."

"Not care, not feel . . . not anything." Gavin shook his head. "I just kept self-medicating until I lost my shit." He paused, but knew he had to say all of it. "Lost my job too. I hit rock bottom when I got a DUI, and ended up in rehab. Used all of my savings between my lawyer and the facility I stayed in. I promised myself if I survived it, I'd get my act together."

CJ looked shaken. "So are you? Together? Because it seems like you do care deeply now, at least for your family."

"Yeah, well, even I can learn something, I guess."

For a long time, he'd played the victim in his own head, assuming the worst in people. He'd convinced himself that his grandma hadn't wanted them, she'd had no choice, that Piper hadn't wanted to be head of the family, she'd had no choice. Wildstone had been too small-minded for him . . . and so on.

But he'd been wrong on all counts. Looking back, he knew how much his grandma had loved him, she'd just been grieving the loss of her daughter, and then her own husband. Piper and Winnie both loved him, madly, and he was fucking lucky considering the long, slow, painful route he'd taken to dubious adulthood. "I owe you an apology," he said quietly. "A big one."

CJ shook his head. "I wasn't in your life when you went to rehab. You don't need to make amends to me."

"Not for that period of time, maybe. But certainly for before. For the way I left."

Again CJ shook his head. "We were too young anyway."

"Don't let me off the hook."

"All right," CJ said with a nod. "I won't. Thank you for the apology. It's accepted." He gave a very small smile. "You're different. A good different."

"Maybe that's because for the first time in my life, I feel like I'm not fighting myself over whether it's okay to slow down, take a deep breath, and be happy. And . . . I am."

"You sound surprised," CJ said.

"Yeah, cuz have you met me?"

CJ gave a very small but warm, easy smile. "I was shot and you're happy. You're a sick man."

"But you love it."

CJ's smile faded, and Gavin once again tried to get up, but in spite of being injured, CJ was strong as hell. "I do love it," he said, holding on to Gavin. "What I don't love is your urge to take off whenever the going gets too good. Think you can knock that the fuck off?"

"I'm working on it."

"I hope that's true."

"Maybe I should prove it to you," Gavin said.

"Maybe you should."

And for the rest of the night, they didn't say another word.

CHAPTER 23

"I've got you this time."

The next morning, Gavin got out of bed way before he wanted to. CJ was still sleeping, so he left him a note telling him that he had a meeting and reminding him to take his antibiotic.

There were several places to eat in Wildstone that were good, but nothing better than Caro's Café. Gavin found Axel in a corner booth, back to the wall, slugging back a hot, black coffee like it was his job. The guy was thirtyish, had wavy dark hair past his shoulders, with a matching beard, and was covered in tats. Good-looking enough to be an actor portraying a rock star, he had both men and women after him, which he definitely made the most of. He was an old friend of Gavin's and they'd reconnected last week when they'd been at the same NA meeting.

Axel had offered to be his Wildstone sponsor and Gavin had taken him up on it.

"You're late," Axel said, wearing his usual perpetual scowl.

"No, I'm not." Gavin waved his phone. "See? It's eight on the dot."

"On time is late. Early is on time."

"Let me guess," Gavin said, taking a seat. "You've been reading self-help books again."

Axel gave a rare grin. "Nah. That came from my fortune cookie last night."

Gavin laughed, and then the waitress showed up to take their order. When she'd gone, Gavin looked at Axel. "How you doing?"

"That was my question for you."

Gavin downed his water and eyeballed the full, noisy diner. "This place is still pretty popular, huh?"

"Best breakfast for fifty miles. You stalling on purpose?"

"Yeah." Gavin met the eyes of the one person in his life who seemed to truly understand where he'd come from, the hole he'd dug himself out of, and how hard it was to stay on level ground. "I'm hanging in there," he said to Axel's patient silence.

"Define 'hanging in there.'"

"I want to stay clean, more than anything."

"But . . . ?"

"But . . . sometimes it's hard."

"No shit," Axel said. "In case you haven't noticed, life's fucking hard."

When their food came, they dug in, and Axel gestured at

Gavin with his fork for Gavin to eat and talk. "Tell me how it's going here in Wildstone."

"I want to be back. I love being home. But it's also bringing up some really bad shit. Losing my parents. Arik. And now me and CJ are . . . well, I'm not actually sure, but we're something. And I like it. But I'm terrified of losing it."

"You talk to him?"

"Yeah."

Axel nodded. "You feel the urge to use again?"

"No. Not exactly. I mean, my brain doesn't want to, but my body isn't always on the same page."

Axel nodded. "We all get that."

"Still?"

"Still. Your present self's just gotta be stronger than your past stupid self."

Gavin laughed roughly. "Yeah."

"Look, an addict's an addict, and unfortunately, we can switch up an addiction for another pretty easily, but sometimes you can replace the need for bad shit with something else." Axel shrugged. "Sex would be my choice. Only I don't mean with me. Nothing personal or anything, but you're a little too pretty for me."

Gavin laughed again, and it felt good.

"But seriously." All smiles aside, Axel leaned in. "You get an urge you can't handle, you call me. I'll be there. Doesn't matter what day or time. Got me?"

Gavin felt gratitude hit him, and he nodded. "Got you. But I've also got this."

"See that you do."

Gavin finished his food and pushed his plate away as he glanced out the window. To his surprise, CJ stood stock-still on the sidewalk, staring at him with an unreadable expression.

Gavin waved.

CJ didn't. In fact, he turned on a heel and walked off. *What the hell?* Standing, he tossed some money on the table. "See you next week?"

Axel nodded. "Unless you need me before."

Gavin headed outside and had to book it to catch up with CJ, who was already getting into his car. For a guy who'd been shot, he was moving pretty good. "Hey, did you get my note?"

CJ turned, his face carefully blank, further assisted by a pair of dark mirrored sunglasses. "The note that said you had a meeting? Yeah, I got it. But that didn't look like a business meeting."

Surprised at both the tone and the implied accusation that he was lying, Gavin shoved his hands into his pockets instead of reaching for the guy, as he'd wanted to do only a second before. "It really was a meeting."

"Okay, so what kind of *business* do you have with a known addict?"

Gavin shook his head. "It's not what you think."

"Really? Cuz what I think is that two years ago I arrested that asshole for assault and battery."

Axel had told Gavin all of this and more, including the fact he'd been stupid enough to resist arrest. "I know. He's clean now."

"Yeah? So who is this guy to you?"

And here is where Gavin made his mistake. He knew it as soon as he hesitated, but Axel was fanatical about his privacy, and Gavin had to honor that. "Just a friend."

"You're lying," CJ said.

More like omitting, but Gavin hadn't asked Axel if he could mention him, and in NA, loyalty was everything. And also, something in the way CJ was looking at him now was really pissing him off. And admittedly, he did not do his best thinking when he was pissed off. "He *is* just a friend. But that's not the real problem, is it, Ceej. You think I'm still sowing some wild oats."

"Not any of my business."

"It sure as hell is. You really think after the time we've spent together since I got back, that I'd do such a thing?"

"You tell me."

Gavin actually staggered a step back, as if he'd been punched in the face. Sure as hell felt like he had been, and he shook his head, going from pissed to . . . hurt. "I haven't done anything wrong here."

"But you can see how I got there, right?"

"I've never cheated on you, CJ. I was an asshole, yeah. But not a cheating asshole." And damn, he was sick of this, of his bad decisions jumping him. Pummeling him. "Look, we both know I have a past. But it's just that, a past. And that the way I left you sucked. But haven't you ever done anything you regret, or are you just perfect, then?"

CJ didn't bother to answer. He just made a disgusted sound and got into his car.

"Are you serious?"

CJ met his gaze. "I realize running off is your MO, but thought I'd beat you to it this time."

When he was gone, Gavin stood there for a beat in shock.

But he shouldn't have been shocked at all. He was pretty sure he was all too easy to walk away from.

He meant to go home. That would've been the smart thing. Something he apparently wasn't, because he drove to CJ's. "You're an idiot," he told himself as he got out and knocked.

No answer. Shock. He tried the door. Unlocked. Fair game then, and he pushed it open and stepped inside.

CJ appeared in the living room, gun in hand. "Jesus," he breathed, then lowered his gun hand, using his other to rub his eyes. "It's like you *want* me to kill you."

Gavin slammed the door behind him. "Okay, yeah, so I *used* to run." He stalked toward CJ, who was still armed and clearly still pissed off as well. Gavin didn't care. He was over this, over paying for his sins and not getting any credit for changing. "But maybe I grew up."

"Maybe?"

"Yeah," Gavin said. "And maybe I *also* know I've got a lot to make up for, but I didn't expect you of all people to not believe in me. Because in spite of how we ended, I've never broken my word to you."

"*Maybe* there's a first time for everything."

This stopped Gavin in his tracks. CJ didn't believe in him. But hell, he'd never believed in himself all that much, so why was he so surprised that CJ didn't? Sick, he pulled off the leather bracelet, tossed it onto the coffee table, and left.

And CJ let him.

On Saturday afternoon, Cam found himself hiking up to Rainbow Peak, a popular hiking area three hundred feet above the lake on the bluffs. He was with his dad, Winnie, Gavin, and Piper, and they weren't there for the spectacular views.

His heart beat heavy in his chest as they bypassed the trailhead for a narrow trail that Emmitt and Piper said only a very few locals knew existed. It led to an overhang where one could stand above the water and get a view of what felt like the entire world. Directly below was the gorgeous blue lake. Beyond that, a blanket of lush green hills holding ranches and wineries for as far as the eye could see.

Cam supposed it was as good a day for a funeral as it could be.

Winnie was wearing the sundress she said was the last thing Rowan had seen her in. But because it was winter, she was also wearing tights, boots, and a jacket—none of it black. She'd forbidden any of them from wearing black, saying Rowan would've hated that.

Emmitt wore shorts and a T-shirt that he'd worn the last time he and Rowan had gone fishing. No jacket.

Piper was in jeans and a sweatshirt that read RIDE THE RAINBOW. Apparently, Rowan had given it to Gavin, who'd shrunk it, and so it'd been passed down to Piper.

Cam, not having had any sort of specific clothing that he associated with Rowan, was in his usual cargoes and T-shirt, but he wore a windbreaker against the gusts and dark lenses against the bright winter sky.

And also to shield his own emotions.

He'd been drunk through Rowan's first funeral. It had felt best to be numb at the time. He hadn't missed the numb until this very moment. His heart ached and felt too heavy for his chest, and he tensed when a hand landed on his shoulder.

His dad's.

He forced himself to relax, wishing he'd gone with being drunk for this service as well. His dad was carrying a small canister that he'd informed the shocked gathering only a few moments before held some of Rowan's ashes.

"This was Rowan's favorite secret spot," Emmitt said. "He'd come out here, sometimes to climb down and then back up just for fun. Sometimes to just sit and breathe. He liked to do that." Emmitt's voice got a little choked up. "He got that from me. I taught him to slow down and smell the flowers. I know it's not a popular opinion, that I should've taught him ambition and forced him to go to college, but those things made me miserable at his age. And as it turns out, life's too fucking short." He sucked in a breath. "So, Rowan, I hope you're in the clouds climbing mountains and smelling the flowers. I'll miss you, son." He swiped at the tears on his cheeks and nodded. He was done. He handed the canister to Winnie.

She drew in a deep breath, but before she could say anything, someone else came along.

CJ. He was in uniform, and his gaze went to Gavin first before eyeing the rest of them, including what Winnie was holding.

"Why aren't you resting?" Gavin asked.

"Yeah, I thought you were off duty for another few days," Piper said.

CJ shook his head, and when he answered, it was to Piper, not Gavin. "Couldn't stay off another second. I'm fine. On desk duty, but fine."

"Doesn't look like desk duty," Gavin said.

CJ shrugged coolly. Clearly something had happened between the two of them to make the air seem suddenly arctic.

"I'm sorry to be intruding on what's clearly personal business," CJ said, "but Mrs. Wilkinson called in that there was something funny going on up on her hill. I took the call and came to check it out."

"Who's Mrs. Wilkinson?" Cam asked.

"The old biddy who lives on the south shore," Gavin said. "She's been there since like the eighteen hundreds. She sits on her lake-front porch with binoculars and spies on people."

"She thinks the lake is hers," Piper said. "And the hills around it, apparently."

CJ nodded. "She said she saw something shiny being waved around up here. She thought it might be an alien invasion." He turned toward the south and waved. "Smile, because you know she's watching."

"Maybe you should jump to conclusions and cuff us," Gavin said.

Even Piper raised a brow at that. Yep, something had definitely gone down.

CJ ignored Gavin entirely and turned to Emmitt. "I'm sorry for your loss." He looked at Winnie next, gesturing to the canister in her hands. "But if you're intending to spread Rowan's ashes into the water below, it's my duty to tell you that you need a permit first."

"What if we have one?" Winnie asked.

CJ looked at her. "Do you?"

"Winnie," Gavin said warningly when his sister went to open her mouth, clearly not wanting her to lie.

The cop grimaced, looking pained as his work collided with his personal life. "Is there or is there not a permit?"

Everyone stared at each other.

"Okay, so here's the thing," Gavin said, after the awkward beat of silence. "Rowan's official funeral was back East, and some of us didn't get to go. We're not trying to break any laws here, we're just trying to honor a kid who died way too young in the best way we know how."

CJ looked at Gavin for a long beat, and then turned to the rest of them. "As I said, you need a permit. Unfortunately, if you don't have one, and someone, say a bored old woman with a powerful set of binoculars, turns you in, there's a big fine. But if that bored old woman happens to receive a visit from a local cop in the next few minutes, who stops by to tell her everything's fine on the lake's perimeter, that there's no alien invasion, and then possibly agrees to her offer of tea so that she's busy and distracted for the next hour, then no harm, no foul."

Gavin watched him leave, something in his expression speaking of a whole lot of pain that had nothing to do with Rowan. Then he nodded at Winnie to continue, who clutched the canister and looked to the water below.

"Hey, Rowan," she whispered, eyes already wet as she pulled a handwritten note from her pocket. "I know, two good-byes and you *hate* good-byes. But I needed to tell you a couple of things." She read from her notes. "First . . . I don't think I appreciated you enough. Actually, I know I didn't. I mean, who else could I have called in the middle of the night about a june bug in my room? You drove two hours to come save me." She sniffed and lost her battle with her tears, but she kept reading.

Not that Cam could understand a single word of it, and given the look on everyone's faces, they couldn't either.

He really wanted to close himself off to her heartfelt, raw grief. Instead, he held his hand out for the paper.

With gratitude, she handed it over, and as he began to speak her words for her, she dropped her head to his chest and sobbed.

"'You always said I needed to reach for the stars,'" he read, his throat on fire as he held her close with one arm. "'And I want you to know, Rowan, I'm going to keep trying. For you. Thanks for being my ride or die. I'll never forget you.'"

"That's sweet, Win," Piper whispered.

Winnie lifted her head and gave her a soggy, grateful smile.

Cam handed her back the note and gently took the canister, looking down at all that was left of his brother. His heart was still beating in that heavy thumping rhythm from a grief he hadn't been able to let go of, didn't know if he'd ever be able to let go. Drawing a deep breath, he stared sightless at the water below, but what he saw was himself on the asphalt that night, holding a dying Rowan, the rain falling on their faces. "I dream about the car accident every night," he said.

He felt Piper's hand on his arm, and when he met her gaze, hers was filled with way too much sympathy and understanding, neither of which he deserved.

"We'd fought," he said through an impossibly tight throat. "He'd been drinking and was acting"—he shook his head—"like Rowan. He could find a good time in doing absolutely nothing, and I snapped." He knew he had to do this, had to say it all or he'd never be able to live with himself. "We got into it." And a lot of that had been because Cam was mad that Rowan had ruined some girl's life getting her pregnant so young, not that he could say that since Piper still didn't know. "I called him immature and ungrateful and lazy. I told him he needed to grow the fuck up. And he"—he forced himself to look at Winnie and his dad—"he told me to stop being a controlling asshole."

His dad made a rough sound deep in his throat, but Cam wasn't sure if it was agreement or anger. He deserved the anger.

Winnie simply closed her eyes.

He didn't dare look at Piper, couldn't face what she must be thinking of him. But nor could he stop now, not until he got it all out. "After we yelled at each other, he tried to leave. He wanted to go home, and instead of making him stay, I drove him to the airport. We didn't make it halfway before—" He broke off and clamped his jaw tight to try to not lose his shit completely.

"No," Winnie said. "That's not on you." She turned him to face her. "You knew Rowan, he was stubborn as hell. He was pissy because he knew you were right. He wouldn't want you to blame yourself for what happened."

Squeezing her hand, he looked down at the canister. "We all miss you," he said and closed his eyes.

At his side, Piper wrapped an arm around him. Winnie was still holding on to him from the other side. But it was his dad who stepped right in front of him, eyes wet, voice raw. "As a dad, as *your* dad, I want to *demand* something of you right here, right now. I know I have no right, but I'm going to do it anyway."

Cam braced for his dad to agree that he was at fault.

But that wasn't what happened. His dad reached up and cupped Cam's face. "Winnie said it best. Rowan wouldn't have blamed you, son. And neither do I. No one blames you for what happened that night. No one. We're just grateful you're alive, so fucking grateful. So even though there's nothing to forgive, you're forgiven anyway. Now all you have to do is forgive yourself. Something I know a little bit about after giving you up to your mom. Forgiving myself for that was a long time coming, and if I'm being honest, I haven't really managed it fully."

"Dad." He shook his head. "It's okay."

His dad pressed their foreheads together. "It's getting there."

When Emmitt finally let him go and stepped back, Cam swiped his eyes with his forearm, opened the canister, and . . . let Rowan go.

When it was done, Winnie took the canister and clutched it to her chest as they all watched the ashes slowly vanish from view. "Now he'll always be here with us," she said softly.

Piper wrapped her arms around Cam, and just like when his dad had touched him, it warmed him. He dropped his head to her shoulder and did something he'd never done in his life.

Took comfort from another human being.

They stood there for a long time, but eventually they all walked home, where Gavin made baked mac and cheese from scratch. And hot dogs. "To eat this time, not throw," he said. "And there's chocolate cake for dessert. Comfort food, from the heart."

The food and company were exactly that, comforting, but halfway through the cake, it happened. He'd been ignoring the signs, the metallic taste in his mouth, the odd aura of lights flashing in his peripheral vision. But suddenly he could no longer ignore it, or the staggering pain. He managed to get to his feet, knowing what he needed, but he'd waited too long.

"What's wrong?" Piper asked, standing with him, taking his hand, looking concerned.

He opened his mouth to answer, but it felt like someone was stabbing a hot poker into his left eyeball, robbing him of thoughts and the ability to speak.

"Migraine," Emmitt said, eyes on Cam. "They're rare, but he gets them when he's stressed. He needs a quiet dark room, no noise."

"Just going to go home," Cam murmured, eyes squinted because it hurt to open them all the way. Both cold and sweating, he had to put a hand on the wall to keep the world from spinning, which pissed him off. He'd learned through some seriously brutal military training how to let pain course through him on its way out of his body, but that didn't mean he didn't feel every inch of it as it went.

"You're not going anywhere," Piper said. "Not when you can barely stand. I've got you this time, Cam."

Having her say that was staggering. No one had ever said such a thing to him. "I just need to sleep it off." He turned to the door.

But Piper had a grip of steel on him. "No way."

He knew he was going to give in, mostly because he was going to pass out. "Bossy," he murmured. And also smart as hell, resourceful, resilient, tough as nails, and she never failed to brighten his day or make him smile. And since he couldn't imagine making it home, he let her take his hand and pull him out of the kitchen.

She took him to her bedroom. Without turning on the lights, she led him to the bed before unbuttoning his shirt. She pushed it off his shoulders and nudged him to sit on the bed, where he narrowly missed squishing Sweet Cheeks.

"Meow," she said in bitchy protest, and jumped down. Which was a hell of a lot better than their first interaction had gone.

Cam bent to untie his boots, but his fingers felt wooden.

"Here," Piper said. "I've got it." And dropped to her knees to tug them off one by one.

He let out a careful breath. "Not exactly what I imagined you doing when I got you into this position."

A smile curved her lips, but her eyes remained worried as she lifted her head. "You imagined me on my knees for you?"

"Once or twice." Or every other minute of the day . . . He let himself fall onto his back when she got his boots off, too shaky to do more. "But just so you don't think I'm a misogynist pig, in my fantasies, I go to my knees and do you first."

She let out a quiet laugh, which said she liked the sound of that. Leaning over him, her face came into view. "Don't move." Then she pulled off his pants.

"I appreciate the sentiment, but I don't think I'm up to the task right now," he managed, his voice already hoarse and rough with the impending freight train in his head.

She gave a soft snort and brushed a warm hand over his cold, clammy forehead before covering him with a light blanket. "You can owe me. Where are your meds?"

"Got 'em." Gavin came quietly into the room with a pill bottle and water. "Emmitt told me where you keep them. Said you needed to take 'em right away or they won't work." He was breathless, as he'd clearly run his ass off to get to their house and back in the time he had.

Cam downed the pills and a very small bit of water, not wanting to throw them up. "Thanks." The only way to get through a migraine was to sleep through it, if he could. Thanks to the military, he could fall asleep at will.

As he drifted off, he heard Gavin ask, "Is he okay?"

"He will be," Piper said, with the same determination she used both on her job and in her personal life.

A personal life that now included him.

He hadn't gone looking for this, for her. But he couldn't have known he'd come home to help his dad deal with the unexpected blow of losing a son, only to also fall in love. With Wildstone. With the people.

With Piper . . .

It wasn't just the off-the-charts sex either, although that was a pretty great perk. But earlier at Rowan's makeshift service, she'd been there for him when he hadn't even realized he'd needed her.

And she was *still* there, sitting silently at his side in the dark, watching over him, making sure he was okay.

No one had ever taken care of him like this, not without wanting or expecting something in return. He had zero idea what to do with that, but he thought maybe he could get into trying to figure it out.

CHAPTER 24

"I think the words you're looking for are *wow* and *amazing*."

Piper woke to her name being said in a gruff whisper.

Cam.

She shot straight up in the chair she'd fallen asleep in, the one she kept near her bed as more of a clean-clothes holder than a place to sit. Her journal fell out of her lap and hit the floor.

It was still dark.

Reaching out with surprising strength, Cam grabbed her hand. "Why are you sleeping in the chair?"

"I wanted to stay close in case you needed me." It'd clearly been a bad migraine, really bad, and she hadn't wanted to leave him alone. She'd done some research and had been making a list in her journal of things she could do to ease his pain. Standing up, she brushed her free hand over his forehead, relieved to find him mildly warm now, not cold and clammy as he'd been. "Is the pain gone?"

"Mostly." He paused. "Not used to being babied."

She snorted. "I'm not babying you."

"You did. All night. And don't get me wrong, I'm grateful. But something's wrong. You're treating me with kid gloves."

She hesitated, because he was right. She'd treated him with kid gloves ever since the service yesterday.

With a speed and force she hadn't thought possible, he tugged her onto the bed, rolled, and had her beneath him, framing her face with his forearms, his fingers in her hair. "*Why?*" he repeated.

"Not kid gloves," she said. "Not exactly."

"Then what?" He frowned. "Is it because of what happened between us?"

She blinked. "Are you referring to the thing we keep . . . *accidentally* doing on your boat?"

His eyes darkened and heated. "I'll never drive that thing again without fantasizing about what's happened there. I might turn it into a shrine."

Lava coursed through her limbs and she had to shake it off. "That's not why I . . . treated you different."

"Then why?"

How to explain? She fiddled with the blanket until he put his hand over hers. "Talk to me, Piper."

"I've been complaining about my siblings since we met," she said. "And then yesterday, I heard your heart-wrenching story about the accident with Rowan." It'd wrecked her.

He shook his head. "I fucked up with Rowan. I didn't, and don't, deserve your sympathy."

"You're wrong. And all I want to do is help ease your pain. Are you telling me you wouldn't feel the same if our situations were reversed?"

He stared at her, his eyes much clearer than they'd been even a minute ago. At his continued silence, she gave him a small "told you" smile.

"You're right," he said. "I'd do anything to take away your pain."

At his incredibly serious and intense tone, she sucked in a breath while he stared at her some more.

"I need you," he said softly.

She rocked a little against the undeniable proof. "Need? Or want?"

"Both. Am I alone on this edge with you?"

"No." The word was barely a whisper, but she couldn't have held it back.

"Is your door locked?"

"Yes, why?"

Dipping his head, he kissed the hollow of her throat, then made his way to her ear, which he nibbled. "Because I'm about to thank you for watching over me," he whispered, his voice and stubble both giving gave her a full body shiver. "And I'm going to be very thorough in giving thanks."

"Cam." Her hands slid into his hair as he kissed his way south. "You should really rest—" She broke off with a low moan when he pushed her shirt up out of his way to capture a breast with his mouth. "Um—"

"You don't understand . . ." Apparently her shirt had to go

because he tugged it off. "No one's ever taken care of me before, not like you did."

She tried to think about what he was saying, tried to grasp the meaning behind it, but suddenly she was naked and he was sliding down her body, his hands on her thighs as he looked his fill. Then he locked eyes with her again. "Pretty," he breathed, and used his mouth to tour her body, mapping it. Every inch.

"Piper."

The full-body Cam experience was incredibly distracting. "Hmm?"

"You with me?"

"Are you kidding me? When I'm with you like this, I can't think of anything else, even if I wanted to."

"Good." He bent his head to her again, his mission clear. When his mouth touched her, heat exploded deep inside, melting everything else away as he performed his special brand of fire and magic. She already knew he liked to touch and taste, and especially liked to linger.

She had zero complaints.

By the time she could once again drag air into her taxed lungs, she was sprawled out, boneless and sated, making contented, purring happy kitten noises.

They dozed, until Piper jerked awake from the realization that she was feeling things she'd never let herself feel before. Terrifying, because this wasn't real, it was temporary—

A pair of arms closed around her and she startled. Cam turned her around to face him and kissed her forehead. "You okay?"

Burying her face in the crook of his neck, she just breathed him in for a long moment, willing herself to let go of the worry and angst about what was to come, and just live in the here and now. The future would be what it would be. No use spoiling the present, since it happened to be pretty damn awesome at the moment.

"Very okay," she whispered, brushing a kiss to his throat.

He took a deep breath and his arms tightened a little, his hand tracing circles over her back, reassuring. Comforting. And she wondered how it was that he always knew what she needed before even she did.

THE NEXT TIME she woke up, she was alone and a little befuddled. The sun was trying to burn her eyelids. Sitting up, she looked at her clock. Dawn had come and gone—three hours ago. She was alone, vaguely remembering Cam pressing a kiss to a bare shoulder, saying something about needing to get to the marina to help his dad because they were busy on Sundays.

She'd gone back to sleep.

She never went back to sleep.

She got up, wrapped herself in a blanket, and felt like a zombie as she staggered to the kitchen toward the scent of coffee. This meant going through the living room, where she jolted to a halt at the sight of Gavin letting a man out the front door.

Ry.

She nearly fell over trying to back up out of sight, but her inadvertent "oh shit" had both men turning toward her.

Gavin's brows went up.

Her ex took a slow sweep of her and said, "About time."

This from the guy who'd once claimed to love her, but had also said she was emotionally deficient. And for a long time Piper had believed him.

Until maybe right now.

Because she was beginning to realize she *wasn't* emotionally deficient, at least not with the right guy. She had no idea why she hadn't been able to let Ry in. He was charismatic, fun to be with, charming as hell . . . But something about his easy availability—and in turn, the ease with which he'd walked away when she'd broken up with him—had closed her off.

With Cam, she'd shockingly had no problem being vulnerable and open. But that didn't mean he was the right guy for her, because he wasn't. He was temporary, a bed of her own making, and so she shook her head at Ry.

"I mean it," he said quietly, his voice free of any cynicism. "It's about time you looked happy. You deserve that, Piper."

And then he was gone.

She looked at Gavin. "What the hell?"

"Just hear me out, okay? I'm trying to step up in a way I haven't before. You deserve that. Ryland's sister works at town hall. Through Ry, she got me all the information we need to turn this place into a B and B. And even better, because this house is so old, it's considered a historical building, which we can use in our flyers and brochures and on the website."

Piper just stared at him. "We still don't have any of those things."

"Yes, we do. Or we have mock-ups. That's what I was showing Ryland, because you know he was a marketing major before becoming a firefighter."

When she continued to just look at him, dumbstruck, he took her hand and brought her to the coffee table, where indeed there were mock-ups of everything spread out in front of her, looking official and . . . damn. Amazing.

"I've got the website up as well." He picked up his tablet and showed it to her. "No one else can see it, but I've got a tentative schedule mapped out and we already have customers."

"What? *How?*"

"Answering phones at the marina. I met an old military friend of Cam's. The guy sends people on corporate retreats. They're always looking for something private, something preferably on the water, something that isn't too close to a big town to give a sense of team building, and guess what? This place checks all the boxes for them. Cam also has a travel-service buddy and said he'd hook me up with him too, who'd recommend us to his clients. It's a shoo-in, Piper." He let out a rough laugh. "How often can any of the three of us say we've ever been a shoo-in for anything?"

She stared down at the gorgeous picture of the house they stood in, the cottages, the lake, the hills, the yard lit with the strings of white lights she'd had up since Christmas. But that wasn't what she was thinking about. She was thinking about Cam helping Gavin find his way. And Emmitt being so helpful to Winnie. Seemed the Hayes men were also fixers.

But in a much better way than she'd ever been. They were constructive about it, not having to control every single thing. In fact, Cam, the master of self-control, never actually tried to control anything around him.

There was something to be learned from that, she knew, but hell if she could figure it out at the moment. She felt befuddled, probably from all the orgasms, but also probably from a nagging sense that while her life was still on the tracks, somehow she'd gotten off at the wrong station.

"I think the words you're looking for are *wow* and *amazing*," Gavin said.

"Okay, yes, both of those things. It was nice of Cam to help."

"He said he can see all the things he didn't do right with Rowan, and he's trying to fix some wrongs."

Piper worked hard at swallowing a huge lump in her throat and failed, so she turned away.

Gavin turned her back to him, and swore at the glimmer of tears. "What the hell are you doing?" he asked, with no little amount of panic.

She blinked rapidly. "Nothing!"

He looked pained. "Hell, Piper, I didn't mean to make you cry. Shit. Forget it. Forget all of it, it's just a pet project I work on when I can't sleep—"

"I'm not crying!" At least not all the way. "And I'm not mad. I'm . . . touched. Because it *is* wow and amazing. *You're* wow and amazing."

"I know," he said, making her let out a soggy laugh. "So what's the problem?"

"Gavin . . . we know nothing about running a B and B."

"Yeah, but why should that stop us? Not knowing how to be *not* a drug addict didn't stop me. Not knowing how to be a mom isn't going to stop Winnie. Is not knowing how to be a physician assistant going to stop you?"

She sighed. "Yes." But not for the reason he thought. If they did this, *that* would stop her.

He looked at her and understanding dawned. "You think this will cost you your dream."

"I'm not sure how else to get tuition, *and* you and Winnie enough money to live on here while I'm gone. Plus this place is expensive to run, there's a lot of maintenance and utilities . . ."

"We'd succeed at the B and B, Piper."

"Okay, and while I do believe that, I don't see it happening as fast as selling."

"Maybe it'd work out better, you ever think of that?"

"We don't have a lot of experience with better."

He nodded, set down the tablet, and turned to go.

"Wait. Gavin—"

"You've made enough sacrifices for us." He turned back. "From when we came here until . . . well, even now you're sacrificing for us, staying when I know you want out because Mom and Dad are gone and you're all we've got. It's our turn to sacrifice."

"How are you going to do that?"

"I don't know yet." He paused and looked at her, really looked at her as if he wanted to see inside. "Please tell me you think about them."

Her chest went tight and she couldn't speak. She thought about them all the time. But what was the use of telling him? She didn't want him to hurt. "Gavin—"

"Never mind." He shook his head. "I can't really even picture them anymore. I try, but it's hard. And . . ."

She closed her eyes. Because what was hard was seeing his pain. "And what?"

"Do you think they'd have been okay with me?"

"Oh, Gavin." She grabbed his hand and pulled him in for a hard hug. "They would've loved you," she said fiercely.

"Even the gay part?"

"Yes, they would've loved every part, I promise."

He let her hug him for longer than he normally would before pulling back with a nod. "Thanks," he said quietly and headed to the door.

"Where are you going?"

"To meet up with my sponsor."

She blinked. "You have a sponsor?"

"Yes. From my NA group." He met her gaze. "I'm taking this seriously, Piper. I need for you to be able to trust me on that." He glanced at the tablet and plans for the B&B. "On everything, just like I trust you."

"But how can you trust me when I didn't even see that you were struggling with drugs?"

"I told you that wasn't your fault. Let it go. I mean it, Piper. For this to work, for any of it to work . . ." He gestured to the table. "Like me running the B and B for us while you're away at school, for example, you've got to be able to trust me."

The door shut behind him and she said to it, "But we can't do both the B and B and school . . ."

"We'll find a way," he said through the wood.

Shaking her head, she went in search of caffeine. If she was going to give up her dreams for Gavin's and Winnie's yet again, she was going to need a lot of it.

CHAPTER 25

"I'm going to take that as a hard yes."

Piper spent the next week working either at the station or on the property. She didn't enter anything new in her journal, which was rare for her. Instead, she worked at checking some things off her various lists. Like not taking extra overtime, buying something frivolous—sexy lingerie, thank you, Victoria's Secret—and . . . actually wearing the sexy lingerie.

And though she'd agreed to think about Gavin and Winnie's plan to turn the place into a B&B, she also still was exploring the option to sell.

At least, that was how she'd spent her days. Her nights, other than the three days Cam had flown back East to train with his unit, she'd spent in his arms exploring their attraction for each other.

But tonight was Emmitt Hayes's fifty-sixth birthday, and

they'd planned a surprise party. Piper had tried to warn everyone that he'd hate it, but Winnie was determined. She'd been in charge of figuring out who to invite, with Gavin being the resident caterer. He cooked while Cam got Emmitt out of the house by taking him fishing. Meanwhile, Piper set everything up, and when Cam texted that they'd docked, she made everyone hide.

A few minutes later, Emmitt and Cam entered the house and everyone jumped out of their hiding spots to yell "Surprise!" and "Happy birthday!"

Emmitt seemed thrilled, and the party got started. Piper was relieved, but not five minutes later, Cam turned to her. "He's gone."

"Who?"

"The birthday boy."

"Are you kidding me?"

"Do you see him?"

Piper looked around. Nope, she did not. The house was full of his friends, including his maybe-girlfriend, Margaret, but there was no Emmitt in sight. He couldn't have gotten far. "You check upstairs," she said. "I'll take a better look down here."

She started in the kitchen, going still just outside the pantry door, where from within she could hear crinkle sounds she recognized all too well. She opened the door and, yep, found Emmitt eating a bag of Cheetos. "Hey," she said, "that's my usual MO, not yours."

He shrugged and kept eating.

With a quick text to Cam that she'd found his dad, she sat on the floor next to him, reaching into the bag for herself.

"Birthdays aren't my thing," he said.

"Also my MO," she said. "But you love being the center of attention. What's going on?"

Before he could answer, the door cracked open and Cam slid in. He stared at his dad and then Piper, who gave him a palms up.

"You okay?" Cam asked his dad.

"Sure."

"Then why are you in the pantry with my girlfriend?"

Piper's heart skipped a beat. *Girlfriend?*

"Needed Cheetos," his dad said. "And you just gave your 'girlfriend'"—he used air quotes for the word—"a heart attack. Did you forget to tell her that's what she is to you?"

Again, Cam looked at Piper, who was indeed trying not to swallow her tongue.

"You scared?" Cam asked.

"No." Liar, liar . . . "Just not sure I'm girlfriend material," she said much more calmly than she felt.

"Maybe you could try it on for size, see how it feels," Cam suggested.

"For temporary size though, right?"

He gave her an almost smile. "Right."

She bit her lower lip, and at the warm and amused look in his eyes, she nodded. Because no matter what happened, he made her smile. And that was worth just about everything, including the label that she wasn't sure she was ready for.

"Okay, now that *that's* solved," Cam said. "Why are we hiding?"

"I'm not," Emmitt said.

"Dad."

"Fine. I'm hiding. You happy?"

"Not yet." Cam took a handful of Cheetos for himself. Before he'd finished, Winnie had joined them.

"Yum," she said, and took the bag of Cheetos.

"Hey," Piper complained.

"What? I'm the one eating for two. And why didn't I get an invite to this private VIP meet and greet?" No one answered her, and she eyed them all. "I'm guessing we have a problem. Why am I the last to know?"

"Apparently we're all the last to know," Cam said, and looked at his dad.

Emmitt avoided his gaze. "Are there more Cheetos?"

Beyond the door, they could hear the party continuing on without them. Music. Laughter. Talking.

Gavin peeked into the closet. They all scooted to make room for him. "What's going on?" he asked. "My food's fuckin' awesome and you're all in here inhaling Cheetos?"

Again, Cam looked at his dad.

Emmitt blew out a sigh. "Okay, I'll tell you. But it's embarrassing."

"More embarrassing than the Bean giving me gas in this tight space?" Winnie asked.

Piper sighed and fanned the air in front of her face.

"Sorry," Winnie said. "I'm growing a parasite. Literally."

"Dear God, man," Gavin said to Emmitt, gagging dramatically. "Tell us the problem so we can get out of here."

"Okay, okay!" Emmitt tossed up his hands. "You invited all my girlfriends to this thing. What the hell were you thinking?"

Piper met everyone's gaze. They were all as confused as she was.

"Girlfriends, as in *plural*?" Cam asked.

Emmitt nodded.

"But I thought you were seeing Margaret."

"Yeah. And Sonya." He grimaced. "And Carol. And Danita."

The look on Cam's face was priceless. "You're dating your dentist, the grocery store clerk, and your barber?"

"What?" Emmitt said defensively. "My doctor told me to live a healthier life, and I am. Sex is healthy." He turned to Piper. "Right?"

Piper opened her mouth, and then shut it.

Cam looked pained. "How in the world are you even finding that many women who want to date you? No, wait, don't answer that. I don't want to know."

"It's all done online now," Emmitt said. "I just searched for all the single women in the area who were on the same dating app as me. Jeez, son, how do I know this and you don't? I'm the old one. And it's not like I'm doing anything wrong. Everyone knows if you connect with someone on an app, you're not exclusive. But that doesn't mean they're going to enjoy running into each other in person."

"You're sleeping with four women," Gavin said slowly. "On your fifty-sixth birthday."

"Well, not at the same time," Emmitt said modestly.

Gavin grinned and tried to high-five him.

Emmitt closed his eyes and *thunked* his head back against the wall a couple of times.

Another bag of Cheetos, unopened, fell onto his head.

Winnie nabbed it for herself before Piper could.

Gavin didn't stop grinning. "You're my idol."

"I've got no idea how to handle this," Emmitt said.

"You think *you* don't?" Cam muttered. "Try being your son."

"*I* know how to handle this," Gavin said. "Watch and learn." He slid out of the closet.

They all crowded up to the door, ears up against it as Gavin hit his first mark, who'd just moved into the kitchen.

"I'm looking for the birthday boy," Sonya cooed at Gavin.

"Yeah, about that . . ." Gavin said, thoughtfully staying near the door so they could all hear. "He wanted me to let you know that you're a *very* special woman in his life, but he's bummed because with so many people here, he won't be able to spend any one-on-one time with you. He's hoping to make it up to you by taking you out to dinner tomorrow night. Just the two of you."

"Somewhere fancy?" Sonya asked hopefully. "Where they put the napkin in your lap and stuff?"

"Absolutely," Gavin said.

"And I can order whatever I want?"

"Whatever you want," Gavin said. "You in?"

"Of course. I'm hungry already!"

"Perfect," Gavin said, steering her toward the back door. "I'll just walk you to your car. He'll call you later to firm up the deets."

"Shee-it," Emmitt muttered. "She's going to make me take her for prime rib and lobster. You know how expensive that is?"

Piper's face was pressed up against the slatted door, watching Gavin work his magic. It reminded her of something she'd forgotten. Her brother was not just great with people, but a *master* at it, in a way she could, would, never be.

He hadn't been an asshole and a flake the past few years. He'd become an addict. And she was still shocked and upset with herself that she hadn't seen his addiction, which was a guilt and shame she'd have to live with.

But he was slowly becoming himself again before her very eyes, and she felt so proud of him. Proud of both of her siblings. Only a month ago, she wasn't sure she'd have thought of them as grown-ups, capable of leading their own lives. But things were changing. *They* were changing, and doing great while they were at it.

Not five minutes later, Gavin had disposed of two more of Emmitt's girlfriends with smooth ease and then opened the pantry door. "Only one left in the house, Birthday Boy. Margaret. So you're safe now. Time to let yourself out of the closet." He grinned at the irony in that statement. "Come on in, the water's fine." He then handed Emmitt a schedule of the week sketched out on a birthday napkin so he could see all his dates lined up at a glance.

Piper couldn't help herself. She grabbed Gavin and hugged him tight, until he made dramatic strangulation noises to be let free.

"What was that?" he asked.

Piper shrugged. "Maybe I'm proud of you."

"Well, that's new," he said, trying and failing to not look pleased.

"Seriously, this is going to cost me a fortune," Emmitt muttered, still eyeballing his schedule. "And you put Sonya and Danita on the same night! Are you crazy? I don't have that kind of stamina!"

"They're separated by two hours," Gavin said. "It's the only night they were both free."

"Fine, but you've got to find a way to cancel Carol on Wednesday."

"Why? You're wide open that night."

"Yes," Emmitt said. "But she was arrested at Walmart last week for driving one of those electric carts while drinking wine from a Pringles can in the parking lot. I don't date felons."

Gavin clapped him on the back. "You play, you pay. Remember, this is your way of apologizing, so don't chintz. Go all in, make them feel special. Do what you've got to do to keep your life status quo."

"Is that how it's done then?" a voice asked, and they all turned in unison to find CJ standing there.

Piper watched the "oh shit" look hit Gavin's face, but he quickly smoothed it over with an easy smile. "You already know how it's done, remember?"

CJ shook his head, turned, and walked out again.

Gavin watched him go, a muscle working in his jaw, but he did not go after him. There was a lot of healing that needed to happen there, she knew, but she also knew that the kind of chemistry and history those two had was worth fighting for. "Nice self-sabotage," she said.

Gavin shook his head at her. "Said the kettle to the pot. And I'm fine, I know what I'm doing."

"Do you?"

"*Yes.*" And with that, he pivoted and strode into the crowded living room. The opposite way that CJ had gone.

So he wasn't going to fight for love. He'd never been much of a fighter. It'd always been easier for him to walk away. She got that. But she also got that some things were worth digging in for and holding on. At least in the movies anyway. She started after him, but could see him talking and laughing with a group of Emmitt's fishing buddies. If he was going to put out the illusion of truly being okay, then she was going to have to let him.

Cam slipped an arm around her. "I was thinking we could slip out for a bit."

She met his heated gaze and thought maybe it wasn't just in the movies after all. "To do what?"

"Anything you want."

"Still standing right here," Winnie said. "Although I have no idea why. You kids be careful now, you hear?" And then she too vanished into the living room crowd.

"*Anything I want?*" Piper repeated to Cam. "That's a lot of power to just hand over."

He laughed. "Babe, the power's *always* been yours."

Since she'd spent most of her life feeling as if it was the exact opposite, this sounded appealing. Very appealing.

"Like that smile," he murmured, wrapping an arm around her, nudging her back against the pantry door.

"Well, I did just realize that my siblings are finally fully functioning adults." She slid her hands along his jaw, loving the feel of his several-day-old beard beneath her fingers. "And that I'm not needed right now."

"I wouldn't say that. Maybe I need you."

She smiled. "How can I help you?"

"I was thinking a few drinks, maybe some food. And"—he

put his mouth to her ear—"me licking either one of those things off your body."

She actually quivered. "So what's stopping you?"

He picked her up and she locked her legs around his waist. Grabbing a bottle of whiskey off the counter, he handed it to her before walking them out the back door.

She held on tight, laughing. "The party—"

"No one will even notice we're gone." He was moving with her at a good pace. A man on a mission. "Besides," he added, "you just agreed to my favorite meal."

"Which is what exactly?"

"You." They were moving down the dock toward his boat now.

With another laugh, she forgot to be afraid of the water as he boarded with her. He took them below deck, setting her on the narrow galley counter.

"Hey," she said. "Do I look like the sort of girl who lets a guy lick whiskey off of her—" She gasped when he gently tipped the bottle a little, letting a few drops of the amber liquid hit her collarbone and throat. Then he lifted her up and licked it off, trailing his tongue up her neck to her ear, before taking the lobe between his teeth, making her moan.

He smiled against her. "I'm going to take that as a hard yes."

PIPER WOKE AT what appeared to be dawn, which meant she'd gotten maybe three hours of sleep after she and Cam had ravished each other. And speaking of Cam, she found him with his head propped up by his hand, watching her sleep. "Oh, crap," she said. "Was I snoring?"

He smiled. "No."

"Drooling?"

"Only a little."

He was kidding. Probably. Just in case, she swiped a hand over her mouth. "Why are you watching me sleep?"

"When I'm stressed, you center me. I told you once before, you're better than swimming the lake."

She took that for the compliment it was. "You don't usually seem to give in to stress like the rest of us mere mortals."

"It's not a productive emotion."

She felt her heart start to pound funny and sat up. "Why am I suddenly the one feeling stressed?"

"These past few weeks have been incredibly important to me," he said, sitting up too. "You've become incredibly important to me."

Yep, that was definitely stress making her heart thump in her ears. Stress, and something else. Something that curled through her in a terrifyingly good way. "Maybe it's the orgasms."

He smiled. "The orgasms are amazing, but it's more than that for me."

"More?"

He ran a finger along her jaw, tucking a stray strand of hair behind her ear. "My unit's being sent out, Piper."

Her heart seized. "Where? For how long?"

He kept his gaze on hers. "Until the job is done. Word is maybe a week, maybe more."

He hadn't said where, and she understood that he couldn't. "When do you leave?"

"Eighteen hundred."

"Tonight?" she squeaked.

"Yes."

She nodded, trying to emulate his quiet calm. This was what he did, put life and limb on the line to protect and serve. And if he could do so with such courage and bravery, then she could do her best to give him the same. "And after? Your leave from the DEA might be over by then. Will you go directly back to the East Coast?"

"If I have to. But it won't be to stay." He paused. "After losing Rowan, I realized something. I've moved every year or two for the Coast Guard, but I don't want that anymore. I want to settle down. I want"—he gestured between them—"this to be more."

There went her heart again. "It was never meant to be more. You know that."

"I do. What I don't know is if you still feel that way now."

She closed her eyes and drew a deep breath. "I feel things I didn't want to feel."

He pulled her into him, entangled their legs. "Piper. Look at me."

She opened her eyes and met his. "There's a lot of things I don't know about those feelings," she whispered.

"Can you tell me what you do know?"

"I know I want you."

"You've had me. Only a few hours ago, in fact," he murmured on a small smile. "I'm sleeping in the wet spot. And you know what I mean."

Did she? The kick of her heart against her ribs certainly suggested she did, that she knew exactly what he wanted to hear. He wanted more. And he wanted to know if she did too. "And if your transfer doesn't come through?"

"Geography isn't a hurdle. Not in my book. I can always leave the DEA and find something here. But I'm pretty sure they'll transfer me."

"You've heard from them then?" she asked.

"Not yet, but they said they intended to keep me, however they could. As for the Coast Guard, I was active duty for twelve years, and have two in the Reserve. I'll be able to retire in two years." He gave a small, dry smile. "Although I can't tell if you're more worried about my transfer not coming through, or that it will."

Yeah, her either. She'd planned on him being nothing more than the fun-time guy to have a little thing with. That's what her bullet journal had him down as. And that shit was in ink, which meant it was gospel. She'd never have done it if she'd known he planned on sticking around. "You'd really retire?"

He shrugged. "I've had my share of excitement. More than." He paused. "So what are you afraid of?"

Only everything, not the least of which was that he could read her like a damn book. She was no longer surprised to realize that he was much deeper and more complicated than she'd ever imagined. So yeah, she *was* scared. Scared to go deeper, and even more scared to lose him, as at the moment, he was the only sane thing in her world. "I'm not sure *afraid* is the right word."

"What is then?"

Good question. What if he decided that if she couldn't give that mysterious "more," would he walk away? It wouldn't be the first time. But unlike with Ry, she was in too deep with Cam to not get hurt if he did. Freaking out a little bit, she slipped out of bed, busying herself looking for her clothes, which she'd been stupid enough—and excited enough—to strew everywhere last night in her hurry to get him naked. "I've got to get to work by seven, sorry."

"Are you?"

She glanced over at him still in the bed, the sheet sunk dangerously low on his hips. His hair was tousled, his stubble delicious, and he looked like the very best thing she'd ever seen. "It's work," she said. "I don't have any control over that."

Cam slid out of the bed. "Are you going to tell me what you're thinking, or keep me hanging while I'm gone?"

Where was her other shoe? Her bra? *Dammit*. She stilled, eyes closed. He was going to go on a mission. It was his job, his life, and yet . . . he was probably being shipped out to a place like where her parents had been killed.

He turned her to face him. He was holding her bra. "Playing games is unlike you, Piper. You're one of the most direct women I've ever known. If you don't want what I want, or if you're not feeling anything, just tell me."

Look at him, *way* overestimating her emotional ability. Had he not met her? In any case, she was *feeling* a whole bunch, thank you very much. But their needs were complete opposites. She'd been planning on going out and getting the life she'd been waiting years to get, and he was looking to sink roots and settle down.

If she gave in to what they had between them, it could mean compromising her life. *Again*.

Footsteps sounded on the deck, and then someone was knocking on the latched door. "Cam?" came Gavin's voice. "Piper's with you, right?"

Cam waited for her to hastily pull on the rest of her clothes before opening the door.

"Hey," her brother said. He took in Piper's state of dishevelment and then Cam in just the sweatpants and expansive bare chest. "I'm interrupting."

"Yes," Cam said at the exact same time Piper shook her head and said, "No." Carefully avoiding looking at Cam, she shook her head again. "I'm going to work."

"I know," Gavin said, still looking unsure, clearly guessing he'd caught them at a bad moment. "Jenna called, said she needed a ride and you weren't picking up. She wanted me to make sure you weren't . . . preoccupied, and not looking at your phone."

"I'm on my way out right now." Piper grabbed her sweatshirt and accidentally made eye contact with Cam. She didn't need a rocket scientist to tell her what he was thinking, that he was irritated because she was suppressing her feelings. And he'd be right.

But that was her only defense. It was all she knew, and she wouldn't apologize for that. She bit her lip. Okay, dammit, she would apologize. "Gavin, we need a minute."

When her brother was gone, she looked at Cam. "I'm sorry I'm so emotionally . . . challenged. I don't mean to be playing a game or to lead you on. The truth is, I . . . like you. A lot. And I think we both know that's more than a little terrifying for me, which I realize makes me a risk, and I'm sure, annoying as hell."

"You like me." He paused. "A lot."

A small, disbelieving laugh escaped her. "Is that all you heard?"

"No, but that was my favorite part."

"Good." She went up on tiptoes and brushed a kiss to his lips. "Can we work on the more part?"

His hands went to her hips and held her still as he took the kiss deeper and hotter. "Absolutely," he said when he was done rendering her stupid.

She kept her arms around him. "Good. Please be careful. Please come back in one piece."

"To you?"

"To me. *One piece*," she reiterated.

He gave her another kiss that curled her toes, and when she got home from work twelve hours later, he was long gone.

CHAPTER 26

It was anyone's guess as to which of their
current mistakes had stopped by.

A few days later, Gavin worked until late afternoon and then
went for a run. He went hard around the lake, until his
legs were quivery and rubbery, and then sat on the rocks facing
the water, watching a thunderstorm move in. A raindrop hit
him and then another. He didn't care. He knew Piper still har-
bored nightmares in storms like this and he hated that for her.
But he wasn't afraid of storms.

He was afraid of loss.

And now that he'd looked into CJ's eyes and seen the same
sense of loss, loss *he'd* caused . . . Damn. He'd thought he'd
created a shield to protect himself, that he'd be bullet-proof to
more pain. But the truth was, life was fucking full of pain.

Feeling sorry for himself, he walked back in the rain, showered, and then made breakfast for dinner. And since he hadn't figured out how to make up with CJ, and Piper was still at work, it was just him and Winnie. And speaking of his pregnant sister, her little baby bump arrived before she did as she came into the kitchen. She had a toolbelt slung around her hips just below her growing tummy, walking and watching a YouTube video on how to repair drywall at the same time.

"Yum," she said, propping her phone up on the napkin holder, the one made of popsicle sticks, which they'd been using since Winnie had made it in kindergarten for Piper. She then began to pour syrup all over the waffles.

Gavin took the syrup from her.

"Hey! The Bean loves syrup."

"Does the Bean love diabetes?"

"The doc says I'm fine, although my jeans are starting to disagree." She ate for a few minutes, putting away a shocking amount of food. Finally sated, she leaned back, hands on her belly. "The place is looking good, right?"

"Really good."

"So what's our next step?"

"You keep growing a baby."

"Yes, but I really want to keep helping around here too," she said.

"You're not exactly quick on your feet right now."

Her eyes narrowed. "Are you saying I'm slow?"

"No," he said carefully. "You're just . . . slower than you used to be."

"And now I'm *fat*?"

Gavin sighed. "You know, I'm starting to understand everything we ever put Piper through."

She grimaced, and he had to laugh. "Just wait until the Bean pulls even a fraction of the shit you've pulled." He stood. "I'm going back to work, I'm planning on finishing up the business plan this week."

"Which we'll use to convince Piper to start up the B and B, right?"

"Right," he said, and hoped that was even possible. It wouldn't be easy. "She still wants to go back to school."

"I know."

"She deserves that, Win. So much."

"I know that too. I told you, I tried to get us a loan to buy her out."

"I know, but I'm not giving up. I'm working on an option that might pan out. *Has* to pan out. Because Piper's never failed us, not once."

Winnie nodded. "So let's not fail her either."

"We won't."

Winnie leaned forward. "So tell me about this option that might pan out."

Gavin started to tell her his thoughts when Winnie's phone buzzed with an incoming text, which she read and froze.

"What?" Gavin asked.

"It's Jenna. She and Piper just left the scene of a horrific car accident. The storm made the roads slick. A family skidded off the highway on the 101, broke through the railing, and rolled down the hill about three hundred feet. The two kids in the back seat survived, ages three and ten. The parents didn't make it."

Gavin felt the nausea roll through him and he set down his fork and pushed away his plate. "Piper?" he asked hoarsely.

Winnie shook her head. "Jenna says she handled the job like a pro, but vanished the minute they got back. She just wanted to give us a heads-up."

Gavin opened the app the three of them had to track each other's locations. Once upon a time, Piper had used it to keep tabs on him. Now they used it out of sheer laziness, like when Gavin checked to see which of his two sisters was closer to the grocery store when he needed something. "She's at the tire swing," he said.

"Where she goes to be alone. What do we do? Do we let her be alone?"

Hell, he actually wasn't sure, but Winnie was looking lost and he knew he had to at least appear like he had his shit together.

"Should we try to get in touch with Cam?" Winnie asked.

"Do you want to live?"

Winnie sighed. "I know, right? She'd kill us if we worried him while he was gone to God knows where doing God knows what."

"She'll come home when she's ready, and we'll be here for her."

But it took her longer than he'd thought it would. It was way past dark, and he was in his room alternately watching TV and eyeballing his phone for both Piper's location and a call or text from CJ when there came a soft knock at his door.

He opened up, not surprised to see Piper in what she called her "birth control outfit": sweats that swallowed her whole, hair piled on top of her head, no makeup, feet stuffed into rainboots.

"Our parents died," she whispered.

He pulled her inside and into his arms as she cracked in half. "I know," he said, throat tight as she shuddered and began to cry against his chest. "I know."

She let him hold her for a long moment, during which time she got his shirt all soggy with her tears, before lifting her face. "I'm sorry."

He gave her a small smile. "Because you just slimed me?"

She managed a weak laugh. "No, I'm not sorry about that." She drew in a deep breath. "I'm sorry I've wasted so much time trying to boss you around into a life you never wanted."

"Hey, it's never a waste of time if you learn something."

She shook her head, not ready for humor. "I've never acted like your sister. And I don't let you talk about Mom and Dad, and I'm sorry for that too. Or if I made you feel like I didn't like taking care of you and Winnie, or that you were a burden—"

"You were thirteen," he interrupted, pulling her farther into his room, sitting her in the chair by the window, turning for the bottle of Jack he used to keep on his dresser back when he was using. But it'd been tossed long ago. And wasn't this a first, wishing for alcohol—not for himself, but to help someone with. "You were put into a terrible, tragic situation that no thirteen-year-old should ever have to deal with. Hell . . ." He rubbed a hand down his face. "If I'd been the oldest . . . Christ, I can't even imagine that responsibility. I'd have lost you and Winnie, or accidentally killed one of you for sure. We were lucky to have you. Now please stop blaming yourself for my problems. I can be a sneaky asshole when I want to be, and I've wanted to be. But I've learned how destructive that is." He paused. "Now you."

"Me? What do you mean? I'm not in the danger zone."

He just looked at her.

"I'm fine, Gavin."

"You're not. You're still pushing away all emotions and reacting to everything like it's . . . I don't know . . . a job."

"Such as?" she asked coolly.

"See? That," he said, pointing at her. "I'm asking for feelings and you're giving me calm logic. Do you know how much it sucks to be someone who loves you but can't reach you?"

She blinked, and he could tell that her first reaction was hurt, and then resignation.

"I know," she said quietly. "But sometimes, I just . . ."

"What?"

She closed her eyes. "Sometimes I feel thirteen again, and I just want Mom."

Gavin felt the ache in his chest for her, for him and Winnie too, because this was way above his pay grade. "I get that."

"I know you do." She swiped at a tear almost angrily. "I tried to make it so that you guys wouldn't miss their presence, but I couldn't. Mostly because I miss them too, so much."

He couldn't speak around the lump in his throat, so he just nodded.

"I need you to know something, Gav. I never minded taking care of you and Winnie. Never," she said fiercely, making him believe her. "But I wasn't done being taken care of either."

He'd have sworn that he was the most screwed up of all of them, but he was starting to realize that the honor might go to his headstrong, irrepressible, smart, prickly, amazing sister. "What can I do to help? Anything. Just tell me."

"I'm supposed to be the one helping you."

"No," he said, shaking his head. "You did your part. Now I'm grown. And that means we're equals. You help me and I help you. It's my turn. So let me help."

"I'm fine."

"Really? Is that why you're freaking out that maybe Cam is coming back to stay? That he wants to? That *you* probably have a lot to do with that?"

He caught a glimpse of anxiety and panic in her eyes before she turned away.

"You're afraid," he realized. "Afraid to let anyone in, afraid to let anyone love you."

She gave a forced laugh. "That's . . . ridiculous. I'd have to be pretty damn broken to feel that way."

"Ah, Piper. It's okay to be broken. Broken can be fixed." He stood just behind her, watching her carefully, not wanting to push her over the edge, but wanting to make her see that she was working with his own MO here—survivor's guilt.

Finally, she huffed out a sigh and shook her head as she turned back to him. "What do you want me to say? That you're right? That I *am* freaking out just a little bit?"

"Or you know, a lot."

She rolled her eyes. "I don't know how to make something like this work. Opening up and letting him see all the corners and the dust in the rafters and the shit I've hidden deep in the basement . . ."

He laughed. "Trust me, if I can do it drug free, then you sure as hell can. Just don't be the you that's, um . . ."

"What?"

"You know. A little anal."

She went brows up. "Excuse me?"

"And don't use that PMS tone either," he said. "Oh, and while you're at it, don't not listen."

"Hey, I listen."

"You pretend to, but you don't, not really. Instead you tell people what to do and how to think."

Her eyes narrowed, but then she paused, chewed on her lower lip. "Dammit. I really hate when you're right."

"The good news is that knowing it is half the battle," he said.

"Maybe you should try heeding your own advice sometime."

At the knock on the front door, they looked at each other, Piper as on edge as he. It was anyone's guess as to which of their current mistakes had stopped by. Piper rolled her eyes at the both of them and they moved to the living room and opened the door.

It was CJ, and Piper visibly sagged with relief. If Gavin hadn't been suddenly so tense he'd lost the ability to breathe, he might've laughed at the stay-of-execution expression on her face as she vanished to leave them alone.

Gavin was having trouble drawing in air as he took in the sight of CJ standing there looking like the best thing he'd ever screwed up. "You come to twist the knife deeper?" he asked, with a calm he didn't feel.

CJ shut the door behind him and came closer, but didn't touch Gavin. Instead, he looked him in the eyes and said, "So Axel showed up at the station today."

This shocked Gavin. Axel hated cops, and probably especially hated CJ, but he'd never say so. "Why would he do that?"

"He wanted to tell me that you'd told him I didn't trust you, but that I *should* trust you because you've got your shit together. He said he's a great sponsor, that he takes pride in it. He also said that you don't really need him, and yet you still make sure to see him every week. Said it was important to you to stay on top of things. For the people you love."

"He shouldn't have done that. He probably got hives just walking into the station."

CJ grimaced and ran a hand over his unshaved scruff that looked far sexier than it had a right to. "He said that he thought it was noble of you to not break confidences, but in this case, also misguided."

Gavin crossed his arms over his chest. "Did he say anything else?"

"That he was flattered I was jealous, but he'd have to be more than a bipolar addict to date you because you're too much for him to handle."

Gavin snorted because that sounded like Axel, but his amusement faded quickly and he looked away. "Yeah, well, most people feel that way about me."

"Not me." CJ came close. "And I'm about as far from perfect as you can get."

"You seem pretty perfect to me."

CJ held his gaze, his own softer now as he shook his head. "You look at me with rose-colored glasses, you always have."

"Maybe that's because I have no idea what attracts you to me." Gavin spread his arms. "I've got literally nothing to offer you. I feel like I get so much from you, and I can't begin to return the favor."

CJ stepped closer and took his hand. "For a long time, I've been nothing but the job. I need to be more than that. When I'm with you, I am. And I like that person. You asked why I never found the One. It was because it's you, Gavin. It's been you all along. You were right. You've done nothing wrong. I got scared, and I'm sorry. I've wanted to say this to you every day since, but I didn't know how."

Gavin felt a rush of something inside him, a mix of relief and hope. "Seems you said it just fine."

"I love that you're dedicated to being the best you that you can be. I'm in awe of that."

"That's not all I'm dedicated to," Gavin said in a lighter, more playful tone.

CJ smiled. "The last time you were that dedicated was in my shower a few weeks back, and you bruised your knees."

"My knees are as tough as the rest of me," Gavin assured him. "And while I love where you're going with this, it's not what I meant." He drew in a shaky breath. "I'm dedicated to *you*," he said. "You once accused me of simply surviving and not really living, and you were right. When I came to Wildstone, I didn't think I was good enough for the people I loved. That in fact, I hurt them just by being who I was. My parents. Arik. My sisters.

You," he said. "It made me keep myself emotionally distanced. And it's an easy step from there to not feel connected enough to care. But there's something about you that blasts away my walls and burrows in. I love you, CJ, I always have. It just took me longer than most to believe in myself enough for this. For us." He tugged CJ in, intending to lay a long, soul-searching kiss on him that would hopefully lead to the rest of their lives, but CJ put a hand to his chest to stop him.

Gavin's heart tripped. "What?"

"I brought food."

Gavin nearly collapsed in relief. "The way to my heart."

"It's the makings for tacos."

Gavin felt the last little pieces of himself fall into place. "A love story in five words."

CHAPTER 27

"Well, that escalated quickly."

A week after he'd left, Cam pulled back into his dad's driveway starving, exhausted, and on edge. In the old days, that had meant he'd been looking for a fight or sex—he hadn't been particularly picky. But with the dubious honor of getting older, he needed more than either of those things. He should've stayed away a few extra days to reacclimate, but he'd wanted to get back to Wildstone.

To Piper.

But her car was gone. Work, probably. So he walked into his dad's kitchen, and then stopped short. His dad and Margaret were at the stove cooking salmon, broccoli, and quinoa.

"Okay," Cam said. "Who are you and what have you done with my dad?"

The guy grinned wide. "I know, right? But Piper says the

green shit's good for circulation, which I translate to mean it's good for bedroom activities, if you know what I mean. And if you don't, it means—"

"Dad." Cam pinched the bridge of his nose. "Let's always assume I know what you mean."

Emmitt studied him a beat and then put down the spatula before glancing at Margaret. "Darlin', would you mind giving us a few minutes?"

Margaret winked. "Take your time. I'll be in the hot tub."

Emmitt watched her go, and then piled up a plate and handed it to Cam. "Rough mission?"

He shrugged as he dug in, grateful for the food. "Business as usual. I'm fine."

"Camden, you're a lot of things. Strong, smart, tough as hell, generous . . . and a shitty liar."

Ignoring that, Cam kept eating.

"I bet it's women troubles. It was only a matter of time with Piper."

Cam stilled and looked at him. "What does that mean?"

"It means that along with being a shitty liar, you're also determined as hell. Once you decide on something, there's no changing your mind. You've decided on her, and you don't understand why she didn't enthusiastically jump on the band-wagon."

Cam opened his mouth to refute that, and then realized he couldn't.

Emmitt's smile was understanding. "See, I get it because we're alike in a lot of ways. The problem is, Piper doesn't think like we do. She's a careful, methodical planner, and slow to engage. Even slower to admit personal emotions. Did you know her own siblings call her the Fixer? It's because she worries about everyone else over her own well-being. That started out of necessity, and I'm guessing it just became habit. And old habits die hard, especially with a woman like that, who'd give you the very shirt off her own back."

Cam blew out a breath and shook his head. "She's making changes for herself. She wants to go back to school, which is great."

"That is great. So what's the problem?"

"She doesn't seem to think she can do that and have a relationship."

Emmitt sat at the table with Cam. "I've got something to say and you might not like it."

Cam had to laugh. "When's that ever stopped you?"

"Good point." Emmitt smiled and clapped him on the shoulder. "In your life, you've been . . . well, free. You left home at sixteen."

"I went into the military," he said dryly. "Not exactly the definition of a free life."

"True, but that was your choice. Piper, on the other hand, never had choices, or even much of a say in her life's path. She's been stuck here since she was a teenager. Now, I get that you're ready to settle down, but she isn't. Hell, she might not even know what she wants."

That it was all true didn't help. He'd had a life of freedom and adventure while her life had been dictated from age thirteen. It was no wonder then that she lived by a set of rules no one else was privy to, and an iron-clad sense of control that manifested in bullet journaling and holding on to the reins of her siblings' lives with both hands.

Now she finally had a shot at being able to live the life she wanted, and he of all people could understand that. Which meant there was only one thing he could do—support her choices. No matter if he wasn't one of those choices.

"What are you thinking?" his dad asked.

"I don't want to lose her. But there's no way I'm going to hold her back either."

His dad nodded. "Good. But when I look over my life, do you know what my biggest regret is?"

Cam shook his head.

"It's that I didn't find a way to make it work with your mom. Yeah, she had her difficulties, but I loved her on the day she died every bit as much as I loved her on the day I married her. It kills me that we spent our years together fighting about why it couldn't work, when we should've been figuring out how to make it work. That, and her unwillingness to stay on her meds, tore us apart, and our family too. I wasted a lot of time, time that I could've spent with you. Yeah, I got Rowan, but as you know, life's short. Too fucking short."

That was the thing about losing someone you loved. It made you appreciate those who really mattered in life. His dad. His future niece or nephew. Winnie. Gavin. *Piper* . . . Yeah, it'd been devastating to lose Rowan, and life would never be the same. But the world didn't stop turning. He could still love. And he'd most definitely found someone special to love in Piper. She was it for him. She made him laugh, she made him feel, and she made him want to be a better man. But he had no idea if she could, or would, feel the same about him. Which made him feel a little bit like he was hanging out there bare-assed naked all on his own.

But she'd said to come home to her, and that gave him hope. As for the rest, she was well worth waiting on the possibility of what could be.

WHEN PIPER WALKED into the house after another long shift at work, she heard voices in the kitchen. It'd been a good day in spite of the long hours. She'd delivered a baby at a rest stop off Highway 46. And then a woman they'd helped last week during a heart attack had brought them cookies. They'd been gluten free, sugar free, and dairy free, but still. They'd been cookies. Plus, she'd heard back about her application to the University of Colorado. She'd been accepted, and could start with their next program in six weeks. All she had to do was figure out how to get either her siblings okay with the sale of the property, or . . . rob a bank.

But since those were both unlikely scenarios, she'd spent a good deal of time thinking about her options, and hedging her bets.

She wished Cam was back. She'd sneak into his bed and rock both of their worlds until thinking too hard wasn't an option. That would help solve everything, for sure. As she walked through the living room toward the kitchen, the voices became clearer.

"I can't tell her now, I waited too long," Winnie said.

Piper stopped in her tracks. God, what now? She couldn't imagine, but from experience knew it would be bad.

It always was.

"Waited too long to tell me what?" she asked, feeling a shock go through her when she realized Cam was also there. "You're back."

"Just got here." He pushed off from the counter he'd been leaning against and came close, during which time her eyes soaked up the sight of him hungrily, but also taking inventory to make sure he was okay. He wore loose, ripped-up jeans and a T-shirt, and a layer of exhaustion that showed in his eyes. She tugged him into the hallway and looked him over very carefully. No obvious injuries.

"You're okay?"

He nodded.

"You sure?" she asked. She'd been so worried, and now that he was here, looking whole, she was having trouble processing and letting go of the stress of it all.

"Hey, you're shaking. Come here." He pulled her in close.

She pressed her face into the crook of his neck. "Just adrenaline letdown. Are you sure, Cam?"

"Piper," he breathed, resting his cheek against her hair.

Okay, so he was sure. "I know it's annoying to be asked if you're okay," she said, "but I can't help myself because . . . apparently I'm not okay. I'm not, and I don't know how to be."

He tightened his grip on her. "I know."

She inhaled him like he was a bucket of double-buttered popcorn. Only he was better than a bucket of double-buttered popcorn, even the jumbo size. "A part of me doesn't know how to deal with how well you know me," she admitted.

He cupped her jaw and lifted her face. "And the other part of you?"

"Loves it," she whispered.

He stilled for a beat and then cuddled her back into him. "Same."

After a wow kiss, during which she nearly climbed him like a jungle gym, she pulled back. "I need to go back in there, don't I?"

Gaze solemn, he nodded, and together they reentered the kitchen.

Gavin was eating out of a gallon ice cream container with a wooden spoon. Winnie had been pacing, but when she saw Piper, she slid down the cabinets and sat on the floor, bending her legs, putting her forehead to her knees.

Cam glanced at Piper, and then without giving away a single thought or clue as to what the actual hell was going on, he crouched at Winnie's side, balanced on the balls of his feet. "Tell her, Winnie. She deserves to know."

"I don't think I can do this," Winnie whispered, and although Piper had no idea what "this" was exactly, it almost seemed like Winnie was saying *everything*, which was heartbreaking.

As was the way that Cam wrapped an arm around her sister and she buried her face in his shoulder, taking strength from him.

Something Piper knew a little bit about.

"It's not fair to her," Cam murmured. "You need to tell her."

Piper agreed, even though she wasn't sure she was strong enough for another hit. But she managed to walk closer on wobbly legs.

Gavin silently offered her the ice cream.

She shook her head, eyes on Winnie and Cam. "Tell me."

"Wait," Gavin said. "Would you prefer a shot of vodka? Because probably, you don't want to do this without a sugar or alcohol rush. If not for you, then do it for me."

Piper watched as Cam kept his gaze on her sister until she nodded. Then he rose to his full height and turned to Piper. Reaching out, he squeezed her hand, but she pulled away. She didn't know why.

Okay, she did know why. Whatever the hell was coming, he knew about it.

And she didn't. "What is it, Winnie? What's happened? Just tell me."

Her sister sighed and lifted her head, eyes wet. "I . . . got something in the mail today. A check. It's from Rowan's life insurance policy, the one none of us knew he had. It's a hundred thousand dollars."

"Wow. Okay," she said, seriously confused. "Why did the check come here? That's probably just a post office delivery mistake, it happens all the time. You can give it to Emmitt."

Winnie shook her head, her eyes overflowing. "The check's written to me. I was his beneficiary. I didn't know he'd done that—" She pressed a hand to her mouth. "He must have done it when he found out I was pregnant."

Piper dropped to her knees beside Winnie. She was incredibly aware of Cam, who'd backed up to give them space but hadn't left the room. It felt like he was both angry and worried, and yet she somehow knew it wasn't directed at her. "That was incredibly generous of Rowan," she said. "But I'm not sure I understand—"

Winnie murmured something so softly that she missed it.

Piper glanced at Gavin, her usual Winnie translator, but he was avoiding her gaze, so she turned back to Winnie. "I'm sorry, honey. I couldn't hear you. What does you being pregnant have to do with Rowan having you down as his beneficiary?"

Winnie lifted her head and pressed both hands to her belly as more tears spilled out of her eyes and ran unchecked down her cheeks.

"Oh," Piper breathed, sitting back on her heels, wondering how the hell she'd missed this. "He's the baby's daddy."

Winnie nodded and it all fell into place. Winnie hiding the pregnancy from her for as long as she could because her sister knew how she'd felt about Rowan not being responsible. Emmitt infusing himself into Winnie's life, teaching her how to do things, being so kind and welcoming—he was going to be a grandpa. Cam being so patient with her because . . . because this baby would be his niece or nephew. And he'd never told her. That hurt. As did the way her mind was spinning.

Gavin didn't meet her gaze.

"You knew," she said. She then turned to Cam, who absolutely met her gaze. In fact, he'd never stopped looking at her. "And you," she said softly, because her throat was tight and on fire. "You knew too."

The answer was in his expression, and the tight, grim set to his mouth.

She nodded, trying to absorb the blows. "I see," she said to the room, even though she didn't. *Everyone* had known about the pregnancy before her. *Everyone* had known about Gavin's rehab before her. And it turned out that *everyone* had also known the baby daddy. They'd all known everything.

And she'd known nothing. She'd been kept out of the loop on purpose by her siblings, whom she'd put her life on hold for. And also by the man she tried not to fall in love with—and failed, by the way. He'd known more about her family than she had.

And hadn't said a word to her. In fact, he'd told her he'd come to help his dad. On the heels of all this, some other uneasy realizations were coming hard and fast. One, Cam was right. He wasn't the no-strings fling she'd set out to have, the no-strings fling she'd been up front about wanting.

Two, and even worse, he'd lied to her, or at least omitted the part about him knowing things about her family that she hadn't. Important, life-altering things.

Which led to a third, extremely hard-to-process realization. The people in her life rarely put importance on her needs. Her parents. Her siblings . . . Now Cam as well, reminding her that once again, she was not important enough to come first, and never had been.

"Piper?" Winnie asked tearfully. "Are you mad at me?"

"No." Okay, maybe a little. "But I'm hurt about the lack of trust and faith in me. But . . ." She rose to her feet, grabbed a tissue box off the counter, and handed it to her sister. "Your baby, your decisions."

"It wasn't about trusting you or having faith in you. It was more about my inability to actually believe I'd ever find my way in life." Winnie blew her nose. "I'm getting there, but . . . there's more."

Piper closed her eyes for a beat. *"Twins?"*

"No." Winnie looked horrified at that. "God, I hope not. But . . ." She bit her lower lip. "Well, the insurance payout was unexpected, but I've decided to put the whole thing into a trust for the baby's education. And in a separate decision, Gavin and I want to buy you out of your third of the property. You can go to school, and we'll stay and start up the B and B."

Piper stared at her. And then Gavin. "What?"

"You wanted to sell so you could go to school, right? After all, you've sacrificed for us to do that very thing, including putting off your schooling for years. So it's important to us that we give you the same chance. We got a property appraisal and a loan." He pulled something from his pocket.

A bank statement of the family account, with a balance bigger than she'd ever seen or dreamed of, thanks to a large deposit dated the day before.

"I know you really wanted to sell," Gavin said while she stared at it. "That this place is too much for you. But you're not alone in it anymore. The three of us are a team now. You made this happen, turned us into functioning adults, and we'll never forget all you've done for us. But this time, *we've* got *you*."

"But a loan," she heard herself say. "The costs, the interest—"

"Manageable," he said. "And worth every penny. The money's yours, Piper."

She stared down at the statement, at her golden ticket to go. "But what are the terms and conditions? Are you sure you got a good deal?"

"Yes," Winnie said. "Because Cam gave us the loan."

Piper felt herself freeze for a single heartbeat, then only her head moved, like she was in the movie *Carrie,* turning to look at Cam. "What?"

"He got his attorney and accountant to look over our whole business plan," Gavin said. "He said it looks solid. Plus, Cam wanted to invest in the B and B, for Rowan. He said Rowan would've wanted that."

Piper hadn't taken her gaze off Cam. He was watching her too, and giving nothing away while he was at it. Absolutely zero. And her heart died a little bit.

"I'm sorry I didn't tell you about Rowan sooner," Winnie said softly.

"Are you?" Piper asked. "Because I think that was a conscious choice, and now I have to live with knowing you didn't trust me enough or want me to know."

"It wasn't like that," Winnie said.

"What was it like?"

Gavin shifted uneasily. "Piper," he said with censure, and she whirled on him.

"Don't," she said tightly. "Don't you dare." She turned back to Winnie. "I'd like an answer."

Winnie looked well and pissed now. Guess they all were, as the room was humming with tension and the weight of so many things left unsaid.

"Honestly?" Winnie asked.

"Sure," Piper said. "Let's try honesty for once."

Winnie winced, but answered. "I didn't want to hear about my bad choices."

Yet another hit. "You really think that I'd do that to you right now?"

"No," Gavin said, showing his middle-child status by interfering and playing peacemaker. "She just means that sometimes you get a little . . . bossy."

Piper pointed at him. "I said *don't*." She pointed at *all* of them. "Each of you kept things from me, purposely."

Cam said her name softly and took a step toward her, and she glared at him. "Are you kidding me? You told me you had my back. You told me I could trust you. You made me feel like we were partners. And then you lied. You lied and you hid stuff. And you . . . *lied*! You all lied to me, and probably laughed about it behind my back!"

"No. Never," Cam said quietly. "And I get and understand why you're upset, but—"

"No buts." She shook her head. "I'm over all of this."

"You're missing the bigger picture here."

"Yeah, I missed that you're an asshole. All of you are."

"Well, that escalated quickly," Winnie murmured to Gavin.

"It is our family motto." Gavin looked at Piper. "Let us tell you everything, okay?"

"No. I don't care. You've surpassed the statute of limitations and I'm done."

"Piper," Cam said, his voice quiet and calm, although interestingly enough, his eyes weren't either. "Before you go to battle, please at least hear everyone out. Because if you speak now without knowing everything, you might say something you shouldn't. I know far more about this than I want to. The last thing I said to Rowan was pretty much 'fuck you,' and now he's gone and I can't take it back. He died with those words in his ears."

Piper understood that, but she couldn't function with the anger and betrayal flowing through her veins. "There's not going to be a battle. I'm done."

He looked at her for a beat, gave a single nod and left through the front door.

Okay, so he was done too, she supposed, and it felt like her heart cracked in half. Letting out a breath, she eyed her siblings, realizing Cam had been right about one thing. "I need a time-out before we do this."

Winnie pushed to her feet. "I know I should've told you everything, but I got scared. And I felt like shit because I knew you'd think that my problems were about to become your problems, like always. And I didn't want that. Not this time. Not after all you've done for me."

"For *us*," Gavin corrected. "Piper, I know we fucked this all up, but I swear, our intentions were the opposite. Please tell me you can get to the place where you believe that."

Piper realized she was holding her breath, and slowly let it out. "I'm going to take my time-out now."

They looked at each other and then nodded and walked away, leaving her alone.

Huh. That was one of the first times they'd ever done something she'd asked without having to nag. Okay, then. She wasn't sure what to do with herself and her newfound knowledge that everyone she knew and loved had betrayed her. She turned and stared out the window at the lake, but found no peace. She knew she needed to talk to Cam. She was still furious, but . . . God. That look in his eyes when he'd talked about Rowan, and it being too late to take back the things he'd said.

She wasn't the only one hurting, and dammit, that was hard to ignore. She went outside to look for him, but he was gone, and so was the boat.

Clearly she hadn't been the only one in need of a time-out.

Hoping she'd find him at the tire swing, she headed that way on foot. She wasn't a runner. She hated running. It was actually her personal idea of hell, but her feet seemed to forget that, because she was suddenly sprinting down to the lake and moving along the path around it at a pace that had her heart bursting out of her chest.

Or maybe that was just the emotions of the day. But when she got to the tire swing, there was no Cam.

So she kept going. After what was probably only half a mile, she got a kink in her side that hurt like hell and slowed her to a walk, but she still didn't stop. She had no idea how long it took her, but she didn't really start thinking again until she got to the hidden cove where she and Cam had moored that day, the one that seemed so long ago now.

She went to the rocky shore, where she sat, with her back to the stones, knees bent, staring out at the water.

It was cloudy. Fitting. The sky matched her mood, dark and turbulent.

With a sigh, she pulled the journal from her pocket and began to write down her feelings. Gavin had kept his secret because he'd wanted to wait until the right moment to tell her. Fine. Winnie had kept her secret/secrets because . . . well, because she was Winnie and she marched to her own beat, no drummer. Piper understood both of them, she got them, she accepted them. She also loved them deeply, which was the only reason they could hurt her at all. Her siblings' needs had changed. They needed comfort and home, and she'd not understood that—which was on her. She stopped writing. Because there was no list for this, for a way to deal with it.

She wasn't in control. Not even a little bit.

Because then there was Cam. She'd thought, mistakenly of course, that he was . . . well, *hers*. Her own little safe haven from the storm that was her life. Okay, yes, when he'd asked for more she'd freaked out a little bit. Or a lot. That was her bad. She'd needed time.

But it was mortifying to know that while she was angsting over whether she could give him all of her including the good, the bad, and the ugly . . . he'd already known it all, and more. He'd known what she hadn't.

And he'd left her in the dark.

Everyone had known everything and she, the oldest, the only one who'd ever tried to keep them all together, hadn't known a thing.

Her phone buzzed. She intended to let it go to voice mail, but it was Jenna. The one person who'd have her back in all this. "Hey."

"Hey yourself," Jenna said. "I'm at the house and your siblings are looking like someone killed the cat. Which isn't true, because the she-devil is yelling at me for food. Where are you?"

"Taking a time-out."

"Why? What's going on?"

Piper told her everything, including the fact that she felt betrayed by everyone going behind her back.

"Okay, so let me get this straight," Jenna said. "In the end,

Gavin and Winnie managed to figure out how to get you the money to go back to school and still keep the property."

"Without my input or knowledge, even though I'm one-third owner of this property."

"Okay, they should have told you, but they did a great thing, Piper. Don't lose perspective on that."

"Cam helped."

"Wow, what a bastard."

Piper sighed. "You're not taking this seriously."

"Piper, they worked together to give you everything you wanted. What's so wrong about that? Unless . . ."

"Unless what?"

"Unless you're afraid."

Piper squeezed her eyes shut tight. "I've gotta go."

"Yes, I imagine you do. It's probably annoying hearing that you're sabotaging your own happiness to prove your deepest fears are true—that no one could possibly love you for you. Which of course is ridiculous since we're all lining up to love you. You can hang up on me now."

So that's what she did.

CHAPTER 28

"You know exactly who you are."

Piper finally left the lake, but she didn't go home. She went to town and straight to the Whiskey River, because sometimes a girl needed a damn drink.

Boomer took one look at her face and made her a Shirley Temple.

Any other day she would've laughed, but this time, now, she was horrified to find her eyes fill with tears.

"Oh, shit." Boomer brought out a box of tissues from beneath the bar and set it in front of her. "Sucky day, huh?"

"I don't want to talk."

"Works for me." He brought her a bowl of peanuts and pretzels.

She stuffed her face for a few minutes and sighed. "Men suck."

"No arguments there. It's a genetic defect, I'm pretty sure. Want me to beat him up for you?"

"No."

"Good, because honestly, I don't think I could. He's pretty badass. Rumor is that on his last mission, his unit took out an entire terrorist cell hiding in the waters off South America, where they were planning attacks on our allies."

She downed her drink. Whether that was accurate or not, she knew the truth was probably even more heroic. "I've got this," she said.

"Do you?" Boomer asked doubtfully.

"Hey, as my bartender, you're supposed to bolster my confidence."

"Sorry. You're right. You've got this."

Not so sure, she left the bar and went to Emmitt's. The boat was back, but no Cam in sight. Emmitt wasn't home either.

So she'd do what she knew Cam would do for her. She waited. After all, she had to learn to face her fears instead of burying them. So she walked back down to the marina and had a little stare down with the water.

Fear number one.

"I'm not afraid of you," she said out loud, lying through her teeth, of course. "But I'll give you this. The sun shining on your pretty white caps is a nice touch." Never one to do things half-assed, she made her feet take her to the end of the longest dock. Heart pounding, she stood there for a long moment watching the way the sun's rays shimmered and danced across the water.

Then, very carefully, so as not to accidentally make a nightmare come true and fall into the water and drown, she sat. And then pulled out her journal and flipped through some of her entries. She had a list of books to read. Her sleep log. A school tracker filled with the classes she needed to take. Her calendar complete with stickers. Her bad-habit tracker . . . Damn. She really was a nut. She paged through to her secret *secret* bucket list and had to shake her head at herself. Maybe she hadn't aimed high enough. She made another entry. Fear number two.

Fall in love.

She stared at the words, having to admit she should probably just go ahead and check that one off right now because it'd already happened. She'd just been too stubborn to realize it. She'd been afraid of commitment in the past because in her mind, committing to someone meant another person whose life would take precedence over hers.

But she wasn't afraid of that with Cam. He'd never try to make her into something she wasn't or put himself before her.

Life as she knew it would only get better.

"Why is this so hard?" she whispered angrily to herself, and pressed her forehead to her knees.

"It doesn't have to be," said an unbearably familiar voice from behind her.

Cam.

She squeezed her eyes shut. He'd found her. Of course he'd found her. Because unlike her, he was in control of himself and always did what needed to be done, hard or easy, big or small.

Damn, she admired that.

He came to a stop beside her, and she made the mistake of looking up at him. His hair was growing out a bit from his military cut and was a windblown mess of perfection. He hadn't shaved in a few days and the scruff and dark sunglasses he favored only added to his bad-boy appeal.

"I'm an asshole?" he asked, reminding her of exactly where they'd left off.

She grimaced and opened her mouth, but he put a hand on her shoulder, gentle but firm.

"Let me rephrase. I *am* an asshole. And I owe you an apology." Their arms and legs brushed as he settled in beside her, calm and relaxed in a way that was beyond her ability, ever. "First," he said, "I need you to know that I wanted to tell you about my brother. I did. But I let the guilt cloud my judgment." He closed his eyes. "Rowan told me he didn't want his kid growing up like we did. He wanted them to have two parents in their life that loved each other. 'Winnie and I are going to make it work,' he told me. And"—Cam met her gaze—"I didn't believe him. I couldn't buy into the notion of love, because it'd never worked for me. But Rowan said it only has to work the one time. A twenty-year-old schooled me."

She felt her heart go a little squishy.

"Rowan wanted me to fill the role for his baby that he knew he wouldn't be able to." He shook his head. "And even then, I wasn't having it. He was bleeding out, dying, and I told him to stop saying goddamn good-bye to me, that he was going to make it, that he'd live to drive me out of my mind another day."

Piper smiled through unshed tears. "And what did he say to that?"

Cam's mouth curved in a grief-filled smile. "For the first time in our lives, he got royally pissed off at me. He grabbed me by my shirt with his bloody fists and shook me. He yelled, 'I need you to listen to me, for once!'"

"Did you?"

"Yeah. I finally stopped reacting instead of listening." He closed his eyes. "And you know the rest."

She tried to hold on to her anger. But in spite of her best efforts, some of it was fading. Actually, a lot of it. "So that's why it's so important to you to listen. It's one of your best qualities."

His smile was wry. "But see, I don't always listen. I didn't listen to you, or my heart. I've got a long history of letting those I care about down. My mom, Rowan, you."

Dammit, there went some more of her bad temper. "No," she said. "Promises mean something to you. I get that. It's . . . noble. You were trying to help Winnie and you'd given her your word. I do that on the job, I keep people's medical secrets, so my sister asking you not to tell me . . . well, I have to accept and understand that. It *was* her story to tell and she thought I'd overreact or tell her what to do rather than listen. Same with Gavin. That's between me and them, and no matter what I might want, I can't control them."

He gave her a small smile. "You letting me off the hook, Piper?"

"No." She paused and shook her head. "Well, maybe just a little. I really do know you were trying to help. Logically. But . . . emotionally? I'm still hurt and angry at being left out."

"Understood."

She nodded, relieved to have gotten that out. He let a companionable silence fill the space between them, along with the small waves slapping rhythmically against the dock. She could hear the wind and a bird squawking at something. The buzz of insects. Her own thoughts . . .

"Everything feels so complicated," she whispered.

"It doesn't have to be."

She looked at him.

"No one meant to hurt anyone," he said. "Least of all me. The loan . . . I came here to Wildstone intending to check on Winnie, you know that now. What you don't know is that I wasn't in a great place. I was . . . needing a connection. Something to ground me, to make me feel. I met you on my second night here, and I knew right then at the bar, Piper. I knew I'd found the connection I was looking for. I wanted to tell you everything, but Winnie needed to do it, in her own time. It was before . . . us." He paused and met her gaze. "But then I started to fall for you, and there I was, holding back from you while asking you not to hold back from me. That's what I'm most sorry about. With the loan, I was just trying to help, trying to give you something you needed. You needed to be free to go. Now you are. You can go find the next good-time guy."

She winced. "You're not just that to me," she said softly. "And I'm sorry I let you think that. You're more. You're . . ."

"*Too* much more?" he asked wryly.

No, you're everything, she wanted to say, but just shook her head.

"Piper, you're one of the strongest people I know. You've had to be. But that's the thing. Now you *don't*. You can let go of everyone else's problems for once, and just live your own life."

"But what if I don't know who I am if I'm not the mom, the sister, the caretaker . . ."

"You know exactly who you are, Piper. Yes, you're those things, but you're also so much more. You're intelligent, resourceful, fiercely independent. You're also beautiful, but that's actually the least interesting thing about you." He looked amused when she blinked. "You make me feel things I didn't think I could feel."

A little overwhelmed and maybe also embarrassed at the compliments, she squirmed. "Yeah, well, aroused doesn't count."

He flashed a quick grin that affected her pulse. "Yes, it does. But it's more than that. You make me—"

"Crazy?"

"I wasn't going to list that first," he said diplomatically.

"Haha." It took her a minute to find the right words. "I'm not the kind of person who believes people are inherently good. I don't trust easily. Or at all. But . . . I trusted you, Cam."

He grimaced. "I know. I—"

She put her fingers to his mouth. "So yeah, when you lied to me, I got angry. But I was angry at myself for not knowing. I should have. I should have seen all of it, but I was too busy and distracted, and didn't take the time for my own brother and sister. So, see, I let myself down. And I want you to know, I still trust you. If anything, I've learned that life's about the little things." She paused, met his gaze. "Like keeping promises."

"Like keeping promises," he agreed, with a serious look on his face as he lightly touched her. "You're too hard on yourself."

Maybe. Okay, yes. She was. She thought about her work, and all she'd seen. How sometimes the simplest choices could have such far-reaching impacts. Like her parents sending their kids to safety, planning to join them soon, but instead being killed before they could. Or someone driving drunk because he lived right around the corner, but in that two-minute drive he hit a car and killed one of two brothers. "Life's too short," she murmured out loud.

"Yes."

She stared at the water and not at Cam. Because looking directly at Cam was oftentimes like looking at a whole pan of buttery soft double-chocolate brownies. Oh so good, and . . . oh so bad for her. "Which is why I've decided to give up my crutch." She lifted her journal.

"Okay. How?"

She bit her lower lip because if he laughed at her, she might have to hurt him.

But his gaze was sympathetic. "You could start slow. Maybe leave it at home once in a while. Or start over and keep journaling without making it a road map of your life that you *have* to live by."

"Or I could go cold turkey and literally toss it." She eyed the lake.

He arched a brow, and she realized she was clutching it to her chest. But the thought of being free of the incessant list-making had her feeling good about her next choice. "I'm serious about this." She slapped the journal against his chest. "But you're going to have to do it."

"Piper—"

"Do it!"

He tossed the journal into the lake. There was a splash, and then it sank beneath the surface of the glassy water, vanishing from view. Piper leapt to her feet. "Oh my God!" She kicked off her shoes. "I can't believe you actually did it!"

"You said—"

That was the last thing she heard because she jumped into the lake, and it wasn't until her body got sucked into the cold water that she remembered.

She hated the water.

CHAPTER 29

Her inner office-supply ho quivered.

Piper spent a horrifyingly long few seconds trying to remember how to swim. But then there was a splash next to her, and suddenly she was being held against another body.

"Okay," Cam said. "I'm moving crazy up to the top of the list. Because what the actual fuck, Piper."

"I wasn't quite ready to let go!"

With a sigh, he swam her to the dock ladder and gave her a not-so-gentle shove up. She climbed to the dock and flopped onto her back, staring up at the sky before realizing he hadn't come up after her. Sitting up, she peered over the side.

He was gone.

Like . . . *gone*. There was no sign of him as far as the eye could see. "Cam!" she yelled.

Nothing.

Oh, shit. She'd killed him. Fear clutched deep in her gut. He was drowning. Dear God, he was going to die and it was all her fault. She got to her feet and was just about to jump back in when he surfaced. He tossed his hair from his eyes with a single shake of his head and lifted a hand out of the water.

He had her journal.

He tossed it at her feet as he effortlessly pulled himself up onto the dock and flopped down at her side.

"Are you insane?" she demanded.

He was drenched, but the look he slid her was one hundred percent dry. "I believe the words you're looking for are *thank you.*"

"Oh my God." She thought he must be furious at her, but when she took a closer look, he was laughing.

"Hey," she said. "It's not funny. I thought I killed you."

"I'm like a cat, I've got a few lives left." He rose to his feet, vanished into the marina storage locker, and came back with two wool blankets. Wrapping one around her, he encouraged her to sit back down.

"I can't believe I made the mistake of telling you to toss the journal into the lake."

He wrapped the other blanket around himself and sat next to her. "I've made more than a few mistakes of my own."

She stopped in the middle of trying to dry off the journal with her blanket and looked over at him in surprise. "You have?"

He let out a mirthless laugh. "Hell, yes. Many. I failed Rowan, and in some ways, my dad too. Finding out he needed me was just another nail in the coffin. Or so I thought. All of it felt like a noose around my neck at first. But I found a relationship with my dad that I didn't know I needed. And then there's Gavin and Winnie, who are family now too. Gavin, who lives unapologetically as he is, owning his mistakes and trying to make right what he can. I admire the hell out of that, Piper. And Winnie . . ." He shook his head with a small smile. "Twenty years old and made of one hundred percent bravado and sarcasm. She's going to be one hell of a mom when she finds her sea legs, but she won't be in it alone. She'll have all of us." He drew a breath. "I've fallen for all of them. And there's something else I fell for too. Someone." He looked at her. "You."

She sucked in a breath. "What?"

"I love you, Piper."

She shook her head. "No. You can't."

He gave a small quirk of his lips. "I know you like to control . . . everything. But not even you can tell me how or when or what to feel."

"But . . ." Boggled, she shook her head. "Why?"

"Why do I love you? Easy. Your energy fuels my soul."

She blinked. "My bad attitude, you mean? That fuels your soul?"

He smiled. "Your everything. You're the calm in the storm."

She stared at him. "Now I know you've lost it."

"I mean every word. I love how you treat people. My dad, for instance. And Sweet Cheeks."

"She's not a people. She's the anti-Christ."

"You know what I mean. You give respect and dignity, even when it's not always deserved. I love how you can always make me laugh, especially when I need it most. I love how you kiss me. I love how you just gathered me in and added me to your core unit." He shook his head. "That means a lot. Actually, it means everything to me."

There was no air. Why was there no air? "I got into U of C," she said inanely.

He smiled. "Good. Congratulations. They're lucky to have you."

"Cam . . ." She closed her eyes because he was so amazing and gracious and kind. And supportive. She didn't even know how to tell him how much that meant to her. "I can't be the girl who changes her plans for the guy," she whispered.

"I know." His hand covered hers. "But I can be the guy who changes his plans for a girl."

Her eyes flew open. "What?"

"I could move to Colorado. With you."

"But the DEA . . ."

"I'll figure it out, but I'm not living for my job."

"But you'd have to move."

"Moving around has always been all I know," he said.

"But you wanted to stop having to do that, you wanted a home base."

"You're my home base."

She stared at him. He made it sound so simple. "You can't do that for me."

"Why not?"

"Why not?" she repeated, nowhere near calm. "Because you need to be here with your dad and Winnie and the baby. I'm not going to ask you to choose." Her breath caught on the word, because in her experience, people didn't choose her, not for their endgame.

"Piper." He took both of her chilled hands in his warm ones now. "I want this to work. I'm willing to make this work, no matter where we live. We're the core, and yeah, right now it needs to be about you, and that's okay."

"But what about you?"

He gave her a smile. "I'll get my turn. Just tell me what you're thinking."

She was mostly thinking that Jenna had been right. Emmitt had been right. Her siblings too. They all knew that life was where you made room for it, and so was love and acceptance. She blew out a breath. "I was fine before you, you know. Just fine."

His smile was unapologetic. "I wasn't."

She brought their joined hands up to her chest and pressed, then lifted her head. "Okay, yeah. Fine. Neither was I."

His smile spread and she shook her head at him. "I actually thought I had all the answers, but I didn't have any. Turns out you had them all."

"If you really believe that," he said on a dry laugh, "you don't know me at all."

But that was the thing—she did know him. Better than she'd ever known anyone. "You've got this way of drawing people in," she said. "And inspiring trust. And love."

He arched a sardonic brow. "Not in *everyone*."

"You drew me in," she admitted. "I trust you." She hesitated. "I know losing Rowan was the hardest thing."

"Yes. So would be losing you."

Heart. Melted. She came up on her knees and put her hands on his shoulders. "I love you too, Cam. I have for a while. I was just scared."

"And you're not now?"

"Terrified. Hold me."

He laughed and pulled her right into his lap. He was warm and his arms felt just right holding her close, like she was everything to him. Cupping his face, she stared into his eyes, feeling all the feels, but unsure how to let them out after a lifetime of holding them in. The man had jumped into the lake to save her *and* her journal. That had to be some kind of a record.

"It's okay, Piper," he said quietly, pushing the wet hair from her face. "Whatever you need to make this work. *Whatever* you want. Just say the word."

He was putting her dreams first and no one had ever done that. He wasn't going to vanish on her. He would come with her. Or even stay here and hold everything together while she was gone, if that's what she wanted. "Word," she whispered, smiling when he looked at her in surprise.

"Yeah?" he asked.

"Yeah. All I need to make this work is my family, which includes you and your dad. But mostly what I need is you. And I need to be here with all of you, in Wildstone."

He was already shaking his head. "No. No way. You're not giving up your dream for—"

"I'm not. I won't. While you were gone, I also applied here at Cal Poly, which I didn't do in the first place because I thought I wanted to leave. I wanted adventure, but *this* is my adventure. *You're* my adventure, Cam."

His gaze searched hers. "You sure?"

She tried to shift even closer, but she was already on top of him. Understanding, he tugged off her blanket and opened his for her, where she made herself at home up against his chest, closing her eyes when his arms came back around her. Winding a hand through her still drenched and tangled hair, he brought her face close to his so he could kiss her, his mouth a hot contrast to hers. They were still kissing, and she was no longer cold, when she heard footsteps on the dock behind them. She looked up and found Emmitt, Gavin, and Winnie staring at them.

"Told you," Winnie said. "They're making up for lost time."

Piper yanked her hands off Cam.

Cam did not yank his hands off Piper. He kept them on her. His gaze too. "What's up?" he asked their audience.

"We could ask you the same thing," Emmitt said. "Or question your sanity, going for a swim in February."

"Love makes you do stupid things," Gavin said sagely.

Winnie gasped, her head swiveling between Cam and Piper. "*Love?*"

"Love," Cam said firmly.

Emmitt grinned.

Gavin grinned.

The old Piper would have rolled her eyes and denied it, and then said something snarky to chase everyone off. The new Piper could only nod with a dopey smile on her face, one that made Cam laugh.

Winnie smiled, but it wavered. "Piper, I'm sorry. I'm *so* sorry. I'd like to blame the Bean, but I'm going to be a mom, so I figure I should probably at least try to grow up. I just want you to know, you're important to me. So important. I love you so much, and I'm sorry I didn't tell you everything sooner. That's not on you, not even a little bit. It's all on me."

Gavin nodded. "What she said. We are assholes, and we're going to do better. You deserve that, and so much more."

Winnie nodded. "And the Bean loves you too. She can't wait to meet her aunt."

"She?" Piper asked softly, throat tight. "It's going to be a she?"

Winnie's eyes filled. "I found out today. She's a she."

"Oh my God," Piper said, and hopped up to hug her.

Winnie squealed with shock when Piper's wet clothes clung to her, but like only a sister would do, Piper tightened her grip. Smiling at the second squeal, she said, "I've got to say some stuff now."

"Uh-oh," both siblings said at the same time.

Piper pulled back to look at them. "What you two did for me, working to get the money to buy me out, that was"—she searched for the right words—"incredible. I'd asked the two of you to grow up, and when I wasn't looking, you both did exactly that."

"So you're not mad that we want to stay and run the B and B?" Winnie asked.

"No, because you're only doing what I wanted for you all along. To have lives that fulfill you. And I want you to know that I'm proud of both of you. Really proud. Winnie, you've made the best of a rough situation, and with those new handywoman skills, you're a serious asset to the property. And, Gavin . . . your charisma and charm make people adore you—you'll be amazing as the face of the B and B. I'm happy we're not selling." She drew a deep breath. "And while I'm confessing, there's more. I thought I had to leave to find that fulfillment for me. But I was wrong. Having you guys back here, being together as a family

as grown-ups, it's"—she shook her head, at a loss for words—
"everything. I . . . want to stay."

Gavin frowned, looking concerned. "But school—"

"I applied to SLO," she said. "It's only thirty minutes from
here. I'll commute."

"Okay, but what does this mean for us?" Winnie asked,
hands on her belly, looking uncertain.

Gavin took Winnie's hand in his. "I think it means we're going to stay together."

Piper nodded. "I love both of you soul-sucking idiots. More
than anything."

"Me too," Winnie said, and flung herself back into Piper's
arms. "So . . . we're okay? Like, we're all finally okay at the same
time?"

Piper's heart squeezed hard as she looked first into Winnie's
hopeful face, and then at Gavin, who looked relaxed and okay
for the first time since . . . well, ever. And then at the smiling
Emmitt. And finally into Cam's eyes. "Yes," she said, holding
Cam's gaze over Winnie's head. "We're all okay."

NOT AN HOUR later, Cam got a notice he was being deployed.
Unusual, he told her, so close to having just gotten back, but not
unheard of. And this time he'd be gone a month, unless his unit
was released early.

During the weeks he was gone, Piper kept herself busy, working on keeping Winnie sane and the baby she was growing
safe, and watching Gavin come into his own right in front of
her eyes. And when they opened the Manning B&B three weeks
after Cam had left, their guests raved about their stay.

Another week went by, and though it was now nearly April and officially spring, they got a hell of a winter storm. Again, there was flooding and the town was a mess. So was the lake.

She and Gavin and some hired help were up to their knees in mud working with Emmitt at the marina. She was wearing one of Cam's T-shirts, pathetically hugging the neckline up over her nose every few minutes to catch his lingering scent.

"I swear, nothing smells better than the person you love," she said.

"Have you ever walked by a Cinnabon?" Winnie asked.

Piper sighed, but suddenly she felt a change in her force field. Whirling from where she was, facing the lake, she stared up at the hill as a single figure worked his way down, in jeans and a sweatshirt, a duffel bag on his shoulder, moving easily and efficiently through the mud like nothing could stop him.

She stilled, but her heart didn't. He wore the usual dark sunglasses, but she could still see the fatigue all over him. Tousled hair, longer than she was used to seeing on him. At least a week's worth of beard on his jaw. His expression fierce and intense, like he was still on a mission.

"Cam," she whispered. She tried to look half as graceful as he while moving toward him, but instead she probably looked like an elephant fighting its way through a lake made of peanut butter.

He closed the distance between them faster than she took a few steps. Dropping the shovel she'd been holding, she launched herself at him. His arms caught her and lifted her off her feet. She was already wrapping herself around him when he murmured her name in a reverent rumble.

"You're home," she murmured, pressing her jaw to his un-shaved, rough one.

"Yeah." He buried his face in her hair, tightening his grip on her. "Missed you, Piper. Missed you so fucking much." Angling his head, he sought her mouth with his.

There was a whole lot in that kiss. Love, affection, relief, hunger—and she'd never been so glad to see anyone in her life. Pulling back, she looked him over for obvious injuries and thankfully didn't see any. "I made you all dirty."

In spite of his clear exhaustion, he gave her a wolf grin and leaned in, for her ears only. "I'll be returning the favor as soon as I get you alone."

"Hey," Gavin called. "You kids going to help, or are you go-ing to make out all day?"

Winnie, also there "supervising" the cleanup, patted her now rounded belly. "The Spicy Bean says get your asses to work!"

Piper very reluctantly started to pull free, but Cam tightened his grip, brushed a kiss to her temple, and then put his mouth to her ear. "Just remember, you've got a date later."

THE NEXT MORNING, Piper woke up slowly, a smile on her face. She was alone in the bed, no doubt because Cam was off swimming or rowing, or something equally nutty. She knew he'd come back eventually, and knowing him and his endless source of energy, he'd talk her into some additional cardio right in this bed.

Not that he'd have to do much to convince her. Smiling at the thought, she looked at the time and found something propped up against the clock.

A beautiful brand-new leather journal, along with a stack of stickers and three different packs of pens and a bunch of pencils.

Her inner office-supply ho quivered and she fell in love all over again.

"I hope the look on your face means you think I'm so amazing that you're going to make breakfast." Cam stood in the doorway in running gear, looking damp with exertion and smiling like he'd had fun—*freak*.

As for the breakfast comment, he was teasing, and they both knew it. If they were eating with the whole gang, Gavin did most of the cooking. If it was just herself and Cam, well, he took up the slack there because he honestly enjoyed it. The only part she enjoyed was the eating.

"Sure," she said, enjoying the view. "I'll do the cooking." She gave him a "come here" crook of her finger as she sat up, letting the sheet fall away from her.

Cam's gaze heated but he didn't move. "Babe, I'm all sweaty."

"Isn't that the point of exercise?"

He laughed. "Yes, but you hate both exercise and sweating."

"Not all kinds." She loved the way his voice sounded when he was at ease. A little lower, a little warmer, a lot sexier. Grabbing him by the front of his shirt, she tugged. He fell over her, but only because he let himself. As she'd learned, when Cam didn't want to budge, he didn't budge.

Except with her. He'd do anything for her, and she was never, ever going to get over the marvel of that. He'd changed since he'd come to Wildstone. In the beginning, he'd been grieving, guarded, and temporary. Very temporary.

And that had worked for her. But she no longer needed or

wanted that. Even when she was an unlovable mess, he looked at her in a way that stole her breath every time.

He was her person.

He hadn't stopped missing Rowan and he never would, but he didn't let it hold him back, and in turn she'd been able to do the same. When she was with him, she felt like she could do anything.

He braced his weight above her with one arm, touching her face with his free hand. "What are you thinking about?"

"That I didn't think anything could still surprise me, but you do. I can't wait to see what comes next."

He grinned. "It's going to be you, babe. You're going to come next."

She laughed and shook her head, but he dipped his to kiss her softly, the laughter gone. "You still surprise me too," he murmured, voice husky the way it got when he was particularly moved. "Every day you show me more about love and life than I thought possible. I don't know what comes next either, but I can't wait for it. I think the next sixty or seventy years should be enough time to see, don't you?"

Her breath caught. "Maybe eighty . . ."

"Yeah. I like the way you think."

EPILOGUE

Two years later

Piper and Winnie stood back from their creation and took a long look at their work.

"Man, we're good," Winnie said.

"We are," Piper agreed.

"Arf, arf, arf!" This came from Chance, the eight-week-old puppy Piper had rescued last week after a work call at the local SPCA. The manager had fallen and broken her leg.

Piper had fallen too. She'd fallen in love with the tiny little puppy in a crate at the front desk giving her the biggest, saddest eyes she'd ever seen. She'd gone back three days in a row just to hold the puppy, until finally the lady who'd broken her leg gently asked Piper if she'd ever considered a dog.

She hadn't until that very moment. She scooped up the puppy and kissed the top of his fuzzy head.

"Ma-ma-ma-ma-ma," garbled the adorable one-and-a-half-year-old in the baby carrier strapped to Winnie's chest.

"Aw," Piper said, bending in to kiss the top of her niece's fuzzy head as well. "And you're right, Ro. It's definitely time for a food break."

"Ma-ma-ma-ma-ma!" This was accompanied by wild arm waving and a smile.

Baby Rowanne, "Ro" for short, had come into the world much like her daddy had lived in it: wild and carefree. And she loved to talk. None of them could actually understand a word, but they all pretended they did.

"You heard that, right?" Piper said. "She's telling us it's lunchtime. In fact, she quite clearly said she's starving and that we are working too hard."

"Arf, arf!" Chance said, chiming in.

Winnie laughed. "You know what? I think you're both right."

Together they stepped back from the marina house to admire what they'd done. A year ago, Emmitt had asked Cam to become an equal partner in the marina, and to sweeten the pot, he'd offered his house to Cam and Piper.

He'd then up and married Margaret and moved in with her.

Gavin ran both the B&B and the marina, and had a few part-time workers for help when he needed it. Winnie was one of them. And when Cam wasn't at the DEA office or on a mission, he and Piper had been renovating the house. He'd been called out a month ago, and to try to fill the time, Piper had wanted to surprise him.

She and Winnie had finished the project he'd been working on before he'd left—painting the master bedroom. But he'd been gone long enough that she was starting to miss him unbearably.

They moved down the stairs and into the kitchen, stopping short at the sight of CJ in full cop gear holding Gavin pressed up against the refrigerator. He was either trying to interrogate Gavin's tonsils, or kissing him hello.

"Again?" Winnie asked.

"I think you mean *still*," Piper said.

"Ba-ba-ba-ba-ba," Ro said.

Winnie smiled down at her girl. "You said it, little mama." To the guys, she said, "Isn't the honeymoon over yet?"

"Nope," CJ said, and smiled into Gavin's dazed-looking eyes.

Gavin grinned dopily back at him. "Definitely nope."

"Come on," Winnie said. "You've been married for months. CJ, you promised to love and cherish and to stop hogging the GameStation. Gavin, you also promised to love and cherish, and to still grab CJ's ass, even when it gets old and wrinkly." She pointed to the proof—the pics taped to the fridge where Gavin had just been held against it.

There was a pic of Gavin and CJ beneath a rainbow altar being married by an Elvis in drag. And one of all of them grinning drunkenly and toasting gallon-sized champagne glasses toward the two grooms. And then another of both of those same two grooms jumping into the hotel pool in their matching tuxes.

But Piper's favorite was a shot someone had gotten of her and Cam slow dancing in a corner beneath a flashing disco ball, eyes only for each other. She was smiling, with a goofy look on her face. Right before, Cam had leaned in and asked her, "What do you think of us being next?"

She'd said, "Next for what?"

He'd just smiled at her, and she'd nearly swallowed her tongue. "Are you serious?"

Cam had dropped to one knee and produced a gorgeous diamond ring, and she'd gasped. "I've loved you for a long time," he'd said. "You make me smile, you make me feel like a superhero, like I can do anything. But the truth is, all I want to do is be with you. I want to sleep with you every night and wake up with you every morning for the rest of my life."

"Yes," Piper had whispered.

"Jeez, Piper, wait until he asks you," Winnie had said.

Cam, not taking his eyes off Piper, had smiled. "Will you—"

"Yes," Piper had said again, softly, past the huge lump of joy and excitement in her throat.

Winnie had shaken her head.

"What if he's asking if you'll do his laundry for the rest of his life?" Gavin had joked.

Cam had dropped his head and stared at his own knees for a beat. Probably second-guessing his desire to join her crazy family. Then he'd tried again. "Piper, will you marry me? And to be clear, that *doesn't* include doing my laundry."

She'd dropped to her knees and kissed him. "*Yes,*" she'd whispered against his mouth.

Remembering this now made her miss him all the more and she moved to the kitchen window, staring out at the lake for a little bit of happy.

Chance, sensing her sadness, whined and licked her chin.

"Thanks, baby." She hated these forced separations so much. She'd never let Cam know, not wanting to add any stress to his plate, but it was getting harder and harder to be apart. That was when she realized there was an odd silence in the kitchen behind her, and she turned around.

Cam was right there in front of her, and with a gasp of surprise, she threw herself at him. He caught her—and Chance—with ease, and then, without any words, their mouths found each other. His kiss was hard and desperate and hungry . . . everything she was feeling, and it said everything that needed to be said. Love. Longing. Desire. Affection. Everything . . .

When they surfaced for air, Cam looked down at the puppy giving him huge eyes. "Who's this?"

"Chance." She held her breath.

"He ours?"

"Yes," she said softly, hoping he'd be okay with that, that he'd understand she'd been lonely as hell and—

"Nice. He's cute." He nuzzled the puppy, looking heart-stoppingly sexy while doing it, then gently set him down. He then picked up Piper and plopped her on the counter, making himself at home between her legs. He was holding her so tight that she couldn't breathe, but hey, who needed to breathe?

They were alone. Well, relatively anyway, as Chance was sitting on one of Cam's feet.

"Never again," he murmured against Piper's lips.

"At least until they call you, right?" she quipped, trying to make light.

"No." His eyes were dark. Serious. "Never again." He pulled a very official envelope from his back pocket and set it on the counter. "I'm out. It's official. I'm a retired man, babe."

"Wow," she breathed. "So I've got you all to myself now?"

"Every inch."

She felt love and happiness fill her heart. "I've got plans for those inches. Lots of plans, Cam."

His smile went a little wicked as he picked her up again and, as she wrapped her legs around his hips, strode with her to their bedroom. He stopped short in the doorway at the fresh paint on the walls and the sheets covering all the furnishings.

"Um," she said. "Surprise."

Without skipping a beat, he took her straight into the bathroom and kicked the door shut. "The shower will do."

"Agreed."

"And then the hot tub."

She nodded eagerly.

"And then—"

She sank her teeth into his lower lip and gave a playful tug. "Let me save you some time, soldier," she whispered, and slid her fingers into his hair. "Anywhere. Anytime. For the rest of my life. I'm all yours."

He let out a breath and pressed his forehead to hers, his eyes soft and warm and full of more emotion than he usually showed. "And I'm yours, Piper. For the rest of our lives."

Sounded like the perfect plan.

Reading Group Guide

1. Piper has a very hard time asking for help. Is this something you have in common with her? Do you think men or women are more prone to not asking for help?

2. Piper loves keeping lists, even if she doesn't always cross everything off them. Do you find to-do lists and journals helpful or harmful? What are the benefits? What are the downsides?

3. Gavin struggles with drug addiction. Is there someone in your life who has dealt with this? How did it affect you?

4. What did you think of the way Piper and her family handled Gavin's situation? Would you have done anything differently?

5. Do you think Winnie was justified in lying to Piper about her pregnancy and dropping out of college? If not, how do you think she should have handled it?

6. Are there situations where you think lying is the right thing to do? How do you decide what those are?

7. Was Piper correct when she made the decision to sell the property without talking about it with her siblings?

8. How much of Cam's decision to help Winnie and Gavin was influenced by the death of his brother?

9. Was Cam right to keep Winnie's secrets? If you were Piper, would you have understood? ❧

You're My Honey Bun Muffins Recipe

In *Almost Just Friends* there's a lot of talk about comfort food. That's probably because comfort food has gotten my family through a lot over the years. It solves problems, eases the tension after family arguments, and brings people together in the kitchen, where good things always seem to happen even on a bad day.

You should know that for me and my family, comfort does not necessarily equal healthy. ☺ It means things like mac and cheese, cinnamon and sugar toast, and anything warm from the oven that includes butter.

In the story, our main character Piper doesn't really cook. She's actually downright bad at it. She leaves that for her brother, Gavin, who's aces at it. But she can pull it together when she needs to. For instance, she's really good at boiling hotdogs to chop up and put in Gavin's homemade mac and cheese.

But I like to think that she could bake the heck out of a good muffin. And I'd like to think that if she could, she'd bake these You're My Honey Bun Muffins (honey banana). It's a recipe I got from an old friend a long time ago and have made a gazillion times for those trying days when you just need something warm and comforting. Give them a try. And think of Piper when you do . . . ☺

Things You'll Need:

12-cup muffin pan
Nonstick cooking spray
½ cup (1 stick) butter
½ cup brown sugar
¼ cup honey
1 egg
3 or 4 ripe bananas
1 teaspoon vanilla extract
½ teaspoon almond extract or black walnut extract
1½ cups self-rising flour

Preheat the oven to 400°F. Prepare a 12-cup muffin pan by coating the cups with nonstick spray or lining them with cupcake holders.

Heat the butter in the microwave until softened. Combine the butter, brown sugar, honey, and egg in a mixing bowl. Peel the bananas and mash them on a plate with a fork. Add them to the bowl and stir until smooth. Add the vanilla and almond or walnut extract. Add the flour and stir until it forms a thick, smooth batter.

Spoon the batter into the muffin pan.

Bake at 400°F for 15 minutes. Remove the muffins from the pan immediately to cool.

Serve the muffins warm with milk and try not to eat all of them in one sitting. ∿

Coming soon . . .
An Excerpt from
The Summer Deal

Chapter 1

Brynn Turner had always wanted to be the girl who had her life together, but so far her talents hadn't gone in that direction—although not for lack of trying.

She mentally recapped the week she'd just endured and let out a stuttered breath. Okay, so her life skills needed some serious work, but as far as she was concerned, that was Future Brynn's problem. Present Brynn had other things on her mind.

Like surviving the rest of the day.

With that goal in mind, she kept her eyes on the road, and three point five long hours and two 7-Eleven hotdogs after leaving Long Beach in her rearview mirror, she pulled into Wildstone, a place that had reinvented itself many times over since it'd been a late 1800s wild, wild west town complete with wooden sidewalks, saloons, and haunted silver mines. It sat smack dab in the middle of California, sandwiched between the Pacific Ocean and the green rolling hills filled with wineries and ranches.

Parking in the driveway of her childhood home, Brynn took a minute. Once upon a time, Wildstone had been her favorite place on earth, but it'd been a decade since she'd lived here. She'd gone off to college and to conquer the world. Only one of those things had happened. She'd been back for visits, though even that had been a while. Six months, in fact. She'd stood in this very spot and had asked both of her well-meaning moms to butt out of her life, that she knew what she was doing.

Note to self: *she'd had no idea what she was doing.*

Clearly she still didn't.

With a sigh, she pulled down her visor and glanced into the mirror, hoping that a miracle had occurred and she'd see someone who had their shit together. Her hair was knotted on top of her head with the string tie from her hoodie because she'd lost her scrunchie. She was wearing her old glasses because she'd run out of contacts. Her face was pale and her eyes were puffy and red from a bad combo of not sleeping and crying. She wore yoga pants that hadn't seen a yoga class since . . . well, ever, and in spite of being nearly thirty, she had a big, fat zit on her chin.

In short, she looked about as far away from knowing what she was doing with her life as she was from solving world hunger.

Knowing her moms—sweet and loving and nosy as hell—were going to see right through her, she pawed through her purse for a miracle. She found some lip gloss that she applied, and then on second thought also dabbed on each cheek for some badly needed color. She also found two peanut M&Ms, and since she didn't believe in wasting food, she ate them. Hoping for more, she shook her purse, but nope, she was out of luck.

The theme of her life.

With a sigh, she once again met her own gaze in the mirror. "Okay, here's the drill. You're okay. You're good. You're happy to be home. You're absolutely *not* crawling back with your tail between your legs to admit to your moms that they were right about Dickhead."

Swallowing hard, she got out of her hunk-o-junk and grabbed her duffle bag and purse. She'd barely made it to the porch before the front door was flung open and there stood her moms in the doorway, some deep maternal instinct having let them know their sole offspring was within smothering distance.

Both in their mid-fifties, their similarities stopped there. Olive was pragmatic, stoic, and God help the person who tried to get anything by her. She was perfectly coifed as always, hair up, her ▶

pants and blazer fitted, giving her a look of someone who'd just walked out of a Wall Street meeting. In sharp comparison, Raina's sundress was loose and flowery and flowing, and she wore beads around her neck and wrists that made her jingle pleasantly whenever she moved. She was soft and loving, and quite possibly the kindest soul on earth. And while Olive was economical with her movements, Raina was in constant motion.

Opposites attract . . .

But actually, her moms did have something in common beyond their age—their warm, loving smiles, both directed at Brynn. It was her own personal miracle, that they loved her madly no matter how many times she'd driven them crazy.

And there'd been a lot of times. Too many to count.

"Sweetheart," Raina said, jewelry indeed jingling, bringing forth welcome memories; growing vegetables in their garden, taking long walks on the beach to chase seagulls, and late night snuggles. Raina opened her arms and Brynn walked right into them, smiling when Olive wrapped her up from behind.

The three of them stood there for a long beat, wrapped up in each other. Catherine The Great Cat wandered in close, her appearance forewarned by the bell around her neck. She might be twelve and seemingly frail and delicate, but as with her moms, looks were deceiving because just beneath Cat's skin lived a mountain lion. Hence the bell, because she hunted like one. No one blamed her instinctual drive to do this, though Raina greatly objected to Cat dropping "presents" at her feet in the form of cricket heads and various other pieces of dead insects.

Yep, Cat was the most adorable murderer who ever lived, and she rubbed her furry face against Brynn's ankles exactly twice.

And then bit.

"Ouch!"

"You know her rules," Olive said. "A little love, a little hate. It's how she is. Now tell us why you're home unannounced, looking like something not even Catherine would've dragged inside."

"*I* think she looks wonderful," Raina said.

"She hasn't been sleeping or eating." Olive's worried eyes never left Brynn.

"I've been eating plenty!"

"Okay, then you aren't sleeping enough or eating the *right* food. You're as pale as . . . well me."

Olive indeed had the pale skin of her English ancestry. In contrast, Raina was Puerto Rican, and an envious golden brown. Since Brynn had been conceived from Raina's egg, not Olive's, along with a sperm donor, her own skin was a few shades lighter than Raina's. Unless she was trying to not hyperventilate, of course. Like now. In which case she probably was whiter than Olive.

"Okay, we can fix the eating right and sleeping, for a start," Raina said with determination. She slipped her hand into Brynn's, and as she'd been doing for as long as Brynn could remember, she took over. She settled Brynn onto the couch with one of her handmade throws, and in less than five minutes had a tray on Brynn's lap with her famous vegan chickpea noodle soup and steaming ginger root tea.

"Truth serum?" Brynn asked, only half joking. Raina was magic in the kitchen—*and* at getting people to spill their guts.

"I don't need truth serum." Raina sat next to her. "You're going to tell me everything."

"How do you know?"

"Because I made peanut butter cups for dessert and you love peanut butter cups."

"You'd withhold dessert from your only child?"

"She wouldn't, she's far too kind," Olive said. "But I would. In a heartbeat." She sat on the coffee table facing Brynn. "Talk."

"How do you know I've got anything to talk about?"

"A mom knows."

This was . . . mostly true. Her moms loved and adored her, they'd never made any secret of that. They'd had her back whenever she'd needed them, except for the times that she'd managed to keep her need a secret. Such as her younger years when she'd been mercilessly bullied for having two moms . . .

She loved them madly but it was a lot of pressure to be their only child, especially given how long and hard they'd fought for the right to have a baby at all. They were both truly amazing, but she could admit it was sometimes hard to live up to their expectations. She could also admit that she often *didn't*. She tended to skate ▶

through life. If she didn't dig too deep into anything, if she kept her life surface-only it was safe there. Her glass house couldn't fall down.

Cat jumped onto her lap and Brynn gave her a long look. "You going to play nice?"

Cat gave her a gentle head butt to the belly, and then tried to put her face in Brynn's soup. The bowl amplified the raspy, old lady purr so that it sounded like a misfiring engine.

"Welcome home," Olive said dryly, scooping up Catherine before she got any soup, gently depositing her onto the floor. "Now let's hear it. Not that we're not thrilled to see you, but what's going on? You've brought a pretty big duffle bag for a weekend's visit. Thought Long Beach was working out for you. You were substitute teaching and living with Darren—"

"Dirk," Brynn said and managed a casual shrug while ignoring the tightness in her chest, the tightness that had been there the whole drive. The whole past week. Maybe months. She was hoping it was a warning sign of an incoming zombie apocalypse and not a panic attack. When she'd been younger, she'd had them a lot. Like every day at summer camp over the course of the twelve years she'd gone, something else she'd managed to keep from her moms. The attacks were infrequent now, but at the thought of the conversation she was going to have to have with her moms, she could feel it building. She'd rather face zombies than worry them. They'd been through enough in their lives. "Just thought I'd come home for a bit," she finally said.

"And you know we love having you," Raina said, putting her hand over Olive's when her wife opened her mouth again. "But we also know that you're a fierce protector of those you love. You'd keel over before worrying us. Something's wrong." She softened her voice. "Did . . . something happen?"

Brynn started shoveling in the soup, even though she hated vegan chickpea noodle soup. "Yum."

Olive hadn't taken her eyes off Brynn. "It was Dustin, wasn't it. Somehow this is all connected to that asshole."

Brynn pushed her glasses farther up her nose. "Dirk."

"Hmm. And you only push your glasses up like that when you're upset."

"Olive," Raina said softly. "Back up, give her a little breathing space." She turned to Brynn. "Honey, you need to inhale."

Right. She was holding her breath. She let it out and gasped in some air. "I'm fine."

"No, you're not." Raina sounded and looked deeply worried. "You're breathing too heavily and your pulse is racing."

Yep, she was in the throes of a good old-fashioned panic attack, her first since last month when she'd realized she'd lost her great grandma's necklace, the one Olive had told her to take the utmost care of as it was not just sentimental, but worth a small fortune. But that hadn't been what had caused the attack. It'd been the unrelenting suspicion that Dirk had taken it.

He'd sworn he hadn't, and had been so hurt and devastated at the accusation that Brynn had started to doubt herself. Maybe she had really lost it.

Now she tried to suck in some more air and failed. "It's just allergies. I'm fine."

"See? She says she's fine," Raina said.

"I *am*," Brynn said, rubbing her chest and the impending freight train in it. "Totally fine."

Olive looked at Raina. "She's not fine. She's not working, her promise ring is no longer on her finger, so I'm assuming David was a huge ass-plant and that she's moving back in here."

"*Dirk*," Brynn whispered.

"None of those things came out of her mouth," Raina said, sounding distressed.

"Well, maybe they would if you'd give her a minute to talk." Olive frowned. "Except she's clutching her chest and looking like she's going to hyperventilate. Honey, are you in pain?"

If by pain she meant the feeling that her ribs were being cracked open by a sledge hammer, then yeah. She was in pain.

Raina crouched in front of her. "On a pain scale of one to ten, where are you at?"

Fifteen sounded about right.

Raina whirled to Olive. "Oh my God, I think she's having a heart attack!"

"No, I'm not." Brynn pulled off her glasses and dropped her face into her hands. "But everything else is all true. The not working ▶

thing. The coming home to stay for a bit thing. The asshole boyfriend thing."

"I'm going to kill Dirk," Olive murmured beneath her breath.

Brynn managed a mirthless laugh at her finally getting his name right.

"Oh honey," Raina whispered. "I'm so sorry."

"The school I was working at closed its doors. And the Dirk thing, it's for the best." Understatement . . . Brynn shook her head. "But I'm okay. Really. I'm just . . ." *Bonkers.* Completely unhinged. Homeless . . . "A-okay."

"She's whiter than you," Raina told Olive. "And clammy but chilled."

"I see it. Sweetheart, breathe," Olive said calmly to Brynn. To Raina, she said, "Call 9-1-1."

"No!" Brynn said. Or tried to. But of course now she really *was* hyperventilating.

Raina was on the phone with 9-1-1. "Hi, yes, my daughter's having a heart attack."

"I'm not!" Brynn wheezed as little black dots danced behind her eyelids.

Olive held both of Brynn's hands. "Breathe," she said again. "Breathe with me."

She was trying. But she couldn't seem to draw air into her lungs, which was now intensifying the sharp throbbing in her chest. Ripping her hands from Olive's, she pressed them against her ribcage, trying to ease the pain.

"Oh my goddess," Raina whispered helplessly, and ran to the door. "What's keeping EMS?"

A few minutes later, two uniforms stood over Brynn, helping her onto a gurney, putting an oxygen mask over her face. She no longer had her glasses and couldn't see past her own nose.

"Honey," Raina yelled as Brynn was stuffed into the back of an ambulance. "We're going to be right behind you, okay? I've got your glasses."

Brynn held out her hand, but couldn't reach them.

"Just relax," one of the EMS said. "Your only job here is to keep breathing."

"I'm fine!" Brynn tried to yell through the mask.

But no one was listening. So she gave up and stared up at the interior roof of the rig that was a blur and did the only thing she could. She breathed.

Forty-five minutes later at the hospital, a doctor and nurse were standing at her cot.

"Looks like it was a panic attack," the doctor said.

Brynn sighed. "That's what I tried to tell everyone."

"We had to be sure. Your moms were adamant."

This was true. They'd been unbudgeable. Brynn had finally made them go to the waiting room because they'd been driving the hospital staff nuts. She sighed. "It doesn't matter. They needed an excuse to cry because I'm home and they missed me."

The doctor looked confused. "It'd have been a lot cheaper to just say that to you."

"Yeah." Like the entire five grand of her insurance deductible cheaper . . .

Half an hour later, she was cleared from her little cubicle in the ER. Her moms had been told the good news and were in the waiting room while she changed back into her clothes. Finally she was winding her way down the white hallways toward the waiting room when she stopped in front of a candy machine, catching sight of her reflection in the glass.

She was clutching the bag the nurse had provided for her to stow her personal belongings like her glasses, phone, and ID. Everything was pretty blurry, but even she could see that she was very pale, and her eyes seemed huge in her face. Embarrassment and humiliation did that to a person.

A freaking panic attack . . . Gah. She now needed a chocolate bar more than she needed her next breath, and considering she almost died from lack of oxygen due to panic, that was saying something.

A tall, lanky, lean guy stood in front of the machine, hands on either side of it as he gave the thing a hard shake.

A candy bar came loose and he caught it, shoving it into one of his cargo pants pockets.

Pockets that looked already quite full.

She couldn't see well enough to know which kid of candy bar he got, but it didn't matter because she liked *all* the candy bars in all the land. "Hey," she said. "Save some for the paying customers."

He turned to face her, his light brown wavy hair falling into his eyes, and . . . something made her fumble into her plastic bag for ▶

her glasses. Self-preservation, maybe, because her instincts were screaming. Clearly not a common occurrence for her, or she wouldn't always be able to detonate her life so thoroughly. When she got her glasses on, the world came into focus again and she breathed a short-lived sigh of relief.

Short-lived because though she hadn't seen Eli Thomas since they were both fifteen, she did indeed know him.

"I put money into the machine," he said. His expression was tight, as if he was highly stressed. And given where they were, in the ER hallway, he in all likelihood *was* highly stressed. "Lots of money, in fact . . ." Stopping, he cocked his head, recognition crossing his face. His eyes softened and he smiled, flashing white teeth and a dimple in his left cheek. "Hey." His voice was different now. Lower, quiet, like the one you used with people you knew. It was also filled with emotion. "It's been awhile."

True story. It *had* been awhile. But not long enough. And in the bad news department, the dimple and smile were still attractive and charismatic as hell, but the good news was that she'd learned how to shut her heart off. She gave him a vague smile, like she didn't remember him.

He arched a brow.

Ignoring this because they so weren't going there, she gestured that he should stand back because it was her turn at the vending machine. She pulled a wrinkled dollar from her pocket and tried to shove it into the slot. She could feel the weight of his stare. He wanted her to recognize him. She was still going with no thank you.

The machine spit her dollar back at her.

"You have to straighten it out first."

Grinding her teeth, she slapped the dollar against her thigh and ironed it flat with her hand before once again attempting to thread the dollar in the machine.

It immediately spit it back out.

Seriously, was it a Monday? Was the universe out to get her?

Eli took her dollar and calmly fed it to the machine.

And of course, the machine accepted it.

Eli started to say something but she held up a finger to stop him, then punched in the corresponding letter and number for the candy bar she wanted.

Nothing happened.

No. Gripping the machine the same way Eli had, she shook it. Nothing.

So she kicked it.

Her audience of one smirked. "So Missy Judgerson goes to the dark side."

She shocked herself by laughing. It was her first laugh in . . . well, she couldn't remember. Life hadn't exactly been a pocket full of pilfered goodies lately.

"Here." Her pretend stranger pulled two fistfuls of goods from his pockets. "You look far more desperate than me. Take your pick."

She took a candy bar. And then snatched a bag of gummy bears as well.

He gave her a look.

"Hey, I'm a pint low, okay?" She stretched out her arm, revealing the band-aid in the crook of her elbow where they'd taken blood.

His smile faded. "You okay?"

Physically, yes. Mentally, the vote was still out. She tore into the candy bar. "I will be."

His eyes were still the most unusual shade of gray, which should have been cold, but they weren't. They were warm and curious. And maybe she'd feel warm and curious about him too, if a lifetime ago he hadn't fooled her into thinking they were friends, when they'd been nothing of the kind because he'd backed her arch nemesis, Kinsey Davis.

Yes, apparently she *could* hold a grudge for years. Maybe it'd stuck with her because she'd written about them often enough in her long-ago camp journal, the one they'd all had to write in every night. She actually still had hers, shoved somewhere deep in her duffle bag. She used it as a reminder of the her she used to be, Past Brynn, who'd been too gullible, too loyal, too forgiving . . . She'd practically been a golden retriever.

But she'd learned. She was tougher now. Present Brynn was a German shepherd.

Eli's phone pinged. He grabbed for it, stared at the screen, and looked stricken. "Gotta go." He took the extra few seconds to empty his pockets, shoving his entire loot into her arms. "In case you need another fix."

And then he was gone, leaving her torn between the humiliating ▶

memories of the past and the hope that whoever he was here for would be okay. She eyed her pilfered goods. The sugar had begun to work its way through her system, slowly giving her the courage she needed to go out and face her moms with the truth.

That once again, she'd failed at life and let down the people she loved. ⌒

Don't miss the perfectly feel-good novel by Jill Shalvis

The Lemon Sisters

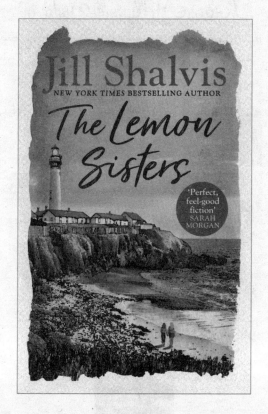

Available now

**HEADLINE
ETERNAL**

$\mathcal{M}$eet the friends of Heartbreaker Bay as they discover that falling in love can be as glorious and tempestuous as the beautiful San Francisco waters.

$\mathcal{M}$eet $\mathcal{P}$rue, $\mathcal{W}$illa, $\mathcal{E}$lla, $\mathcal{C}$olbie, $\mathcal{K}$ylie, $\mathcal{M}$olly and $\mathcal{S}$adie in

HEADLINE
ETERNAL

Welcome to Cedar Ridge, Colorado, where the only thing more rugged than the glorious Rocky Mountains are the rough-and-tumble Kincaid brothers.

Meet Aidan, Hudson and Jacob in

  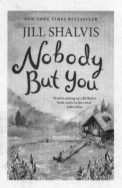

'Humor, intrigue, and scintillating sex.
Jill Shalvis is a total original'
Suzanne Forster

HEADLINE
ETERNAL

HEADLINE
ETERNAL

FIND YOUR HEART'S DESIRE...

VISIT OUR WEBSITE: www.headlineeternal.com
FIND US ON FACEBOOK: facebook.com/eternalromance
CONNECT WITH US ON TWITTER: @eternal_books
FOLLOW US ON INSTAGRAM: @headlineeternal
EMAIL US: eternalromance@headline.co.uk